S0-AEF-897

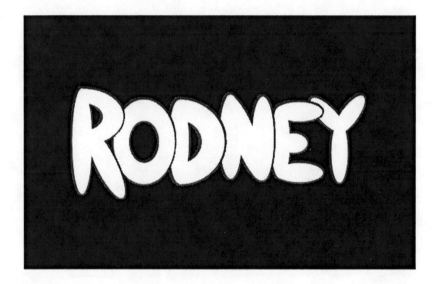

A Novel

Dick Baldwin

iUniverse, Inc.
New York Lincoln Shanghai

RODNEY

Copyright © 2007 by Dick Baldwin

All rights reserved. No part of this book may be used or reproduced by any means, graphic, electronic, or mechanical, including photocopying, recording, taping or by any information storage retrieval system without the written permission of the publisher except in the case of brief quotations embodied in critical articles and reviews.

iUniverse books may be ordered through booksellers or by contacting:

iUniverse
2021 Pine Lake Road, Suite 100
Lincoln, NE 68512
www.iuniverse.com
1-800-Authors (1-800-288-4677)

This is a work of fiction. All of the characters, names, incidents, organizations, and dialogue in this novel are either the products of the author's imagination or are used fictitiously.

ISBN-13: 978-0-595-41420-8 (pbk)
ISBN-13: 978-0-595-85772-2 (ebk)
ISBN-10: 0-595-41420-6 (pbk)
ISBN-10: 0-595-85772-8 (ebk)

Printed in the United States of America

Let no one say it,
And say it to your shame,
That all was beauty here
Until you came

—Val Lewton

ONE

So far, so good.

He'd gotten up Main Street unmolested, and all the way down Lochomocha Lane to Gulpolina Drive looked safe. Rod Rodoggio, the sexiest man on earth, sighed in relief. Arousing every woman who set eyes upon you may seem like heaven to the plebeians, but in reality it is a burden of responsibility he would wish upon no one. Being accosted by beautiful women, day after grueling day, having clothes ripped from your body in pure sexual frenzy, having countless hands caress your most intimate areas, and dozens of sweet lips smothering your flesh with hot kisses ... it is a tribulation beyond belief. Taking a simple junket to Main Street and home again for the newspaper was risky, he knew well, but Oh! to live the life of Common Man, to shuck this gift of beauty, grace, style and wit once and for all. But who would fill his boots? Who *could*? For Rod Rodoggio, in addition to being the most desirable man alive, was also the most sensitive individual ever to grace this life. He yearned to make dreams come true for the mass of poor creatures long denied the pleasure of his magnificence, but, alas, he was a lone lighthouse of joy struggling against an overwhelming ocean of need.

Walking briskly, he turned off Lochomocha onto Gulpolina. Now he moved openly, boldly allowing caution to dissipate with the late afternoon sun. The Rodoggio Estate was ahead. He watched the gold-edged spires glistening in the sunlight above the treetops, coming ever closer to home.

Ah, at last. The comfort of my servants, my library of fine books, my in-home Movie Theater. And within awaits my own True Love!

Walking past the Krémcorn family homestead, a shabby little affair with the smelly over-fertilized front lawn, terrible apprehension slowed his step. Before he could turn, run, or find a place to hide, three lascivious lasses leapt on him from behind. They must have been stalking him for blocks, awaiting an opportunity to pounce, like hungry panthers on an antelope.

Now he would pay the price supreme for his arrogant carelessness!

Rod wanted to scream out for help, but past experience taught him the uselessness of such an act. His screams were like a Siren lure, always bringing forth more unrigged females.

Oh, God give me strength. For Betty ...

And God, who adored Rod, heard his prayer. He helped Rod break free of the trio through a weak link, suddenly provided by the dark-hair sweet smelling vixen of the group, who was too busy rubbing her lithe body with her hands, drooling over his sexiness and not paying attention to her duty. His legs pumping for all they were worth (which was considerable according to Lloyd's Of London), he ran toward the big wrought-iron gate surrounding his property. He ran swift as the wind, but they were faster, more cunning than he. In less than a heartbeat he found himself boxed-in by these haughty beauties grinning over their prize.

He watched them, studying movements and body structures for vulnerabilities. They were young. Healthy and strong. It was going to be virtually impossible getting away from them chaste. One was blonde, her hair cut short in a cute tomboyish-way. Her cutoff jeans accented shapely legs, nicely tanned. She was nineteen or so. Her full, red lips smooched at him lustfully. Another, the one with long dark hair cascading over bare, creamy white shoulders, reached out to fondle his ultra-handsome face. Her tube-top could barely contain the bountiful bosom swelling from her chest. She wore a very, very short skirt and high, spike heels that made her legs look sooo long and gorgeous. It was hard to tell: she looked to be twenty, but might be as young as seventeen. The third was a yummy redhead. She obviously was the leader of the pack, perhaps twenty-four years old. A real woman. She filled perfectly a chic black cocktail gown, very adult, which was backless and strapless. A daring fashion statement. Her hair, he could tell, was normally the color of autumn sunset, but in this rosy afternoon sunlight it reminded him more of the familiar fire's glow from the big mahogany mantled fireplace in the Playboy mansion living room, where Rod spends much of his free time enchanting the girls and giving advice to Hef.

They were so beautiful; his blood ran cold thinking of the ramifications.

The redhead moved in, licking her chops. Rod backed instinctively away, falling over the kneeling blonde behind him. Immediately, she of the dark-hair and the redhead ringleader grabbed one leg each, dragging Rod off the sidewalk into the dense clump of shrubs in front of Mr. and Mrs. Loodelay's house. There, the blonde assailed him, raking the pleated white shirt under his jacket with her long nails while covering his face with wet, passionate kisses. This breech of protocol angered the redhead.

"*I'm first,*" she announced, wrenching the blonde bimbo off the stud. Blondie did not take this in good grace, fighting back by beating the leader with her fists. The dark one instantly took this opportunity to selfishly hog Rod for herself, kissing his exposed, manly chest, rubbing her greedy hands on his hips and inside his legs, all the while moaning with pleasure.

Whimpers issued from his mouth as the girl nibbled his neck and gyrated her hips against his groin. She tore the white dinner jacket clean from his body in an enormous show of lust and strength. She unraveled the black butterfly bow tie from around his neck, groping for his black dress slacks, succeeding eventually by making them fall away to the wayside. She chortled in victory, and then gasped with appreciation seeing that Rod brazenly wore no underpants. Unfortunately, her coos of delight snapped to attention the other two.

They stopped fighting long enough to observe what their companion was up to. They regarded her with frightful malice.

"Why fight, sisters, when we can *love?*" she laughed. They advanced. "There's plenty for all! Come, partake of the best the world has to offer!"

Seeing the hellcats agree with the dark-hair vixen, Rod painfully understood that this would be the spot of his defeat, his Waterloo. Pinned to the ground under the weight of such amour, he tossed reserve away.

Let them do as they will with my body. They cannot *make me love them as I do my own sweet Betty.*

Bitter tears welled in his eyes. There was something he needed to feel, and his searching fingertips found its hardness. Stoked, he wrapped his hand around it, feeling its contour and thickness, feeling it sway and bend with pliancy as he stroked it, testing both length and durability. He yanked it roughly while the girls squealed with enraptured joy, kissing him, caressing him, and generally exploring each inch of paradise.

Holding it tightly in his fist, he wrenched it out from the hedges. It was a big, brambly branch and he began whacking off, fighting back with as much power as purity of soul can bring. The redhead squealed like a pig poked with a pin—but wait!—she was enjoying this! She quickly tore off the upper part of her gown, forcing her nudity between the other two thus giving herself the lion's share of his thorny strokes. Her cries of absolute ecstasy abruptly ceased when the brunette rammed her selfishly aside, straddling Rod as if he were a stallion and she a naughty cowgirl begging for punishment. She entreated him to whip her, whip her *hard*. Miss Blondie, who'd been running her mouth over Rod's muscular body, using him as if he were a giant tube of Chap Stick, decided that wasn't enough for her. She wanted a slice of this tantalizing branch action. To her deep anger she discovered the raven-tress tart had no intention whatsoever of relinquishing her plumb position, so to get this usurper off *her* man, Blondie, with flashing fire in her green eyes and ice crackling in her blood, punched the bitch a good one on the side of the head.

She kicked the redheaded for good measure, in case she had any ideas.

One heck of a catfight ensued.

They fought wickedly, pulling each other's hair, tugging each other's clothes until the air was filled with sounds of delicate fabric tearing away from astonishingly well-endowed bodies, as well as the hissing, virulent screams of mortal struggle. Neighbors up and down the block, hoping to see a murder, peeked through their windows. Disappointed wives turned away while many husbands continued watching until their ears were pulled and blinds quickly closed.

Rod Rodoggio was fascinated by the scene played out before him. He was feeling a surge of warmth in the center of his stomach and thrill chills slithered up and down his spine like the press of an ice cube on the back of his neck. His manliness stirred to life.

He was turned on.

Ah, but there was that stabbing self-disappointment, that remorse for having a weakness he should be far above. Allowing the sight of three naked women fighting with lust-crazed fury to arouse him tarnishes the cherished love of his life, and if he did not do something quickly to save himself, he knew his tenuous hold on fidelity would end.

He could see himself wallowing in lust with these hellcats.

Blondie broke away from the fight. Belly flopping upon Rod, yet landing gently as a goose down pillow floating on air, she took possession of him purring and squirming her silky body up and down.

Rod caught the rhythm. Watching the girl's loveblimps sway back and forth, he reached out to grab them with eager, impatient hands.

"Betty, forgive mee-eee-eee!" he implored with his rich, deep masculine voice, preparing to engage in the old humpity-doo-dah with this delicious piece of blonde fluff.

"Why?" Betty asked sarcastically.

Rod looked up. Towering over them all, like some kind of avenging colossus, there she was, Betty, his own True Love. With her tightly fisted hands pressed authoritatively to her hips and suppressed rage playing across her face like molten lava dancing on a volcano, she awaited an answer. When none came, her upper lip curled in a snarl of fury. She dislodged the blonde and tossed her into the other two, making a sorry heap of them all in the middle of Gulpolina Drive. Betty raised her fist to the sky and proclaimed sonorously, "*HE IS MINE!*" Windows rattled in their casements as far away as Lame Lane on the other side of town.

A far different redhead, a remorseful creature taking the place of the lusty and vicious hellion of only a minute ago, got to her knees before almighty Betty. She clasped her hands together in supplication, sniveling, beseeching The Woman to show her mercy. "Forgive me! Forgive me!"

"Please, o please, Mistress Betty. I am innocent," whined the brunette, climbing aboard the bandwagon. "Excuse my lack of control … he's … he's …"

"So overpoweringly virile and attractive," the blonde continued, her voice cracking with fear. "The mere sight of such a manly man was too much for me to bear."

She pointed a pretty, albeit accusatory, finger at her companions. "It was them who forced me into this mad act. I would have been content only to gaze upon his beauty but for them. Punish them, but spare me!" She wept openly, snot bubbles coming out of her nose.

Betty looked away from this disgusting specimen of womanhood.

Despite her earlier repentance, the redhead trollop now had a cocky demeanor. She sulked and fumed about sitting in the gutter like a worthless dog; on the other hand, the dark hair girl, laying in the fetal position not too far away, tearfully expressed her shame and guilt.

Betty's heart was moved. "How often," she mused aloud within earshot of the three unfortunate wenches. "How often have I been driven to the same extreme passion from one mere glimpse of him, a glance in his direction. Ah, yes the thought of his male perfection is a difficult thing for us unworthy girls to comprehend. It is harder still to encounter and then walk away from."

Betty piteously shook her head. "There but for fate go I." She turned her attention to the assemblage, firmly reminding them that Rod was hers, and that no one else will ever have him. "*EVER,*" she warned. "And if I so much as hear that any of you have been sniffing the ground he's walked upon, I will teach you a lesson you will never forget. Now get out of my sight."

"Can we at *least* gather up our clothes?" the redhead asked with a rather snippy tone.

"*NO!*" Betty yelled, disturbing the peace even in the cemetery on Cobblywobble Road. "I was prepared to treat you with leniency, but I see you need a lesson." Betty cleared her voice. Everyone trembled, fearful of the punishment ahead.

"For the act of looking upon my man, I sentence you to go to your homes. There you will take red hot pokers and poke your eyeballs out. Be grateful I have not passed sentence on the offense of touching him."

Although there was gratitude, there were also tears, and much begging for mercy. And many, many apologies. But the time for clemency had passed. Betty stood firm. Soon the trio, much sadder and hopefully much wiser, lifted themselves off the ground. "Mistress Betty," asked the humbled brunette. "May I have one last look at him? One last look at the supreme perfection of the sexiest man on earth to last me my lifetime in darkness?"

"Absolutely NOT! Now go before I decide to give you some real punishment!"

Rod scrutinized their every move as they inched their cute naked butts down the block. Craving had not abated since Betty appeared. If anything it was much stronger now.

Too bad Betty wasn't in on the catfight.

He watched them, drooling, until he discovered Betty watching him watch them and decided that it might be wise instead to gather up his own clothes.

Maybe I can find that redhead later?

"Have you been faithful to me," Betty asked. He stepped back as if punched in the heart, dropping his gathered clothes. Clutching his chest in mortal pain, he lied, avoiding those eyes. "Of course I have!"

"HAVE YOU?"

"Noooo," he confessed quicker than a sinner in a coin-operated confessional box who's just discovered his dime was running out. Falling to his knees, covering his face, he whined, "Those tramps turned me on! If you hadn't come along, I would have boffed 'em all!"

Betty bellowed obscenities at the sky. She grabbed the thick branch, the one with all the jagged, pointy thorns, each still razor-sharp even after the tremendous workout they had endured against nubile female flesh. Bits of gore clung to the club.

Betty shook off the debris. She lifted it high above her head.

"It's time for *your* lesson, mister!" She brought the club down, fully prepared to strike the sexiest man on earth, but she saw his wonderful face, his unclothed godlike body. The club fell from her hand. Betty collapsed in a flurry of tears.

What could he do? Perhaps it's true that he deserved some form of punishment for his lascivious thoughts, but marring his perfect body would be a tad extreme, *oui*?

Thank God Betty realized that, too.

Putting his arm around her delightful waist, he smoozed away, gently saying that Betty would be the only woman he'd ever love. There could be no one else ever in his life. He pulled her close, close enough to gaze into her lovely face. Tears careened down her cheeks and into her mouth. Unattractive puffy bags appeared under her eyes, similar to those under the eyes of his detested father.

Rod kissed her and watched as anger melted away into sweetness.

"*I should be whipped,*" she blubbered in a strange voice, one that sounded like Pinocchio under water calling for Geppetto. "*You should be whipped,*" she repeated.

Her voice changed. And why was she hitting him with that damn branch? He closed his eyes, concentrating, focusing on the answer.

Whoa-ee, that branch felt just like a big log! Stings like the devil!

"Wake up," she growled. "Think you're better than the rest o' the world?" Smack-smack-smack. "Think you can sleep the day away??" Pound-pound-pound. "Get UP, you worthless gum!"

"Scum," Rodney corrected automatically, chilled suddenly with sick apprehension.

Whack-whack-whack.

Boy, Rod thought, *something is really out o' kilter here.* There was something he needed to remember, something he could not quite put his finger on. If only she'd stop whacking him with that branch he could have a chance to think.

She did stop whacking him. Now she was poking and jabbing him.

Ooouch!

He reached up to caress her dear ears, using them like handles to bring her face close to his, puckering up for a big anger-melting kiss. He pressed his lips to her rough and chapped, food-gooey mouth.

He opened his eyes.

Betty had turned into his father! Coarse thick lips, bloodshot eyes, hairy ears and all. Even though Rodney had a firm grip on those chimp like ears, the old bastard could still get the leverage he needed to use his rolled-up newspaper effectively. A thrust to Rodney's throat aborted the anger-melting kiss.

Rodney wanted to cry.

Maybe he could get back to sleep just long enough to hump Betty?

"WAKE UP," Jab-jab-jab. Poke-poke-poke. Smack-smack-smack. "Wake up, wake up, wake up, wake up, wake up, wake up, wake up, wake up, wake up …"

TWO

Rodney sat up. It took a moment to get the cobwebs out of his eyes and his vision to clear before recognizing the overly familiar, dreadfully bland, detail of the Rodoggio family living room. *I must've been in some deep sleep,* he said to himself. Yet it seemed only a moment ago that he went to lie down on the sofa. His father continued swatting him with his rolled-up newspaper.

"It's four o'clock," Ralph Rodoggio informed him. "In the afternoon."

Four o'clock??! Impossible! It can't be four o' goddam clock!!

At two thirty-five he left his lackey $1.60-an-hour job at the EverRipe Super-market—he would have left at two had those stream of ballbusting customers abated—and got home by quarter to three. Over one whole hour was shot to shit now because he fell asleep. He knew he'd have to call Betty pronto, or miss the chance of maybe getting a date with her tonight. That was the one annoying thing about Betty Bunz: she never plans dates ahead of time. You have to call her the same day and hope she's free. After years of trying, Rodney hit it lucky only once.

That was two years ago, back in '71, when they were both seniors at Gulpo Plains High. Rodney had set his alarm clock for six a.m. this particular Saturday, but ended up oversleeping until eleven-thirty because he was up till four watching horror movies on television. He called Betty before his eyes were even fully opened, and learned dismally that he had missed the boat. However, she said, if he wanted to take her to lunch over at Manny's Juicyburgers and could pick her up before she left the house to go food shopping with her doofy parents, she wouldn't mind too much. But he'd better hurry over because mama Bunz was just getting her purse.

Rodney dressed quickly in yesterday's dirty clothes and was almost down the stairs when he remembered that he had no spending money. He was getting a trifling 50¢ weekly allowance from his cheap-o father, which Ralph held out giving him until Sunday so that half can go into the lousy church collection plate. Not that twenty-five crummy cents would go very far at overpriced Manny's Juicyburgers, but without something in your pants you can't even pretend you're escorting a date. Rodney tore through the house like a maniac looking for anything at all resembling cash, eventually ending up in his sister's room rummaging through her drawers. Ordinarily, this was one of his favorite leisure-time activities. He enjoyed driving Roweena crazy looking through her stuff and mussing it all up. He especially enjoyed running his fingers over her soft, fragrant underwear. But today there wasn't time to have fun.

She has about a thousand sets of those Days of the Week panties that she never wears, presents from miscellaneous aunts and family members. Underneath them was the real stash, Roweena's wardrobe of wearable undergarments. Sexy little bits of sheer, lace trimmed crotch-huggers, some with an easy access opening in front. Under these he spotted some he'd never seen before. They turned out to be tightly rolled pairs of gossamer hot pink panties so sheer you could read the small, fine print of *THIS NOTE IS LEGAL TENDER* through several layers of material. They had the most delicate black lace trim around the waist, leg and crotch openings and stitched in shiny blue silk thread across the crotch was the word *Fun*day. The best thing about them though, was that tucked inside each was a wad of money, at least $150.00 worth of green skins. How Roweena, two full years younger than him, was able to save this kind of loot on a 35¢ allowance was beyond him. If she could accumulate this much over seventeen years, he should have, by all rights (here he stopped long enough to figure the math on his fingers) $200.00. Yet, his savings fell a little short at zilch.

This discovery really pulled his chain. But this was no time to think of injustices. Rodney just pocketed a hefty portion of bills, stuffed crap back in her drawers, and took off to catch Betty before she left with her parents.

Downstairs, flinging open the front door, he was stopped dead in his tracks by the slow moving old fart of a mailman, Mr. Pursnikky, blocking-up the doorway, putting one piece of mail at a time in the frigging mailbox. Rodney diplomatically opened the screen door, pushing the old geezer a bit to give him a hint that he was in the way, but, of course, Mr. Pursnikky's ass could be on fire and he wouldn't get the hint to sit in a pail of water.

"How'de'doodle-do, Master Rodoggio," Mr. Pursnikky said in his snarky, patronizing way. Rodney hated that *master* crap ever since his sixth birthday, when meddling Auntie Clarissa sent him a birthday card addressed *Master Rodney W. Rodoggio*. This tickled the jumping bejesus out of the mailman no end. Rodney remembered Mr. Pursnikky standing on the stoop clutching his sides laughing hysterically. He called Rodney *master* ever since.

"I'm in a hurry. If you could please …"

"Almost done. Almost done," Mr. Pursnikky sighed as if he had the hardest job in the world, continuing to study each piece of mail carefully before lifting the mailbox flap, placing it in, closing the flap, then reopening it for the next letter until Rodney wanted to shriek like a loony. In a fit of inspiration, he realized it would more expeditious to leave the house through the kitchen back door than wait around for the mailman to finish.

It was three whole blocks to Betty's house on Cowbell Place. He got there, winded and wheezing, just in time to see the Bunz family station wagon pull out of the driveway. Rodney ran toward it, signaling wildly with his flailing arms. Unable to get their attention he tried outrunning the car, which by this time was moving at a good clip. The best he could do was reach out and give the taillight a smart smack with his hand, cracking the red plastic.

Betty's father, Herbert Bunz, was not the most patient of men. He beeped his horn, politely warning the lunatic kid to back off, but when that didn't work he lost his temper. He threw the car into reverse and stepped on the gas. Rodney was fortunate not to be run over. Mr. Bunz yelled a lot of nasty things at him through his rolled down window because, in spite of the near mishap, Rodney was not giving up. He continued running after the car screaming for it to stop. Finally, at the main intersection of Cobblywobble Road and Netherland Avenue, Herbert Bunz had enough. He screeched to a stop, halting the massive Saturday morning traffic in all directions. There was plenty of horn honking, curse yelling, and objects thrown viciously at the Bunz station wagon. Herbert Bunz jumped out of his car, cursing, yelling, and throwing things back at the other motorists, screaming orders at Mrs. Bunz to honk the horn loudly and steadily.

Rodney frantically checked inside the car, practically ripping the door off its hinges.

"Betty is not with us," Mrs. Bunz said testily above the cacophony of tooting horns. "She went over to Manny's Jewyburgers for lunch. Now, leave us alone." She rolled up the window and locked the door against him.

This was terrible. Manny's was clear across town.

"Any chance for a ride to Manny's Juicyburgers?" Rodney asked Mr. Bunz as he got back into his car.

"You're just lucky I don't KILL you!" Mr. Bunz shouted, roaring off with his car, narrowly missing Rodney's feet with his left rear tire.

What to do? What to do? Rodney fretted, standing in the middle of Cobbly-wobble Road, cars zooming past him. *Hey! I'm a man of means by no means!* he sang to himself, feeling the plunder from Roweena's panty drawer lumped in his pocket, and seeing the Klownie Kab stand just across the street.

Ten minutes later a bright yellow car with a gooney looking clown face painted on its side pulled into the parking lot of Manny's Juicyburgers. Nearly every kid Rodney knew from school was hanging out here, and all of them watched to see what kind of idiot took a cab to a fast food restaurant. Some kids sat cross-legged on the ground, some draped comfortably over the hoods of parked cars and trucks. Some just stood around like lawn jockeys with Manny's bags in their hands instead of lanterns. Kids were everywhere, except inside Manny's, the fire-hazard deathtrap where they cooked and served the abominations that passed for food. Marty Martex was here (without his mother for a change), so was Freddie Anasambole and his sister Adele, Sally Glonk, Muller Maxwell Molt, Sandy Queezenok, Dan O'Pazil, and that little turd Alan Cusp. Crazy Eddie Scrotagg was blowing up Mannyburgers with firecrackers. George Washington Niggle, Iris Callump (who Rodney had the hots for until he discovered Betty had grown tits), Bellvue Snickerton, Tervoin Kittycatt, Helen Poddopisin, Vickie Tromeach, Vernon Fosleaf, and God-knows-who-all-else. Even his own damn sister Roweena was here with that drip Benny Fossert and his pack of dingoesque friends.

Rodney hated Benny Fossert with a passion. There was something very shifty about a guy whose eyebrows joined in the middle like a big hairy worm over beady eyes—that in itself was enough to give anyone the willies—but what really got up Rodney's nose was that Benny Fossert was a first-class Mr. Personality, the ultimate happychap. He was a joke telling, hee-hawing son of a bitch bastard. Rodney had no idea how Roweena could possibly stand him, and it just proved what sort of lamebrain she was that she did. She was sitting on a patch of dried grass, surrounded by Fossert's hyenaheaded pals, laughing her ass off while Benny, wearing one of those idiotic Manny Moose giveaway hats with silly cardboard antlers jutting out at right angles, cavorted spastically around like Jerry Lewis high on drugs. He knocked into people, tipped over bicycles and trashcans pretending like the hat was so heavy it threw him off balance. Everyone thought he was hilarious.

Jerks.

Betty, thank the good Lord, wasn't among these gaggle of goons. Pressing his face against the window, afraid now that she might be inside Manny's Deathtrap, he peered intently into the murky interior. The windows were cluttered by millions of advertising broadsides and dopey Manny Moose posters. The glass itself was streaked with old grime and it was impossible to tell if she was there. Everything seen through the smeary glass window appeared wavy and distorted, a funhouse mirror view of hell. Blobs of color wobbled around, stretching up one moment and compressing down the next. He'd have to bite the bullet and go inside.

What a dump, he thought sourly, opening the door to the musky scent of singed fur. It was dark and smoky inside. Hot, steamy and uncomfortable. Everything had a greasy film on it, and some kind of crusty stuff adhered to the tables, chairs, walls, and especially the floor, which crunched as you moved around, like you were walking on peanut shells. The clientele wasn't much better. Construction workers, truck drivers, a real rough crowd. Rodney's Klownie Kab driver, an awful, ugly, massive, man who could easily be a convicted criminal, had stopped in to grab a little something—

Betty.

She was sitting at one of the window tables, eating soggy MannyFries dripping with gooey ketchup. The Klownie Kab driver flirted with her, making a big show of wiping away with a napkin ketchup that had dribbled onto her chest. Betty laughed and laughed as he dabbed that napkin with his felonious hand all over her chest, getting lots of free feels.

Rodney was outraged. He marched to the table. Unwisely, he slapped his rather small and bony hand on the driver's massive shoulder. "Get your filthy hands off her," he demanded, trying to make his squeaky soprano sound more an authoritative basso.

The driver turned to Rodney, missing a big glob of ketchup just as Betty let it dribble onto her shirt. Betty clucked her tongue with disgust, rolling her eyes upward. "Of all the dumb *morons!*" she said to the intruder. "Look what you did! There's sticky, disgusting catch-UP all over my front! What are you? A re-tart or something?"

"This creep is getting his *JOLLIES* off you. But not while I'm around!"

"This *creep* is my Uncle Altoid," Betty said coldly. "And he gave me this shirt last Chris'mas. It's my *favorite* shirt and he was trying to help me keep it *clean*. I hope you're *happy* now that there's a big stupid STAIN on it." She angrily wiped at the ketchup, spreading it around and around in circles.

"I gotta get back to work, dolly," Uncle Altoid said. He had a funny, cartoonish voice, sounding something like Woody Woodpecker after sucking on a helium balloon. "Good going, kid," he said, slapping Rodney painfully hard on the back.

"Yeah, good *going* … uh, uh … *what's* your name?" Betty said.

"Rodney."

"Oh, never mind. I'll think of it."

"Look, Betty, you don't want to stay in here, do you?" Everybody was looking at them. Rodney heard some snickering and crude comments. *Boy, this place really is the pits.* He couldn't wait to get her outside.

Into the bushes.

Next to Manny's was a vacant lot overgrowing with weeds and bramble bushes, offering the perfect secluded make-out spot for Gulpinian youth. It was almost an unwritten rule, as Rodney understood it, established among these young folk, that a girl coming to Manny's Juicyburgers with a boy probably would go next door to hump away in the great outdoors.

"Well I want to have *lunch*." Betty expressed caustically, tossing back her shoulders and fisting her hands tightly against her hips.

But of course! Providing food was part of the humping ritual, a justification for being in this god awful place to begin with, because nobody in their right mind would actually want to eat this slop. To Rodney, reading between the lines with great illiteracy, Betty's desire for lunch was a positive indication that he was *in*. *Ohboyohboyohboy!* he thought, rubbing his hands together and grinning, watching her get up from the table.

Betty told him she wanted a plain Mannyburger. Then changed her order to a Cap'n Sharky Fillet O' Fish sandwich, and then changed it back to a Mannyburger but this time with cheese. When her Wheel-o'-Fortune mind was made up, she settled herself down at one of the single-seat Formica tables. Waiting.

Rodney rushed to the service line.

"Wait," Betty called across the restaurant, attracting everyone's attention. "I want a Big Bugger!"

"I'll bet you DO!" some truck driver called back.

Everyone laughed except Rodney. Betty chuckled, blushing slightly. Rodney was thinking, *those damn Big Bugger Burgers cost $4.75 … it'll just get tossed aside in the bushes … so how come she didn't order something cheaper? Aw, who cares? It's Roweena's money!* Hearing the fading laughter, it occurred to him, as he stood in line with some really smelly, unsavory men, that it might not be too smart a move leaving Betty sitting at a table alone. The idea of eating a Big Bugger Burger wasn't nearly half as revolting as the thought of some jackass putting the make on her while he was stuck waiting here. He tried to cut ahead. One of the customers objected.

"Eat shit," Rodney said under his breath. Suddenly everything grew dim. Something large, hairy and hard was in his face and his neck snapped back.

Betty was getting tired of waiting. Finally looking over to the serving counter, she was annoyed to see the fool *outside* the service line, kneeling on the floor and rubbing his nose with a paper napkin. In Betty's view, he should be up there paying through his nose rather than *playing* with it. She yelled to him to hurry it up.

By the time Rodney was able to stop the blood flow from his probably broken honker, Betty was on top of him saying in no uncertain terms that she'd rather place her own order than wait for him to stop clowning around. Rodney begged like a dog for another chance, but Betty brushed past his kneeling body as if he didn't exist. Jumping up to follow, he slipped in a puddle of something—grease, or more likely his own blood—and slid forward into her. His groin smashed her from behind just as she leaned forward to place her order. The counter boy and many nearby customers thought this was the funniest thing they'd ever seen, hooting hysterically. Betty, however, did not find the humor and flashed Rodney a dangerous look of warning.

"I don't like being laughed at, you know," she told him harshly. Noticing his soiled high school jacket, she recoiled, bouncing backwards away from him. "Ugh! You have BLOOD on your Gulpo High Gold 'n' Green! I don't want to be in here with a slobby pig that has *blood* all over him!"

"Meet me outside … I'll get the food …" Rodney said, nauseous either from the stink of sweat mixed with the terrible frying smell in the air, or from the loss of blood. He wasn't sure, but whichever it was it made him feel like puking.

"Oh, OKAY, Ronco," Betty sighed irritably. "Get me a Supermannyburger with xtra sauce, MannyFries with plenty o' catch-up, and a large Orange Frappe Fizz. And make sure that the hamburger isn't overcooked! And tell them not so much chewy crap, like that elastic lettuce they use, and definitely NO ice."

Rodney's head was spinning. "Ice in the hamburger?"

"No, *idge-jit*, no ice in the Orange Frappe FIZZ! If you can't remember a simple order, I'll ask someone else."

"No, no, it's okay—really, go ahead," he said eagerly.

"And ask them to put some extra salt in it, too."

"In the Fizz Filled Frappe?"

Betty pressed her tongue to the roof of her mouth and clucked it hard with a startling, revolted snap to prove how very bored, how very annoyed, and how very disgusted she was by all this. "Yeah, that's right, Ronco. Have 'em put SALT into my drink. While you're at it, why don't you have them pee on my french fries? I'm going outside."

It was getting harder by the moment to concentrate, but he made sure he was getting the order just as she requested it, giving directions to the counter boy and correcting him frequently. Rodney snatched up and paid for the bag containing his exact order: a Supermannyburger with no sauce and extra lettuce, fries with the standard amount (little or no) ketchup, and a Grape Slogg with ice and salt. He hurried outside to look for Betty Bunz and found her sitting by a trashcan chatting with that loser Marty Martex. Benny Fossert popped out of nowhere still wearing that stupid Manny Moose hat.

"Hey, Roderoo! Are you going to eat that in the bush," Benny said jovially, waggling his Manny Moose antlers at the grease stained Manny's Juicyburgers bag. There were sniggers all around.

"How 'bout it, Bet? Wanna go eat in the bushes?" Rodney said, winking at her.

"What are you? Nuts? Eat in the bushes, with all those bugs and crawly things out there? No, *thank you*! And don't ever call me Bet. I detest that name."

"It's not *so* buggy there," Rodney said smoothly. "As a matter of fact …"

"Not so buggy, huh?" She hitched her thumb toward the vacant lot. Rodney followed her indication and saw what looked like thousands of flying bugs hovering over the field. While he watched, Selena Coombiya was coming through an opening from the lot followed by towheaded Harvey Palooka. As they crossed Manny's parking lot Benny Fossert's animalistic friends cavorted around them like jackaloons, braying and howling, making all sorts of crude sexual noises at Harvey. Selena brushed dirt off her clothes with the back of her hand, while Harvey reached down inside his pants to adjust his pecker. Betty poked Rodney hard with her finger. "Why don't you ask Selena if it isn't so buggy out there? She's flickin' 'em off her left 'n' right. And look at poor Harvey! Those crawly things actually got inside his *pants*." She made a noise deep in her throat, a cross between a growl and a hiss. "*Bugs.*"

It might not be so easy to get Betty into the bushes after all.

He sat, cross-legged, on the ground next to her. Betty unwrapped her Supermannyburger, and pushing the straw into her drink saw viscous blue stuff bubble up. "Hey! This is GRAPE … and look at all the garbage on my hamburger! What do you think I am, Ronco? A rabbit?"

"Those imbeciles," Rodney said with indignant fury. "Can't they EVER get an order right?"

"I hate grape," she stated, tossing the drink over her shoulder. The container burst into blue goo on the tarmac of the parking lot.

"Hey, Bet, how about if ..." Suddenly, his face was full of dry, ketchupless MannyFries.

"I told you NEVER to call me Bet. Got it NOW??"

The look on her face made his blood run cold. Oh, yes. He got it. "How would you like an Orange Fizz-uh-Flip with that?" he asked, adding quickly and cleverly, "or would you rather go into the bushes?"

"Oh, yes!" said Betty

"Great!" Rodney got up from the ground and waited for her to follow.

"Well?" she asked curtly.

"Don't you think you should get up if we're going to go?"

Betty's eyes narrowed to hard little slits. Her teeth clamped together tightly. She spoke seemingly without moving her lips. "You want *me* to get up and get my own Orange Frappe Fizz?" She stood up angrily.

"No," he said, aghast.

"So?" she said.

"So?"

"So give me some damn money!" Betty bellowed, kicking him in the shin and holding out her hand. Rodney fished out a bill. It was ten dollars. Surely he had something smaller. While he fished again, Betty hooked the money out of his hand and marched into Manny's followed by Roweena, Benny, and Benny's pals. Benny discarded his Manny Moose hat, placing it over the naked lady hood ornament of a Gulpo Plains Fruit 'N' Produce truck. As he walked through Manny's door he turned to Rodney. Putting his left hand behind his head he created a feather headdress, wiggling his fingers wildly in salute.

"Woo-woo! Rod-o-reenoo! Heep Big Chief Eat-In-Bush sez try'um, you like 'um!" Then he pressed his hand down flat to his head, like it was a Frenchman's beret. "You zould try ate-ting in zee boosh, monsewer! It is, how you zay?—dee-licious!"

Rodney fixed him with a distasteful look. Benny crossed his eyes and added a goofy grin to his face, patting the top of his head with his hand. It dawned on Rodney that this supercilious scumbag might be making fun of him. Rodney was going to yell "eat shit" to him as he started a new line of ridicule, but that big bastard of a truck driver, the one with the free fist, came out of Manny's just as he opened his mouth. Pushing past Benny, who was blocking the doorway, and noticing his antics, the trucker gave a sidelong glance to see who was the object of such mockery. He was amused to see that it was that punky little scarecrow kid who thought service line rules didn't apply to himself. He guffawed heartily and tossed Benny a cigar.

Rodney wished he could throw his voice like Paul Winchell, to make it sound like Benny Fossert was saying "eat shit" to the big bastard. It would be real nice to see Fossert have his smiley face punched in. The truck driver was still yocking it up until he saw the Manny Moose hood decoration on his truck then he stopped laughing. He took out a blackjack.

Betty soon returned with Benny, Roweena, and a herd of Benny's pals, one who carried a bottle of Manny's Own Orange Crunch for her. "They were out o' Frappe," she said bitterly. "Give me your bottle opener." She held out her cute little hand to Rodney.

Jeezus! What kind o' jackass carries a bottle opener around in their POCKET? Rodney asked himself, sitting miserably on the ground, trying to regain his breath while nursing his tender, blackjack-sore, solar plexus.

"I have one," Benny said.

"Oh, sir," Betty said demurely, batting her eyes playfully at Benny. "I cannot accept your kind offer. Since I am socially embarrassed by my escort's lack of pre-paredness, I am in a vulnerable position. However, should you offer to buy me my libation, I may accept your kindness opening it for me."

Huh?

Benny laughed and handed Betty two dimes and a nickel, the price of the bottle of soda. She put the coins in her bluejeans pocket, where they merged with her other money, including all of Rodney's change from the ten. The coins jingled in her jeans religiously. "Does anyone have a dollar bill for a bunch o' change?" she asked sweetly.

After the bottle opener faux pas, Rodney was anxious to redeem himself. He quickly dug out his dwindling cash, looking for a single dollar bill. He proudly flagged one at Betty. She plucked it out of his fingertips and in return dumped an annoying pile of coins, mostly pennies and Canadian nickels, into his lap.

"Ready for another bite in the bush?" Benny asked Roweena.

"Ooo! How can you stand going over there?" Betty asked. "I mean, with all those repulsive bugs crawling all over the place with their lousy little legs, and their hairy, creepy arms! And those other flying ones, comin' at you with those unnatural wings they have on their backs! Eee-*ooo!* Gives me the clititty-clacks just thinking about 'em!"

"I didn't notice any bugaloos over there. Did you, Ro?"

Roweena shook her head.

"Aren't you worried that they'll fly into your mouth?"

"My mouth was pretty full," Roweena said. "There wouldn't be room for a bug."

This remark, and, of course Roweena's perfect timing and delivery, elicited a big, big laugh from Benny's pals. Rodney started getting mighty hot under the collar.

"Of course," Benny said seriously. "If you went over there with big, strong Rodorooney, I'll bet he'd protect you from those giant hairy spiders."

"SPIDERS???! They HAVE spiders over there???"

Red spots floated before Rodney's eyes. He was choking on active thoughts of murder, knowing full well that his frustrated anger would make him lose control soon. It's inevitable. The handwriting was on the wall, as clear as the shiteating grin on Manny Moose's grotesque face. All it's gonna take is one little thing to push him over. One little thing.

"So, maybe you'd feel safer with me, eh? What'cha say, Bettina? Wanna go into the lot and have a bite to eat?"

That was it.

Rodney grabbed Betty's hand and yanked her to her feet. "YOU'RE NOT GOING ANYWHERE UNTIL YOU GO INTO THOSE BUSHES AND EAT ME!" He screamed so loud that even the illegal aliens working behind the counter inside Manny's heard him. Some of them had to translate to others what the loco gringo was yelling. It took quite a long while for all the laughter to stop, and when it was reasonably quiet again, Betty told Rodney what a filthy disgusting mouth he had. It took a great deal of explaining and coaxing, but Rodney did manage to convince her that what he said was only a slip of the tongue. During his heartfelt apology, Benny and his goons huddled around, listening attentively to Rodney's each and every word, nodding affirmatively at all the salient points. When the slip of the tongue line came out Fossert raised his one solid eyebrow.

"Our Betty likes a slip o' the tongue now and then, don't'cha, babe?"

Betty smiled in spite of the fact that she was furious with Rodney. Benny's humor mellowed her out, relaxing her and making her hungry for her lunch. "Well, Ronco, I'll forgive you on one condition." Rodney waited to hear what she had to say. "That you give me an apology present. Give me *SuperBig* Bugger."

Somebody in Fossert's group howled like a wolf in response.

Wiseguy. Maybe someday you'll howl your throat muscles out. "I'll get you a Big Bugger, but you have to promise to come with me into the bushes," he said lightly, trying to strike a bargain with her. Betty's displeased look made him add, "… I know for a fact there are no bugs over there."

"Yeah? What did they do? Pack up their wings and hairy arms and go south?"

Sarcasm did not look good on Betty Bunz. The ends of her lipsticked mouth curled down like inverted fishhooks, and the tip of her plump tongue darted as she spat out the words.

"There are no bugs out there," he said firmly.

"How do you know?" she asked even more so.

"Yes, Roddyrink—how *do* you know?"

"Uh," Rodney said desperately. "Uh ... there's no bugs out there because ... because ..."

Everybody was waiting to hear. Dozens of questioning eyes were upon him. He felt sweat pour down the back of his neck.

Think of something. Think, think, think ...

"... because ... the rats ate 'em all."

Betty sighed.

Finding a small, but almost clean spot amongst some odorific bushes, Rodney took off his jacket for Betty to sit on, then plopped himself down onto bare dirt upon a broken Carnival Cola bottle. He wondered what the big deal was, why everyone thought it was so sexy here. It was just about as sexy as Miss Phibes the school librarian. All types of used and discarded condoms hung off branches everywhere, making the place look like a demented Christmas Wonderland. There were multi-colored Cutesy-Cons, French Ticklers by the score, one or two Big Johns, an awful lot of Wee Willie Winkies, even some Blast-O-Fun Flavored Lovegloves. While Betty peeled away the gluey wax wrapper from her SuperBig Bugger, Rodney squirmed around on broken glass trying to find a comfortable position. That hamburger looked vile. Tons of congealed, vanilla-colored fat adhered to the sides of a moldy bun.

He watched with repugnance as Betty took a big gloppy bite, chewing it with her mouth open. The mess mushing inside there, like a cement mixer full of produce, made Rodney's stomach churn. He wondered why he was attracted to her. His eyes left that mouth, following a dribble of Manny's Secret Mannysauce down her chin dripping onto her shirt between her two big bazooms. He licked his lips.

Carefully, oh so carefully, he put his arm around her shoulders. Betty, cheeks puffed out, mouth full of SuperBig Bugger Burger, smiled happily at him. She reminded him of a chipmunk working on its nuts. The feel of her shoulder under his hand, the sight of her balloons a'bobbin as she chewed, gulped, and swallowed made Rodney's left eye twitch, flipping up and down like a mechanical shutter. This eye-twitching business was a brand new load in his life. Lately, whenever he starts getting hot 'n' horny his left eye starts winkin' 'n' blinkin'.

"You look cute like that," Betty remarked, not bothering to clear her mouth first, making it impossible to understand what she said. Rodney asked her nicely to repeat it. Instead she took another chomp of burger.

"What did you say?" he asked again, thinking that perhaps she hadn't heard him.

"Noffink," she huffed angrily, spraying some food out in the process. "Libbon ub ness dime."

She kept chewing and chewing, her lower jaw grinding sideways. Rodney was fascinated, thinking of *Mutual Of Omaha's Wild Kingdom* for a while, then getting bored. His twitching eye slowed to a standstill. His arm stiffened across her broad shoulders, cramping up until it ached.

That mouthful gave her quite a workout. Rodney reflected that it had to be the cheap, lousy meat Manny's uses. *It's all gristle, or maybe muscle. I would not be surprised if the State Board Of Health discovered that it was KANGAROO meat they were using. Perhaps something even more unsavory. Like wolf, or owl. Probably it's monkey meat. Jeez! Monkey meat!* He could picture that damn cartoon Manny Moose on TV in one of his hard-sell Manny's Juicyburgers commercials saying "Try it—it's CHIMPLY delicious!" *They should throw Manny Moose's ass in jail and close this hellhole forever. Godfearin' people thinking they're eating a good, wholesome American hamburger and these sneaky wetbacks were giving 'em ANIMAL meat! Disgraceful!* Because he was uncomfortable, and wasn't paying much attention to what he was doing, he let his hand dangle down level with one of her globelike boobs. She turned to look at him—

—and screamed out the entire contents of her mouth into his face. The next thing Rodney knew, Betty was on her feet running out of the lot, screeching like a fire engine on fire. Rodney was mystified. He thought she might have seen one of those big, awful rats that used to sniff around Manny's garbage dumpsters and looked around nervously. Even though nobody's seen one for a long, long time doesn't mean they couldn't've come back. He felt a slight tickle on his forehead and scratched it. The tickle came away on his fingers.

It was a ladybug.

One of those cute li'l critters they used to sing about when he was a goo-goo kid in kindergarten. It had been crawling on his forehead. No wonder Betty acted the way she did. This red-with-black-dots bastard scared her away.

Well, Mr. Ladybug, do I have a surprise for you!

He placed the bug carefully on the ground. Using the biggest, heaviest rock around, Rodney socked it to the bug, smashing the rock down hard on it.

Over

and

over.

Again and again.

Your lesson for today: Don't Screw with Me. He left the rock as a makeshift grave marker for the interloper, giving it a hard twist down into the dirt. *Here lies Mr. Cocksucker Ladybastardbug.* Rodney could not believe his eyes when less than a moment later, the goddamn thing crawled out. It seemed dazed, but unharmed. First it walked in teeny circles one way, and then in teeny circles the other, as if trying to reorient its tiny little self. It spread its wings and deliberately flew up his sore nose. He could feel it buzzing around in his sinus cavity. Gingerly picking at it with his index finger, trying not to start the blood flowing again, he felt a sharp rap on the back of his head. Out zoomed the bug. Rodney turned, smiling, to thank whoever it was who lent him the helping hand. A cop's night stick was playfully chucked under his chin.

"Hey there Kitty-kat, what's the scoop?" The policeman asked this with a friendly smile on his face.

"I had a bug up my nose …"

"No, no, no, no, no-o!" the cop sang, tapping the club into Rodney's throat. "I'm asking you what you did just now."

"Did?"

The friendly smile faded. "With that broad. That piece of stuff that just ran out o' here screaming her knockers off. So, what-did-you-DO?" He emphasized each word by jabbing his night stick into Rodney's nose. "Don't play games with me, jack. I heard her scream. I saw her run. And here you sit with your finger up your nose. So what kind of perverted teenage crap did'ya pull? What'cha do? Show her your *dingle?*"

"I didn't do anything, officer, sir!" Rodney whined. "Honestly! We were sitting here having lunch when she saw a bug."

"You were eating lunch out here?"

"Uh-huh."

"In these dirty bushes?"

Rodney nodded.

"And a bug scared the bitch away?"

"Yes."

The policeman noticed that there was a glob of blood on the tip of his night stick. He wiped it off on Rodney's shirt, then holstered the stick. Next, he removed his hat and dabbed at his sweat-dewed brow with his uniform shirtsleeve. He spent many moments in deep concentration studying Rodney. He said, "Hmmm."

Rodney squirmed on the broken bottle glass. He was afraid to move.

"Let me see if I have this straight. You and Pussy Galore decide *not* to have lunch in Manny's, but instead come out here to this rat-infested, insect-filled vacant lot where you can sit in dirt and smell rotting animal corpses while you eat. Of course, it *is* tastefully decorated. What would you call this? Post-Modern Scumbag? Sounds like a perfect lunch date to me. But, O My! The snatch sees an itsy-bitsy bug and runs out of here screaming bloody blue murder! Does this about sum it up?"

Rodney sat miserably silent.

The cop beamed, a big wide smile spread across his face.

"Good! We understand one another! Now that we both know what a crock o' shit that is, and what the truth is we can get on with business." He began chuckling in a low, frightening way.

Rodney sensed that this guy might be nuts.

Soon the cop began shaking his head sadly. "But guess what, bunky? I gotta let you go. I should be marching your scrawny, perverted ass down to the jailhouse, but the law says I gotta let you go. The *law*. The *jackass* law that says teenagers like you can do whatevertheflamingfuck they want to do with my wife and get away with it." He laughed real deep, from his chest cavity. His eyes glazed over. "Yes sirree, bobby! Whatever they want. Diddle my wife. That's OKAY because it's the LAW."

Rodney was getting scared.

"The LAW. Ha-ha-ha-ha-HAHAHAHAHA! Oh, but one day … one fine day I'll catch you in the act, Kitty-kat. And then—"he whipped out his service revolver, pointing the muzzle between Rodney's eyes. "BANG-BANG! The *law* says I can! Got it?"

Rodney nodded weakly.

"Good." He replaced his pistol, took out his night stick. Starting to twirl it, whistling that old ragtime tune *The Boy and His Dog*, he sauntered away.

God alone knows how long Rodney sat there without moving. When he did find the strength and the courage to move, he couldn't remember which way led out of the lot. He went off in an arbitrary direction. His path was soon blocked by a patch of brush so dense that it was virtually impossible to get past it without getting down on his hands and knees and squiggling through gaps of exposed roots and poison sumac. Wiggling on his belly, Rodney heard a familiar voice. It didn't sound very far away.

"Oooo, babeareeni, do THAT some more … ah-hhh-hhhhh!"

It was wormbrow Benny Fossert, obviously getting some off Roweena. Perhaps Rodney ought to teach them both a lesson. Scare the living crap out of them. He reckoned by the sound that they were in a patch about three bush clumps over to the left. Creeping inch by scratchy inch he came to a small opening in the clustered foliage. Looking through he was shocked to see a picture-perfect clearing. A secluded meadow out of a friggin' storybook. Green, green grass. Bright colorful flowers. A delightful blue sky overhead. Not a soiled condom in sight. The only thing missing was friendly butterflies flittering about. Instead there were hundreds of those flying and buzzing bugs, but what really shattered the beauty of the scene, placing it firmly into reality, was the sight of Benny Fossert's naked hairy bottom chugging up and down.

Rodney had to hold his hand over his mouth to keep from laughing out loud at the thought of Benny and Roweena scrambling when they think a cop has caught them.

Composing himself, taking a deep breath, he said very loudly and authoritatively in as deep a voice as he could, "WHAT'S GOING ON HERE? AN ACT O' PERVERSION?"

Benny Fossert rolled over. They looked at Rodney, who wasn't hidden very well.

"Ronco!! What the HELL do you think you're doing?? Are you trying to be funny?" Betty modestly attempted to cover herself with Benny's discarded shirt.

Rodney tried to speak. He wanted to say, "But, you're my girl." Instead he got stuck on the first word which he stammered out as "Bug … bug … bug …"

"What?" she said with a definite chill toward him. "Bugs? Where?"

Over the course of time, in Rodney Rodoggio's chuckleheaded memory, this first date with Betty Bunz had the rosy glow of near perfection. When he thinks of that golden afternoon at Manny's Juicyburgers, which is very often, he pictures Betty's smiling face (sans the food lumped in her cheeks). It would have been an absolutely perfect date, according to Rodney's remembrance, if Benny Fossert had not been all over the place causing tons of trouble. But Fossert was a problem no more. He was gone. Gone forever. He went and joined the Navy, and, to Rodney's surprise and delight, the Navy actually took him! Right this moment, ol' Wormbrow was probably a billion miles away in some leaky ship in some godforsaken part of the world peeling potatoes on KP duty. Thoughts like this always brought a smile to Rodney's lips and a spring to Rodney's step.

But making Rodney happy now, at this moment, was knowing that he formulated the perfect, fool-proof date imaginable. It came to him at work, as he sat on a milk crate in the breads aisle pretending to price items, sneaking bites of donut out of a box he'd open on the shelf. He'd take Betty to the Gulpo Plains All-Weather Drive-In Movie Theater, where a brilliant double feature was playing. *Affairs d'Amour*, a new release, one of those artsy asshole foreign craps, paired with *Killer Zombies From Planet-X*, which has been held over yet again, making it the longest running movie in Gulpo Plains history. Betty will be so bored and disgusted reading subtitles, trying to figure out all the goofy symbolism that his advances will be a welcome diversion. Then there'll be a hot humpin' time in the old town tonight! Those foreign yawnfests run on and on forever, which means there will be plenty of time for rolling around on the backseat of the car before the good movie begins.

A first class canoodle, followed by some relaxing entertainment. The American Dream Date.

And it all begins with a telephone call.

THREE

There were three telephones in the Rodoggio household. The nearest, scant inches away on a flimsy table by the foot of the stairs next to the sofa upon which Ralph Rodoggio sat grunting over his tattered newspaper, was not to be considered. At any moment Ralph would start expostulating with his big booming voice, damning all the criminals, politicians, and overpaid entertainers he read about, calling them all sorts of lunatic names while invoking God to give him five minutes alone with the muskrats (he meant miscreants). Very distracting, to say the least, when you're on an important phone call. The next closest was the useless piece of junk kitchen phone mounted on the wall adjacent to the rattling, banging dinosaur of a refrigerator. As if the hoots, pops, and whistling death throes of the thing didn't make it difficult enough to carry out a conversation, the phone itself transmitted sound at a level audible only to dogs. You had to yell your nuts off so loudly to be heard that all the nosy neighbors up and down the block knew who you were talking to and what you were talking about.

Rodney was set on using the Princess phone upstairs in his parents' bedroom anyway. The old folks' boudoir has a nice thick door that can be closed for those special romantic moments with your *fillet* (he meant *fille*) during enchanting telephone conversations. As she whispers sweet little nothings filled with dirty words, there is the additional thrill of rolling around on a real, honest-to-God bed. There was, however, one gigantic, ballbusting problem with using the Princess phone: right now his stupid pain-in-the-ass mother was cluttering up the bedroom napping. After a hard day of soaps 'n' sips, she needs to unwind before slopping together one of her famous inedible dinners. Normally, he would have gotten to the telephone before the end of her last dopey soapy, but today because he just had to sit down and kick off his shoes, and then was silly enough to watch some of that crap on television with her, he'd been lulled into a deathlike sleep. It would be hard coming up with a ruse to get the dragon out of the cave, *but, hey!* he told himself, racing for the stairs, *if I can't trick 'er out, I'll simply kick 'er out!*

O, the happy thoughts that flowed through Rodney's mind as he dashed hell-bent-for-leather to his parents' bedroom. Rodney literally flew on the wings of love up those thirteen uncarpeted, worn-shiny wooden steps with his stocking feet. Happily hopping up to the top, his rayon-covered toes skimmed the step's edge with slick ease. He tumbled ass over teacup backwards, landing in a heap at the bottom. His head seemed bent at an unusual angle. It was tucked under his left arm. Or under his right leg, he couldn't tell for sure which.

"What the HECK are you doing?" his father screeched from the living room sofa. "Do you WANT to wake your mother up? Pray quietly, for crying out Christ!"

"That's play, daddy," Rodney squeaked. Although he was now nineteen, Rodney's voice had never bothered to change. He had the falsetto squeak of a eunuch, another little gift from God.

"Pray, pay … what's the difference? Just do it QUIETLY!" Ralph rolled his already severely damaged newspaper into a tight club, smacking the palm of his hand with it to give Rodney an indication what was in store for him if he didn't watch it.

Rodney located his feet. When he saw that he could wiggle his toes he took it as a good sign. He righted himself, twisting one limb over the other until he thought he achieved a more natural posture. Intense pain flowed through every bone in his body. He feared he may never walk, nor move his arms again. Starting to whimper over the terrible tragedy fate had dealt him, an even more horrible thought came to his mind. His pecker might be broken. It would be just like God to make him fall down these crappy stairs and break his pecker just when he needed it most. He jumped up and started probing with his hands until he was assured that it was in working order.

In the living room Ralph smacked his lips, clucked his tongue, then shook his head with disbelief over what he was seeing. "I said, pray quietly, not pray with yourself."

Attentively climbing the stairs this time, he managed to get up them and down the hallway without breaking anything. Rodney stood outside his mother's door, listening to see if the harpy was snoring. There it was through the thick wood, that awful sound like a warthog in heat. A snort-grunt-wheeze combination, meaning she was out cold. He opened the door to peek in. Good GRIEF—in the late afternoon sun slating through the blinds, the sight of her was enough to make him gag. She lay atop the bedcovers, her skinny little body decked-out in a gay, brightly colored floral muumuu. Soft, fluffy green mules adorned her hoof-like feet. Surrealistically, she wore a blue scarf around her throat, its end fluttering in the breeze from her gaping mouth as she breathed in and snorted out, her cheeks puffing and deflating. She looked like a rainbow trout out of water. And, *ugh*, she was wearing one of those pink sleepmasks, like the ugly blindfold Arlene Francis used to wear on *What's My Boring Line* every tedious Sunday night before the celebrity asshole signed-in.

If there was a bright side to the hideousness of his mother, it was that someday beautiful Roweena might look just like her. He gently closed the door. Tapping lightly with his knuckle just under the thumbtacked *Quiet* sign, he hoped she'd hear and wake up.

There was no response.

"Yoo-hoo, mommy ..." he tapped a little louder.

"Is that you, Roweena, dear?" Rhonda called sweetly.

He clucked his tongue silently. *Unbelievable! My own goddam mother couldn't tell the difference between me and my miserable sister.*

She seemed to be in a fairly decent mood, though. Vacating her might be easier than he'd thought. Opening the door boldly, he saw she was sitting up on the side of her bed, one bony chicken leg crossed over the other, still wearing her sleepmask and groping around with both hands on her nightstand for cigarettes.

"It's me, mommy. Rodney."

"Who?" she asked. After several beats, she clucked her tongue and tilted her head back. "Rodney? I might o' known," she said acidly. "What do you want?"

"Well, it's after four o'clock. I thought you'd like to get up now and fix some dinner ..."

The heavy ornate cigarette lighter just barely missed his head. Jeez!—even blindfolded she had tremendous aim. He closed the door quickly, before something else could get him. Sure enough, he heard a thud hit the back of the door where his face had been just a millisecond ago. With Betty waiting, there wasn't time to play games with this demented battle-ax. Rodney gave up the idea of using the Princess in favor of the phone in the living room ... *and if Ralph so much as gives me one ounce of trouble—well, a punch to the heart would shut him up for a while.*

"Daddy?" he called, "can I use the telephone down there?"

No answer. Maybe the old lunk had a heart attack and was dead on the living room floor? *Jesus McChrist! I hope not! It would be awful trying to talk to Betty with a goddam corpse rotting all over the place.*

Back downstairs, Rodney was relieved to discover that his father's body wasn't laying around cluttering up the living room. He probably went outside and was pretending to do yard work so he could spy on neighbors. What a break! He thanked God in Heaven for gracing him with this tremendous stroke of fortune and in return for Rodney's sincere thanks, God sent Brucie sauntering into the living room from the kitchen. Brucie, Roweena's screwed-up mutant of a dog, was an animal only Ripley could love. He had a long, squat body with tufts of wiry billygoat hair on top of his head, under his chin, and down his turd-brown back like clown suit buttons. But what else would a poodle/dachshund mix look like? Rin-Tin-Tin? Brucie wandered around the living room sniffing chair legs while brushing his pointy little tail against the yellow carpet looking for an unstained spot to mess.

He found it.

What a nutcruncher, Rodney thought, watching Brucie's ass dispense shit like a Tastee-Freeze machine. Rodney was royally disgusted, but he had more important things to do than contemplate the awfulness of this animal and the swirling pile of yuck it was producing. He picked up the telephone and dialed. It rang once, then again. He cleared his throat.

"Hulloo?" a woman said.

"Hulloo," Rodney said back, politely, wondering why the signal was still ringing on the line. "May I speak to Betty?"

"I'm sorry, miss, but you must have the wrong number. There is nobody here by that name."

Oh, NO! The Bunz family moved away and Betty didn't tell me! Now there was a click on the line. "Is this 244-8487?"

"Why, yes it is," a different woman said. "Hulloo?"

"Is that you, Grace?"

"And who are *you*?" Mrs. Bunz barked nastily. In addition to a myriad of physical infirmities, Betty's mother also was hard of hearing.

"Rhonda Rodoggio ... Ralph's wife ..."

"Rhonda? Rhonda *Rodoggio*? Oh ... yes. I was just about the call you."

"That's peculiar. I picked up the phone to call you, and you were already on the line."

"That's nice. How is everything, dear?"

"Just wonder-full-*l-l-l* ! Blah-blah-blah-blah-blah-blah, blab, blah-blah-blah. Ha, ha, ha!"

"Tee-hee! Blitherie-blab, yak-yak-yak-yak-yak-yak. Blabble-blab-blab ..."

Rodney hung up. This was a revolting development. Once his mother and Betty's got to yakking and laughing it would be hours before they'd get off the friggin' phone, letting their poor families starve to death for dinner and blocking up the telephone lines from important calls.

Those mothers.

Maybe he could do the world a favor and end their worthless jabber by pretending to be an operator with an emergency telephone call for Betty?

Yes, but what kind of emergency? Mr. Bunz having a work accident at the construction site? A death in the Bunz family? Who? Betty's richbitch Aunt Hornessa?

She's older than the hills!

A perfectly credible passing. Her last words were: "Tell Betty ..." *What? Tell Betty what?* Well, he'd think of something.

He picked up the phone.

"Oh, shit," he said into the mouthpiece, thinking of something he should've remembered. The old moneybag had already pinched her last penny. Rodney hung up softly, hoping the ladies would not hear and think they were being eavesdropped upon. How could he forget all the hubbub attached to dear departed Nessie? She made the *Gulpo Plainsman* front page, a big deal in itself, and the Bunzes threw a spectacular Requiem party which turned out to be the social event of the season. The party was held at Lake Loon Country Club. It had fancy dining, and dancing to the Phil Smackley Orchestra until the wee hours of the morning. It was so lavish that it, like its benefactress, made front page news. Ralph cried for a week over the poor departed woman, slowly becoming angrier and angrier that his picture wasn't in the newspaper along with all the other dancing mourners at Lake Loon. The Rodoggio family had not been invited to the funeral. Nor to the party. And Ralph blamed this oversight on Hornessa Bunz herself for not leaving instructions in her will. ("Nobody leaves invitations to a party in their wills," Rhonda told him. "But that's what wills are for," he maintained.) Soon he was yelling at her front page newspaper picture, believing that her smiling kisser was flouting him. His fury did not abate until it was understood by one and all in the Rodoggio family that the name Hornessa Bunz shall never be uttered in his household again. To prove he meant business, he destroyed the little shrine set up to her on top of the television, ripping the newspaper picture into tiny bits. He prayed to God O'Mighty that her crap-filled soul be plunged into the darkest corner of damnation, so dark in fact that for eternity she'd never be able to see the difference between a single and a five dollar bill, and that there be plenty of bellhops, waiters, and doormen she'd have to tip.

Rodney tried to think. What other kind of emergency break-ins are there? A long distance call? An overseas one! Betty's batty old mother always crowed that someday somebody would discover Betty and put her into the movies. Rodney could try to convince Mrs. Bunz that he was some foreign movie director interested in Betty's career. The more famous the name he'd use, certainly, the easier it would be to get them to put Betty on the phone. He wracked his brain. A foreign movie director? Who directed *Affairs d'Amour*? Wait—he had a better idea. A couple of weeks ago on TV they had this werewolf movie called *Howl of the Wolf*, which turned out to be one big boring, foreign dudOrama. In the first place, a knucklehead at the TV studio renamed it *Hour of the Wolf*, but that didn't matter as much as the fact that all the werewolf scenes were cut out to make room for a ton of commercials. Without the good stuff, that movie was moving sl-o-o-o-o-w. As for the guy that directed it, Rodney jotted down his name, thinking he'd write to him care of the TV station to ask about what he missed. Here it was, right where he wrote it, on the wall behind the TV set. Ingmar Bergman.

Brucie sniffed his load of cooling poop, licking his black little lips. Rodney threw an ashtray at him and he scampered off. Picking up the ashtray for later tossing, but leaving the mess of cigar ash and cigarette butts on the carpet, Rodney considered his plan of action. Brucie traipsed back into the living room, interested now in chewing on a cigar stub. Perhaps he'd try out a foreign accent on Brucie. In a lower voice, one which made him sound like a munchkin with a headcold, he said, "Eh, leetle bustard, you want for mee to push your noze into zhat pile o' shet?"

Not bad. Not bad at all.

Gently, he picked up the telephone, pinching his already pinched little nose, he said, "Soddy to break in on your conbersation. There id an urgent oberseas call for a Miss Beddy Bunz from Baris, France."

"Who is this?" Grace Bunz asked suspiciously.

"Uh ... uh ... obverseas oberator 277."

"What's this about?" Rhonda inquired in a curious way.

Mrs. Bunz echoed the question. "Yes, what is this about?"

Rodney began sweating. "I'll switch you to the pardy that wishes to talk with MISS BEDDY BUNZ." He snapped, crackled and popped his fingers into the mouthpiece, making noises that would add credibility to this being an expensive overseas call, then came back on with a his deep French accent. "Allo, thiz iz ze whirl famoose feelm deerectori Ingmar Bergman. I'd like to, how you zay?—talk to Mizz Bettee Bunzez."

"Why?" Rhonda asked.

"Yes, why?"

"Uh, I happened to bee in zee Gulpoo Plainzez several yearz ago and I wuz lookey enuf to haz ze 'onor of zeeing Mizz Bettee Bunzez in zhat wonnerful play at zee Gulpoo Plainzez High Schools, *Ze Fates of ze Leetle Loosie.* Ah, oui-oui, I remember eet well! I would like to zign her up for my next moofee."

"Oh, how wonderful," cried Mrs. Bunz.

"When did you say you saw Betty act, Miss Bergen?" Rhonda asked.

"Miss Bergen??" Rodney asked, amazed at his mother's stupidity. "Who do you zink I yam?"

"Didn't she say she was Polly Bergen, Grace?"

"Yes. That's what I thought."

Oh, CHRIST. Polly Bergen. He was getting angry now. "This is NOT Polly Bergen," he said in his normal voice. "This is Ing-O-mar Bergen."

"Oooo!" shouted Mrs. Bunz gleefully. "He's doing his Charlie McCarthy voice for us!"

Rodney lost his temper. He screamed into the phone, "I AM NOT EDGAR GODDAM BERGEN … I AM NOT POLLY EAT ME BERGMAN! I AM INGRID BERGMAN AND I WANT TO TRY TO GET A DATE WITH BETTY SO PUT HER ON THIS SHITEATING PHONE RIGHT THIS FARFELFUCKIN' MINUTE!"

The women gasped. They never heard anything like this before.

"Sally Clumdyke's niece Minty got almost the same kind of phone call from a lady truck driver recently … but I *never* thought Ingrid Bergman was one of *those!*"

"She certainly is NOT. She's a BIG movie star!" Grace Bunz told Rhonda icily. "She probably wants to have a cup o' coffee with Betty."

"I don't know. Why don't you ask her?"

"You think I should?"

"Of course! If she were my daughter, I'd want to know why a big Hollywood actress wants a date with her."

"I guess you're right. So, Miss Bergen, why *do* you want a date with Betty?"

"Because I want to HUMP her ass off, you stupid old cow!" he said oh-so-softly with his mouth far, far away from the phone.

"HOW DARE YOU!!!" Mrs. Bunz screamed. "I HAVE A GOOD MIND TO ..."

"Rodney?" Rhonda hissed. "What's *Rodney* doing on this line?" He jammed the phone down onto the hook.

FOUR

Rodney strained his ears listening for snatches of his mother's conversation. Brucie, meanwhile, sniffed the pile of mess, dunking his pink nose right into it for inspiration. He slinkyied over to the coffee table and lifted his stubby right rear leg. After forty-five seconds of solid pissing, he finally finished and climbed up the slipcovers to the top of the sofa where he gave his attention to a duck-shaped throw pillow. Rodney was too distracted to notice him. Once or twice he heard his mother's braying laughter, but that was about all. He was terribly unhappy and gave up trying to hear anything useful. *I'll never get a date with Betty now. Five whole years of trying and it's come to this.*

He needed a stiff drink.

Thinking he'd go to the kitchen and hit his mother's secret stash of Old Hen's Foot under the sink, he turned away from his post at the foot of the stairs and bashed his toes on the corner of the staircase.

Now tears came. *And as far as humping her, I might as well forget it.*

Leaning against the banister for support, he buried his face in the crook of his arm and let out his pent-up frustration. Tears flowed freely, without shame. It wasn't long before bitterness overcame him. He shook his fist at heaven saying out loud, "I'll show her! I'm gonna HUMP every girl in Gulpo Plains ..." Then something caught his eye.

... what the HELL ...

Brucie was straddling the duck pillow, pollywollydoodling the feathers out of it.

Anger blurred Rodney's vision. He grabbed the 14k gold letter opener, a Rodoggio family heirloom much too precious to despoil with the common act of opening letters, from its display rack in the bookcase under the big picture window. He flung it at Brucie, watching as it whizzed harmlessly past the dog's ecstasy-filled face, planting itself deep into the back of the sofa. Brucie scrambled off, onto the one spot on the coffee table not cluttered with Rhonda's caboodle of crap, putting some nice deep scratches into the finish with his claws. Jumping down to the floor, he proceeded to bend his body like a pretzel so he could lick his little red Popsicle.

"Christ-in-a-*kilt*," Rodney hissed, trudging over to pull out the letter opener. En route he took a moment's detour to give Brucie a swift kick, then shrieked in pain as needle-sharp little teeth sank his into his flesh. Rodney flipped his foot instinctively. Brucie, plus his sock, sailed away into the dining room. He examined his injured toe. Thank God the skin wasn't broken. *Now to take care of that bastard letter opener.* It required some hard tugging to get it out of the upholstery, and when it finally did come free, suction dragged out about a million pounds of sofa stuffing with it. Carcinogenic fuzz flew in the air, clumps of the stuff snowed over the sofa seat and floor. There was a big gash in the fabric and a hollow spot beneath it. Unfortunately, the 14k gold Rodoggio family heirloom letter opener got somewhat bent in the struggle, some of the yellow metal had peeled away revealing underneath a grayish-green substance. Stepping over the wet piss pool, dogdump, ashes, and whatnot, he replaced it on the bookshelf, turning the display this way and that until the damage was least noticeable.

He picked up the telephone.

"Excuse me, ladies," he said as nicely as he could. "I would like to …"

The ladies continued chatting without pause.

"… may I *please* interrupt …" Rodney could not believe his ears! Not only were they ignoring him, but they were actually talking louder to override his voice! "LISTEN," he shouted, and that brought instant, cold, silence. "Will you two hammerhead bitches get off the phone so that I can talk to Betty?"

"I'll hang up, dear," Rhonda said pleasantly. "Since someone is *so* anxious to speak with you."

"It was nice talking to you, Mrs. Rodoggio. I'm so sorry mommy got upset and had to leave off with you."

"Think nothing of it, dear. If *I* had a hunchback like your mother, and someone used *that* word around me, I'd be very upset too. Toodle-loo for now." There was a click on the line. Rodney was alone with Betty Bunz.

"So what's the big deal about talking to me, Rory?"

"Rodney," he corrected meekly.

"Yes, I know!" she snapped. "Hurry it up. I haven't got all day." Her tone was not inviting, it was like an icepick jabbed into his eardrum. Nevertheless, and with great suavity, he told her how much he'd enjoy seeing her, that being in her company was like having a slice of heaven right here on earth. "—say!—there's a nifty double feature at the drive-in, why not catch it with me tonight?"

"Get to the point! I'm waiting for an important phone call." Her tone had changed. It wasn't so pointed now, it was more like annoyed irritation. "Well, RORY?"

"It's not Rory, it's Rodney, and the point is that I thought you'd like to spend the evening with me at the drive-in."

"The drive-in?? I've got better things to do than sit around that stupid drive-in, sniffing swamp gas and having bugs fly in the car windows at my face. Besides," here her voice took on a soft, lovesick quality, "I'm waiting for someone *special* to ask me out tonight."

"WHO?" he roared loud enough to make the vase on top of the TV rattle.

"If you must know, it's Marty Martex."

Rodney wanted to barf. *Marty Martex? That mama's boy creep? The homeliest guy in Gulpo Plains? Next she'll be telling me she's going out with Crazy Eddie!* Crazy Eddie was Edward Scrotagg, and he earned his sobriquet by having a deep and profound love of firecrackers. He accidentally blew out his eyes with cherry bombs one July Fourth, and has damaged his hearing, lost fingers, and generally blown himself away on many another non-National Holiday days—it didn't have to be Arbor Day to have a blast, you know. Rodney had a sudden and horrible vision of Betty's big boobs being launched into outer space by skyrockets.

"You haven't had any accidents lately," he asked nervously. "I mean, you haven't been around any skyrockets, have you?"

"Skyrockets? Are you sick, Rufus? Is that the big deal question you needed to talk to me about? Goo'bye."

Click-k-k.

The phone went dead in his hand. He instantly redialed.

"Hull-oo-o," Betty answered musically. It was hard to believe that this was the same Betty he'd just been talking to; she sure can get over a crankiness fast.

"It's me-*ee*-e," Rodney sang back.

She clucked her tongue. "What now?"

"IfMartydoesn'tcallwillyougowithmetothedrive-in??" he rattled off before she had the chance to hang up.

"Oh, OKAY, as long as you keep the car windows closed tight. Got me? T-i-t-e: *tight*. Call me back in an hour." She finished with a bored sigh, then hung up without saying goodbye.

Rodney was elated. A date with Betty! He kissed the telephone. Plopping down on the sofa, giggling and breathing hard, he stared mindlessly at the blank TV screen. He imagined he saw Betty Bunz on television, blowing him kisses off her hand. Now she began a seductive little dance for his viewing pleasure. *Ahhh!* She was taking off her clothes. Slowly, piece by silky piece … he could almost feel the softness of these things as they left her fingertips and floated by his face. *Oooo!*

Wisps of Betty's shimmery gold hair caressed her lovely face, swaying sensuously with each movement of her head and shoulders as she continued to peel off layers of clothes. How her red, full lips glistened when she licked them with the tip of her sexy tongue … how they invited him with small little smooches! And her eyes, big and blue, winking at him—a doorway to a world of enchantment.

Now she was NUDE!

And she was no longer on TV, but kneeling wantonly before him, begging for his attention. She lifted one of her bulbous dollywaggles to him. Rodney's face lit up like a grinning jack-o-lantern, and behind his closed left eyelid was the inevitable flutter of the hated eyetwitch. He reached out to touch her offering, and felt her firm nipple in his fingertips. It was moist, round, and stiff. He tweaked it playfully and it bit his thumb. His eyes shot open. His thumb was tightly clenched in Brucie's mouth, his fingers still wrapped in abandoned caress around the dog's snoot. He flicked his wrist and Brucie flew off his hand into the television, knocking the vase to the floor, where it shattered to bits.

Oh, balls-a-poppin' he fretted, but recovered quickly, reasoning that who has time to care about such trivialities when there were important things to do?

Next on the agenda was Mr. Marty Martex. Rodney looked up mama Martex's number in his brown-nosing mother's address book, then spun the rotary. After three or four rings, the silky, sickening voice of Marty the Slug Martex said hulloo.

"Is this Marty Martex?" Rodney asked in the raspy voice of Herbert Bunz. Mr. Bunz's voice was damaged from years of inhaling asbestos sawdust at construction sites, although, oddly, his wife and daughter have similar vocal traits. When they were all talking together, their loud, annoying buzz-saw intonations made it sound like you're standing in the middle of a lumber mill. Rodney was able to duplicate the rasp rather well, so good in fact that he once successfully tricked Mrs. Bunz into thinking that it was her husband calling on the phone to talk to

Betty—until she realized that Herbert was sitting in the kitchen sucking down a beer.

"Why, yes it 'tis. How may I help you?" Marty Martex said cordially.

"This is Herbert Bunz. Do you know who I am?"

Marty gulped hard enough to be heard over the phone. "Yes ..." he said anxiously.

"Do you know why I'm calling?"

"Uh ... uh ... (gulp) ... I believe I do, sir ..."

"I'm WARNING you: keep away from my girl if you know what's good for you!"

The silence on the line was broken only by the nervous, deep-throated gurgles Marty Martex was making. Finally, in a voice filled with shame, dread, and apprehension, he moaned, "I've only done it with her a couple o' times, sir. She BEGGED me! Honest t'God! It will never happen again, I swear!!"

A couple o' times??! Rodney was so angry he nearly dropped his Herbert Bunz voice. At the crucial moment he regained his control.

"WHAT? YOU'VE STOLEN HER VIRTUE? I'M COMING OVER THERE RIGHT THIS MINUTE TO KILL YOU, UNLESS YOU PROMISE NEVER EVER TO CALL MY DAUGHTER AGAIN!"

"Your daughter, sir?" Marty asked, confused. "Aren't we talking about your wife?"

Rodney felt sick to his stomach, like he was going to heave up his guts. "Just keep away from Betty," he stammered, then hung up.

What a toad! Of all the crudchewing, backstabbing bastards! How in the name of all that was holy could he do such a despicable thing? There weren't words strong enough in the English language to describe the utter perversity of Marty Martex, the most revolting ... scumsucking ... asslicking ... moron ever to walk the face of the earth! Imagine putting your own sweet lovewand into that hunchbacked, flabby old bag o' misery known as Grace Bunz?

Jeez-us K. Kee-rist!

But—so WHAT? If that asshole wants to haghump that's his problem. It just leaves the field of young ladies wide open for us stallions.

Rodney burst with joy. Marty won't be calling the Bunz household today or any other day from now on. "Good Things Happen to He Who Waits," Grandpa Rodoggio used to say when Rodney was a small boy sitting on the old man's lap. Until now, Rodney never believed that crock o' crap, or anything else Gramps told him: it was hard to take seriously someone who got genuine delight feeding a little kid pepper-laced candy and then waited for a reaction (and when it finally came, the old creep would finish his proverb by saying, "… Time and Time Again.")

"It's TRUE! Good things DO happen to He Who Waits!" he sang out, dancing around the living room like Fred Astaire. He danced to the bookcase, and then into the dining room. He samba-ed to the kitchen and mamboed out again. He twirled, en pointe, around the smelly pile of Brucie shit and leapt like Nijinsky onto the coffee table, scattering magazines, coasters, bud vases, and other junk. Skipping off the table he spun once, twice, and on the third time he spun into the angry visage of Ralph Rodoggio.

Ralph was no longer in a good mood. Since his newspaper had been torn and tattered to the degree that reading it was not the civilized pleasure it ought to be, he had to suffer the humiliation of going back to the damn Hokey-Dokey Magazine Shop with his tail between his legs for a replacement. Naturally, they were out of newspapers by the time he got there so he could not exchange his defective one for a fresh copy. And did that salesclerk hee-haw at Ralph's predicament! To be chortled at by someone far beneath him was terrible enough, but having the lout then refuse to take back the paper for a cash refund, causing Ralph to yell and argue in public, was an embarrassment he won't soon forget. Then, to have the honor of marching home again with the same raggy newspaper tucked under his arm—it's no wonder he disposed of it in the gutter.

Now *this*.

Ralph looked around for a newspaper substitute. "You're lucky my paper got slabby from hitting you," he said heavily.

"Uh, I think you mean shabby."

"Oh, yes. Shabby. Shabby. Shabby. Shabby. Shabby. That's right. Shabby." He sat down on Rhonda's easy chair. "I forgot you were the brain of the family. Yes, sir-eee. I must remember that correct word slabby. Slabby. Slabby. Slabby …" Ralph Rodoggio burst into tears. "Why?" he implored, "Why must all the nice things that happen to us be spoiled? I'd have the perfect American family if only I had a different son."

"Uh … what's the matter, daddy?"

"What's the MATTER?" Ralph exploded. He snatched up one of the magazines Rhonda kept handy by her chair and rolled it into a flimsy little tube. Even though it was not as sturdy as a newspaper, the glossy stock stings like the devil. "Mrs. Grace Bunz, who I had the shame of humping into on the street, tells me that you broke into a lovely three-way conversation she was having with your mother and Miss Ingrid Bergman of HOLLYWOOD to shit out some FILTHY words! A famous movie star. Our chance to mangle with greatness, and you've got to dwarf it all up!"

"Bumping into … spit out … mingle … and freak it all up …" Rodney corrected, backing away from his advancing father. The only thing between Rodney and his father's wrath was the pile of doggie muck, which Ralph stepped squishingly upon.

"AND WHO PUT THIS HERE?" he thundered, walking on the back of his heel to the sofa so he could wipe his shoe on the slipcovers. Then he saw the hole in the sofa, plus all the leaked stuffing. Ralph Rodoggio's face became bright, bright red. His teeth clenched tightly. Shallow breath issued through his expanding nostrils.

"Brucie did that!" Rodney managed to get out before the words and a magazine were shoved down his throat.

FIVE

Uncirculating air, dense and humid, and body heat mixing with an external temperature in the upper nineties made it sweltering hot in the closed car. Sweat dripped off Rodney's brow into his eyes, burning like acid. The plastic steering wheel felt wet and sticky, as did the door armrest, and especially the damn vinyl carseat. Breathing was difficult. This thermal metal tomb was so airless that when he opened the door to get out, being careful not to bump his door into the car parked right on top of him, the inrush of fetid gas from the Samuel A. Gulpo Memorial Swamp straight behind the screen half a mile away felt like a refreshing breeze.

Betty playfully shook her finger, smiling. "Now, don't be too long."

He squeezed out through the narrow opening, trying not to dislodge the speaker dangling by its cord over the doorframe so that the window could be rolled-up tight against bugs.

"Because I'm starving t'death," she added strongly, watching him struggle, the smile completely gone. He gazed at her through the open car door, his mouth agape, his tongue lolling out. "And CLOSE that door before BUGS get in! Jumpiny Cracket, are you *dumb*."

"Jiminy Cricket," Rodney corrected without thinking, closing the door.

"*What* did you call me?" she asked sharply. Rodney babbled through the thick safety-glass windshield, trying to get her attention and explain about Ralph's unhinged articulation, and about Pinocchio's little friend, but Betty's patience and good nature were at the end of its rope. She screamed at him to get off the hood of the car and just go get the popcorn before the movie starts.

Looking eastward, Rodney attempted to judge by the setting sun when the show would start. He reckoned about fifteen minutes. He didn't need to rush. The Refreshment Center was going to be packed anyway, a regular zoo, and besides, absence makes the hump grow harder. If he played it right she'd really be missing him by the time he got back. Whistling a chorus of *Zipp-a-Dee-Doo-Dah*, he worked his way through one jammed row of cars after another. Rodney wondered why the drive-in was so busy tonight as compared to all the other times he'd been here with his family, when their's was virtually the only car in the field. Just last week they'd come to see *The Garry Moore Story* with Donald O'Connor, and damn if the place wasn't as empty as Durward Kirby's pockets.

As he was weaving through the rows of parked cars, Rodney merrily reran his memory of that magical moment this evening when he picked Betty up. He sat in his father's turquoise Studebaker outside her house, calling loudly and blowing his horn to let her know he was there. As Betty appeared at the front door, flipping her hand at him to be quiet, Rodney could hardly take his eyes off her. She was a vision of loveliness. Her honey-blonde hair was piled tightly atop her head in a sexy beehive number, one of those cute little pink bows placed front and center on the crest. He noticed she had taken the time to dress extra-specially nice, too, with a hot pink halter top, real tight purple capri slacks, and those spiky-heeled shoes that drive manly men crazy. She fairly sailed down the stoop steps, and Rodney gulped in awe at her wondrous beauty. As she floated nearer, he saw that her two tremendous love buoys bobbed braless under her halter top. Rodney jumped out of the car, and the only thing keeping him from anchoring her on the Bunzes weedy front lawn was the sight of crabby Mr. Bunz looking at them from over the backyard fence. Rodney waved cordially, and Mr. Bunz growled something unintelligible.

The Refreshment Center was chock-full of people, most of them waiting on a long line. It took Rodney quite a while to find the end of it, passing a myriad of grumbling, impatient people with clucking tongues. Rodney felt his excitement ebb away. The festering horde of pajama-clad little trolls overrunning the place *really* got on his nerves.

He saw these little kids clogging up the service line.

Little kids knocking into people, making them spill their orders.

Little kids slopping sticky soda on the floor.

Rodney tried to ignore them, put them out of his mind like they didn't exist, but one of the turdlickers was impossible to avoid. He was wearing, of all things, cowboy pajamas. He chased, or was being chased, by another mutant wearing Batman sleepers. In and out between people's legs, yelling, screaming, shoving.

Soon both of them were bumping and pushing against Rodney's legs. He clucked his tongue, thinking with distaste how cheap these parents were to bring their damn parasitic offspring to the drive-in to sleep just to save a few measly bucks on a babysitter.

Tight as they may be with babysitters, the parents of the cowboy apparently did not believe in stinting on fashion accessories to compliment the kid's sleep ensemble. On his tiny brainless head he wore a red felt cowboy hat. And, of course, he had a deluxe two-hip holster set with matching cap pistols, one of which he flourished wildly, popping caps like crazy. Batman had no bat-cessories to protect himself against the cowboy who, it seemed, was intent on shooting the guano out of him. The idiot kid didn't think he needed help dodging bullets. Around and around they went, an endless loop of laughing and kneeknocks.

The line stepped forward. Cowboy wedged himself in front of Rodney, preventing him from moving ahead and the resulting gap was filled immediately by a linecutter.

Cowboy scampered playfully off. Rodney lifted his fist to punch the linecutting jerk's kidneys just as Batman squeezed in, hooting at the cowboy while jumping up and down on Rodney's toes. Cowboy tried getting under Rodney's arm for a better shot at Batman, but Rodney wasn't affording him an opening.

"No fair," the cowboy pouted. "Come out here so I can shoot you!"

"You can't shoot me! I'm behind my BATSHIELD!" Batman thumped his pygmy fist proudly on his Batshield, and the Batshield debated if he could pinch the little bugger and get away with it.

Kicking the impenetrable Batshield in the back of its leg, cowboy said with venom: "Okay, Batfag, you ax'd for it. I'm gonna blast you and your doo-doo-head Batshield into the middle o' Kingdom Come." He shoved his cap pistol into Rodney's ass and rapid-fired a thousand rounds or so. Each minute percussion felt like a jab from a fiery finger. Rodney looked around to see if it was safe, then dropped his fist onto Batman's head, bending a pointy ear on the stupid plastic Batman hat. He spun around, quickly grabbing the cowboy around his neck with the crook of his arm.

Batman's loud howling attracted the attention of all the responsible grownups, including Mr. Linecutter. Turning immediately, he saw Rodney about to shoot the cap pistol up the cowboy's small nose. If Rodney didn't have any doubts, or hesitations, or second thoughts, regarding the sagacity of punishing a child in such a manner, the hard sock to his mouth from the linecutting clown convinced him that this *might* not be the proper approach. Dropping the pistol to nurse his hurt mouth, he received a hard punch to his nuts from Batman's diminutive fist, followed by another from the cowboy. Walking and talking were going to be difficult for a while. Meanwhile, the two kids scampered off, playing as if nothing at all traumatic or individuality-inhibiting had happened to them.

Twenty minutes later, the sharp pains subsiding into dull aches, Rodney stood at the counter looking at the billions of posted ads trying to determine the price of popcorn. A Yummy Jumbo Hot Dog cost $1.25; a Large 8 oz. Soda, 75¢; a yuckky-looking meatball sandwich "With Special Secret Sauce" would take a bite out of your wallet to the tune of $6.50 ... but there was not one single ad for popcorn anywhere.

"What'cha want." the lady behind the counter snapped at him. It was a declarative statement rather than a question. She looked to be at least seventy years old, having a scalpful of thinning, matted white hair patched with old blonde dye. Her frowning face was as lined and as cracked as a dried-up river bed. Her red, crusty nose, which she wiped incessantly with the palm of her right hand, dripped snot like a molasses spout.

"Do you have any popcorn?"

The women clicked her tongue impatiently while shaking her head in disbelief. A glob of stuff from her nose flew out, leaving a long slimy trail over her shoulder. "What are you, sonny? Some kind o' *retart*? Can't'cha read signs?"

"There isn't one for popcorn."

"No? What's that—the Declaration O' Independence?" She flicked her thumb at an extremely tiny ad placard above the door to the public ladies room, about twenty feet away on Rodney's extreme left side. He strained his eyeballs, pinching his lids half shut for sharper focus:

UMM-MMM!
DEE-LISH-OUS FRESH POPPITY-POP-POPCORN!
A FAMILY FAVORITE!
EACH KERNEL OF TENDER-SWEET POPCORN
SWIMS IN IT'S OWN POOL OF GOLDEN, CREAMY
BUTTER!!!
A REAL TASTE TREAT!
GIANT BUCKET ONLY 75¢

Reading the sign, squinting like a fool, Rodney was distracted by the ladies room door opening. Out came a very thin woman who, as the door closed behind her, jumped as if she'd been goosed by an electric cattle prod. When she saw Rodney looking in her direction, she gasped and ran off.

The counter lady tapped her knurled knuckles for Rodney's attention. "Well? Did'ja make up that brilliant mind o' yours?" He ordered a giant bucket of popcorn and watched the woman open a steam cabinet. Reaching in and bringing out a small container of soggy, limp popcorn, her old arthritic hand must have brushed against a hot surface because suddenly she yelped in pain, dropping the container and spilling almost the entire contents onto the floor.

"Aw, damnaroo," she hissed, shooting Rodney an annoyed look as if it was his fault. She bent down to scoop up the mess, grunting and groaning with the effort. When she came back up, Rodney saw she still had a fistful of popcorn clutched in her right hand, which she dumped into the container, wiping salt and butter substance off her palm onto its lip. She angrily thrust it at Rodney, staring at him expectantly and finally inquiring snidely if payment was forthcoming.

"But this stuff is dirty," he whined. "Aren't you going to give me a new bucket?"

"Where the Sam Diddily Hill do'ya think you are? The Waldorf Ass-toria? Think I'm here just to serve *you*? There are *decent* people waiting in line, you inconsiderate PUNK." Decent people on line behind Rodney started complaining, pushing forward. He gave the woman a dollar bill and was squeezed away from the counter before he got his change. "Thanks for the tip, sonny!" she called to him, grinning.

Rodney walked down the line carrying his container of crappy popcorn, noticing many a hostile glance aimed at him.

"Some people have no consideration for others," a wife said loudly to her husband as Rodney passed.

"And all he bought was POPCORN." someone behind the husband said.

These comments started a flurry of conversation.

"Well, what do you expect from a *teen*ager?"

"Teenager my Auntie Sloo. Look at the way he's dressed, and that shaggy, sloppy hair. That's no teenager, that's an ANIMAL!"

"He's probably a commie aggravator from the Soviet Union."

"Eating POPCORN instead of wholesome food. No wonder he's inconsiderate."

"That's true, you know—how can you be considerate of others when you care so little for your own self?"

"Those teenagers *eat* dope, you know. It's what they live on. That and CRIME."

"You can just tell he's a dope addict. Hopheads loose their taste for normal food and all they want is JUNK like popcorn to eat."

"Why d'ya think they call them JUNKIES?"

They went on and on and on, and were still discussing the disgustingness of Rodney as he went through the door and out into the dark evening air. He wished he had the magical power to make the roof collapse on them all, crushing their mouths to silence, shoving their idiotic opinions back down their tongue-clucking throats.

The program had started. A *Mister Magoo* cartoon was playing on the big screen and Rodney got involved watching it, setting off for the car in the wrong direction. Watching the movie, walking further afield, Rodney became quite panicky when he looked and couldn't spot his father's Studebaker. His cold fear was not based so much on the fact that he had borrowed the car without his parents' knowledge or consent, or that should the car turn up missing his life at home would not be worth a plug nickel, what really scared the b'jeepin Jesus out of him was the idea that Betty may have been kidnapped.

Frantically rushing up and down aisles, searching, the miserable thought popped into his brain that she may not have been kidnapped after all, that she may have, in fact, gotten bored waiting for him and drove off home. He cursed himself for leaving the keys in the ignition.

"Betty!" he wailed loudly, and cars all over honked their horns angrily, flipping on and off headlights, those well-known indications that movie-disturbing noise will not be tolerated. Rodney sprinted away aimlessly. He couldn't even begin trying to locate the position of the car from the location of the Refreshment Center because, now, he didn't even know where the hell *that* was. Just about to give up, throw in the towel and lay down in the gravel, he spotted the car's dented roof in reflected light from the screen. It was only about five rows over. Joyously jogging toward it, his heart fluttering wildly, a drive-in security officer on a motor scooter cut him off. That skinny woman from the ladies room sat on the back of the scooter, her fingers gripping the driver's seat, her pipe-cleaner legs tightly wrapped around the officer's waist like a straight jacket.

"THAT'S HIM!" she screeched.

"Are you sure, ma'm?" asked the security officer.

"I'm a cop's wife, I ought to know how to identify *kittykat* perverts. That creep was peeking into the ladies room, trying to see women in their underwear. Now look at him, going up and down rows of cars filled with good Jesus Loving folk, peeking in at them hoping to see God knows what. An act of perversion if ever there was one. You should take out your gun and shoot the perp right between his sneaky-pete eyes."

A crowd of people gathered from out of their cars, watching the live show unfold before them as they nibbled their snacks.

Rodney was dumfounded. "Are you talking about me, lady?"

(The crowd laughed.)

"Watch who you're calling names." she fumed. "I'm not one of your sluts you know."

(Ooos and ahhhs.)

She continued ranting. "Oh, do I know your type very, very well. Sex, sex, *sex* all over the place with every poor girl you can get your filthy dingle into. Never mind that they have *husbands* who pistol-whip them and handcuff them naked to the bumper of the family car then drive around the neighborhood until their knees are scraped fleshless. Never mind that so long as you get your *piggy* pleasure. Disgusting!" She raised her massive pocketbook to smack Rodney, but the security officer grabbed her arm.

(Scattered whistles and applause.)

"Is this boy guilty of some crime or not, ma'm?" the security officer asked.

The woman sputtered. "Well … he …"

"I haven't done anything!" Rodney cried.

(Hearty laughter.)

"*Oh, yeah?*" The loony woman ripped her dress at the shoulder. "HE RAPE-RAPE-RAPED ME!" she whooped delightedly, pointing an accusing finger at Rodney.

(Assorted gasps.)

The security officer unholstered his nightstick and smacked it against the top of the Woman's head, knocking her unconscious. He strapped the limp body down to the back of his scooter, apologizing to Rodney for the inconvenience. "Remember: movies are your best entertainment value. Enjoy the show," he said, puttering off.

Yes sir, Rodney thought sourly, then wiggled his way through the crowd of applauding, backslapping people to the next row of parked cars.

SIX

"Ugh," Betty said tasting the popcorn. "It's cold and soggy." She popped a few more kernels into her mouth. "And *slimy*." She made an angry face at him. "I told you not to be too long." She tossed the inedible popcorn over her shoulder into the backseat of the car.

"I'm sorry, baby."

"BETTY," Betty corrected nastily.

Rodney hastily started talking about his hardships at the Refreshment Center. He told her about Batman and the cowboy, the linecutting peckerhead, and especially all about the bastard people who pushed him out of line before he could get his change. Then he tearfully told her how horrible it was getting lost, being worried that she'd been kidnapped.

"… then this crazy lady told a security officer that I *raped* her!"

Betty flared. "Listen, who's your date tonight? Me or some crazy lady? I expect consideration—not popcorn I wouldn't even give *you* to eat." She crossed her arms across her chest, stared straight ahead, fuming.

Rodney sensed that this time Betty was really angry.

Goddam bastard people …

A delightful vision popped into his puny brain. The cranky old hag who gave him the disagreeable popcorn, slipping on a puddle of snot and falling headfirst into a steam cabinet. Or maybe she'd be pushed into it by Batman and the cowboy.

Like the old bitch in that idiot fairy tale Hansel & Gretchy. That'd make her years golden all right.

He chuckled, and Betty gave him a sour stare.

The *Mister Magoo* cartoon ended. Next came an excruciatingly long travelogue to the land of Boredom, followed by a zillion coming attractions. Then the screen went blank. Three spots of light, like large flashlight beams, appeared. They circled the screen, chasing one another, in a well-worn attempt to attract attention. Rodney noticed that there wasn't an overload of people rushing back to their cars. The spotlights continued for many minutes before the screen went blank again. Rodney looked at his watch. Eight-forty-five.

He smiled.

It'll take about fifteen minutes for her to get over her pique, another fifteen for the movie to start, fifteen more for her to get bored. Let's see … in a little over an hour it'll be HUMPTIME!

A blaring, brassy fanfare sounded from the cheap, tinny speaker, echoing over the rows and rows of cars like stage thunder in a high school production. A dull gray background slide appeared on the screen, over which was superimposed:

The
Gulpo Plains All-Weather Drive-In
Theater
—Douglas D. Dunky, Manager—

At the last harsh fanfare note, the overly chipper cosmetic voice of Mr. Dunky started his usual moronic spiel.

> *Welcome to the Gulpo Plains All-Weather Drive-In Mo-oo-vie*
> *Theater, presenting the finest family entertainment your money*
> *can buy. Remember, 'movies are your best entertainment value'.*
> *The Gulpo Plains Chamber o' Commerce reminds you 'God Saves'*
> *so attend church regularly.*
> *Tonight's feature in our exclusive* Sensual Erotica *series will*
> *begin in a moment, but before it starts there is still time to visit our*
> *modern and sanitary Refreshment Center. Come on over and join*
> *us for a* Yummy Jumbo Hot Dog *and a* Gulpa-Cola. *Or, if you prefer,*
> *a* Big 'N' Beefy Hamburger *and* Gulpa-Cola. *Don't forget our World*
> *Famous* Gulpolino Submarino Sandwich! *Tender meatballs smothered*
> *in a special secret sauce served warm on a loaf of crusty Italian-style*
> *bread. Mama-Mia, everybody'a'love this'a taste'a Italy! It tastes*
> *better, naturally, with a big cool cup of Gulpa-Cola. Be sure to load*
> *up on everyone's favorite—POPCORN! Each hot, crisp poppin'*

fresh kernel of corn is popped just for you and swims in a pool of
golden creamy butter! M-mmm-mmm! They don't call it Dee-Lish-Ous
for nothing, folks! Wash it down with a fizzy sip o' Gulp, 'the Drink O'
Today', *accept no substitutes.*
And … now …
       … It's …
          … ShowTime …
             … ShowTime …
                … ShowTime …

The irritating voice faded dramatically. There was rhythmic deep breathing on the soundtrack, although it sounded more like someone chewing Reynolds Wrap than erotically-charged sighs over this crackling speaker. The screen suddenly filled with what looked like a gigantic close-up of a human female breast. It was hard to tell since that stupid Gulpo Plains All-Weather Drive-In Theater slide was still on screen along with the movie. Rodney tooted his horn and flashed his headlights to show his annoyance. Cars from all over the field joined in, honking and flashing their headlights at the screen, washing out the projected images. The slide was removed. The headlights ceased. Now everyone could see the heaving mammary without the annoying interference, although the film itself wasn't much clearer. The color had faded to an orangey red, with the picture and sound jumping at every foot spliced together by Scotch tape. Black line scratches veiled a lot of the image, as if Peggy Flemming used the negative to clean her ice skates. The film was terribly warped, going in and out of focus. But no matter how awful the film quality, Rodney's eyes were glued on that forty foot by eighty foot tit.

The camera teased around the nippley-doo-dah, slowly pulling back to show more. When the girl's naked, writhing body occupied the entire screen, the picture froze into a still, then opening titles appeared over her. Some breathless sexy-voiced girl began singing about *Amour* in a Euro-peon language. The jazzy/blues music pulsed, the singer moaned with soft, rapturous sighs, and Rodney squirmed uncomfortably on his hot, sticky seat.

"I'm hungry," Betty said. "Go up to the Refreshment Center and get me a Gulpolino Submarino San'wich."

Rodney, hypnotized by the music, could not take his eyes off that girl on the screen.

"DID YOU HEAR ME?"

"Huh?"

"I said, did you HEAR me! What are you? Deaf? Go up to the Refreshment Center and get me one of them Gulpolino Submarino San'wiches."

She huffed angrily. Rodney, staring at Betty's heaving chest, his left eye twitching, reached out almost beyond his free will to grab a handful of mushy Betty boob. She gave his hand a hard slap.

"Don't you *dare* put out your hand to me for money, mister! You're escorting me, remember?"

Rodney came to what little senses he had. Wisely looking at the broken and chipped plastic dashboard instead of at the movie screen or at the rack of Betty he said, "Uh, that was a Gulpareena Saltina Sandwich … anything else?"

Betty thought for a moment. "Yes. A *large* Gulpa-Cola."

When Rodney shifted to get out of the car he discovered he had a nice, big, stiff, embarrassing hard-on. Moving so Betty wouldn't notice, he succeeded in jiggling his ass all over the car seat, noisily sticking and unsticking to the goddamn vinyl. Betty was staring at him. He opened the door a crack, put his left foot out onto the gravel and shifted his weight enough to work his way out.

A moth flew into the car, attracted by the interior light. It flapped around in his hair.

"Eeee-eeeee-k a BUG!" Betty screeched, pushing Rodney out the door with her foot, then deftly hooking the handle and pulling it shut, nearly clipping off his trailing right leg. From outside, Rodney could hear the sound of all the door-locks snapping.

"Wha—?" he started to say quizzically, not having a clue as to what was going on. The circling moth veered into his open mouth, fluttering around in a frenzy, before diving down his throat, leaving a bitter, powdery taste in his mouth and throat which neither spitting nor coughing relieved.

SEVEN

Rodney returned within half an hour, this time with nothing awful to add to his storehouse of miserable memories. As he navigated back to the car with his unbalanced cardboard tray of food, he reflected how extraordinarily lucky he was that there was anything left to buy at the refreshment center considering the desperation for snacks that besets the American moviegoer in the last minutes before a movie starts, and how positively amazing it is to see the speed in which a place teeming with people can become a desolate wasteland of geriatric serving personnel.

Rodney approached the Studebaker from Betty's side, and he was somewhat perturbed to see that she had become seriously engrossed in the movie, which by now had turned into a regular humpfest between that naked young girl and three extremely greasy guys. He avoided looking at the arousing images on the screen, knocking on the passenger window with his elbow for Betty's attention ... then pounding hard enough to severely crunch his funnybone, which made holding the flimsy tray loaded with heavy food mighty difficult. Betty turned away from the movie and pulled up the lock, but only after she saw the precarious tray in his hands. Juggling the door open, passing the tray to her, he requested that she reach over to unlock his side, but she quickly closed the door.

He went around and watched her through his window, waiting. Noting the dangling car keys in the ignition, he again cursed himself for leaving them there even after God had given him a clear warning before. As she unwrapped the sandwich, Rodney called her name over and over again. Betty ignored it, but someone in a nearby car yelled for him to shut the fuck up. Rodney tapped his finger on the thick safety glass, pointing to the doorlock and mouthing the words *let me in* while she was licking sauce from the foil wrap. She took a big bite of the sloppy mess then whipped her head around to shoot him a dirty look. "This is terrible," she complained bitterly, slapping the Gulpolino Submarino Sandwich down on top of the dashboard. "Where's my Gulp?"

Rodney was holding it. He had taken a couple of slugs as he walked back to the car, but the highly carbonated sugary soda did little more than bring out the full tang of acrid mothdust. She flipped up the lock. Rodney got in and handed her the cup, smiling.

"You call this a *large* Gulpa-Cola? Look—half of it is missing …"

"I also bought you some more popcorn," he said quickly.

Betty smiled warmly. He was encouraged to feel that the evening was not going as badly as he had feared, although that damn six dollar and fifty cent sandwich wasting away on the dashboard was distracting. "If you're not going to eat that …" Rodney said, delicately indicating the sandwich by reaching out for it just as Betty noticed gooey secret sauce dribbling down the dashboard and onto her pants. Before he could touch it, the sandwich went flying over her shoulder. Rodney turned to look. Meatballs, secret sauce, soggy popcorn, uncrusty Italian-style bread all over the upholstery. More than seven bucks worth of food just to end up a mess on the backseat of the old man's car. Well, so what? Soon, he'll be getting much, much more than seven dollars worth of sweet Betty flesh.

He stole a glance at the movie. A slick old geezer and some Joan Crawford-type lady were engaged in a violent argument. Their voices, dubbed into English a millisecond too late, raised angrily and intensely above the crappy music score of squealing violins and underlay of tubas. The Joan Crawford lady was constantly moving, flitting about in a dopey negligee, the kind that puffs out and trails behind like gossamer wings and are supposed to drive men nuts with hornyness. Rodney hooted derisively. Joan Crawford in one of those things was still Joan Crawford underneath it. A *real* pecker-killer if ever there was one. And who was this lady anyway? Maybe the naked girl's mother? Was the man the naked girl's daddy? He dressed like an organ-grinder's monkey. Tweed pants, bright red gold trimmed vest, a plain shirt with a string tie and a round little tasseled hat on top of his head. His dyed black hair with snow white fluffy sideburns, and thin red lips didn't help much either. All he needed was a tin cup in his hand.

The scene went on and on and on. Rodney yawned, played with the car keys, tapped his fingers on the steering wheel, anything to help pass the time. This had to be one of the most boring duds ever made. His mind wandered.

This grasswatcher's delight is so slow moving that the only action Betty's going to see will be right here on the front seat.

Heh-heh-heh, he smirked.

Putting his head back against the headrest, Rodney reviewed the technique he'd chosen for tonight's Extra Zesty HumpOrama. First, slipping his arm around her shoulder he'd draw her close. Next, an intense gaze steadily and deeply into her big blue (*or are they brown?*) eyes for a dash of romance. Then their lips would lock in a sexy, suction-filled, kiss. A little tongue waggling would give her a taste of things to come.

Ooo, yes! There'll be some handy handwork, and then …

"Turn up the volume. *Pu-l-l-ezze.*" Betty's mouth was full of popcorn, but Rodney got the gist of her request. He continued daydreaming, turning the little plastic knob on the old, much used, metal speaker. He wondered why the people on screen had suddenly stopped yelling, reasoning that it was a cinematic statement. *It figures. These fruity foreign filmmakers would have to throw in some bizarro art crap just as I'm trying to adjust the volume.*

"Louder, I said. Not *off*!" Betty clucked, but her tongue slipped on popcorn grease adhering to the roof of her mouth. All she could manage was a little slurping noise which hardly sounded annoyed, so she told him she was very annoyed, shaking the container of popcorn at his face for emphasis.

Rodney misinterpreted, helping himself to a handful. Betty rolled her eyes heavenward, sighed deeply in disbelief, and inquired with strained patience if he intended to turn the sound back on. Rodney checked. Sure enough, he had turned the speaker off accidentally. Nothing happened twisting the knob with his popcorn-buttered fingers. They kept skittering off, so he pinched down hard. The momentum of the knob sluicing over his fingertips propelled it all the way around, now blasting sound at them.

"THAT'S TOO LOUD!" Betty yelled, covering her ears and spilling her popcorn.

Rodney quickly wiped his hand on his pants and bore down on the troublemaking, sonofabitch, little bastard knob. The cheap plastic casing broke apart.

"Turn it DOWN!"

Rodney thought of punching his fist through the speaker box, but ruled that out rather quickly. Not only did he fear it wouldn't do the trick, but the damn drive-in would make him pay for the damage. His only hope was turning the bare metal stem. What felt like ten thousand volts flowed through his body.

"Shit*shit*DAMN—shitshit*DAMN*—SHITshit*DAMN*—!" he ejaculated.

Betty told him to watch his filthy mouth.

His whole body vibrated. Muscles tightened, loosened irresponsibly, shaking him like Saint Vitus at a hoedown. With tremendous willpower he twisted his hand, turning the sound down to a reasonable level. His fingers were soldered to the stem by electromagnetic current. Pulling, he managed to pry them open. Surprisingly, there was no pain in his body, although his teeth seemed to be buzzing. He guessed that once shock wore off he was in for it big time. He vowed to compensate for the pain to come with additional pleasure from Betty's body *now*.

In the movie, the man was raising his hand to strike the woman. "I know what is mine," his dubbed voice said. The woman laughed sardonically out of synch.

Rodney stifled his anxiousness. *As soon as she finishes that popcorn …*

Monkey-man repeated his last line, this time pounding his chest forcefully. Rodney giggled. Doing an Italian accented imitation of the old geezer, adding monkey grunts while beating his chest, he looked over at Betty, believing that his whimsy would be striking her fancy.

It wasn't. She looked at him as if he *was* a monkey.

Rodney sat in embarrassed silence for a long time, finally lifting his hands above his head to stretch. There was a ripping noise. Alarmed, he felt under his arms to see how badly his shirt was damaged when he realized that the sound had come from the movie. J. Fred Oldie was holding Joan Crawford-Lady's tattered negligee. Very slowly, the camera pulled back to reveal her laying naked on the bed, exactly the way the young girl had.

She looked pretty good—but that's because Joan Crawford had turned into the young girl!

There were cuts back and forth between closeups of their eyes, showing the viewer that the couple were re-evaluating one another. Betty leaned forward, eating her popcorn at a faster pace.

Rodney's left eye twitched.

The man threw down the negligee. Peeling off his own clothes, he shouted, "A man takes what is his," and dived onto the bed. The camera zoomed in for some juicy close shots of female body parts and of big, hairy male hands squeezing them. Rodney drooled, wanting to lunge at Betty. He was at the bursting point. With his last remaining bit of self-restraint, he forced his view away from the movie.

He looked into the next car.

A boy and girl were in that car, looking pretty damn cozy. The boy was Larry Ladle, one of Benny Fossert's old pals, and the girl was unmistakably Sandy Queezenok … but, wait, no!—these were different kids. These were *high school* kids, a few years younger than Rodney and everybody else he knew from school.

They were kissing with wild abandon, the boy's arm around the girl's neck, her hand stroking his hair. Rodney gasped seeing the boy's other hand go under her blouse. They soon disappeared below view onto the carseat. Rodney returned his gaze to the movie screen, poking at his eye. The man and girl rolled around, rutting on the stupid bed, grunting and moaning like pigs in a pen who have just been slopped.

He looked at Betty.

She stared, entranced, at the screen and had stopped eating. She breathed deeply, her untethered pleasurepuffs rising and falling.

"A MAN TAKES WHAT HE KNOWS HE WANTS," Rodney screamed, leaping across the seat, pushing her down against the door in a shower of damp popcorn while she kicked and struggled with her legs. He tried to smooch her voluptuous mouth. Betty's foot entwined with the steering wheel, and as Rodney went to grab a breast, Betty went to kick his ass. Her long spiky heel caught the hornbar, jamming it into a blaring wail. Irked horns sounded, accompanied by angrily flashing headlights.

Rodney sat up quickly, trying to unjam his horn by smacking the steering wheel, which somehow managed to increase the horn's volume. It kept escalating to an earsplitting level while Betty sat up. Brushing the popcorn out of her hair, she composed herself.

"THAT'S THE TROUBLE WITH YOU, ROLLO," she said above the din, opening the car door, "YOU DON'T EVEN HAVE THE *CLASS* TO WAIT UNTIL I'VE FINISHED MY POPCORN. GOO'NIGHT!"

She left the car door wide open.

EIGHT

Television presented the best entertainment Ralph Rodoggio could ever imagine, and this evening there was a whole hour of the very finest. At ten o'clock *Serial Killers In Your Life* aired. It was a half-hour Special featuring stories of mass murderers around the world and one segment, about a Los Angeles looloo running a hippie commune, was *especially* entertaining. Ralph slapped his knee, getting a tremendous kick every time the scraggly bearded loon was on screen. His appetite whetted, enjoying the warm and cozy feeling in his tummy only quality television provides, he couldn't wait for *Mortimer Morbane's News of the Day* to begin. Watching the endless line-up of commercials and becoming more and more irritated, he clenched the purloined newspaper resting on the snack table before him. Earlier, about the same time Rodney (who Ralph thought was upstairs in his room) last jaunted to the refreshment center, Ralph was outside getting a nosy looksee at the neighbors. Although dusk settled in, and light was scarce, he pretended to be trimming his nearly dead-by-neglect bushes while looking into other people's yards. Electric light coming through the dining room window next door fell like manna upon the forgotten newspaper resting neatly on their well-kept lawn—so, as God (who sounds a little like Popeye the Sailorman in Ralph's mind) says: "*I helps those that helps themselves*", Ralph had helped himself to Helman Droogie's *Gulpo Plainsman*.

He turned his vision away from the TV in disgust. Television, a wonderful American Privilege, would be perfect if those dangdarn politicians didn't crump up the airwaves trying to sell stuff. Gazing over his living room at all the nice things American life has brought him, his sight happened to fall upon the sofa and its unsightly gaping hole. Anger burst up from his stomach, demolishing all trace of the good feeling he had just moments ago. His grip on the newspaper tightened. He rolled it into a thick log, picturing himself dashing upstairs to mete out some well-deserved punishment before the Mortimer Morbane show began.

Rhonda, sitting in her easy chair next to Ralph, knitting an ice bucket cover, asked, "What's the matter, dear?"

For a mad moment, Ralph thought she was Rodney. He lifted the paper to wallop her, but caught a glimpse of Roweena lounging on some pillows at their feet on the floor. His heart softened immediately. His agitation bubbled down like stomach acid in Bromo Seltzer. "We may have been given a rotten break with our son, but God in His grave saw fit to grant us a wonderful little girl," he said lovingly.

"*Grace*, dear."

"Nooo," Ralph said with strained patience, clucking his tongue slightly at Rhonda. "*Grace* is married to that nutty Herbert Bunz."

Roweena, adjusting her shoulder-length brown hair, which fell demurely down her neck and over the shoulders of her Yogi Bear bathrobe, gave him a wink. Ralph petted her head tenderly and she stretched her long legs, rubbing her head against his palm. As soon as he heard the clacking teletype, introducing the start of *Mortimer Morbane's News of the Day*, Ralph snapped his hand back and turned his full attention to the TV screen.

The first few minutes were hogged up with boring news from around the world, then came national headlines. After a tedious commercial break, finally it was time for local news. The gravedigger's strike at the EternOrest Cemetery was now in its fifth month. Residents were advised to avoid going near the intersection of Cobblywobble Road and Netherland Avenue because the odor resulting from unburied bodies is said to be extremely unpleasant.

Ralph shook his head sadly. "Those poor unburied people. Is there no rest for the dreary?"

"Weary, dear," Rhonda said.

The high cost of meat, how people were trying to stretch their shopping dollars, was discussed in minute detail. On-the-scene newscaster Tony Donameche, a slick and smoozing individual, reported from the Droupe' family house outside town, near Siftracht City, unfolding a solution to this discouraging situation. "Clumpy, their Newfoundland dog weighing in at three hundred ten pounds, cost one hundred and seventy-five dollars when bought from a breeder as a pup. After cooking, and allowing for two years' worth of upkeep, the bottom line is that this alternative to store-bought meat comes out costing less than one dollar per pound."

Mrs. Rodoggio looked at Brucie.

"Mrs. Ilka Droupe´ thinks the government should begin breeding Newfoundlands for an inexpensive source of meat. According to her, everybody will love the taste of what she is calling clumproast.

"Another city family, the Leon Bastardos, say that their dog Spuffy has nothing to worry about. The idea of eating a family pet is so repugnant to them that Mr. and Mrs. Bastardo and their twelve, now eleven, children have found another meat substitute by cooking and eating—"

And whatever was said next will never be known by the Rodoggios. Somewhere down the block a non-stop automobile horn blasted, drawing their attention away from the low sound on the television. Ralph jumped to his feet, brandishing his rolled newspaper.

"IF I CATCH THE LOUSE THAT'S MAKING THAT NOISE," he bellowed. "I'LL TEACH HIM A THING OR TWO ABOUT RESPECT FOR DECENT TAX-PAYING CITIZENS!"

"Please don't," Rhonda pleaded fearfully. "What if it's one o' those serial killers, like on tel'o'vision? What if it's Charlie Manson? You might inflame his sick mind to murder us all if you start bashing him with that newspaper!"

"Are you *loopy*, Rhonda? There's NO such thing as cereal killers. It's made up. Like the *Beverly Hillbillies*. What do you think? We have hillbillies living here in those big houses over on Gookinn Place?"

"Charles Manson is a real person, daddy." Roweena told him.

The horn was getting louder *and* closer.

Ralph paled, sweating. From this moment on, for the rest of his life, Ralph not only believed that there were people in the world that went about helter skelter, loving Rice Krusties cereal and murdering folks for no reason, but also that everyone who lived on wealthy Gookinn Place, including the mayor of Gulpo Plains, were hillbillies from down south who ate possums for breakfast and weee-doggies for dinner like old Jed Clampett. The two facts were now inseparable in his mind. He sat nervously, waiting for the car full of killers to pass by.

The vehicle was close enough to the Rodoggio house that the unmistakable croak of a car engine could be heard along with the keening horn. With unbearable horror, Ralph heard the car pull up his own driveway.

"IT'S CHARLIE MANSON," he screamed. "TURN OFF THE LIGHTS! MAYBE HE'LL THINK WE'RE NOT HOME AND GO AWAY."

Ralph and Rhonda rushed around the living room shutting off lights, closing drapes. Ralph pulled forward his big easy chair and huddled his family behind it, clutching his newspaper as a makeshift weapon. The living room was dark and quiet except for the eerie glow from the television, casting strange shadows on the walls and ceiling, and the low mumbling monotone of Mortimer Morbane.

The car engine stopped coughing. A car door slammed. The garage door was thrown forcibly open. Ralph, Rhonda and Roweena heard clattering garden tools and lawn equipment tumbling on the cement floor inside the garage. Aside from the lunatic bee-eee-eee-eeeep of the car horn, there followed peace for a second or two. Then came the awful hullabaloo of crashing glass and crunching metal.

The car horn ceased to beep.

"He's got my ax," Ralph whispered. "I think he just murdered his car with it."

The garage door banged down. Angry footfalls reverberated up the front walk from the driveway, and then onto the stoop.

"When he rings the doorbell, we won't answer."

But the intruder didn't ring the doorbell. Instead, he boldly came right into the house through the unlocked front door and headed straight up the stairs. Ralph sighed in relief. The killer would be so busy murdering Rodney the rest of them could get out of the house unnoticed.

"Is that *you*, Rodney?" Rhonda asked with some vexation. Astonished by her stupidity, flagging their presence to a terrible killer, Ralph smacked the side of her head with his newspaper, flipping her eyeglasses off across the living room floor.

"No," came a sarcastic voice from the landing. "It's Walter Cronkite."

Ralph jumped up. He slicked down his thinning gray hair with a spit-damp palm. "Walter Cronkite was making that noise?" he beamed, turning on a lamp.

"No. It's only *Rodney*," chortled Roweena.

"I should have known," Ralph snarled, belting the back of the easy chair cruelly. "Wherever there's noise, there's *Rodney*."

Rodney stood on the stairs, patiently listening to Rhonda scold him for disturbing his father's favorite TV show. Ralph added bitterly that it didn't matter any more, because being burdened with a son like Rodney he was used to missing out on all the joys of American Life. Rhonda lifted her arms heavenward, pleading with God to tell her what she had done to deserve such a lousy life. Ralph curtly informed her that the only person she had to blame for Rodney was Rhonda herself.

"Me," she screeched. "I suppose *you* had nothing to do with it!"

"Yes! I had *nothing* to do with his conscription."

"Rodney's a bastard … Rodney's a bastard," Roweena chanted.

Rodney, absorbed in gloom, standing on this step just waiting for someone to get around to yelling directly at him, contemplated going back out to the garage for the ax to chop Roweena's chanting head off. Leaning forward to sit down, several papers slipped from his shirt pocket. One was a repair bill from the drive-in for the speaker torn off its post as he hastily pulled out in an effort to escape a mob of movie lovers intent on lynching him for ruining their fine entertainment. The other papers were, of course, various traffic tickets ("Beeping at an Intersection", "Horn Honking Past Ten O'clock at Night", "Joy Beeping" and other infractions of the law) plus a summons to appear in court for disturbing the peace.

"Rodney's a bastard ... Rodney's a bastard ... Rodney's a bastard ... Rodney's a bastard ..."

Ralph's tirade escalated. Indicating the twelve inch black & white television set to Rhonda, illustrating a salient point, he had the sublime sorrow of seeing that *Mortimer Morbane's News of the Day* was over. The Late Movie was on. Clenching his chest, shrieking in agony, Ralph wobbled over to plop down into a chair. Rodney dashed into the living room to see if the old scumbo was dead. He was greeted with a mighty thump across his face with Helman Droogie's newspaper, now wielded by his sobbing mother.

"If you hadn't been such a rotten son your father would still be alive!" Tears streamed down her face. Wrapping both her petite hands around the newspaper club she swung at Rodney for all she was worth. But not being familiar with the process of smacking her son with a rolled-up newspaper, Rhonda connected only with air, losing her balance and spinning forward. She fell atop Ralph's lifeless body.

A miracle occurred.

Ralph grunted an "*oomph*" as air escaped his body through just about every opening. His eyes sprang open. Mumbling something into Rhonda's ear, he then asked softly for his son's ear to his mouth. Rodney stupidly bent low.

"YOU'LL PAY FOR THIS, MISTER!" Ralph thundered. Rodney bolted upright, cradling his ringing ear. He felt some kind of warm liquid drain through his fingers. "BECAUSE OF YOU, I'VE MISSED *THE MORTIMER MORBANE NEWS O' THE DAY SHOW* ... NOW I'LL HAVE TO GET ALL THE MORNING PAPERS TO CATCH UP WITH WHAT'S HAPPENING IN THE WORLD. I'LL TELL YOU THIS: YOU'LL PAY FOR EACH ONE OF THOSE NEWSPAPERS PLUS PAY FOR THE WASTED ELECTRICITY USED RUNNING THE TEL'O'VISION FOR NOTHING!" He held his hand out. Rodney reached into his pocket and pulled out a quarter. Ralph's jaw dropped. "A QUARTER?? DO YOU SEE *THAT*? HE GIVES ME A LOUSY QUARTER FOR *ALL* THE MORNING NEWSPAPERS! THEY COST AT LEAST A *DOLLAR* AND HE GIVES ME A FALLOPIAN QUARTER." (Nobody would hazard a guess as to what he meant to say in place of *fallopian*.) Sobbing quietly, taking consolation in the sight of his sweet little girl, he said with a tremolo "My Roweena wouldn't give her daddy a lousy quarter, would she?"

Roweena gasped. "Oh, no, daddy!"

"You want a dollar?" Rodney howled. He took out his wallet and zipped out the last bit of money he had on earth. "There's your dollar!"

"Thank you," Ralph said. "Now, about the electricity. Five dollars." Rodney wrote him an I.O.U.

"Can I go to my room now?"

"See that?!" Ralph implored, holding his hands up to the fates, letting them know the tribulations he has been through. "My own son, flesh o' my flesh, fruit o' my loom, won't *even* stay and watch the Late Movie with us!"

Rodney loudly smacked his lips. He kicked Brucie from his place on the floor, dropping down to sit crosslegged, staring at the damn TV. It was some kind of idiot musical with Gene Fucking Kelly. Ol' Gene was tap-tap-tap dancing away, a big eat-my-ass grin on his face.

"And look! It's got GENE KELLY in it! He's click-clacking with his *feet*!" Ralph laughed delightedly, tapping his own slippered feet on the floor. "How do'ya suppose he makes that click-clack sound?"

"Well, it's just the sound his shoes make on that shiny floor he's dancing on," Rhonda offered.

"I don't know. I've danced on shiny floors and my feet don't click-clack. It's something else. Maybe the click-clacks are in the music?"

It was bad enough having to sit and watch this boring crap, let alone be witness to one of the most inane conversations his parents ever had. Rodney couldn't stand it. It was like being skinned alive and dipped in brine. "They're shoes," he said. "Special shoes. *Tap* shoes."

"Yeah, really," Ralph said suspiciously.

"That's true, daddy," Roweena chirped.

"Wow! *Really*? First thing in the morning, I'm getting myself a pair o' TAP shoes!"

Rodney heard Brucie sniffing behind him. He ignored the horrific monster of a dog—until he felt a stubby leg lift against his back. He gave Brucie a shot with his elbow, mocking a sneeze to make it look like an accident.

Brucie, somewhat smarter than all the Rodoggios put together, knew this was no accident; *retaliation* in dogspeak is a four-letter word best said with flashing teeth.

NINE

Ninety some-odd minutes later, in his dinky bedroom, his own private corner of the world, rubbing the still-sore dog bite on the back of his neck with his still-sore electrically-burned fingers, Rodney thought about what a dismal thing dating was. The pain of self-pity soon transcended his physical discomfort. Indulging himself in some well-deserved, albeit sloppy, solace, his lower lip quivered while his fuscous orbs filled with tears and snot dribbled from his nose.

Searching his messy room with glum-clouded eyes, Rodney longed for something familiar and comforting. He found delight in his largely unused toys, which were racked higgledy-piggledy on a cheap pressboard bookshelf beside the window. Fondling these treasures, his brain seized upon the far less miserable days of his boyhood. Here were gyroscopes and broken Slinkys, some G.I. Joe figures, a dollhouse senile old Aunt Grewl gave him believing Rodney was a girl, his Mr. Twinkie stuffed animal, and, of course, his model airplanes.

Lovingly, gently, he picked up the Wright Brothers plane, *Kitty Hawk*. He built it when he was ten, following the instructions closely, doing everything patiently the right way. Looking now at the workmanship and remembering what a bitch it was to glue all those small damn pieces together, he marveled at the fine job he'd done and how long it took him to finish the intricate model. What a sense of pride he felt holding it, what a supreme accomplishment! You had to be *very* careful handling these models, though, because the Aurora airplane glue was by now dried out and the model could come apart in your hands, fragmenting into a zillion pain-in-the-ass pieces. *It's funny*, he ruminated with irritation, *how the goddam glue sticks to everything while putting it together* … his fingers, his hair, the dinning room table … *and now the crap can't even hold these little plastic doodahs in place.*

Lofting the *Kitty Hawk* high above his head, he jogged the few steps to in front of his dresser, making zoom-zoom airplane noises with his mouth. God! He loved this model! He almost tripped over the bunched-up dirty clothes on the floor, but veered past them to his bedroom door, turning sharply before crashing into the wall. Flying it the length of the room to his bed, he plopped down on his knees, bouncing up and down on the mattress while performing several loop-de-loops and other aerobatics. Uttering a happy little laugh, Rodney fell forward landing on his belly, his chin and arms hanging off the foot of the bed.

His short-lived euphoria ended. The misery of life flowed over him in waves as the *Kitty Hawk* fell from his inattentive fingers, landing miraculously unbroken on soft carpet. Yes sir, his childhood may have been the trots, but it certainly was better than what he has now.

Rodney moaned unhappily.

There was one thing that might cheer him up. He flopped around on top of his unmade bed so that his head was on the pillow and he reclined on his right side. Reaching down behind the headboard, Rodney plucked out the well-worn copy of *Playboy* magazine he bought for the price of twenty-five firecrackers from Crazy Eddie when they were both in the ninth grade. He turned quickly to page 105, to the photo showing a beautiful blonde girl standing nude behind a diaphanous curtain. The caption along side identified her as Celeste Yahootie, a Bunny at the New York City Playboy Club. Rodney fantasized coming into her bedroom unexpectedly, finding her lounging around all nuded up. She was pleased as punch to see him, running teasingly to hide behind the curtain.

The little vixen!

She was playfully peeking out. From the way she was standing you could see her delightful blissblimps as clear as day, erect nipples and all, as well as part of her tender, tight bottom. Rodney brought out his expensive Japanese *Mammyyokum* camera and snapped this picture.

He sighed. Someday he'll leave Gulpo Plains, heading for New York City to get a great paying job, probably as an executive. He'd be a *What Kind of Man Reads Playboy* guy, earning a hundred smackeroonies a week. With his very first paycheck he'll buy himself a Playboy Club Key and go there every night until he meets Celeste Yahootie in person. With his wonderful success and manly charm, he'll seduce the hell out of her. She will fall madly in love, and as she washes his dirty underwear by hand in the kitchen sink, he tells her all about his childhood. They laugh together, laugh their asses off, thinking how Big City Rod came from such a jerkwater asshole town like *Gulpo Plains*. When Celeste Yahootie, an international celebrity, hears that Betty Bunz, an intergalactic nobody, snubbed him, she would write a haughty letter telling Betty what great humpiness Rod possesses. Betty, remorseful everafter to have missed such pleasure in her mundane life, would pack her bags, rushing to Rodney's gigantic Manhattan penthouse apartment. She'd kneel on the welcome mat outside the door and plead for forgiveness, begging the Bunny to let her have a roll in the sack with Big Rod for old time's sake.

Naturally, Mrs. Celeste Rodoggio, née Yahootie, will snort derisively, spitting in Betty's face. Betty would return roll-in-the sackless to Gulpo Plains, having to make do with local yokels like Marty Martex while Rodney and Celeste live humpily ever after.

"Oh, Celeste … *sweetiepuss*," he murmured, flipping onto his back, undoing his pants. In a moment, he was panting like a wildebeest doing 51 mph on the Serengeti Plain. His hand twitched in rhythm with his defective eye. Faster …

… faster still …

… until—

The bedroom door opened.

Rodney, so startled that he didn't know what to do next, rolled quickly onto his left side. The last thing in the world he needed was the extreme mortification of his jackass parents catching him in the act of whacking his willie off. Trying to pull up his bedspread entangled pants, he simultaneously pushed the dirty magazine under his pillow. Poising himself to appear as if he was turning over nonchalantly, tugging furtively at his spiteful pants, he didn't realize that he was turning over onto air until he was flat out on the floor looking up into the sarcastic face of his sister.

Roweena, minus her Yogi Bear bathrobe, wearing only a very short, very flimsy powder blue nightie, giggled. "Well, I see you didn't get any tonight. Who'd you go out with? *Betty?*"

Rodney angrily got to his feet, pulling up his pants and sitting down on his bed. "That's none of your business."

"How is ol' Flossie these days?"

"What the hell are you doing in my room anyway? GOO'BYE!" he made a shooing gesture with his hand.

Roweena didn't cotton to this type treatment. Smugly, she told him so, adding that He'd better hurry his scarecrow ass out of here because she was tired.

"What'd'ya mean, 'hurry my ass out o' here'?" he asked acidly.

"Why, I'm sleeping here tonight," Roweena said with wide-eyed innocence.

He grimaced, giving her the shooing gesture again, this time with much more shoo behind it. Roweena ignored his ill-temper and glided over to the dresser. After admiring herself in the mirror she shoved the ton of crap on top to the side and hoisted herself up to sit. As she crossed her shapely legs the lacy nightie hem rode up, revealing her luscious bare thighs. She insisted that tonight she was indeed sleeping in his bed. Roweena brushed an errant lock of her shimmery hair away from her eye with a delicate stroke of her left hand as Rodney fumed and sputtered before her.

"Who says?"

She smiled mysteriously.

God, Rodney hated his sister. He hated how her hair fell behind her ears, how her legs dangled over his dresser as if they were just meant to be there, and especially how her pert breasts filled out fabric.

His face got red. His left eye started to tear.

"Daddy," she said simply. Her hand moved sensually up her side, flowing with each curve, then across her chest to the top of three bows on her nightie. She tugged playfully at it, daring it to open. Roweena laughed her silky sex laugh, the one she reserves for only the worst of her taunts. If Rodney had a gun, he'd shoot the shit out of her right this moment.

"He said you're sleeping in my room tonight," she told him distractedly, then seemed surprised when her bow came undone. "Oh, *my*!"

"Sleep in your room? With the smell of all that cheap perfume on everything! Christ in a cabaret! The stench of your room is bad enough this far away. What makes you think I want to be *in* it?"

"*Au contraire*! I happen to know how much you love sneaking into my room when I'm not around. Your greasy fingerprints are on every undie I own. Let's face it, my room smells like heaven to you."

"Only if heaven happens to be an Avon factory in Whoreville, Indiana. There's NO way I'm swapping rooms with you."

She started fiddling with the second bow. "You'd better, or daddy will be mighty angry."

"Give me one good reason why I have to sleep in your lousy room," he whined.

"I've been hearing strange noises at my window the last couple o' nights, and Daddy's worried now that a serial killer is trying to get me."

Rodney clucked his tongue. "That's ridiculous! What serial killer in his right mind would want you?"

"Oops," she said as the second bow fell open. She turned her attention to her hair, gathering a big handful and sweeping it over her left shoulder. Now tilting her head forward with calculated theatrics, moving her perfect chin down ever so slightly to keep the lustrous bunches from shifting unattractively, she went for the third bow.

Rodney looked at the miscellany of junk littering the floor, the stacks of old comic books, and even his pile of dirty underwear. He looked everywhere, except at Roweena. "Why are you home anyway?" he said petulantly. "How come you're not out on one of your marathon dates?"

She didn't like that snippy tone. "I ran out of BCs, if you must know," she said sharply. Regrouping her composure she added, "But to be honest, I wanted to be *here*." She let her right shoulder wiggle out of the nightie.

Catching a glimpse of her would be fatal. Rodney knew exactly what she was doing; what he didn't know was how far she'd go this time.

He looked.

She pounced like a lioness on a dik-dik. She flung her head back in that casual, alluring, mouthwatering way that she does, so that all the hair resting on her left flew en masse over to the right, cascading down her soft creamy white bare shoulder. Regardless of the fact that she's an absolute bitch, Roweena was completely and totally gorgeous. And desirable.

He needed something strong to counter her maneuver, something that would make her angry enough to lose her footing. He cackled ruthlessly, remembering the little joke he played on her and Rhonda together.

"What are you laughing at?" she asked harshly, quickly appraising herself in the dresser mirror to see if something was ruining her controlled exterior appearance.

"I know *something* you don't know … I know *something* you don't know … I know *something* you don't know …" he sang at her. "… about a little white round *pill*."

She didn't like the sound of this. "What are you talking about, you moron?"

"Dear old mom's been using them in her coffee. *You've* been taking saccharin!"

"WHAT?" she screeched.

"It's called the switcheroo, Rowie, old girl. It's purpose is to screw-eroo-you.!"

Roweena watched her brother laugh himself silly. This was awful, a revolting development. "If I'm …" she trailed off between clenched teeth. "Do you have any idea just who the father is?"

Rodney couldn't catch his breath to talk; he shook his head, holding his sides, laughing all the louder.

"Marty Martex, that's who."

He stopped laughing immediately. Marty Martex? No wonder she sounded annoyed.

"Well, there is a bright side, I guess," Roweena said. "I *could* marry Marty."

Rodney was flabbergasted. Why would she want to marry that twit? Drab, dull, tubby, toothy, stupid Marty Martex? Benny Fossert was almost understandable. Pushing it a bit, even Crazy Eddie. But Marty Martex???

"God, this is awful," she hissed. "It'll destroy my looks!" She was seething.

Everything before was child's play, now she's going to play rough. Rodney braced himself.

She slid down off the dresser, deftly twisting her torso so her nightie slithered down to her feet. "Oh, dear," she said in mock coyness.

Rodney averted his eyes as if she were Medusa—or someone much uglier than Medusa, someone like fossilized Auntie Clarissa for example; it actually would be far better for him if Roweena was a Gorgon because Rodney would much, much rather be turned to stone than to jelly, which will happen soon if he didn't get rid of his sister. He grabbed her roughly by the arm, pulling her to his door. He pushed her out. "Goo'bye," he told her, slamming it shut. The feel of her skin under his hand was amazing; his fingertips fairly tingled and his stomach churned. His left eye twitched.

What next?

He stretched out, laying down and breathing hard. His chin rested on the foot of the bed, his feet on his pillow. He stared at Roweena's discarded nightie, shifting his gaze quickly to the *Kitty Hawk*. He imagined himself piloting the plane, sailing through fluffy soft clouds back to his New York apartment and to Celeste, who awaited him in the bedroom behind a sheer curtain. Rodney hastily wiggled his pants down.

This time he didn't need to look at pictures in *Playboy*, he just shut his eyes and felt her tender flesh under his groping fingers, but he unwillingly pictured a hybrid creature having the body of Celeste, the massive fleshy chest of Betty, and the face of Roweena. He drifted away in the arms of eros.

He violently pumped his organ toward crescendo, hearing the sound of a snapping crunch. Hysterical that he may have broken his dong off with his unbridled passion, his eyes sprung open to discover, with momentary relief, that it was only a slippered foot stepping on his cherished model airplane. Rodney looked up and saw the familiar, angry face of his father.

TEN

Ralph Rodoggio knuckled his son on top of the head. "Time to go to your mister's room, sister." Rodney scrambled to pull up his pants.

Behind Ralph, Roweena, in her Yogi Bear bathrobe, sobbed realistically. "Rodney refuses to go ... and I'm sooo sleepy ... and that's not all! Rodney tore and ripped at my nice blue nightie until it fell off me, leaving me there all *naked* in front of him." She pointed to her fallen nightie, right there on Rodney's bedroom floor, hard evidence of her brother's perversion. Turning purple with rage, Ralph grabbed Rodney by his hair, yanking him to his feet with such force that he practically pulled the boy out of his pants and underwear. As Rodney stood looking into the glowering face of his father, his scalp smarting like crazy from the vise-like grip, he felt those turncoat pants slide down his legs, bunching up at his ankles. Rodney was in a humiliating and vulnerable position.

"YOU *ANIMAL*! DO YOU THINK THESE NIGHTIES GROW ON TREES? THEY COST MONEY, YOU KNOW!"

"It's late, da-a-dddeeee," Roweena cried. "I need my beauty sleep! That Gene Kelly movie was on way too long."

"Aren't they all?" Rodney muttered.

"Get a MOVE ON!" Ralph hissed, giving Rodney's hair a good, strong, encouraging tug.

"Why do I have to move? Why can't she go sleep on the sofa or something?"

"The *sofa*!" Ralph snurffed audibly, a sound of contempt that is produced by a sharp intake of air into snot-filled nasal passages. "That's the very first place a guy who kills for Kix will look. You've got to show some respect for your little sister, protect her from all the dangers of her bedroom at night!"

"Ho-ho! What dangers?"

"How about cats flapping against her window? Is that *dangerous* enough for you, smartypants?"

Roweena clucked her tongue impatiently. "Bats, daddy. Bats."

"The only bats around here are in her stupid head." Rodney chortled. The strong hand clasping his hair released its grip in favor of smacking him across his disrespectful mouth. The hand quickly returned a grasp much stronger than before, only this time to Rodney's throat.

"Apologize to your baby sister."

Rodney nodded, not wanting to talk in case some teeth were loosened. The hand squeezed his neck. "I'm sorry," he croaked.

"I'm sorry, dear *who*?"

"I'm sorry, dear Ro-eatme!"

"That's better," said Ralph relaxing his grasp.

"He called me Ro-*eatme*!" Roweena wailed.

A couple of close-handed smacks to his head later, Rodney was shuffling around his bedroom, attempting to fix his pants while picking stuff up off the floor to take with him for the night. Roweena had decided, and let everyone know it too, that she did not intend to sleep in a pigsty. Ralph, yelling constantly, told Rodney to stop fiddling with his pants, otherwise there would be even more smacks in store for him.

Roweena opened her mouth in a super phony yawn.

Ralph flicked his lazy son's earlobe. "Can't you see she's tired? Hurry UP!"

Rodney could hardly wait to be rid of the old crud. Sometimes at night, before he falls asleep, he thinks about what a wonderful world it would be without Ralph Rodoggio in it. Now as he struggled to pick up another pile of crap in his already full arms, he pictured the funeral. Ralph is laid out in a very uncomfortable coffin, an ill-fitting one that Rodney picked out especially for him. Rodney saunters up to the funeral display, looking down on his poor dead daddy and punches ol' Ralph right in his nuts. Slamming down the coffin lid, he jumps up on top of it, dancing away like Gene Kelly, tap-tap-tapping merrily over his father's lifeless corpse.

"Are you going to be ALL night?" Ralph inquired in his customary way, snapping Rodney out of his reverie. Rodney bent down to pick up his JokesAhoy! Dribble Glass. "What's it to you, slobface?" he whispered toward the floor.

Ralph saw Rodney's lips move, but couldn't quite hear him. He reiterated his question, highlighting the finale, *all night*, with knuckles jabbed sharply into Rodney's forehead. Several items of apparel tumbled from Rodney's grasp, including the dribble glass which broke upon contact with the edge of his dresser.

"I'm just going!" he grumbled, retrieving as much of his fallen things as he could and thinking how much pleasanter it would be baling hay in Alabama in August. Naturally, struggling to get to the door, the old hooplehead followed at his heels, berating and browbeating him every step of the way.

And, of course, the bedroom door was closed tighter than a cork up a flea's ass. Rodney balanced his load on one arm. Reaching to turn the knob with his free hand, he felt everything shift. It all dumped onto the floor, right in front of the door.

Roweena yawned and cried and pouted; Ralph poked and yelled and kicked.

Rodney hastily turned the doorknob, but could not pull the door open until picking up the stuff blocking it. With both arms once again full, prying open the door with his foot, it occurred to him that in the context of a social setting such as this, being severely unbalanced holding tons of personal effects while standing on one's foot with one's pants and underpants bunched down around one's ankles, being kicked roundly in the posterior by one's incensed pater, was not conducive to the well-bred and accepted manner of exiting a bedroom. No, sir-ee, *Bob*. For one thing, as you fall forward through the open door into the hallway each item of your impedimenta tends to clatter obstreperously to the floor. For another, it hurts like hell to have your bare pecker squashed as you fall upon it. Through a haze of discomfort, Rodney saw his Mudcat Grant auto-graphed baseball roll toward the staircase and bounce bumpingly down each step.

Across the hall, the door to his parents bedroom flew open. Rhonda stood looking out and queried with great nastiness just what all this stinking noise was about.

Ralph rammed his foot into Rodney's appendix. "I hope you're satisfied. Now you woke up your crummy mother."

Managing to pull his pants up, unfortunately neglecting to fasten them well enough, Rodney got to his feet. The pants skiddled down. He was standing semi-nude in the hallway, his arms full of crap, both parents screaming at him, his lousy sister laughing, and to top it off his crushed and broken *Kitty Hawk* model tumbled down from the heap. As he bent to pick it up, Brucie stuck his wet, icy-cold nose up his ass. Rodney sprung upright, lifting a foot to kick Brucie, but his mother cautioned him to stop playing with the dog and *get to bed*. Rod-ney maneuvered himself to Roweena's door as best he could. Apparently he wasn't maneuvering fast enough to suit Ralph because suddenly he was spirited forward faster than he thought possible. He was squished flat between Roweena's closed door and his steam-breathing father. Items of nostalgia in his arms dug and poked into his flesh.

"Now get yourself into that room. I don't want to hear another BEEP out of you. Understand?"

"Peep, not beep," Rhonda said wearily.

Rodney turned his head, scowling defiantly at the old crudlicker. Ralph made a nice big warning fist in Rodney's face then galloped off to his bedroom, kicking Brucie out of the way and practically knocking Rhonda over in the process. He reappeared seconds later with Helman Droogie's missing newspaper tight in his fist. Waving it over his head like an Indian with a tomahawk, he whooped, "Are you getting into that room, or do I have to wallop you?"

Rodney spent the next couple of minutes working at opening the door while getting walloped with the newspaper. The push/lean method resulted in the door finally swinging inward unexpectedly. Rodney, still pushing/leaning, took a noisy header into Roweena's dark room.

Ralph and Rhonda exchanged disgusted looks and irritated tongue cluckings.

"What an Oboe," Ralph muttered contemptuously. Rhonda and Roweena glanced questioningly at one another, then at Rodney.

"HE MEANS 'BOZO'," Rodney screeched, kicking the door shut, leaving himself in the pitch black. Stepping out of his annoying clumped pants and underwear, climbing carefully over the pile of crap just deposited on the floor, he fumbled for the bedside table lamp. The stench of cheap perfume tickled his nose and went straight to his head, making him sluggish. The room seemed a million times bigger than it actually was; walking, walking, walking, never finding the stupid bedside table—until he stumbled over his expensive Deke Molyvin pro tennis racket. He fell forward, smashing his head on a sharp corner of the goddamn nightstand and ricocheted, falling over backwards.

He continued falling, and falling without hitting anything discernibly solid, finally coming to a doughy standstill, engulfed in foamy softness something like a mound of marshmallows wrapped in a sponge.

… Roweena's idiotic, overly-soft, boxspringless bed with a mattress so loose you might as well be sleeping in a hammock. This was a hand-me-down from Uncle Filbert and his famous bad back. Rodney was sunk down so deeply in the middle of this trap, that his ass practically kissed the floor with the rest of him bent, forming a backcrunching 'V'. Two gigantic, sneeze-producing, duck-feather pillows inundated his face.

I'm supposed to sleep like this??!

But his eyes did grow heavy. The sickly-sweet milieu of *Eau d'harlot By Prince Mogglicella* lured him into deep sleep.

The Roweena-Celeste-Betty creature appeared to his sleepy brain. Nothing in the world seemed as real as this vibrant female floating against a backdrop of deep purple, not even his sister's brown-nosing call of "Goo'night, mommy!" through a closed door across the hall. The sound only skated across Rodney's subconscious dream perception. Roweena's clear soprano became the purl of a crystalline waterfall, causing the deep purple to transform into a nocturnal wonderland filled with mystery and romance. Rodney followed the girl through a maze of unidentifiable objects, falling deeper and deeper into the marshy softness of the bed as she led him deeper and deeper into the Land O' Nod. The musical sloshing of water magnified in volume. Entering a clearing up ahead, Rodney found himself in a tranquil woodsy setting, peeking out at the idyllic scene from behind a fragrant flower bush. The girl, Rocelbet, standing brazenly at the edge of the waterpool beneath the beautiful waterfall stripped off all her clothes for a refreshing dip. Dropping the last bit of her coverings, looking over her shoulder and seeing Rodney, she winked, encouraging him to join her. Rodney's r.e.m.-filled left eye twitched, but in dreamland that particular annoyance was completely dissociated from the reality he was enjoying: it became a speck of dirt or perhaps a flying bug crashing into his eye, nothing more. Rhonda calling goo'night back to Roweena from the room next door became the squawk of a scrawny bird somewhere off in the distance. Rocelbet's sweet splashes in the water were culled from Roweena's goo'night to daddy.

Boyoboy! Does she look sexy! Rodney's hand instinctively set forth to find a log to flog. Now he was in the water with her, running his dream hands over her smooth delightful body as his real hands bopped his baloney.

"Goo'night, Rodney," bellowed a bear from somewhere in the woods.

Rodney grunted, groaned, and pumped faster.

"Goo'night, Rodney!" the bear growled.

Rodney awoke long enough to pant goodnight.

"What? I can't hear you."

"I said, goo'night, you old nuthook."

"*What* did you say?" Ralph called quizzically.

"He said, '*Goo'night, you OLD NUTHOOK*', daddy."

The sweet woodsy setting, with Rocelbet frolicking in the water, disappeared completely when Rodney heard commotion from his parent's bedroom. Angry footsteps echoed through the house. The door to Roweena's room flew open. Rodney could just about make out a dim, shadowy figure in the hallway.

It was Ralph, and he meant business.

He stepped dictatorially into the room, and painfully onto the cusp of a hardcover library book Rodney had neglected to return ages ago. In adjusting his step, Ralph slipped with his bare feet on a valuable mint condition issue of *Li'l Loony Comics*, ripping off the cover as he fell rump-first to the floor. Ralph screamed in horrified surprise; he screamed as though the boogieman was taking a big chomp out of his ass, but it was only an overwound set of JokesAhoy! Yakkity-Yak teeth biting him. He quivered, groaning.

Maybe he'll just fall asleep there, Rodney hoped, letting his eyes drift shut, willing himself to return to the world of Rocelbet. Before his eyes were even half-closed, Rhonda was in the room. Upon seeing her poor prone husband, she let out a banshee-like shriek of anguish. Pain-in-the-ass Roweena quickly followed, immediately switching on her table lamp.

"Rhon-n-nda-a-a!" Ralph moaned pathetically. "Hel-l-lp meeee! I can't mo-o-ove! I think I'm polarized!"

She wasn't strong enough to pry the newspaper from his frozen grip, but seeing the tennis racket handle she wrenched it up to use in its stead, not realizing that Ralph's head was pushed squarely through the mesh. He yelped like a puppy dog whose tail has been crunched. Furious and frustrated, she let go and went for the table lamp.

Hot, burning sparks showered over Rodney's body from the breaking light bulb, each one leaving a tiny brown burnhole on his skin where they landed. Luckily, he could not feel them because he'd been knocked unconscious by the lamp base smashing down onto his head. Ralph stirred, lifting his arms weakly.

"THANK YOU GOD *AND* THANK YOU KATHRYN KHULMAN!!" he screamed joyfully, loud enough to wake the dead. "I WON'T BE SPENDING THE REST O' MY LIFE IN A WHEELBARROW! '*I BEELEEEVE IN MIRACLES*'!"

Rhonda, rushing to his side, inadvertently stepped on the tennis racket handle, pushing the thing down further and more excruciatingly into his scalp. She helped him to his feet. Assured that Ralph was stable, she tugged the racket handle to get it off his head. Unfortunately, it had a pretty strong grip on him. He was wearing it like a sunvisor with a very, very long brim, and the sight gave Roweena quite a chuckle. She giggled so hard she almost couldn't help her mother walk Ralph over the scattered junk. Stopping just outside the room, Ralph turned to look back at his son through the open door.

"One more sound out o' you tonight, and I'm copping the calls ... capping the cocks ... I mean clipping the *clops*! Do I make myself clear?" With a wag of his chin toward the bedroom door, indicating his wishes psychically, Ralph looked demandingly to his wife. Rhonda understood completely. She reached over and pulled the door closed with a bang.

ELEVEN

Rodney wafted away on a weightless cloud, drifting in a starfield of pulsing colored lights playing against a rich background of deep dark purple sky. *Ooo Dreamland*, he thought to himself, floating along serenely on buoyant air. The icky stench of perfume was gone, replaced by a fresh, delicate scent of something wistful. *Oleander? Perhaps wisteria. Or something heliotrope? Bloodstone?*

Startled by this sudden ability to find articulate words, he opened his eyes. The dreamland vanished into the stark outlines of his sister's room.

Where the hell did that come from? Now I'm an expert on flowers? One o' those whozitt guys? A phlebotomist?? He yawned, wanting to go back to sleep.

Caught now between sleep and wakefulness, hovering in the dark, Rodney found it disturbing, to say the least, that in a stupor he could be smarter than when he was awake. Most likely this intelligence was dredged up from some deep gorge in his mind; maybe all that boring school crap shoved down his throat ended up in his subconscious after all? Now, for some reason, they were puking up from his narrow brainpan. Any further thoughts about his mind's capacity were instantly put on the back burner. His attention was riveted on an alluring green cloud misting over his view.

Were his eyes opened or closed?

He didn't remember.

The cloud expanded, spreading out everywhere. Arm-like tendrils of wisp extended from its main mass to snoop around Roweena's room, looking into every corner, getting familiar with the layout. Having a snootful, they streamed back together into the cloud, which became more of a luminous green fog suspended over the bed close to the ceiling. Apparently it was studying him. He felt uneasy, beginning to think that he wasn't sleeping at all.

Good Christ O' Mighty! I must have a goddam concussion!

Without further adieu, the apparition set about spinning like a gyroscope, developing speed until it was a whirling funnel. A stationary cyclone that disturbed not even the air around it.

Forget about concussion—what if it's brain damage?!!

As it rotated, the fog seemed to congeal. The faster it spun, the more tangible it became. Rodney's eyes grew heavy from watching. He heard a high pitch whistle in his ears. The center became a cone, melding all the ethereal foggy stuff onto it. Rodney was reminded of one of those carnival machines that makes cotton candy. There would be all this wavy, thready air in a big silver metal dish, then the grubby salesguy twirls around a paper cone and poof there's a mass of hot, sticky, pink goo on the end of it.

The cyclone slowed. The revolutions became less frenetic, the fog more dense. It was less misty, forming a solid flat surface looking to Rodney like a stage curtain. The fog split apart from the bottom, just like in a theater, and out stepped …

… a green Betty Bunz!

He was asleep and having one beaut of a dream.

Clumps of tacky spun-fog glommed onto her, but she didn't seem to mind a bit. She stood at the foot of the bed, holding out her hand, beckoning him to join her in the sticky green mess. Although he tried mightily, he could not move forward. He was too weak, his body ached from countless pains, and the bed mattress held him captive like a Venus fly trap.

Come heer-r-e to me, she said with a gesture of her hand. I will make you feel better-r-r.

She sounded like Doris Day impersonating Frank Gorshin impersonating Bela Lugosi. He struggled, reaching, and eventually was able to touch a part of the hem on her green gown. To his surprise it wasn't sticky at all. It felt vaporous. Dank and clammy. But in touching her, all the pain in his body disappeared like magic. Laying there, trapped hopelessly on the bastard bed, he saw what looked like a smoky green version of himself curl up into the air and join Betty Bunz. Although he could only watch the other Rodney cavort with her, all his tactile senses responded as if he was groping her in person. When the doppelgänger buried its face deep into Betty's pulpous chest, Rodney felt the mush of her bazoomkas pressing into his mouth.

After some moments of sublime smotheration, something disquieting came over him. He realized that the taste was off, all wrong. Instead of the sweat-salty, fleshy, flavor he expected, this tasted more like his mother's Thanksgiving dinner. He coughed profusely. Up came half a dozen tickle producing raw duck feathers. He viciously tossed the chewed and leaking sonofabitch pillow from the bed.

He was awake. All the wonderful visions gone. It was a dream after all, not an hallucination brought about by head injury. He closed his eyes. The colorful starfield against deep purple background was gone ... the green fog was gone ... and, *o' course*, green Betty was gone. Tears rolled down his face. His brain reeled. Physical pain assailed him from every angle.

Oh, yes. He was wide awake now.

Life's just GRAND, isn't it? Get plenty o' all the stuff you don't want and don't get any of what you do. ANYthing would be better than this misery ...

Angrily lifting his head up off the remaining pillow he felt a stabbing throb skewer his brain. Thousands of Christmas treelike lights danced behind his eyelids. His head tilted like a lopsided merry-go-round. *Voilà!*—the green fog reappeared! Once again the strange stuff eddied, forming a cone within but it lost power, fizzling and fading before Betty could step from it.

He wasn't quite as woozy as before, so he lifted up his head as high as possible and brought it down sharply on the headboard.

That seemed to help.

The fog returned, then again melted before Betty appeared. Rodney got the definite impression something was toying with him, like it was getting some huge cosmic chuckle. *So what? Laugh your NUTS off—just bring Betty back.* He gave his head several more hard strikes. Finally, after a half-dozen headsmacks the green fog clicked-in, staying long enough to spin its cone.

"I'm coming," Betty said darkly from very far away.

"Hurry!" Rodney begged.

"I'm almost there," she said with an even odder voice than before.

This time there was an undisguised odor to the green fog, similar to low tide or closer still to the chemical experiment in Mr. Tottsy's eleventh grade science class that went room-clearingly sour. In fact, everything about the fog was way less attractive now. It had a murky, sinister look to it, dull and dirty like a poor copy of itself, not the lush, vibrant thing it was before. It didn't even have density. Rodney could see the bedroom window straight across from the bed, it was plainly visible through the wispy fog. The glass panes shone brightly like somebody was aiming a flashlight at the window from outside. The light hurt his head.

He closed his eyes, but that did not shut out the pain of that light streaming through the window. It crossed his mind that this new fog might be a separate dream, a lousy road-company version of the wonderful green cloud dream. Rodney quickly opened his eyes again. *Of course*, he reasoned, *I'm asleep and dreaming everything.*

That made sense.

Sort of. Could he be dreaming with his eyes open?

It shouldn't matter if my stupid eyes are open or closed anyway, or what they're doing in this dream. They could twirl around like coins spinning on a table for all I care as long as it brings Betty.

And through the haze he saw a figure weaving from separate green mist filaments outside the bedroom window. It tapped and scratched at the glass with long, sharp nails.

"Betty!" Rodney said, or thought he said.

"Here I AM!" she replied with an evil, deep throated chuckle. "Aren't you going to invite me in?"

"Come in! Come in!"

The window flew up on its sash. A nasty dead smell entered the room, a smell so awful he let go of his pecker to hold his nose. The figure shrunk, compressing into itself, its arms getting longer than its body. The gassy mist cleared. Rodney saw a large bat flap-flapping ugly batty wings just outside the open window.

Clearly, this wasn't a dream.

"Shoo …" he hissed. "Get away! Get out of here!" He threw Roweena's alarm clock but missed. The clock sailed through the open window, crashing to the ground two stories below. Chuckling and laughing in an obnoxious high-pitched voice, the bat flew into the room. Rodney grabbed at it, but it did a mocking loop-de-loop outside his reach then flew into Rodney's face, flapping its wings against his cheeks mockingly. It flew off to circle the room, dropping smelly liquid guano all over the place.

"I'm gonna rip your goddam wings off," Rodney threatened, trying to push himself up from the marshy mattress. He sank in deeper.

The bat laughed merrily at Rodney's distress.

Holding onto the bedside table for support, he was able to hoist himself up. All at once, though, he was tumbling off the bed onto the floor. He felt around for something to throw at the thing. Finding a paperback porno book under Roweena's bed, he pitched it. The bat flipped it away using its wing as a paddle.

Flying to the ceiling, the bat began a descending circle leaving in its wake a trail of guano and green fog; soon the flying rodent was completely obscured.

From out of the dense cloud stepped a man dressed in old-timey formal clothes, complete with top hat and red-satin lined opera cape.

"Goood eve-nnning-gg-g," he said.

TWELVE

Rodney has seen enough Christopher Lee movies in his lifetime to know instantly that this smiling jackaloon was an honest-to-God, genuine, bloodsucking *vampire*.

Looking up at the ghastly sallow face with the bright yellow eyeballs shining like coach lamps in the dark, Rodney was frozen with fright. Every horrid detail was plainly visible in that preternatural yellow-eyes light. You could see that he had a mouthful of pointy teeth, not just two fangs like in the movies, but every tooth in his head had a dangerous tip. His anemic-looking lips and baby's butt-smooth chin were covered with flecks of what looked like dried blood.

Ugh!

Rodney pushed away instinctively, backing himself up against Roweena's bedside table. God must have been with him, for in jiggling the table Roweena's First Place prize in the $50,000.00 Church Raffle—a cheap little plastic crucifix (nobody but the church got the fifty grand: it was a fine-print rule that the winner donate *that* back to the church.)—jiggled and fell right into his lap.

This will scare the jumping bejesus out of him, he thought with confidence. *One look, and he'll cover his ugly face with his cape and before you can say "eat my ass" he's out the window.*

The vampire pounced. Clutching Rodney by the shoulders, he lifted him with unbelievable strength. Rodney waved the cross wildly.

Taking one look at the ridiculous religious icon, the creature laughed so hard he actually dropped Rodney. Now Rodney understood the source of that terrible odor. It was vampire breath. It smelled like all those unburied bodies at EternOrest Cemetery mixed with the stench from the EverRipe dumpster. He pinched his nose shut with both hands, the sight of which made the vampire laugh even harder, as if this was the funniest thing he'd ever seen in his afterlife. More putrid breath billowed into Rodney's face. Then, with some embarrassment, Rodney remembered he was standing here in front of this stranger absolutely naked from the waist down. With one hand, he attempted to cover himself.

The monster let out another hearty guffaw, a deep, unearthly, bellow, practically holding onto his sides. Rodney's hand soared back to his nose.

"IF YOU DON'T STOP THAT LAUGHING," Ralph's voice boomed through the wall separating the two rooms, "I'LL COME IN THERE AND GIVE YOU SOMETHING TO LAUGH ABOUT!"

The vampire shut up. A worried look crossed his cadaverous face. Obviously, he wasn't dead so long as to have forgotten what bastards angry fathers can be. After a bit, he licked his lips, quietly advancing. Rodney thought pitifully that if he could make the bloodsucker laugh again, his father would charge into the room hell-bent-for-leather and frighten the vampire out of the house. He hooked his right thumb and index finger into his mouth and pulled down the corners while sticking out his tongue. At the same time, he pushed up the tip of his nose with his left thumb and made gobble-gobble noises in his throat, lolling his head moronically.

The vampire clucked his tongue and rolled his yellow eyes, shaking his head in disbelief.

Before Rodney could pull out another knee-slapper from his arsenal of hilarious visual effects, the vampire had him up against the bedroom wall. Rodney kicked frantically with his feet, somehow managing to knock the creature off balance momentarily. As it lunged, Rodney ducked. The vampire smacked into the wall.

"WHAT IN THE NAME O' GOD ARE YOU DOING IN THERE NOW?? BOUNCING BALLS AGAINST THE WALL? IF I HAVE TO GET UP, YOU'LL REGRET IT!"

Rodney was in a good position to reach the door. He gave the monster an additional shove into the wall for good measure and raced toward safety.

Needless to say, he didn't make it. He stumbled, of course, over his pile of clothes, books, sporting equipment, toys, and whatnot, ending up by falling back onto Roweena's deathtrap bed.

The vampire grinned, gleefully rubbing his undead hands together.

"Please," Rodney sobbed, "spare me! I'm too young to bite the big one … I've never even had sex yet …!"

The vampire jumped him.
"With a GIRL …!"

THIRTEEN

Ralph Rodoggio, rubbing the sleepcrust from his eyes, shuffled down the stairs in his comfy old maroon slippers as the pounding on his front door increased tremendously. *"OPEN UP, POLICE!"*

Reaching the bottom step, Ralph flipped on the hall light switch and looked at his watch. Four fifteen. He called the Police Station several hours ago, explaining to the curt desk sergeant that he thought his son had gone lazy.

"You're calling *us* at two in the morning to say your son isn't doing his chores? What are you, Mack? Some kind of a-hole?"

"No, no," Ralph corrected. "I mean, I think my son might be …" He searched for just the right word. In his sleep befuddled brain he pictured all the ones he could remember that had the double *x* in the middle. "Craxxy. That's it."

"Cracksy?"

"No," Ralph said, starting to get very annoyed. "Oh, hold on a second. RHONDA …!" he shook her awake.

"What is *it*?" she yelled back.

"What's that other word for lazy?"

"How the heck do I know? I'm sleeping, not doing a doodleydamn crossword puzzle. Indolent?"

"No," he clucked his tongue impatiently. "That's a disease, for fryin' out loud! This word's got a couple of Xs in the middle of it … you know, like when someone's loopy or nutty or something …"

"You mean crazy?" the desk sergeant said.

"Yes, that's right!"

"Daffy … dippy … goofy … batty … cuckoo … bananas …"

He huffed a deep, theatrical sigh as she continued listing words, waiting oh-so patiently for her to run out of steam until, finally, he said sarcastically, "It's okay, now … we've got the word.

"*Wives,*" he whispered derisively into the mouthpiece. The desk sergeant agreed. Wives were indeed a royal pain in the old derry-air.

"I'll send someone right over, chum. In the meantime, sit tight and don't provoke the bastard. He could be dangerous."

The hubbub outside the door escalated to gale force. Ralph reached to unlatch it just as gunshots fired through the door handle, twisting metal and splintering wood. The door flew open in a gust of blue smoke. Ralph jumped back, his right foot catching the curve of Rodney's Mudcat Grant autographed baseball. He stumbled wildly, trying to catch his balance as his arms flailed the air like an exotic dancer from the middle-east doing the *Hootchie-Kootchie.*

Five uniformed cops barrelassing into the house were followed by a detective wearing a beige trench coat and battered fedora hat.

"THAT'S HIM, BOYS!" the detective screamed, lifting the barrel of his smoking revolver toward the lurching maniac coming at them. The cops grabbed Ralph, wrestling him to the floor before he could kill someone. They were just about to haul his sorry ass off to prison when Rhonda appeared at the top of the stairs.

"Don't worry, lady," the detective told her. "We've got the perp under control. He tried to attack us, but my men are much sharper than any drug-infested, loony-livered lunkhead."

"But … you have the wrong, uh, perp."

"Hmmm," he said, flipping open a note pad with the tip of his gun barrel. Holding gun and pad together in one hand, he reached into his pocket with the other and brought out a Bic Clic. "Wrong perp? How can you be sure?"

"It's my *son* who's gone crazy."

The detective took a long, hard look at Ralph, spread-eagled on the floor with his arms bent up behind him, wrists bound with handcuffs. "Well, isn't *this* your son, lady?"

"I'm his WIFE … Rhonda Rodoggio."

He appraised Rhonda for a number of seconds, then looked pityingly down at Ralph. "I guess you are. Okay, boys get those 'cuffs off the poor bastard."

Once Ralph was uncuffed and brought to his feet, he thanked the officers for coming. He told them that he feared for their lives, afraid Rodney might be turning into a cereal killer. "I thought we'd all be dead in our beds. That boy was packing up."

"Running out, huh?" the detective made a note of that fact.

"No, he means cracking up, officer."

The detective clucked his tongue, scratching out the information he just noted. "I'd like to see the loony's room." He moved toward the stairs, stepping on the Mudcat Grant autographed baseball. Sliding, his revolver discharged, shooting one of the uniformed cops through the head. "Goddammit to HELL!" he hissed.

In order for the rest of the cops to get to the stairs they were forced to step over the body of their fallen comrade. The last man up stumbled, his foot striking the corpse. He danced back a little to avoid additional contact, but it was too late. The damage was done. "Aw, SHIT! Look at that," he cursed, "*blood* all over my regulation uniform shoes!"

"Would you like a towel?" Rhonda offered nervously.

"No, *thanks*," he snapped. "I'll just use your carpet." He wiped the crown of his shoe vigorously on the carpet leaving a big ground-in stain. This time he stepped over carefully. Ralph and Rhonda followed.

Upstairs, the detective waited patiently, smoking a cigarette and flicking ashes onto the floor. When Ralph pointed out Roweena's room, the detective dropped the cigarette to the floor, crushing it out with his shoe heel. Kicking open the door with the same foot he rushed in prepared for an ambush. Tripping and falling over Rodney's stuff, he snarled "Turn on some goddam lights, you morons!"

"I don't know where they are, Lieutenant."

"I wasn't talking to you, I was talking to those cocksuckers who live here!"

Rhonda apologized profusely, stepping into the room and going over to the desk lamp. Once the room was illuminated, everyone screamed in horror at what they saw laying on the bed.

Rodney was situated in a bunch of jumbled white bedsheets, his arms and legs bent at an unnatural angle. His head was twisted somewhat to the right, his throat torn open at the jugular with an ugly stomach-turning wound.

There was not one drop of blood to be seen anywhere.

Over the sounds of retching cops, the detective inquired if the deceased had acted strange in any way this past evening.

Ralph spent the next ten minutes detailing Rodney's interruption of the *Mortimer Morbane News Of the Day* show, and how reluctant he was to watch a fine upstanding, American movie starring Gene Kelly. During the narrative the detective grunted affirmatively and doodled drawings of penises in his note pad.

"What else, bud," he said finally, cutting Ralph off in mid-sentence. "Did he act weird? Do anything out o' the ordinary?"

"Well," Ralph said, scratching his head pensively. "He was laughing in the wee small hours o' the morning."

"Laughing, huh? What kind o' laughing?"

Ralph tried to imitate the deep guffaws he heard, but the strain on his vocal chords caused him to cough hard.

"I thought you said he was laughing," the Lieutenant said with irritation, using angry strokes to eradicate the word "laughing" from his notes.

"Yes … he was! Real deep heehaws." Ralph said diffidently, meaning guffaws.

The detective turned to his crew. "Heehaws? Does a braying donkey sound like he's laughing to you, boys?"

They looked at one another.

"No way!"

"Hell, no!"

"Laughing, my ass!"

"What about you, O'Runkly? Do heehaws sound like laughter to you?"

"Can he do that jackass impression again, Lieutenant?" O'Runkly asked.

"Well, can'ya, bub?"

Ralph cleared his throat and tried a deep guffaw. Again he hacked out a scratchy cough partway into his imitation.

"Yeah, that sounds like laughing, all right … like someone with tuberculosis laughing." The men snickered at O'Runkly's sarcastic gibe, and Ralph colored with embarrassment.

"Okay," the man in the trench coat said to Ralph, his finger tapping the pistol trigger. "Which is it? Laughing or coughing?"

"Laughing," Ralph stuttered. "Don't you believe me?"

"Okay, okay. Keep your tits on." He rewrote "laughing" into his note pad. "Now, what kind o' laughing was it?"

Ralph tried again, quickening his pace to get it all in, but, unfortunately he coughed violently before he got very far. The detective angrily jabbed the nib of his hardnose Bic Clic into the meaty portion of Ralph's arm. A small drop of blood appeared on the surface, but it didn't flow. The area under the puncture turned bright purple.

"Laughed or coughed?"

"Coughed," Ralph agreed miserably. The detective turned to a new page of his pad and made some scribbles. The pen wrote bright red for a second or two, then purple, and finally returned to its normal blue color. "Hey! This pen really does work like on TV!"

Rhonda was busy sucking the ink out of Ralph's wound when the Lieutenant tapped his pen against her forehead for attention. "Anything else?"

"My husband said that it sounded like he was bouncing balls against the wall."

The policemen let out whistling gasps of breath. To a man, each one pressed his knees together, clutching their groins with their hands. "God," one of them, probably O'Runkly, said. "Bouncing his *balls* against the wall!"

"That must hur-r-rt!" said another, sweating and grimacing at the thought.

The detective said aloud as he wrote, "'extreme odd behavior: laughing while bouncing a delicate part of his anatomy against the bedroom wall, bringing about in the deceased youth a strong coughing fit.' That sound about right?"

"Actually," Ralph said, "he was laugh … er, coughing before he was bouncing the ball off the wall."

"This sounds right." the detective said rigidly, lifting the point of his pen eye level, pondering it.

"Ooo, yesss," Ralph replied uneasily

"That's *good*, chumly." First examining his notes, then glancing once more at the body, the detective snapped shut his notepad. He informed Ralph and Rhonda that their son died as a result of ingesting illegal mindwarping drugs.

Ralph asked nervously if there was any chance that Rodney might have been done-in by a killer. "That neck wound looks mighty auspicious."

"No chance. He was a druggie. He was shooting up through his neck. Pretty common in cases like these. I've seen it dozens o' times."

"A drug attic! In my house!" Ralph gasped.

"Okay, boys! You heard it! The stash is in the attic!" Cops spread out all over, looking for the entrance to the attic. The detective quietly brought back out his notepad, turning quickly to the last page where he had his list of quantities and buyers.

"My husband meant addict, officer, not attic," Rhonda explained.

"We'll have to check the attic anyway, ma'm."

"Well … we don't really have one."

Jamming the notepad angrily into his pocket without even closing it, he regarded Rhonda with a steely cold gaze. "You bastard," he said to her, then yelled to the cops. "Knock off the search, boys! There's nothing more we can do here. That junkie's dead."

The policemen halted their search, preparing to follow the detective leaving the premises. Two of the more industrious cops began rolling Rodney's lifeless body in bedsheets.

"What happens to him now?" Rhonda asked one of them.

"Why, he goes to *hell*, o' course."

"No, no—I mean his, uh, remains."

"Police Morgue," interjected the detective. "The medical examiner will want to toodle around with him." He gave his men a slight, nodding gesture. Immediately, they stopped wrapping Rodney, pulling their hands back almost as if he was a hot tamale and leaving him mostly uncovered. "We'll take the stiff with us …" he waved his men out of the room, continuing to Ralph and Rhonda in private, "… just bring it down to the patrol car. There's plenty o' room in the trunk. But make sure you wrap him up *real* good, because I can't stand touching naked deadies." He meandered out into the hall.

Ralph, following, asked if he should bring the dead officer out too.

The detective clucked his tongue and rolled his eyes upward. "What d'ya think we have out there? A meat wagon? We've *got* to take Danny Drughead to the police morgue, but that officer killed in the line o' duty on *your* property is *your* problem. Maybe the fire department will help you get him to the hospital morgue … but I doubt it. However, if you insist we take another body with us, we'll take *hers!*"

He was referring to Roweena, who just came out of Rodney's room in her short nightie, long legs and thighs exposed, rubbing the sleep from her eyes and asking what was going on.

There were howls and whistles and energetic expressions of delight at the prospect of handling this corpus delectable.

"It's nothing. Go back to bed." Rhonda snapped at her. Roweena shrugged. A shoulder strap fell, almost exposing her left breast. She went back into the room and shut the door.

A violently disappointed band of policemen, now in very bad moods, went outside to wait in the patrol car. It took Ralph and Rhonda many minutes to get their dead-weight son off the bed to floor, and then to lug him down the stairs to the front door. Their burden was underscored by impatient horn-honking and siren blasts from the patrol car, making them much more fretful and nervous.

"HURRY UP YOU MOTHEREATERS," the detective yelled. "THINK WE GOT ALL NIGHT HERE?"

FOURTEEN

Almost an hour later Rodney's remains was delivered to the night-shift attendants at the police morgue located in the basement of the Gulpo Plains Police Station, which was about five minutes away from the Rodoggio house. He spent the rest of the night laid out on a hard metal drain table until the day shift reported for work at seven a.m. After having coffee, they rolled up their sleeves for the task ahead.

It was now nine-thirty a.m.

The two attendants began by washing down the body with a normal saline solution, cleansing all the bruises, burns, and other injuries he sustained in life, including the anemic neck wound. Leaving it to air dry on the drain table, they went to play Gin for an hour or so.

When the cadaver was mostly dry, the attendants got out a commercial shroud kit from the supply closet. The pouch was tough to open so one of them used his teeth, ripping at the clear mylar plastic like it was a slab of Bonomo's Turkish Taffy. They laid out the bag's contents: a large plastic sheet, several strips of black cloth, tags and whatnot, and started their task by first binding the legs tightly at the ankles with one of the thin, but strong, black ribbons. They folded arms across chest tying them at the wrists. A third piece of the cloth tied the hanging jaw shut, but because they made a stupid mistake, using the wrong size ribbon for the legs, the longest piece of the three was left. They tied the excess in several bows and knots on top of the head, giving the lifeless thing a somewhat Rastafarian look. Proceeding to the next step in the preparation for storage, one of the attendants noticed that the tongue was sticking out. They undid the knots and bows. They used the flat end of an autopsy knife to push the slippery tongue back inside the mouth and retied the bows and knots. The tongue managed to dribble back out.

What a pain in the ass.

The less patient of the two went looking for the bone snippers, but the other, more practical, attendant just twisted the appendage over onto itself into a fat roll and shut the mouth around it, clamping it firmly between teeth. He tied the ribbon with many little knots crisscrossing on top.

Now the eyes would not close no matter what they did. Each time they pulled the lids down, the eyes sprang open again. One of them bopped the side of the head. Still no luck. After a few more attempts, one of the attendants let out a sudden, hearty laugh.

"What's so funny?" the other asked, in no mood for levity.

"You see the way his eyes cross like he's staring at the tip o' his nose ... and how his cheeks are puffed out from the way the band squishes his mouth shut ... and the way I rolled his tongue into his mouth?"

"Yeah ..."

"Well, there was this old Marx Brothers movie on the tube last night, and in it Harpoon made a face just like this. It was hysterical."

"Harpoon? Which one was *that*? There was ... what's his name?—Gunko. And Cheapo?"

"Gunko was one of the seven dwarfs, dopey ... you're thinking of Grouchy. Grouchy, Chimpo, and Harpoon. Anyway, the guy that doesn't talk, the one who honks his hooter all the time. That one."

His workmate stared dumbly, his jaw sagging, his eyes fixed on infinity.

"CHRIST on a SILVER *DOLLAR*! He has CURLY hair ... ya' know? Wears a raincoat with big pockets ... Jeez, I might as well be asking a squirrel the time o' day!"

Then the lightbulb came on. Someone *was* home. "Oh, YEAH! That GUY ... the real funny one! Now that you mention it, he does look a helluvalot like ol' Harpy ... it's sort of like having a celebrity here ... hey!! You know what we should do? We should get Klackkie to bring a camera down from criminology and take a picture of this bird ... we can hang it up over the sink. Too bad he can't autograph it for us."

The Criminology boys were bored shitless. They were sitting around on their spindly old office chairs, getting on each other's nerves bitching and moaning over the paucity of murders when the morgue attendants called to tell them about the comical corpse they wanted to photograph. Although they all hated being anywhere near the creepy morgue, the diversion was too hard to resist. They flew down those thirteen basement steps so quickly, one might think girls with free booze were down there throwing a party in the Den of Deadies.

Larry Klackker, the crime scene and mug shot photographer, couldn't stop laughing over the sight. The scrawny teenager was sitting up on the edge of the drain table, naked and lolling to the left. He had a ridiculous-looking bow wig on his head, eyes popped and crossed … and that tongue! … rolled-up like a thick slice of baloney sticking halfway out of his mouth!

"Hurry up, Klackkie," the creative morgue attendant said, worried that the body might tumble off the drain table. This stiff was not stable.

Klackkie, guffawing, was having trouble focusing his camera. His hands and stomach danced up and down. "Just a second, guys …" he choked out, doubling over, flailing his free hand at them as he tried to catch his breath. Suddenly, with inspiration, he snapped his pudgy little fingers and asked excitedly, "Do you guys have any other corpsesicles in the fridge?" The attendants shook their heads. Klackkie, dejected, muttered, "Too bad. We could've set two others up around him to make 'em look like the whole damn bunch o' Marx Brothers."

Now Eddie Furnox, the lanky chief criminologist, snapped his fingers. "We don't need deadies to pull that off! I can dress up like Groucho, and Billy can do Chico. It'll be a riot!"

Everyone except Rodney rocked with laughter.

Eddie Furnox and Billy Meach went back upstairs. Several minutes later, they returned in makeup and costume. Eddie did a Groucho walk all around the morgue, while Billy called after him with a half-assed Italian accent, "Hey-a, boss!"

"Man, Eddie! That's GREAT! Where'd you get that stuff?"

Eddie told them that he used fingerprint dust powder to make his mustache and eyebrows. "The clothes were stored in the evidence cabinet and are left over from some hom-o-cides. I even found this cigar in an overcoat pocket. The bloodstains don't show, do they? Do I look okay?"

"Perfect," Larry Klackker said.

A Harpo costume was put on Rodney, complete with a battered top hat and one of Detective Lieutenant Claude LoBloud's beige trench coats. Several pictures were snapped in various poses, and Klackkie hurried off to develop them and make prints for everyone. Groucho and Chico were slow to leave, hanging around the morgue until it got just as boring there as it had been in the criminology lab.

"Well, you're a lovely couple, but, hello, I must be going," Eddie 'Groucho' Furnox said, wagging his bloodsoaked cigar and raising his fingerprint dust eyebrows one last time.

After everyone was gone, the attendants tagged and wrapped the last remaining Marx Brother in a milk-white, opaque shroud and wheeled him on the ancient gurney to freezer compartment # 61. As they hurriedly slid the body from the table to the freezer slab, not minding too much that it was getting banged-up in the process, the compartment's intense cold made their teeth chatter. They slammed the door shut. The practical attendant placed an "Embalm Immediately" note on the door handle for the night shift. The other wrote out a body ID tag to insert into the slot in the center of the heavy metal door.

Then the two attendants went back to the routine business of playing cards.

FIFTEEN

At the same moment Klackkie snapped those last photographs of her son, Rhonda was on the telephone with the Chief Medical Examiner inquiring about the cost of an autopsy. It was a very busy morning. She already made a zillion phone calls, and there still were a *host* of others to make, plus all her errands yet to run.

"Who the hell has time to mess around cutting open junkies? We'll send you a bill for embalming and storage. That's as much as I can do for you."

Rhonda thanked him quickly, but politely, hanging up the phone before he could change his mind. She dreaded calling the church because she was sure they would want her to come in person to make arrangements for a service. Rhonda bit the bullet, dialed the church's number, and grimaced as it rang ten thousand times before it was answered by young Father Sassi. She was happily surprised to be given the fee list right over the telephone, and Rhonda picked out what she believed to be a tasteful yet economic showing. The young priest offered to stop by this afternoon to pick up her cash payment, sparing her the trip to Main Street. "But," Rhonda told him, "waiting here all afternoon will put a terrible crimp in my errand running."

"Not to worry, Mrs. Rodoggio," Father Sassi said, "I'm sure your lovely daughter will be home *alone* when I call."

"Yes! O' course! I'll make sure she is."

Rhonda needed to get to the bank for cash, and also to Sippy Nollic's Fine Spirits and Liquor Shoppe, then she'd have to go grocery shopping, stocking up on supplies for all the diddlydamn entertaining she was going to have to do for townsfolk who'll want to drop by with their diddlydamn sympathies.

So much extra work, she thought bitterly.

And, of course, she had to get to the Gulpo Plains Woodworks. Rhonda called there first thing this morning, explaining to the snooty sales manager that she needed to buy a coffin, something unassuming and reasonable. Preferably a second-hand one, or a floor model. All he would offer her was a pre-fab baroque style casket for fifteen hundred big, green dollars, the only coffin they produced, but it was made-upon-order. Regardless of the fact that it was far too fancy and expensive to suit her taste, she was going to take it anyway … until she discovered that it couldn't possibly be ready for the next day.

"You know, Mrs. Robbidolo, we usually get six weeks worktime on that coffin," he told her bluntly. However, if she was willing to pay the total cost in full before noon today, plus an additional express service charge, he would personally see to it that the item would be constructed, finished, and delivered to the church by five that afternoon. Rhonda haggled over the outrageous price tag, and haggled with such rampant consumerism that in the end she was able to get him to agree to make a from-scratch plain wooden casket for only seven hundred, including express service plus church delivery.

The only niggling detail left was Rodney himself.

Upon the recommendation of Pippa Frappé, the busybody neighbor from around the corner who called bright and early this morning, disturbing everyone's sleep wanting to know what the hullabaloo last night was about, Rhonda called Selma Krinklis, Pippa's cousin and professional mid-wife who was now doing freelance corpse-dressing. Pippa said that Selma's ministrations were mucho cheapo, including pickup from the morgue and preparation for funeral presentation at a wake (or burial for those using their backyards).

Mrs. Krinklis was a cheery woman with a deep, husky voice. "Will you require the service of a Sin Eater, dear?"

"Nooo," Rhonda said hesitantly, not sure what a Sin Eater was but knowing full well that not a penny more will be put out than absolutely necessary.

The woman checked her schedule while Rhonda waited on the line. Yes, she was free this evening. She'd go to the Police Morgue sometime after supper to fetch Rodney. Arrangements were made, fees agreed upon. Mrs. Krinklis then asked delicately about the Rodoggio post-service plans. Rhonda said frankly that she really didn't know, that they hadn't given it much thought yet. The midwife/ corpse-dresser swooped-in like a hungry vulture. She gave Rhonda a bubbly pitch about storage, explaining that she was currently in negotiation to rent space at the huge FurLand Mink Storage facility outside Sogg City in Docsville.

"I'll be able to offer cold storage until this *damn* cemetery strike is over," she said, sounding quite sincere in her anger toward the strike, although she was certainly profiteering from it. "If you could put off the funeral, honey, for, say, a week or two then you won't have to dig a big ol' hole in your backyard, or leave the kid to molt in his room. You certainly don't want him hanging around EternOrest with all those undesirables! Storage is *very* sensible, don't'cha know ... and at $53.50 a week you can't get a better deal."

"We're anxious to have this over and done with," Rhonda told her mercurially. "We'll probably just take him to the park."

"Well, suit yourself," the woman replied stiffly, no longer as friendly sounding as she was even a moment ago. "The coffin *will* be at Our Lady when I get there, correct? I don't want to end up waiting around all night for delivery, sitting on the church steps with your son's body in my lap, like the damn *Pietà*,"

"I am assured that it will be."

"And you said his suit o' clothes will be in the coffin?"

"Yes," Rhonda replied. She almost asked if Selma could arrange the removal of the dead policeman from her living room, but thought better of it. Why pay for something when the fire department can do it for free? She said goodbye to Selma Krinklis. Now, aside from phone calls to neighbors inviting them to the funeral, Rhonda's phone chores were through. She celebrated with a little toot from the bottle of Old Hen's Foot under the kitchen sink. And another. After licking her lips dry, she put on some lipstick.

The bank line wasn't too bad, but it took *forever* for the stupid teller to count out five hundred dollars, and Rhonda was able to hurry off to her next stop in jig-time. Praise be to God, Sippy Nollic's chatty wife Lucinda was on the telephone bending someone else's ear when Rhonda entered the liquor store, otherwise she might never have gotten out of there and she'd still be at the cash register listening to the old hag flap her lips as all the alcohol evaporated out of her purchases.

Rhonda got to the Woodworks just after the noon deadline. She carried Rodney's neatly folded blue suit like a veteran's flag in her gloved hands as she briskly walked from the car to the front sales office. Sawdust in the air collected on the Navy Blue fabric like dandruff. *It could use a good dry-cleaning*, she thought, brushing some of the chaff away. There just wasn't time enough as it was to get things done without worrying about persnickety details on top of it all.

While she waited for the manager to tally her bill, she hurriedly wrote a note of instructions to pin to the jacket lapel, asking that the suit be placed inside the coffin. Then she idly browsed through a showroom catalog, which she found on the counter, and saw an illustration of the baroque casket she refused. It really wasn't that bad. Not bad at all! It was a handsome mahogany piece with brass handles and a plush silk lining. There were some tasteful frills and carvings in the wood, but these accented the luster of the wood rather than make it look gauche. It would make a splendid Hope Chest. Flipping ahead several pages, Rhonda spotted a darling antique writing desk. Asking about it, she was told the cost was nine hundred and fifty dollars. She simply *must* have it! The manager remarked that there might be one in stock she could have for nine hundred if she bought it today, otherwise the waiting time for construction was about three months.

"Ooo," Rhonda cooed. "I'll take it! Can I pay on delivery?"

He shook his head. "First off, there's no delivery on this item unless you're willing to pay an additional two hundred. Second, if you want it, you'll have to pay up before closing time today otherwise the price jumps back up to nine-seventy-five. I'd let you leave a goodwill deposit of two-thirds now and come back with the balance. *I* trust you … BUT I can't guarantee someone else won't come in off the street and buy it before you get back, in which case your deposit will be refunded, o' course, except for a 10% service charge. That's 10% of the total product price, not 10% of your deposit."

Rhonda gazed longingly at the catalog picture. What a dilemma! She had twelve hundred and fifty dollars in her personal checking account, which would cover either writing desk or coffin nicely, but not both. Her joint checking account with her mother had about four hundred in it, but that checkbook was at home, little use to her now even if it had a bigger balance, which it did just yesterday until Rhonda wrote checks from it for her mother's bills.

Damn that gas and electric usage!

Well, under the circumstances it would be best to put off paying for the coffin until Ralph could come in later and write out a check from his personal account. She'd pay for the writing desk in full now, just to be on the safe side.

"Eleven hundred, lady," the manager said writing up the receipt. "We can't continue work on that box you commissioned until it's paid for in full. If it gets any later I doubt we can finish it today."

"My husband will be in by three this afternoon. Is that too late?" she asked with a definite edge in her voice.

"*Eeeuuufff,*" the manager replied, taking a sharp gulp of air and sounding like someone just punched him hard in his solar plexus. "That's cutting it close.

Rushing construction like that, you run the risk of the thing looking like a pile o' crap, not to mention that it'll probably be as stable as a fart in a windstorm."

Rhonda told him she'd take her chances.

SIXTEEN

When Doug and Larry, the morgue's night shift attendants, arrived at work precisely on time, five p.m. sharp, they found the morgue completely deserted. Attendants were required to wait until the new shift arrives before leaving their post, but the day shift rarely did what was required of them.

It was typical that they split early, and even more typical that today they left behind a mess of pizza boxes, crumpled paper towels, and half-eaten crap all over the place ... but, as an extra-added annoying touch, there was that silly black and white photo hanging above the sink.

Doug spent a moment or two looking at the picture in shocked disbelief. He clucked his tongue. "A couple of real sick puppies," he said. "And I thought they went too far the time we found the corpses sitting around the drain table with canasta cards in their paws." He shook his head disdainfully.

Larry shrugged it off. He knew better than to be shocked by those idiots on the day shift. So while Doug methodically checked out the worksheet, he moved a couple of stools to the drain table in preparation for their day's activities. Doug, coming over and sitting down, tossed a bit of crumpled paper toward the waste basket next to the sink. It missed and fell to the floor. Larry watched it bounce and roll away as he took a well-worn deck of playing cards out of his freshly starched uniform pants' pocket.

"What was that?"

Doug told him offhandedly that it was just an *Embalm Immediately* tag those clowns stuck on sixty-one. "Look, we'll play a couple of hands, then we'll start work. Okay?"

"You bet, partner."

"Great! I'm gonna win back everything I lost from you yesterday. I feel lucky tonight. Deal 'em!"

By seven fifteen, with the sun nothing more than a red ember in the sky outside, Larry had won each game of Rummy and quite a few dollars. Doug threw down his cards in a fit of bad temper. "That's it."

"Aw, c'mon Doug. One more hand."

"We have work to do," he said crossly.

"We're gonna be here all night, aren't we? That tenant there in freezer sixty-one isn't going anywhere. He's in no hurry, right?" Larry scooped up the cards and shuffled them. In freezer number sixty-one, the late Rodney Rodoggio was stirring awake, wondering what happened to Betty, the waterfall, and that delightful woodsy setting.

Then he remembered the green fog, the smell of death, and the vampire. All of it, including this, must be a dream. Maybe he was in a coma? He was puzzled by the new sensations in his body: a strong and fast moving current of energy, as if all his blood was replaced by pulsing light. He felt tremendous power, but physically too weak to even lift a finger. There was no pain, although his mouth throbbed uncomfortably. He cautiously moved his tongue to probe the area and discovered that his tongue *was* the problem. His teeth had grown razor sharp and were impaling it. When he attempted to release the helpless organ by opening his mouth he found that his jaw was clamped shut.

It was pitch black wherever he was. *Cold?* It was cold in an abstract way, more a concept then a real feeling. He could see perfectly although the only thing in sight was an opaque milky whiteness. With a shock, Rodney realized that something filmy was covering his head and whole body. He could feel its slick ickiness next to his skin.

Someone's stuffed me inside that giant Ramitin brand condom display from Fooster's Rexall...

He was distracted by voices heard clearly from someplace off in the distance. Two men arguing.

"... you're just sore because I won every hand ..."

"Bulldinggy! We're getting paid to run this morgue, not to play crummy Rummy."

Morgue??! Holy SHIT—Am I DEAD?!!! Of course not, he reasoned. He didn't feel dead. He tried to remember that this is all a dream, but, *goddammit*, it all seemed so real.

"What's the big deal? One more hand, then we'll do some FUN work ..."

"Fun … You mean like that old guy last month? The one they shipped off by bus to bury in Minnesota?"

The two men laughed merrily.

"Whew! That was a close one! It's a damn good thing they had a closed-coffin service. We could've lost our jobs."

"Aw, so what."

"So what?? Listen, I don't know about you, but that forty-eight dollar-a-week check means something to me. I'm not taking any more chances."

"Yeah," the other mumbled, sulking. "Those day shift bastards may be real sick creeps, but they get to have some laughs. Looks like they had fun setting up that Marx Brothers picture with ol' Harpo."

"I didn't say we weren't going to have some chuckles here, Larry, I just said I didn't want to take any high risks with little jokes. That's all."

Larry, Rodney thought. *One of them is named Larry.*

"I admit, not embalming that old guy before his trip was risky, but just imagine the paying customers on that Greyhound bus out to Minnesota!"

They laughed again.

"There's something very poetic about a dead old man sitting on a Greyhound bus to Minnesota turning green and purple and decomposing all the way across America," Larry continued and Rodney imagined a busload of pretentious oldies sniffing each other to see who it was rotting under their very noses. He tried to smile.

"We agree, no more risks?"

"Okay, okay. As long as you don't stiff me on our Rummy games."

"It's a deal. Now about sixty-one … let's take care o' him! Any ideas?"

"How 'bout an Oldie but still a Goody?"

"You mean like some snipped off toes stuffed up the *KAZOO*? Yes'sir'ree'*bobbie!*"

Rodney heard them belching out bursts of high hilarity until almost all the breath left their bodies and they gasped for air. He pictured a sixty-one year old dead guy with toes sticking out of his asshole and laughed at the thought himself despite the awful feeling it caused his tongue.

Doug and Larry busily prepared for their embalming task; they got out tanks and tubes, washed probes and pipes. Searching for the bone snippers, Doug got real peeved thinking that those scumbag day attendants probably borrowed them for use in the outside world until he saw the silver stainless steel handles sticking out of a pizza box.

Larry, washing a twelve inch probe at the sink, gazed at the Marx Brothers photo. "Hmm, I wonder if this guy is Mr. Sixty-One?"

"Could be," Doug said. They looked at one another, caught each other's eye. Doug dropped the bone snippers nosily to the floor and clutched his sides. Larry started singing.

> O, Sixty-One,
> O, Sixty-One!
> It's So Much Fun
> Embalming Sixty-One!

Larry sang to the tune of *O, Christmas Tree*, accompanying himself with taps on the dirty drain table with the tip of a clean probe. The two attendants strived for a new level of mirth as they sang round after round of *O, Sixty-One* during final embalming preparations. "What's Sixty-One's name?" Larry asked, thinking he might like to create a second stanza. Doug waltzed over to the freezer and read the name off the tag.

"It just says 'Harpoon'." he sneered. Rodney heard the voice good and loud, as if it was right behind his head. *Harpoon? Didn't I have a school teacher named Mrs. Harpoon? Second grade? Maybe it's her husband?*

"Those morons can't even tag a corpse properly. I've got a good mind to complain to the Mayor."

But Larry wasn't listening. He was trying to get a second stanza going. "How's this …"

> O, Sixty-One,
> O, Sixty-One!
> Harpoon is Fun in
> Getting Done …

"Ugh," said Doug. He thought for a moment, then hummed *Deck the Halls*.

> Stuff the Ass with Toes
>   of Harpoon
> Fa-la-la-la-la-la—La-la-la-la
> He Will Be Impacted
>   Real Soon
> Fa-la-la-la-la-la—La-la-la-la
> First We Snip His Toes Off
>   Smartly

> Fa-la-la-la-la-la—La-la-la-la
> Then We Stick'em Where He Used
>   To Fartly
> Fa-la-la-la-la-la—La-la-la-la
> Watch Yourself if Gas
>   He Passes
> Fa-la-la-la-la-la—La-la-la-la …
> Flying Toes Might Break Your
>   Glasses
> Fa-la-la-la-la-la—La-la-la-la

"Hey!" said Larry, "that's pretty good. You've got talent."

Doug pushed the dilapidated gurney over to the compartment. Actually, it was more like dragging the dilapidated gurney, even on this slick linoleum because the goddamn thing was so old that the wheels hardly turned anymore. It was handmade back in the dawn of time by Elmer Tittinsel, one of the first police morgue attendants, who got sick and tired of carrying corpses in his arms from the drain table to the ice cooled cabinets they used to use outside in back of the station. This dopey gurney, a warped wooden platform nailed to spindly buckled legs with large rusty wheels attached, was bound to collapse one fine day and break apart into a million splinters. Doug dragged/pushed it to the edge of the freezer door praying that today wasn't going to be that fine day.

Rodney heard what sounded like banging pipes amid the off-key caroling, followed by the ratchety squeals of the gurney wheels coming closer. *The trolley o' death is coming to get YOU Mr. Harpoon! Man, I wish I could see his toes snipping off! Maybe I can get a job in the morgue once I'm out of the coma.*

"ONE NUMBER SIXTY-ONE COMING UP!" the voice he recognized as Larry cried from right behind his head. "THE HARPO SPECIAL!"

Rodney could barely contain his amusement. He felt like he was going to wet himself from wanting to laugh so hard. There was a deep metallic clang behind his head and the sickening noise of inrushing air. Rodney was startled by the sudden burst of blue-gray fluorescent light around and over him.

Those jerks opened the wrong … whoaaa …! The metal slab he rested upon slid out with such swiftness that Rodney felt his whole body jiggle like Jello. *Play dead,* he wisely counseled himself.

Larry gave the corpse a little hello punch on the face. "Howdy Doody, Harpo."

If he could still sweat, Rodney would be sweating *now*. Playing dead wasn't such a great idea after all.

They attempted to hoist the wrapped body off the freezer slab onto the gurney, but the shroud stuck to the metal tenaciously.

"Someone glued him down," Larry observed.

"THAT'S THE CHEESIEST JOKE IN THE BOOK! IF THOSE DAY BASTARDS THINK THEY CAN GET AWAY WITH THAT ..." Doug screamed.

Larry poked and probed under the shroud and discovered that it was being held in place by frost.

"I see those assholes didn't bother to let the table drain completely before they slapped the sheet on," Doug muttered, a little embarrassed by his outburst. They roughly wobbled the body back and forth to loosen the ice.

Some of Rodney's new strength flooded through his being. He felt power surging, flowing like molten lava.

This was good.

This was *real* good because he needed to get out of this place very soon, otherwise he'd be spending time plucking his toes out of his rectum. As he was being jerked around he rocked back and forth for momentum. If he could swing his legs over and get up onto his feet ...

That didn't seem to be working, so he wedged his joined feet between the slab and gurney and gave a hard push. The gurney shot between the attendants and trundled unsteadily across the room. Rodney fell to the floor.

"Fuckadoodledoo," Larry hissed. He gave the corpse a good kick. They hefted the body and slammed it back down onto the slab. Doug retrieved the gurney. Bracing the rickety thing with their bodies flush against the buckled platform they unceremoniously dumped Rodney onto it.

"Let's get this mothereating shroud off him!" Doug sang out with glee.

"NO," Larry protested. "I love jabbing a knife through the plastic into the tummy and watch the gut juices bubble up through the plastic."

Doug looked at his partner as if he'd never seen him before. "Are you NUTS? It's more fun without the damn plastic getting in the way."

"Baloney! It makes that nice squishy sound through the plastic."

"But the bile and gutcrap don't BUBBLE UP through the shroud, moron! You don't get to see a damn thing."

Larry flung a scalpel at Doug, nicking his shoulder.

Doug ran to the sink to see his reflected image in the stainless steel cabinets. The boring white of his uniform's shoulder was rapidly disappearing beneath tendrils of the bright red liquid bubbling out through the slit in the fabric. He had to admit, the effect was far more interesting than had he been watching the blood dribble down his naked flesh.

"See! I told you." Larry said proudly.

"Okay, okay!" Doug conceded. "We'll leave the plastic on."

Larry danced over to pick up the scalpel. He wiped the ultra-sharp edge on his leg, being careful not to slice his pants. He bowed deeply to Doug, and presented him with the instrument now resting cleanly and elegantly on his outstretched arm. "Your blade, Monsieur."

"Tut-tut," Doug cautioned. "What have we forgotten?"

Larry laughed. There was a cassette player in one of the cabinets, along with some selected tapes. Larry fished through them until he found the right one.

Rodney saw their blurry shapes through the milky wrap. Their arms were raised high, flourishing tools that glinted sharply. They tapped their heels on the linoleum. Spinning around, lifting their legs, they came at him dancing the lusty *Boléro* like a pair of hellish flamenco dancers. Beyond them, over to the right he could make out a dark rectangle against a gray field. It looked like a door.

Doug stopped short and gasped. The corpse was swinging its legs off the gurney, trying to stand upright! The dripping condensation on the shroud gave the thing a shiny, supernatural look. He felt something wet dribble down his pants leg.

Rodney, using a combination hop and shuffle, waddled drippingly toward the door leaving a slippery trail behind him.

"Come back here, you!" Larry ordered, stalking it cautiously. Not exactly sure what a reanimated corpse was capable of doing, he didn't want to take any chances. He gestured vehemently for Doug's help, but Doug wanted no part of this particular business.

"Leave it alone," he pleaded. "It's some kind o' miserable *ghost*!"

Larry ignored that feeble-minded bullcracky. "C'mon, give me a hand, will'ya! Chase it from the other side …"

"I'm not chasing that!" He looked at the thing, which was at the door trying to prize it open with a number of moves. The creature looked like that picture of Jesus at the house door calling on sinners, his body glowing with celestial light. All the sins of his past floated by Doug's horrified eyes. He fell to his knees, praying to God for forgiveness. Larry cursed, tried a flying tackle and ended up slipping off Rodney as if he were a greased hog. Rodney lurched away from the door.

The floor was getting difficult to maneuver on, as Doug found out when he cringingly attempted to avoid the hopping corpse. He jumped to his feet like a

Lutheran after a hymn. Moving quickly and changing directions suddenly, he glided in a puddle of shroud drippings right smack into the revenant. He screamed shrilly, bounced away and collided with Larry. They fell onto the floor together in a tangled heap. Rodney hopped to the door and got out by using his elbow to turn and pull the doorknob while his ass wedged the door open. He skittered out backward.

"*Eeeee-yahhhh! Get off meeee!*" Larry screeched. When it became apparent it was a warm-bodied human he was tumbling with, Larry became livid with rage, but also very relieved that it was only Doug atop him. He got to his feet, leaving his partner trembling and repentful.

Seeing that Harpo flew the coop, Larry said darkly: "He got out. What the hell am I going to embalm now?" He glared down at Doug. It didn't look like he'd mind a trip to heaven. A bit of fun, Larry said to himself, a peculiar little half-smile on his face. Then a quick trip to the swamp. Who'd know? But he'd have no one to share the fun with.

Just then, in walked Selma Krinklis. Larry's half-smile ripened into a full one.

SEVENTEEN

A heavy mitt fell upon Rodney's shoulder as he skittled backwards through the morgue door. The door closed with a hydraulic whoosh in his face.

"You're under arrest!" the voice attached to the mitt said. It was deep, adenoidal, scary. Rodney was forcefully turned around. Two wavy silhouettes in the dim hallway light stood in front of him. One, a big oafish Yogi Bear of a figure, the other short and squat with hands on hips.

Boo-Boo?

The big one shook with jolly retarded laughter. "What you guys won't do," he said loudly in the small corridor. His voice bounced around like neutrons in an atom splitter. He put his great big mug right up to the shroud, right into Rodney's covered face. "Is that Doug or Larry in there? It's me ... Ogden Bialystock ..."

Rodney nodded broadly, hoping to indicate that, yes, he was one of the lunatic morgue attendants. The numbnutted idiot thought Rodney was nodding at the squat figure beside him.

"Oh, her," the giant said disinterestedly. "This is Mrs. Crinkles."

Selma laughed politely. "*Krinklis.* How dee'do, hon."

"I had to escort Mrs. Crinkleless to the morgue," he grumbled. "She's here to pick up somebody's crappy body. Hey! Not a bad idea! Picking up a body!!" He picked Rodney up by the shroud-tie around his midsection and carried him like a purloined picnic basket. "Let's go show the guys upstairs!"

Officer Bialystock ran up the steps, two at a time, barely containing his toggle-headed giggles. At the main desk the package was dropped down and held upright by Ogden's extra large paw clenching the back of Rodney's neck.

"Look what I caught trying to rob the morgue."

"That'll be sixty days in the *cooler*, me fine young man," the desk sergeant said with a phony Irish brogue, throwing a hardback book of Gulpo Plains Laws and Regulations playfully at Rodney. It hit his forehead and bounced off, falling to the floor with a smart thud. "I'm throwing the book at'cha!"

Everyone laughed hysterically, even the felons brought in from the city on drug and murder charges.

"You need a little humor to break up the monotony," the desk sergeant told a sourpussed hooker named Glenda, the only one not laughing. She was very annoyed that her pimp hasn't shown up yet to get her tit out of this ringer.

All the cops in the place gathered around Rodney, leaving their duties (which included securing dangerous criminals) unattended. They slapped him on the back, patted his ass, and told him he was a great looking dead guy. They waxed poetically about what terrific morgue attendants they were to share such funny jokes with "us poor working stiffs". Someone mentioned the photo shoot, already a classic in Gulpo Plains Police Annals, and invited him and his partner to the big party following next Friday night's prostitution sting.

"There'll be plenty o' girls," the desk sergeant winked. "You don't wanna miss it!"

Rodney stood dumbly throughout all this, sometimes nodding, sometimes grunting until interest in him finally abated. When he was standing there for moments on end with no attention paid to him, he shuffled over to the door and worked it open. All the officers and the few remaining criminals called goodbye as he left.

Outside on the street, in the dark, Rodney found his sense of direction very much impaired. Although he knew the Police Station was not too far from home, he had trouble determining just which way to go. He turned right, hopping away along the grass curbstrip in an effort to avoid scraping his feet on the uneven cement sidewalk.

He hadn't journeyed long before bright light diffusing through the plastic of his shroud warned him of an upcoming streetlight. Navigating around the pole with a minimum of effort, a dexterity that impressed him considerably, Rodney found confidence enough to increase his speed. He hopped roughly twenty-five fast hops when he rammed flat-out into the next streetlight, one in which the lamp had burnt out eons ago and was never replaced. There were a lot of these burnt-out lamp posts all over Gulpo Plains and Rodney cursed his bad luck for not remembering this little tidbit. It was lucky for him he didn't topple over backwards because it would be a real bitch to get back up again. He'd be like a turtle on its back, waving his feet impotently in the air trying to flip over. Maybe the straight and narrow cement was the best path after all. Twisting his feet one way while turning his torso the other, he Chubby Checkered himself onto the sidewalk.

The undead travel swiftly, he might have known if he paid more attention to those horror movies he watched instead of just looking at the half-dressed girls who popped up in them. Unbeknownst to himself, he'd already traversed the entire length of the town. It wasn't until his feet left the secure firmness of sidewalk, coming down mid-hop in the soft, oatmealy ooze of Samuel A. Gulpo Memorial Swamp, that he realized first, that he was traveling so quickly and second, that he was going in the wrong direction.

Fighting against the suction pulling him under the disgusting goo, Rodney frantically wondered just how-in-hell he was going to get out of this particular mess. It crossed his mind briefly that since he was in a coma, this sensation was probably nothing more than Roweena's bed sucking him down. Still, sinking rapidly, he was pushing against the downspiral tug. Every move dragged him down deeper, and deeper still, until with one mighty push of his body he succeeded in propelling himself to the very bottom of the swamp, where not only was the smell incomprehensibly awful, like sewer turds and overcooked cabbage, but he was assaulted by a host of human body parts suspended in the mire around him. Disembodied hands poked at him, feet kicked at his nuts. For some lucky reason, the shroud began ballooning up around him with trapped air. He lifted toward the surface at a dizzying speed, bobbing on the surface like a marshmallow in hot cocoa. He got his elbows up on the edge of land, hoisting himself out of the swamp. Bellyflopping on cement, his feet dangling over the edge, his shroud was a dank, sticky, smelly mess around him.

Christ alone knows how bad it looks … I probably look like one o' those used Kotexes wrapped in toilet paper I have to fish out of the clogged toilet because those idiot supermarket ladies insist on flushing them …

He lay there for many moments, rancid swamp breeze drifting over him, the lap of rushing quicksand at his feet. He was trying to decide the best way to get home once he managed to regain his feet, hopefully without falling over backwards into the swamp.

A gunshot rang out just up ahead. An answer to his prayers for help!

"NNSSSESSS. GOOMMMBOKKAAA!" he called joyfully through his sealed mouth.

Mrs. Grummbacher lives in the only house on Gulpo Swamp Road. Back about a million years ago, sometime in the 1930s, when the swamp extended its boundaries due to a deep-earth fissure, all the houses on Gulpo Swamp Road were swallowed up. That is, all the houses except for Mrs. Grummbacher's. According to local legend, she sat on her porchswing, rocking back and forth, watching as one houseful of neighbors after another vanished into the tidal wave of gloop. "Toodle-loo!" she'd call to them cheerfully above their terror-ridden screams.

If she wasn't bonkers then, when a whole block of families were mulched to swampmeal, she certainly was *now*. And Rodney knew this better than anyone in town. He'd spent most of his boyhood delivering her damn *Gulpo Plainsman* newspaper every day, and after he stopped being a picayune paper boy and got himself a real job as a stockboy, was stuck delivering her heavy damn groceries from EverRipe.

Mrs. Grummbacher would often coax Rodney to stay and keep her company after making his delivery. He was forced to listen to the old bag twitter on about her youth and her marriage to Xaxier Grummbacher, the most wonderful man who ever lived. These never-ending stories had no discernible point, going absolutely nowhere—except on and on and on. All the while she talked she kept passing him the oatmeal cookies she baked, and watched like a hawk to make sure he'd eat one after another until the plate was crumbless. Oatmeal cookies that tasted awful were one thing, but these not only tasted like soggy swamp patties, they also gave him severe diarrhea. Rodney never knew, or figured it out, that Mrs. Grummbacher's secret cookie ingredient was scouring powder used in place of baking soda. Even when he was delivering eight cans of Comet a week to her, it didn't sink in.

He tried refusing the cookies once, but Mrs. Grummbacher cried and cried until he yielded. She watched with a warm, satisfied smile as Rodney ate all six dozen cookies she'd made that very morning especially for him. Boy, was it hard getting through the rest of *that* day, which included a family dinner at stuffy old Auntie Clarissa's house where a child's use the bathroom was considered very bad manners and subject to much criticism.

Rodney started wiggleassing on his belly toward her. "NNSSSESSS. GOOM-MMBOKKAAA ... NNSSSESSS. GOOMMMBOKKAAA ... NNSSSESSS. GOOMMMBOKKAAA!"

EIGHTEEN

"My, how pleasant it is tonight," Mrs. Grummbacher commented aloud, breathing in a lungful of stagnant swamp air. Mrs. Grummbacher had the bad habit of talking aloud to herself, but since she often became engaged in meaningful and witty conversations this way she did nothing to correct it.

"It certainly is," she responded. "An early evening constitutional is every bit as enjoyable as a late night pre-sleep walk," Mrs. Grummbacher pointed out to Mrs. Grummbacher. The old woman had recently changed her walk schedule due to the increase of thugs hanging out at the swamp. Reprehensible young people from Loodyville or the city would arrive just around midnight and stay through to the wee hours of the morning, hooting and caterwauling disgracefully. How was a girl to get her beauty sleep with all that ruckus going on? She called the police every night. Sometimes fifty times a night, but the police started calling her a nutburger, slamming down the telephone in her ear.

They did nothing to remove these usurpers.

She wrote letters to the newspaper. Long editorials filled with swamplore and facts as well as a plea to make our swamp safe again.

They went unpublished.

She went to the Mayor's house to complain, but those big, vicious guard dogs of his prevented her from getting anywhere near the front door. It was very frustrating, to say the least.

Mrs. Grummbacher certainly had no objections to people coming to the swamp to enjoy the scenery, but when they made horrible slurping and cackling noises night after night after night, drinking bottles and bottles of beer, molesting her in the middle of her dear walks, that was taking fun a little *too* far if you wanted to know the truth. Something had to be done.

She paused for a moment to put down the large satchel-type pocketbook she carried in her left hand. Tucking her cane under her arm, she rubbed vigorously the gnarly knuckles on that arthritically pain-afflicted hand. Her brow knitted down over her milky gray eyes in an expression of displeasure.

"The only *un*enjoyable feature of my little walks is having to carry around this stupid pocketbook," she grumbled.

"Ah, but one never leaves one's home undressed, my dear."

"Yes, that's true," she sighed.

"Yes it *is*. What would dear Xavier say if he saw you cavorting around town improperly dressed?"

"You have a point."

Xavier Polidori Grummbacher disappeared one day fifty years ago. Some folk say he'd gotten squiffy and fell into the swamp, others maintain that he ran off with that awful Lucy Odalisque and set up a cozy little love nest in her house over on Strumpet Lane. They say you can still see him through Lucy's big picture window at certain times of the day, when it is neither too light nor too dark. When the day melts into twilight, there he is brazenly sitting in his underpants, a dopey satisfied expression on his face, looking at the TV.

But Mrs. Grummbacher, who was his wife after all, knew the whole horrible truth of Xaxier's disappearance, regardless of what the "good folk" of Gulpo Plains might think. She knows that he was abducted by a revolting, slimy thing that lives under the quicksand, a furious swampsnake hideous to behold.

Xaxier Grummbacher left the house one day in 1923, going for a pack of cigarettes and it must have been the lure of sweet Grummbacher flesh that brought the creature to the surface licking its chops, meaning to devour Xaxier clean to the bone. But Grummbacher men are made of sterner stuff. They do not give their flesh away so easily. There must have been quite a tussle as Xaxier was carried off down into the murky recesses of the swamp. Down to the secret cavern where the abomination lives. All the while, as she sat in their comfy little home patiently awaiting his return, she was unaware of the terrible fate befalling her dear husband. Mrs. Grummbacher envisions the year-to-year struggle, a war to the finish between her brave, loving Xaxier and that unholy thing. She knows that once he defeats the creature he will return victorious to Gulpo Plains and to his own true love.

Mrs. Grummbacher, infused with terror, lives in fear that the evil swampsnake will come back to the surface looking for *her*—a trump card it would use to thwart Xaxier once and for all. She will never forget the very first time she saw it with her own two eyes; although now her memory seems a little out of kilter, it's basically as clear as the picture on her antennaless television.

Right after she'd given up her attempt at getting the authorities to remove those undesirable teenage hoodlums, she took the bull by the horns and went to ask them personally to behave or leave the swamp. Just as they accosted her with wolfie-whistles and kissy sounds, rubbing their grubby thumbs lustily over their even grubbier fingertips at her, up from the swamp rose the horrible creature! It routed out all the hoodlums, cutting them up with a great big butcher knife and tossing their pieces into the bubbling swamp, laughing and laughing all the while, it's little gnarled hands dripping with thug blood. Then the swampsnake had the audacity to go into Mrs. Grummbacher's very own home! It slithered into the bathroom and washed up at the sink, ruining one of her favorite towels, leaving it crumpled and dirty on the floor. Mrs. Grummbacher took that gesture to be an omen.

As she lifted her heavy pocketbook off the sidewalk, one of its two straps snapped. The bag tilted open dumping some of its contents out onto the ground. A sharp metallic bang echoed out over the swamp.

"Oh, cookies," she grumbled, bending over to pick up the fallen and discharged .38 snubnose handgun along with her wallet and her comb. As she stuffed them back into the pocketbook her fingers slid across the blade of one of the great big butcher knives inside.

"*Monkeyballs!!*"

Blood dribbled from her cut fingers. She instinctively put them up to her mouth, sucking it back into her old body. Just then, she heard the slithering snakelike sound of something squirming on the sidewalk up ahead and saw the hideous swampsnake come out of the mist. A creature with vile white skin covered with fresh swamp ooze. It was coming right at her. "NNSSSESSS GOOM-MMBOKKAAA!" it called. To her ancient and dried-up ears it sounded like it was bellowing, "HISSSSSS ... COMIN' TO GET YA!"

Mrs. Grummbacher gulped hard, her trembling hand reached into her pocketbook.

"Come and get THIS!" she screeched, pointing the .38, squinting her eyes for aim. She was glad now that she never made it a habit to engage the safety mechanism, even though she's had many an accident with the gun shooting itself off all over the place, even once just barely missing that nice supermarket delivery boy. Who'd want to waste time fiddling around with a doggone lever or latch or whatever it was when you really needed it? Point and shoot, that's the name of the game.

She fired the gun and the recoil sent her frail body flipping over backwards. The bullet, however, must have found its mark because the slime monster stopped dead.

"Yah-HOOOO!" Mrs. Grummbacher cried in victory, getting up and hopping around, waving her decrepit fists in the air. "Yah-HOOO, you flesheating weeniesucker! YAH-HOOOOOOOO!!!!"

The thing was not vanquished … it was moving.

Coming at her with vengeance.

She fired the gun, this time bracing herself against the pressure. She fired until every shell was spent. Still it came, hissing in its snaky voice, "NNSSSESSS. GOOMMMBOKKAAA … NNSSSESSS. GOOMMMBOKKAAA … NNS-SSESSS. GOOMMMBOKKAAA". She threw the gun, hitting it on its noggin. It stopped, momentarily dazed. Dumping the contents of her pocketbook out onto the sidewalk, she picked up three of the largest knives she carried. She hurled one of them, missing by a mile. The second did no better, but the third knife found its mark. It struck the center of its horrible head, the handle sticking up out of it like the horn on a Ray Harryhausen Cyclops. The enraged creature struggled to stand upright. Twitching forward like a disgusting hobbling slug, it advanced on Mrs. Grummbacher.

Mrs. Grummbacher was filled with fear and loathing. She lost heart and wanted to turn to run for the safety of her home, but the smiling visage of Xaxier Grummbacher floated before her eyes. Her fear evaporated like a suppository left out on the porch on a fine July day, and she firmly stayed her ground.

When all that was left in her arsenal were the explosives she had purchased from that crazy boy with no eyes, Mrs. Grummbacher lit the fuse of a cherry bomb. Chucking it as hard as she could muster, she watched in dismay as it sailed over the snake and landed in the swamp. A moment later brown icky goo showered down on the old woman and her combatant.

But it was too late. It was upon her. Garbled sounds came from deep within it … she clutched her thick, hard cane in her pain-ridden hand …

Whack … whack … whack … whack …

NINETEEN

After dinner Ralph Rodoggio and his family retired to the living room. With his wife and daughter settled around him, he prepared to watch an evening of fine television. Ralph clicked on the ancient set using the little plastic volume knob, then turned and jogged to the easy chair awaiting him. Relaxing in the chair's familiar contour, he watched the TV set warm up. A tiny gray dot appeared in the middle of the screen. Ralph studied it with eager anticipation, waiting for the dot to expand into a full, glorious, TV picture.

The dot flickered, refusing to expand for quite a long while. Finally, the screen began filling with murky gray light. There was sound, some people laughing in an audience and having a high old time, but Ralph sat fuming not knowing *what* was so funny, looking at indistinct dark globs amidst the gray.

He sighed deeply from his diaphragm, arose from his chair with the *Gulpo Plainsman* firmly in his grasp. Several firm whomps to the side of the set snapped-in the picture strong and clear. It was *Gilligan's Island!* No wonder the audience sitting in the lagoon were laughing so hard! He went back to his seat. After ten minutes the picture flipped and began rolling. He flung his slipper hard at the television screen, but the disturbance persisted. Removing his remaining slipper, Ralph stood up and marched czaristically toward the Sylvania. Almost there, his hand raised to come down hard on top of its traitorous cabinet, the picture suddenly stopped tumbling. He smacked the TV set anyway.

Ralph Rodoggio was in no mood to fool around tonight. His dinner was ruined by the off-putting smell of that dead policeman still decorating the stair

- 116 -

landing, and now he was extremely annoyed that this repeat of *Gilligan's Island* wasn't making *him* laugh. Roweena, too, was quiet and sulky.

On the other hand, Rhonda Rodoggio hummed a never-ending tuneless little song, happy as a lark. When her gaze drifted over to the other end of the living room, which it did quite often, and she saw her brand new writing desk placed at a jaunty angle in the corner, her lips arced upward into a big spontaneous smile, making her hum all the louder.

But as midevening rolled around, when the weekly *Mortimer Morbane's Gulpo Plains In Focus News Special* started, Rhonda's mood deteriorated, affected considerably by the sourness of Ralph and Roweena. Neither one acknowledged the presence of the writing desk let alone compliment her wise buy.

"*Your many cards and letters,*" Mortimer Morbane said, looking right into the Rodoggio living room, "*suggesting ways of alleviating the accumulation of bodies at the EternOrest Cemetery have been very useful in trying to resolve a deplorable situation.*

"*As everyone knows, due to the rash of coffin robberies last month our dearly departed neighbors have been laying all over the EternOrest grounds in heaps, coffinless and exposed to sun and rain and godknowswhatall types of terrible weather. In one rare instance, a crime was committed that has yet to be explained by puzzled authorities. A body was stolen from the cemetery instead of its coffin. Cute li'l sixteen year old Belinda Scoophaven's remains disappeared from her coffin shortly after being placed there two weeks ago. Her whereabouts are unknown.*

"*Belinda passed on during a botched attempt to remove her unborn baby with a wire hanger by Hal Feenmaster, ex captain of the Weasels, Gulpo Plains High School's football team. In a statement to police, Belinda's stepfather Elroy Pudpul said, quote, 'that wherever she is, I'm sure they are taking care of her tender young body REAL good, giving it all the sweet loving it deserves' end quote. He went on to say that his daughter's needless death should serve as an example of the evils of legalizing abortion.*

"*Be that as it may, this robbery makes one less nuisance for Plainsians who live near the cemetery or, like me, have to pass by it every couple of months. Unfortunately, we cannot expect such good luck with all the other cadavers still piled there, tangled in a mess of humanity.*

"*The viewers writing in suggesting that corpses could be made more attractive to robbers have rocks in their well meaning but stupid heads. We all know how unrealistic it would be to decorate them with jewelry. Squirrels and other packrat predators who have been feasting on the bodies would take the jewelry to their tree-nests and leave the corpses behind. And it would be impossible to sew money inside them because stitches would not hold the unstable flesh together.*

"*By and large, the majority of your letters contained ideas like these. Ideas that not only are not feasible …*" Mortimer Morbane smiled warmly. "*… they're just plain DAFFY. Shipping them to Russia, for example, would place such a heavy burden on the town budget that we'd feel the tax bite for years to come, not to mention how much we'd hate it if those Russkies started sending us dead commies in some kind of bizarre exchange program.*

"*Likewise, it would be ridiculous to entertain the idea of using the high school gymnasium for storage during school's summer recess. Moving crumbling bodies all the way from EternOrest to the High School, then from the High School back to EternOrest once school started would take manpower, which costs money. Big money.*

"*One viewer suggested that the cemetery workers who went out on strike, causing this ghastly mess in the first place, should be made to take them home and keep them. See how fast those crybaby cemetery workers decide to grow up and go back to work then! Frankly, we were leaning toward this idea as a sensible solution and would have applied pressure in the right places to bring this about, but a better solution has been found without our intervention.*

"*Today the fine folks at EternOrest held a public auction, with bidders coming from as far away as Queezemore in Alaska! Surprise of surprises, however—the top bidder proved to be a local man. Mr. Leon Bastardo, shown here with his wife and nine children, won the lot for just eight hundred fifty dollars and twenty-nine cents!*"

Ralph perked up. "Say, I wonder if this fellow might be interested in buying the policeman? Why wait for the fire department if we can get rid of him sooner?"

"And make a tidy little profit," Rhonda continued. "An excellent idea. Why not call him right now?"

Keeping an eye on the TV screen so he didn't miss a thing, Ralph crabwalked over to the telephone table and dialed the operator.

"How may I help you?"

"Yes, operator. I'd like the telephone number of Mr. Leon Bastardo."

"Look in your directory. Under *B*," she said curtly. There was a loud click on the line, then the dial tone. Ralph flipped open the Greater Gulpo Plains Area Telephone Directory and turned to the *B*s. There were at least fifty Bastardos listed, twenty-six of them Leons. Ralph was not going to call each and every one of them personally, that's for sure. He dialed "O" again.

"How may I help you?" It was the same snotty operator.

"Yes, operator, I just looked in my directory. It's filled with Bastardos."

"So? What the hell do you want me to do? Call 'em all?"

Ralph stuttered in disbelief. "Can't you help me, miss …"

"MS," the woman corrected harshly, making Ralph's eardrum tickle. "*Mizzz*, got it? Listen, Mr. Male Chauvinist Pig, don't give ME any of that MISS crap."

He forced himself to be courteous. "Well, Mizzz Crap can you help me?"

"And if I don't, Mr. PIGGY?"

Ralph's face flushed scarlet with anger. He grit his teeth. He counted to ten.

"IF YOU WON'T HELP ME, I WON'T PAY MY PHONE BILL!" He blasted into the phone.

The operator chortled loudly. "Okey-dokey, funnyboy. What's the name o' the party?"

Ralph told her.

"Here you go, bub. Have a blast."

The line went blank for a moment, then connection was made. Ralph counted forty-one rings before a breathless woman answered the telephone.

"Hello," Ralph said politely. "I'd like to speak to Mr. Leon Bastardo please."

"OH MY GOD! ARE YOU HIS WIFE??"

Ralph heard the receiver drop to the floor, the woman crying hysterically. "FORGIVE ME, GOD … FORGIVE ME, GOD … FORGIVE ME, GOD!!"

"Listen, Meranda," a nasty voice suddenly said to Ralph over the telephone as the caterwauling continued in the background, "I thought I told you NOT to call here to check up on me!"

"Excuse me," Ralph said. "I think you're …"

"That's the trouble with you, Meranda. You think that the MOMENT you leave the damn house I'm going to bring in some other woman. I've got a big, fat NEWSFLASH for you: I'm all alone here. Yes. Completely and utterly alone. Does THAT satisfy you now?"

"I'm RALPH RODOGGIO," Ralph interjected.

"Oh. So now my wife has hired some private *dick* to check up on me. Very, very nice. Let me tell you something, Mannix, you're working for a genuine fruit-cake." The man went on to list all her follies and foibles, stressing time and again that this asshole wife of his had absolutely, positively no cause for jealousy what-sofuckingever.

"I'm here alone," Mr. Bastardo concluded. "You can come right over here and see for yourself. Hold on …" Now Ralph heard the man telling the crying woman to get out quickly followed by the heavy slam of a door. "Come over right this minute!" Leon Bastardo said defiantly when he got back on the line.

It took Ralph many minutes to convince the man that he wasn't a private eye or Meranda disguising her voice trying to trick him into a confession. Finally, Ralph told him that the only reason for his phone call was to inquire if he, Mr. Bastardo, would be interested in buying the dead policeman's body.

"A dead body? Why would I want to buy a *dead* body?"

That was a very good question. The body on the stair landing was taking up space ... it didn't look very good either ... and the smell it gave off certainly was not an attractive feature.

Who *would* want to buy one of these things?

"I don't know, Mr. Bastardo," Ralph said, trying hard to think of uses for the thing. "Maybe you can muff it?"

"Stuff it!" Rhonda hissed from the living room.

"MUFF it?? What do you think I am? Some kind o' lousy pervert? I don't muff guys, let alone DEAD ones, you goddam piece o' ..."

Ralph hung up the phone.

"What did he say, dear?" Rhonda asked as Ralph sat back down in his chair. He grunted and swung the newspaper at her head.

"*... And now,*" Mortimer Morbane bleated, "*some good news in the meat department. The elevating cost of beef and pork has created a market for suitable alternates. As a result, substitute meat shops have opened everywhere. They freshly butcher and sell acceptable substitutes like horse and buffalo, as well as other unusual products. Opossum and chipmunk are mighty cute critters, but did you know they were good eating? Late today it was announced that the first Meat Substitute Market would open here in our fair city of Gulpo Plains. BastardOmeats ...*" A graphic appeared on the screen showing a jolly cartoon of a BastardOmeats butcher shooing away apparently well dressed and prosperous cartoon cows and pigs trailing dollar bills behind them. The butcher clutched a mittful of these dollars, saying in a word balloon over his head:

LEON BASTARDO SEZ:
"GOO'BYE HIGH PRICED MEATS!
I'LL GIVE THESE SAVINGS TO ALL MY
NEW CUSTOMERS!
COME SEE ME AT
BASTARDOMEATS
ON MAIN STREET
(right next to Gluupick's House O' Treats)
328-6328

REMEMBER:
NOBODY CAN BEAT MY MEAT!"

Rhonda rubbed her chin hairs thoughtfully. "I wonder if that BastardOmeats man is the same Leon Bastrado who bought all those dead people at EternOrest?" She jotted down the phone number.

"Are you NUTS?" Ralph snapped back at her. "There are THOUSANDS of Bastardos in the world. What would make you think this would be the same man?"

"Speaking of bastardos," Roweena said bitterly, deciding now was as good a time as any to break the news Dr. Monklee gave her this afternoon. "I'm going to have a baby."

Ralph stared at his little girl. He stood up. Walked forward, dazed. His eyes revolved twice in their sockets before rolling back. Air rushed out of him through his nose and mouth and ears. He fell to his knees. He lost consciousness, pitching forward. Ralph Rodoggio's face met Mortimer Morbane's, then pushed through it. Glass shattered all over the floor while television innards sizzled and fizzed electronically around Ralph's head.

Rhonda rushed forward to pull her husband's head out of the TV set, smiling at Roweena with motherly affection as she passed. Roweena complained nonstop about her dismal situation while Rhonda extracted slivers of glass from Ralph's face with the tweezers she always kept handy. Each of the deeply embedded slivers caused a tiny geyser of blood to spurt as it was plucked out. Ralph stirred a little, opened his dazed eyes and grunted. He stroked Roweena's arm tenderly. In a voice choked with emotion, he told his precious daughter how happy he was to know he'd have a hair to his umpire. A hissing sound from inside the television, followed by a foul chemical odor gave Rhonda cause to worry that poison gas might be escaping from some darn tube or something, so she scooted everyone out into the dining room where they could plan Roweena's future in perfect safety.

Nearly tripping over the policeman, Ralph decided then and there to call BastardOmeats. He rashly returned to the living room, retrieving Rhonda's writing pad from the little snack table next to her chair. He was forced to step over Brucie, asleep in front of Rhonda's chair, clucking his tongue in disgust as he rammed his uplifted toes into the edge of her chair. He went to the telephone and dialed BastardOmeats.

"Hiya, Hiya, Hiya! BastardOmeats!" someone said with an intensely cheery voice. "Watch for our BIG gala opening! Bring the wife and all your kiddies!

Twerpsetta the hilarious Juggling Clown will 'meat' and greet you with a free sample of delicious substitute meat! Plus, there will be Ba-a-lo-oo-ons for one and all, and a gigantic raffle for the special Albert Fish Buffet Platter, big enough for any Donner Party! Ha-ha-ha! Help us celebrate the best and freshest meat substitutes in town! Nobody can beat my meat!"

"Mr. Bastardo?" Ralph asked. "Mr. Leon Bastardo?"

"Yessireebobby!"

"The same Mr. Leon Bastardo who won the action today at the EternOrest Cemetery?"

"Yes sir, one-in-the-same! Although there wasn't much action to speak of. Just me and some guy from Alaska who misunderstood what they were auctioning until almost the end. How can I help ya, bud?"

Ralph told him that he had a dead policeman. "What's he worth? A hundred?"

"Naw … twenty-five tops."

"Seventy-five."

"Thirty, and that's pushing it. Cops are tough, you know."

"Okay, thirty it is," Ralph said. He was going to ask Leon Bastardo what on earth he wanted with all these dead bodies, but his vision was blurring from the television gas and his tongue felt like a duffel bag in his mouth. After quickly giving Leon Bastardo their address, Ralph hung up the phone. The TV set exploded just as he was leaving the living room sending Brucie flying through the air over Ralph's head.

"What did he say, dear?" Rhonda asked, catching the little dog in one hand.

"He'll give us thirty dollars."

"That's *all*?" she snurffed. "Didn't you haggle with him?"

"O' course I did! But he's a real sick businessman. This was the best deal I could get. Ooo, I wish I knew what he was doing with those dead bodies. It's like one o' those irritating diddles … you know the kind. 'When is a dump truck like a dairy queen?'."

"That's riddle, and how the heck do I know when a dump truck is like a dairy queen!" Rhonda's lips were suddenly very parched. "I'm going to the kitchen to make sure the stove is all right … lord above knows we don't need THAT exploding next." She quickly moved the sugarbowl aside, plopped Brucie down on the table, and hurried off into the kitchen.

Roweena huffed, wondering when they were going to get around to her little problem.

Rhonda returned a few minutes later, bright-eyed and extra-smiley. She misfired snapping her fingers, rushed to the kitchen once again, wobbling back with a writing tablet. Mother and daughter talked of the many things they needed to buy while Rhonda made a list of all the paraphernalia she squirreled away from Roweena's babyhood. Most of these things would be quite useful, although Roweena wanted everything new and was irritable. They talked of names, boy names and girl names beginning with the letter *R*.

It was a lively and fruitful conversation.

As a matter of curiosity, Rhonda asked Roweena why she hadn't been taking that little antipregnantness pill of hers. Roweena self-righteously informed her mother that Rodney can be blamed for this particular kettle of fish, since he thought it was sooo knee-slappingly funny to switch her birth control pills with Rhonda's saccharin.

"I KNEW my morning coffee tasted strange," Rhonda burbled.

Ralph took his daughter's hand lovingly into his own. "Maybe it's just as well. I've heard that sometimes you can get very nasty special effects taking those pills."

"*Side* effects?" Rhonda asked.

"Uh … sometimes …"

Rhonda breathed a sigh of relief. She was worried that the hair growing on the bottoms of her feet was caused by menopause.

"It was rotten of Rodney to do this to me!" Roweena screamed, pounding the table with her cute little fist upsetting the salt shaker. She started crying.

Ralph shook his own fist in the air. "*Rodney*," he made the name sound like a cussword. "We should've sold *him* to Leon Bastardo. Instead, he's getting a nice, expensive funeral."

"Appearances, dear," Rhonda reminded him. "We have to. For the sake of our standing in the community. What would the neighbors think if we did otherwise?"

"Ahh, slew the neighbors," Ralph hissed.

"Oh, be quiet!" Rhonda whispered angrily. "Can't you see Roweena is upset enough without you making it worse?" Ralph petulantly crossed his arms against his chest, refusing to look at his wife. Rhonda, meanwhile, wrapped her arms around her little girl, cooing soothingly to her that every cloud has a silver lining.

"Look at Brucie! If that TV set didn't explode he'd still be in the living room, *dead* from that awful gas. But it did explode. And mommy was here to catch him." She placed a finger beside each corner of Roweena's scowling mouth, pushing up to form a very hostile smile. "Make sure *YOUR* umbrella is upside-down!"

Rhonda looked at the tiny dog on the table. Even Ralph bent forward for a good, close look. It would be really nice, he thought, to prove Rhonda wrong for once. Discover that the dog was dead anyway. *That* would shoot apart all this sappy happy-crappy stuff spurting out of her mouth.

As if on cue, Brucie opened his eyes. He sneezed into the pile of spilt salt, sending most of it stingingly up into the nicked and bleeding face of Ralph Rodoggio.

TWENTY

After Ralph quit making that pain-ridden screeching noise, a combination of yowl mixed with ooohs and awws, sort of like an Alpine Yodeler with his foot caught in a bear trap, Ralph crooned into his daughter's ear, "Tell us who the proud popper is."

"Oh, Ralph! What a silly question," Rhonda said with deep disgust. "What difference does it make? Maybe she doesn't even know who the father is. Did you stop to think about that?" Rhonda brought her attention back to the more important issue of organizing pages of notes into a shopping list.

"O' course it makes a difference. I want to know who he is."

Rhonda rolled her eyes ceilingward. "Well, whichever one of her creepy boy-friends it is, you can bet your boots Roweena will be saying *adieu* to him."

"ROWEENA WON'T BE SAYING 'I DO' TO ANYONE UNLESS I APPROVE!" Ralph screamed into his wife's face.

Roweena clucked her tongue. "It's Marty Martex."

"Oooo!" Rhonda gasped.

Ralph thought for a moment, taking time to savor those three little words hanging in the air like the scent of sweet clover.

It's Marty Martex.

He could contain himself no longer. He stood up straight and tall, raising his arms thankfully to God in Heaven, crying out Marty Martex's name in hosanna at the top of his lungs. Dishes rattled in the china cabinet.

"Well, well, well!" he exhaled, sitting down and leaning back on his chair. Because he had no suspenders to hook his thumbs into, Ralph Rodoggio folded his arms across his puffed chest. "A bine young fuck."

"A FINE YOUNG BUCK!" Rhonda bellowed.

"… whatever … and oh, sooo handsome. He'll make a my-tee-fine son-in law!"

Roweena blushed, her face glowing. "Well, you know, it isn't so much that Marty is handsome. It's that he's sensitive … caring. He knows how to make you feel like a *real* woman."

Rhonda blushed too, grinning warmly to herself.

A wave of goodwill and happiness washed over Ralph. He was thrilled to the bone at the thought of his wonderful daughter and the young man she picked out to be the father of his grandchild, the grandest grandchild that ever would be. *Absolutely* the greatest one. A *great* grandchild! Overjoyed, he felt like jumping up on the highly polished dining room table to dance like Gene Kelly would if Gene Kelly was in Ralph Rodoggio's tap shoes. The only thing stopping him was that they (a brand-spanking new pair) were in the poison-gas-filled living room right now, next to his easy chair.

"Yes indeed! Martex. A fine, fine young cad …"

"Lad, dear."

"… *lad* …" He gave Rhonda the look of daggers. "… and now," he continued as if he'd never been interrupted, "… he's gone and given our Roweena a little clap …"

Roweena swallowed hard.

"Your idiot father means chap," Rhonda corrected sweetly. She glared at Ralph. "You know, it might not be a boy."

Ralph looked for something to shake angrily in Rhonda's face. He picked Brucie up. "It'll be a boy, all right." Brucie uttered a small yelp. Ralph sheepishly put him back down on the table. "It butter be. Yesss, sirrrr! That Marty Martex will make a wonderful scum-in-law!"

"Yes, he certainly will," Rhonda added. She winked at Roweena. "His lucky wife will ride the coat-tails of his success to great glory."

"She sure will!"

"Oh, yes!"

"Yes, indeedy-doo …"

"Yes," Roweena concurred with just the proper amount of tartness, "Betty Bunz is a *very* lucky girl."

A hush fell over the dining room table. Ralph and Rhonda sat motionless, mouths agape, stunned. Roweena enlightened them with the news: everyone was saying that the Martex-Bunz pairing was a match made in heaven, and without doubt, Betty's life as Mrs. Marty Martex will be a charmed one. Noetha, Doctor Monklee's talky receptionist, told Roweena that the wedding ceremony tomorrow is slated to be the social event of the season.

"*Tooomor-r-row!*" Rhonda yelped in surprise. "Why tomorrow? Well, I guess if I was Betty I wouldn't let any grass grow under my feet either. I certainly hope they don't count on us being there," she said with deep disgust. "We've got *other* plans."

Roweena added that the local gossip was that even Mayor Horvath J. Pindoughie himself would attend.

"Just think," Rhonda bubbled enthusiastically, "the Mayor o' Gulpo Plains himself!"

"Well it is just a rumor." Roweena chided.

"Nonsense! If Mayor Pindoughie says he'll be someplace, there he'll be," Ralph pronounced. He tapped his chest with his index finger. "And I oughta know—I voted for him!"

"Some girls have all the luck," Rhonda mumbled.

The family fell into reflective silence.

A warm tear trickled from Rhonda's eye remembering how deliriously blissful she'd been at Roweena's birth. She snuggled into her seat, conjuring up memories of her little girl, running a mental slide-show of Roweena growing into the beautiful young thing she is today.

Ralph plucked at a needle of television screen glass still in his eyelid. It stung like craxxy, but neither the deeply embedded slivers, nor the flow of blood from the open cuts, nor the salt crusting each laceration could bother him now. He was a hap-hap-happy man. Ralph beamed, smiling wider and wider, like an ape in the process of discovering another use for its pecker.

Roweena sat forward, planting her elbows firmly on the table. She contemplated calling someone on the High School football team.

The knock on the front door ended all their reveries.

TWENTY-ONE

"I wonder who'd be knocking on our door this time o' night?" Rhonda asked expectantly, arising from her chair as if she was sitting on a joybuzzer. Hurrying hostess-like to the front door, fluffing her hair as she went, she thought that perhaps it was a hand delivered engraved invitation to the Bunz-Martex nuptials.

Rhonda was appalled to see just who it was who disturbed their peace, still she smiled nicely, saying in her most cordial and measured voice through the screen of the storm door, "I'm truly sorry, but we're not interested today. Thank *you!*" She shut the inside door quickly before another word could be uttered.

When she returned to the table, visibly cranky, Ralph inquired who was at the door.

"A stupid foreign kitchen knife salesman, that's who," she snapped back. "What galls me is the *fudgin'* tactics they use to get your attention. As if cutesy-wootesy gimmicks worked on me."

"What kind o' gimmicks, Rhonda?"

"This one was wrapped up like a Thanksgiving Day Turkey with a big butcher knife sticking out of his head."

Ralph clucked his tongue, highly incensed.

Breeze from the slamming door spun him around on slippery shroud heels. Leaning against the stoop's handrail for support, he cursed the difficulty of coma-induced delusional adventures.

It was one tough time getting home. Not as tough, mind you, as moving a goddamn rock from the goddamn flowerbed to the front of the goddamn stoop, and then trying to kick it at the goddamn front door with both goddamn feet tied together with goddamn strong ribbon, but *goddamn* tough nonetheless.

That crazy old Grummbacher bag smacked him at least a thousand times with her cane, and might have smacked him a thousand times more had she not had a stroke or seizure of some kind which made her fall into the Samuel A. Gulpo Memorial Swamp. He'd gotten his ass out of there *posthaste*, hopping away like a madman. Naturally, he kept going in one wrong direction after another, traveling all over town before finally finding a landmark guiding him to Gulpolina Drive. Arriving at the Rodoggio home, he crossed the lawn hopping around the dangerous dips. Somewhere in the middle of the lawn, as he veered away from a sink hole, his feet came down on the tines of the grass rake he left there only the day before yesterday. Fortunately, the rusty points did not dig too deeply into his feet and one small hop freed him, although unfortunately, coming back down to earth he caught the rake's edge and its handle sprang up into his face. He kicked the rake out of his way into the flower bed next to the stoop.

He assessed the situation. There were three steep steps to climb in order to get up the red brick stoop to the front door. A high hop got him up the first step, but he flubbed the second, missing and tumbling down to the concrete walk. Propping his elbows on the lowest step, he lifted himself back to his feet. The next attempt got him up the first and second steps, but the top hop killed him. Over the cast iron railing he went, right into his mother's jaggy, branchy rose bush. Dragging most of the plant with him, depositing it in a thorny heap across the walkway, he positioned himself for another attempt. This time he made it all the way. Twisting his feet to and fro, moving ever closer to the door, the pride of accomplishment sang in his ears.

It wasn't a very long song.

As his elbow touched the doorbell something repelled him and he fell backwards down the steps and onto the walk.

Obviously, the doorbell was defective and he would have to knock on the door.

He bent his knees, leaned forward, and thrust hard to get up the steps. His propulsion was mightier than he could have imagined. With that one push forward he was airborne, flying fast as a bullet not touching the stoop steps, zooming straight at the front door. Within micromillimeters of making contact with the storm door's screen panel, Rodney was tossed backward with a momentum greater than what he exerted, a momentum that would have tossed him clear across the street except for the catching his heels on a step and flipping him over the iron handrail into the thorny remains of the rosebush. Bouncing hard, Rodney landed smack-dab in the middle of the flower bed, right onto the rake which simultaneously dug into his back and smacked the rear of his head.

Struggling up, lurching forward, he tripped over a rock pile Ralph left there three summers ago, a little Better Homes & Garden flower bed border envisioned but never executed. Rodney, in a huff, shoved one of the rocks away with a flip-jump motion of his feet. He heard the stone thud down somewhere in the middle of the lawn, and the brilliant idea of using one of them to knock on the door was born. Easing a rock out of the pile, working it around into position, and with a deft movement of feet and hips, he shoved it. It was a gray-black blob against a dark blurry background in his sight, but he saw it hit the storm door with a perfect *clong* of dented aluminum. He cautiously hopped up the steps. The front door opened and hallway light spilled out over him. He stood stock still, caught, like a moth in candle wax. He was thrilled to see his mother.

"Mmmmieeeee," he said, approximating the word *mommy* with his clenched tongue. "Ids Blaahhdee ..." *("It's Rodney ... ")*.

Rhonda chirped out her message to him, slammed shut the door, and Rodney was left with the task of finding another rock.

The second one, like the first, went straight for the door. And like the first, put another big dent in the aluminum panel. Within seconds, the inside door flew open and Rodney's father stood there, a wavy dark mass through the milky plastic in Rodney's vision.

"Hulloo," Ralph said, pleasantly enough. "As my wife told you, we're not interested. Thank you for calling."

The door was open, Rodney seized the opportunity.

"Addee, ipps mee!" *("Daddy, it's me!")*. He cried, hopping up and down.

Ralph shut the door hard.

Rodney kicked another rock.

This time Ralph appeared holding what looked like a white club with black speckles all over it. The rolled newspaper.

"Goo'bye, Mr. Salesman," Ralph waved the paper menacingly. "I'm sure they need plenty o' knives next door."

"ADDEE, OON'T UDDD DEE OAAR!!" *("Daddy, don't shut the door!!")*.

"Ooggie-boogie walla-walla!" *("Learn to speak English!")* Ralph said, clucking his tongue loudly. He lowered the rolled newspaper to the inside doorknob and used it to push the door closed.

Rodney kicked one of the rocks on the stoop back against the storm door, bringing Ralph screamingly back.

"YOU WERE TOLD TO GET LOST, YOU PERKY FOREIGNER? NOW YOU'LL SEE WHAT IT MEANS TO DEAL WITH RALPH RODOGGIO!" He opened the screen door to step outside.

"Ralph! Don't you DARE go out there! Not in that damp night air!"

"Well what the heck d'ya want me to do? Let this guy bother us all night until we buy a *knife*? If I don't put a stop to it now, he'll be back with all his fiddler friends."

"Obbleer," *("Peddler,")* Rodney corrected.

"Peddler," said Rhonda, annoyed. "I don't want you sneezing and snorting all night long. You stay inside."

Ralph turned back to Rodney. Even in the dim light his cut and bleeding face looked delicious.

Delicious??!

Rodney moved forward. Something held him frozen in place.

"My wife says I can't come out to take care o' you," He thumped the newspaper club against his palm, "so you'll have to come in."

Rodney was suddenly pitched through the open door smack into Ralph, who began a Custer-style massacre all over him with the newspaper club. Swamp goop flew off his shroud in all directions.

"Look what you're doing to my walls!" Rhonda yelled. Ralph stopped for a moment, saw the mess, and discontinued whacking the salesman. Instead he jabbed him in the stomach.

"Ah! You like *that*, don't you, Mr. Ooggie-Boogie?"

These blows were not such a bad thing for Rodney: the shroud, weakened in many places from the Grummbacher caning, soon tore away. The jaw ribbon broke under one of Ralph's thwacks, and now there wasn't much left on Rodney except for the binding strips around his ankles and wrists along with a small bit of shroud pinned to his forehead by the butcher knife.

"Omystars! an EXHIBITIONIST!" screeched Rhonda, closing her eyes and directing her daughter to do the same. Ralph halted, looking at the foreign knife salesman and saw the visage of his late son. His mouth drooped open, drool poured over its corners; his eyes crossed and glazed over. Gently, Ralph sat himself down on the floor then lay back, curling into a fetal position, hugging his newspaper like a Teddy Bear.

Rhonda, eyes tightly shut, heard the awful silence. She groped her way forward. Tripping over Ralph and thinking it was the dead policeman's corpse, she gave the body a violent kick out of the way. Ralph uttered a loonlike chuckle.

Gingerly moving this way and that, afraid of barking her shins on furniture, she finally found someone. Rhonda struck out with her fists, beating furiously.

"Mommy you're hitting ME!" Roweena squealed. "In *my* condition!"

Rhonda peeked to be sure it was Roweena. "Sorry, dear," she murmured, closing her eyes once more and continuing on, blindly searching for the pervert invading their home.

"Mommy you're hitting ME! In my condition!" Rodney said, imitating Roweena's nasty trill as Rhonda's bony fists found him. Rhonda peeked out once again. Seeing that it was only Rodney, who was chewing at the black ribbon binding his wrists with his pointy teeth, and not some Euro-peon knife salesman, she opened both her eyes.

Roweena whistled derisively. "Hey! Dig those sharp teeth!"

"I'll dig them into you," Rodney growled. He was cut off mid-sentence by a sharp punch to the stomach.

"Don't you DARE talk to your pregnant sister that way. And take that silly knife out of your head."

"Yes, you look like a can o' corn," Ralph said giddily, sitting up suddenly. Rhonda looked questioningly at Roweena, then they both looked at Rodney.

"Unicorn," Rodney offered, but Ralph did not confirm or deny it because he lay back down on the floor and was off to loonland once again.

Rodney kicked off the ankle ribbon, then grasped the handle of the knife. He gave it a hard tug. It didn't budge. With one mighty pull it slipped out quickly and smoothly. There was a strange sound coming from the open wound in Rodney's head, a sort of gurgling hiss, a fizzy sound much like the effervesce of Auntie Clarissa's favorite dinner beverage, Alka-Seltzer in Gulpa-Cola. The noise subsided and there followed a spray of green mist. Rhonda, immediately disgusted by this, reached over for the tissues.

"Now you look like Moby Dick," Roweena laughed. Even Rhonda chuckled, handing him the box of EverRipe Snotties. Rodney dropped the knife like a hot poker. It just missed Ralph's foot, planting itself deeply in the hardwood floor instead. He pressed his hands tightly over the geyser, trying to stop it, but it kept on streaming away through his fingers. Finally he gave up, just letting one tissue after another saturate and fall to the floor. The flow slowed eventually, ending with a bubble of thick green sludge bursting against his forehead, drying instantly and patching the wound with a layer of fresh green colored skin. This patch gradually lightened to match his ashen gray complexion.

Leaping over the dead cop, Rodney rushed up the stairs to his room. He was horrified and dismayed to see that it was stripped clean, totally barren. Even his bed was gone. It was sucked clean, like a collection plate in the hands of a minister.

"Where are all my things?" he bellowed down the stairs.

"We gave them to the Salvation Army," Rhonda called back.

"THE SALVATION ARMY??? YOU GAVE AWAY MY THINGS??!! JUMPIN' JEEZUS GOD A'PLENTY!! WHY THE HELL DID YOU DO THAT FOR?! DIDN'T YOU THINK I WAS GOING TO NEED MY CLOTHES??"

"Well, how am I *supposed* to know you weren't going to stay dead?" She screamed back at him, then clucked her tongue loudly enough for him to hear all the way up the stairs, down the hall, and into his room. "We didn't WANT all that *clutter* in our house, you know!"

"I'm DEAD?" It wasn't a dream or coma-induced delusions, all this was happening? "I'm real-l-ly-y *dead*," he wailed. He cried and carried on for a while, then looked back at his room woefully

"I hope those shitlicking poor people enjoy my things," Rodney yelled, his voice echoing in the empty room like Lou Gherig's at Yankee Stadium. "I guess it's just my fate to walk the earth with my pecker swinging in the breeze." He slammed the door behind him.

Inspiration hit him like a rolled newspaper on the side of the head.

Fate!

The costume from his Senior Class play, *Little Lucy's Fate*—costing him $32.50 at that ripoff Gluupick's House O' Treats—was downstairs in the basement safe and sound, surreptitiously stored in a box containing all his Betty Bunz memorabilia. It was *the* perfect afterlife wear.

Little Lucy's Fate, as reviewed by Rodney W. Rodoggio, most likely the crummiest high school Senior Class play given anywhere, anytime, in the whole history of crummy high school Senior Class plays, was about Otis Cannerby, a tight old bastard, who had the hornyhots for the beautiful young and innocent Little Lucy. Because Otis holds the mortgage to Little Lucy's mother's house, and because Little Lucy's haggy failure of a mother, who has a hundred children to feed and no visible source of income, can't meet her mortgage payment, Otis threatens to dump the whole miserable family out onto the street—unless Little Lucy agrees to marry him. In exchange for this guarantee of a lifetime of blowjobs, Otis will hand over the house deed to Little Lucy's mother. Little Lucy's shitheaded boyfriend Beauregard shows up at the last minute, bringing with him the family's long-lost deadbeat dad. He saves the day for Little Lucy, the crappy mother, and all the dopey children, giving the audience one big dildo of a smiley-puss happy-crappy ending. Real corny junk, worse even than the stuff on television.

Rodney played the part of the evil Otis. His role called for an old timey black dress-suit costume, and one of those long opera capes and a top hat. The closest thing Gluupick had in stock was the DeeLuxe Dracula Hall-O-ween costume, which was constructed of cheap, itchy felt. It was a one piece slip-on thing that buttoned up the back and didn't come with a top hat, so Rodney make one for himself out of rolled cardboard and scotch tape. The bastardy hat, naturally, kept unrolling and falling apart throughout the show's run, which was supposed to be for four performances, but only lasted three because something happened during the third performance. Something so shocking and horrible that everyone in the audience and backstage (and probably everyone in Gulpo Plains that read about it in the *Plainsman* the next day) was sent into an apoplectic fit. It caused the early cancellation of the show and gave Rodney many a sleepless night thereafter.

The countdown to disaster began when the drama coach, Miss Luffty, instructed her Little Lucy (portrayed by Betty Bunz) specifically *not* to wear a brassiere under her costume blouse, the costume blouse which Miss Luffty personally ordered from Gluupick's two sizes smaller than Betty's considerable figure required. Without the uplift support, the tightness of the blouse was supposed to bind her, flatten those bombshells to give Betty the illusion of a young maiden. Miss Luffty called this a bit of *stage magic*.

She underestimated the Houdiniesque nature of Betty's boobs, for at the climatic point in that historic third performance, when it appears that Little Lucy is doomed to life with Otis' pecker in her mouth, Betty had to deliver her "Do with me as you will," speech. She played it just as directed, just as she played it successfully for two performances and countless rehearsals prior. She threw back her head in despair, uttering her line oozing with virtue. This was Rodney's cue to lift his cape, swooping in for the symbolic taking of Little Lucy. The audience sees her angelic face above Otis' encroaching cape. She flings her upstage arm across her noble brow, a gesture of submission.

What Rodney saw behind that cape was the real stage magic: as her arm lifted, all the over-stressed buttons on that too tight blouse popped. Mounds of flesh escaped, tumbling out in what seemed like a neverending cascade. Rodney gulped, as did everyone watching from the wings.

In the script by school janitor Hank Pederasty, Otis was to kiss Little Lucy's lips—but Rodney's mouth headed south. He was stopped by two fingers poked powerfully into his Adam's apple. Quickly adjusting his aim, reaching up for a handful of pleasure, he was thwarted by Marty "Beauregard" Martex arriving on stage severely off cue. Holding Little Lucy close against his chest with her back to the audience, he banished the villain off stage and covered her embarrassment in one fell swoop. Rodney was left with empty hands and a twitching eye. Worse, from the wings, he could see Martex's slimy fat hand rubbing all over Betty's chest, pretending to the audience that he was comforting her.

The play ended.

The curtain fell.

And nobody would have been any the wiser

IF …

Rodney had not rushed back out onto the stage, wrenching Marty away forcibly enough to make the poor lad tumble to his ass. Grabbing at Betty's delightful dumplings himself, the curtain lifted, pulled up by the confused curtain puller for curtain calls for which nobody was ready.

There were gasps, cries of outrage, and even several shrieks from the unsuspecting audience at what appeared to be the wanton defilement of the star performer by a senior class high school boy who was, indeed, a real-life villain! In an effort to duck all the playbills and other things flying at him from all directions, Rodney's cape brushed Betty Bunz's breasts, the closest thing Rodney ever had that *actually* touched her lovelumps. The entire cast was on stage by now, kicking, smacking, and generally walloping the daylights out of him. Although he was plenty bruised and sore, miraculously the costume was completely unharmed, a treasure for all time.

The Betty Bunz box was nowhere to be found. "Where's that *Personal! Do NOT Open!!* box??" he called up to his mother.

"You mean the box with all those lewd pictures and obscene letters inside? Or do you mean the box with your Foo-Dog hand puppets?"

"I'm looking for my *Little Lucy's Fate* costume!"

"That old rag?" Rhonda yelled down the stairs. "I'm using it to line the bottom o' Brucie's bed!"

Rodney bounded back up the steps. Brucie's little wicker sleeping basket was next to the pantry in the kitchen. Five years ago, when Roweena first showed it to the hybrid dog, Brucie growled, refusing to go anywhere near it. For all this time he avoided the bed as if it were an overgrown Venus Flytrap for dogs. Now the mean and spiteful hellspawn was fast asleep in it, a corner of the costume cape just visible under his little body. Rhonda called Roweena into the kitchen.

"Ooo! How cute!" Roweena gushed.

Rodney gave the corner of the cape a swift yank. Most of the costume came free, but part of it was stuck on something: Brucie's clenched teeth. Rodney tugged harder, the costume snaked upward. With a low meaningful snarl, Brucie tugged back.

Roweena clapped her hands. "Look, mommy! He wants to play!"

"Sic 'em, boy!" Rhonda cheered.

Rodney raised his hand to smack the dog and Brucie's shifty little reptile eyes followed his hand upward. Rodney, fascinated, let down his guard for a moment. There was a sudden jerk and what little cape fabric he clutched zipped out of his grasp. In front of Rodney's startled eyes, Brucie scratched, bit, chewed, and tore the villain costume to shreds, much to the delight of his chuckleheaded sister and mother.

"Isn't that just too, too adorable?" Rhonda prattled delightedly.

Rodney flung open the refrigerator door and tossed Brucie in among the leftovers. As the two clucking hens ran to the rescue, Rodney surveyed the damage. There wasn't enough costume left in one piece to cover an earlobe.

Ralph wobbled into the kitchen, massaging his temples. "Can I have an icepick for my head?" he moaned.

"Now what am I supposed to do?" Rodney complained bitterly. "I haven't got one bit o' clothes to wear! How can I go through eternity like this?"

"What are you in such a *snit* about?" Rhonda asked testily. "There's a perfectly good suit in your coffin, so don't go around screaming you have nothing to wear."

"My coffin," he croaked. Rodney never once considered the idea that now he might have to get into a coffin and really be dead. "I'm dead!" he wailed again. "How will I ever get laid now?"

"Keep that voice down!" Rhonda screamed. "Can't you see your father isn't feeling well? If you're *sooo* worried about clothes, I suggest you go get your suit." She wrapped some ice in a towel for Ralph.

"Where is my … eehhh*hhh* … coffin?" Rodney whined.

Rhonda clicked her tongue smartly off the roof of her mouth. "At the church, o' course. Where do you think it would be? In the living room?"

"At the church!!? That's just GREAT! How am I going to get to the goddam church to get something to wear if I have nothing to put on now?"

"Watch that mouth o' yours," Ralph told him weakly. "Go borrow something of Roweena's. She'll be happy to lend you her old clothes, especially since she'll soon be too big to fit into them."

"That's a very good idea," Rhonda said.

"Oh, mommy! Can't he take something o' yours? I don't want my clothes ruined."

Rodney inquired just why it was that he couldn't borrow something from Ralph.

"BECAUSE I'M SICK O' PAYING FOR YOUR MISTAKES, SONNY BOY!" Ralph accented this logic with a swinging towel full of hard, cold ice cubes, smacking Rodney soundly on the back of his head. "Besides, all of Ro's clothes are going to be thrown away." He looked tenderly at Roweena's shocked face. "Because her daddy-waddy is gonna buy her all newy-wewy things! I'm even gonna get her a paternity suit."

"Maternity."

"Aw, what's the dif?" Ralph sneered.

"So," Rodney sniffed. "That's the way it is, huh? An undead creature attacks and kills me so that now I can't even have peace in death, and to top it off I have to go parading around through eternity stark naked, while *she* gets a ton of new clothes as a reward for getting knocked up."

Rhonda rolled her eyes heavenward, shaking her tightly clenched fists. "What are you babbling about? Undead creatures! It's that mindrot junk you watch on tel'o'vison. Stop your bellyaching … Roweena will give you something to wear, then go and get your precious blue suit at the church. It figures. My son is the only one in town who just can't be dead without a lot o' problems."

"I will *not* start my afterlife dressed like a girl!"

TWENTY-TWO

It wasn't a long walk to the church. Not a long walk at all.

You take a little saunter down Gulpolina Drive to Lochomocha Lane, then a few brisk paces up Lochomocha Lane to Main Street. Now just a few lively steps on Main Street and, *voilà!* there you are at the Church of Our Lady Of Perpetual Misery, ready to give your soul to Christ and your money to a priest. But Rodney, dressed less-than-trendy in a yellow vinyl blouse with brown-pinstripes, a hot neon pink mini-skirt, and an old pair of powder blue, overly-tight, high-heeled go-go boots, opted to take the long way around. Why? Because Main Street, where the church nestles among sleazy storefronts and bars, is brightly lit at night, as are most major streets in Gulpo Plains, including Lochomocha Lane, in contrast to the residential streets with their burnt-out lampposts; according to local statistics, bright stadium lighting discourages potential muggers and rapists, who, also according to local statistics, frequent only major streets. Ralph, on the other hand, swore that the tremendous power usage was in reality a ploy to drive taxes up and put more money into the deep pockets of crooked politicians out to destroy America.

Darting in and out of house shadows, behind bushes and trees, Rodney zig-zagged his way to Sumac Avenue, a street intercepting Main Street about eight blocks away from the church. While he successfully avoided the bright lights of Lochomocha, he actually ended up further away from the church. Not only did he have a much longer walk now in the glaring artificial daylight of Main Street, but he was also in a dangerous area, a part of town filled with all sorts of vermin and low life.

Rodney pressed close to the store fronts, rapidly making his way forward. He hadn't gone very far, almost to The Barrels O' Fun Bar & Grill, a real rough hangout, when he heard the disquieting sound of footsteps behind him. Rodney nervously stopped and looked.

Right there, not three inches away, was a horribly familiar face, a face with big, wet, puckered smootchie lips. The wormlike eyebrow arcing down over beady eyes rippled up and down suggestively beneath a sailor's cap drunkenly cocked to the left side of his head.

"Hul-l-loooo, Baby!" the sailor cooed, then hiccuped. Obviously the asshole was looking for a quick pickup. *Eau d'Rhonda* lasted in the air several seconds while Rodney feverishly tried to figure the best way out of this sticky situation.

"Buzz off, creep," he said, imitating Iris Callump in the seventh grade when, standing behind her on the cafeteria line, he asked if she might care to have lunch with him.

"Aww, don't be like that, honey," the sailor said in a smoozy voice, reaching out for Rodney's flat chest. "I've been out to sea for sooo lo-oo-ng ." He rubbed his barnacled hand all over Roweena's blouse front, squeezing and fondling the vinyl. Rodney moved away, but the creep followed in lecherous synchronization, jumping out in front of him to block his path. Rodney had a terrific view of The Barrels O' Fun front door over the drunk's shoulder, and couldn't miss seeing the peachy picture of guys from the Gulpo Plains Construction Company night crew heading right toward it.

This could be *very* bad. Rodney was not dressed to greet these burly bastions of the community, for next to all non-whites and non-Americans and non-Christians, the civic-minded construction crew workers hated non-hetrosexual males the most.

Colorful round plastic blouse buttons were pried open under the sailor's thick fingers, but Rodney was too busy counting construction workers to notice. There were sixteen of the gorilla-like psychos, each one looking meaner than the other, although it was difficult to tell them apart: they were almost identical from their bald bulletheads and unshaven mugs to their thick muscley arms and tremendous beer-bellies. Each man was carrying a big black metal lunch basket.

"HEY," the astute Naval man exclaimed in surprise and anger. "YOU AREN'T A GIRL! WHY THE FLAMIN' FUCK ARE YOU DRESSED UP LIKE A BROAD IF YOU AIN'T ONE?"

"Be quiet," Rodney whispered, his eyes glued to the construction crew milling around in front of the bar.

"YOU'RE NOT A GIRL, GODDAMIT!"

"Very bright, asshole." Rodney hissed. "Now shut up!"

A light bulb seemed to switch on in the empty rooms of the sailor's head. "That voice … I KNOW you!"

Rodney sighed. He was afraid of this. "Who, *me?*" he said in a deep voice.

The sailor clapped his hands. "Rod Rodoggio!"

Rodney moved back, trying to duck into the recess of a darkened doorway. The sailor pulled him forward. "You don't have to be embarrassed," he sousingly slurred. "Take it from your old pal—you do remember me, don't you? I used to go out with your sister." Benny Fossert licked his lips. "By the way, how is Roweena?"

"Pregnant."

"Oooo. That's too bad."

"Yes it is, isn't it," Rodney said, distracted, watching the movements of the men outside The Barrels O' Fun. They were yakking it up, laughing and punching each other like a pack of jackaloons high on dope. They paid no attention at all to him and the sailor. *Thank God.*

Benny Fossert yanked Rodney into the glaring light of a Main Street spotlight. "I meant it was too bad she's not open for business," he grumbled. "Casara-sara, funicculli-funicculla. That's what I always say. Let's go have a drinkie-poo. Dutch, o' course." Placing an arm of camaraderie around Rodney's shoulder, Benny pushed him toward the bar. Resistance would be futile, as well as attention-getting, so Rodney shuffled along trying to keep a low profile.

"You know, Rodo," he continued, "I've been all over this mothereatin' world, and I've seen a lot o' perverted stuff in my time. Guys who've had their banana split so they could be girls, girls with three tits, and a whole bunch of he-shes who have a lot of extra stuff on 'em—man, are they repulsive!—so you don't have to be ashamed around me just because you like to dress up in girl's clothes and look for guys. Hey, this is the modern age! Anything goes. Right? People around here are way too uptight anyway, they need to loosen up and understand where someone like you is coming from. It's a matter o' …."

Benny stopped talking abruptly. He stared straight ahead, walking mechanically in a zombielike trance.

What a break! Benny Fossert was a moron, and now that he was also very drunk his brain stopped sending stupid messages to his big troublemaking mouth. As they got nearer to the forest of sequoia-like men, Rodney cuddled in closer, hoping that the muscle and mush brained jerks would see them as nothing more than a boyfriend and girlfriend out for a stroll.

It seemed to be working. The construction workers caught sight of them and made jovial obscene remarks. They whistled, pinching Rodney's ass as he and Benny walked right past the bar. It was going very smoothly with just one more man to get by, but this last bullethead was one mean-looking hombre. He stood somewhat apart from his chums, observing the scene with all the aplomb of a New York Times Drama Critic. As the young couple passed, he shifted his intense gaze to Rodney, staring with ice-cold eyes, looking Rodney up and down. Suddenly his meaty paw was under the miniskirt, kneading Rodney's buttocks affectionately. His fingertips felt like sandpaper.

"Nice," the man cooed in that raspy, asbestos-damaged construction worker voice they all had.

Rodney swallowed hard and kept moving.

"TOO DAMN CLOSED-MINDED," Benny Fossert shouted loudly, not ten feet past the milling men. "LIKE THOSE CHOWDERHEAD CON-STRUCTION GUYS!" He stopped dead, crossed his arms against his chest and clucked his tongue thickly. Rodney tried pulling him forward, but it was as if Benny's feet were planted in the uneven concrete sidewalk.

"If *they* weren't so upfuckingtight, *you* wouldn't have to try fooling normal guys like *me*! There'd be plenty o' other pervos around here for you to have fun with!"

Rodney looked back over his shoulder.

Yup.

That last guy, the beefed-up Mr. Clean with the extra sweaty bald head and big ironlike muscles was looking at them.

"What did you say, sailorboy?" he called over harshly.

Benny stared ahead, concentrating. Whatever gears shifted in that whacked-up head of his, he was now in low drive. He didn't even seem to know where he was. "Uh … that those construction guys are chowderheads?" He asked.

"No. After that. A little something about this girl o' yours being a PERVO."

That snapped Benny out of his stupor and back into high gear. It was like he was seeing the construction workers for the first time. "Hey! Hi'ya, fellas!" he smiled largely. It was easy to see he was well-lubricated.

The men grunted and impatiently stepped up to the door of The Barrels O' Fun Bar & Grill. Even Mr. Clean followed, abandoning the sailor and his cute little girlfriend.

"HEY …" Fossert called. The men stopped, not at all happy with the delay.

"What is it, Mack?" someone from within the group rasped with the clear indication that this better be good.

Rodney guessed that now would be a great time to think about leaving, but Fossert had a tight handclamp on his shoulder. A sharp turn broke loose Benny's tenuous hold and Rodney veered away, right into a weasely little guy smoking a big smelly cigar. His pencil-thin lips curled into a smile around the cigar, his fingertips stroked up and down it's length as he winked at Rodney.

"Pssst, honey ... ya wanna make some BIG buckeroos? Come with me, I got a job for ya in the city that'd be jus-s-st up yer alley."

Benny meantime waved the sixteen guys over. They encircled Benny and Rodney, fisted hands on hips, elbows pointed out touching one another's: a sinewy fence no one could break through.

"We usually like to punch people *after* a couple o' drinks. It makes us more sociable," someone said. "I don't like to fight before I've had my drinks. I get too damn angry." A buzz of agreement went around the circle.

"Wait, fellas! This is AMERICA, right?" Fossert asked.

There were enthusiastic handclaps, whistles and cheers. The little weasely guy whistled through his fingers, making a shrill birdlike noise. Benny continued. "Don't you believe that everyone in America is entitled to freedom and the pursuit o' good times?"

There was some chatter in the group. This was an interesting issue. "Sure.... So long as they ain't a wetback or something."

"And this you believe? Speaking as good American citizens?"

Mr. Clean stepped forward. He smiled warmly and said, "O' course. Anyone normal and American is okay with us." The smile fell from his face abruptly. He dropped his black metal lunch bucket to the sidewalk. It sounded heavy, echoing up and down Main Street, clanging like it was filled with bowling balls. Staring directly at the smug little sailor, he rubbed the knuckles on his big hamlike fist with the palm of his other hand.

When his fist was primed, he reached out and grabbed Fossert by the throat lifting him several inches off the ground. Putting his cinderblock fist into the ashen little face, Mr. Clean asked if Benny was one of those fairies.

Sweat dribbled off Benny's forehead and collected in his wormlike eyebrow. "Hell no," he greeped, "I'm a SAILOR in the U.S. NAVY."

Benny thudded back to earth.

Nervously, Rodney backed away. He was halted by a gigantic hand cupping his behind. He looked around. A homely kissy mouth came at him. Rodney averted his face, but too late. A big juicy one caught him smack on the cheek.

"Hey, Mack," the Romeo behind Rodney asked Benny, "is this your girly? Is she up for grabs?"

All eyes turned toward Rodney.

"She's cute," someone rasped. "Woo-woo," said another. This was followed by many sentiments of approval, comments such as: "Come over here, babycakes.", "Look at them titties! Mmm-mmm!", "How 'bout a smootch, dollface?", and the ever-popular tongue flag accompanied by a juicy slurpy noise.

"This is not my *girl*," Benny announced.

The sound of zippers floated on the breeze, but Benny's upraised hand halted any further advance toward Rodney.

"In fact, there is something else *she* isn't …"

"Oh?" Rasped Mr. Clean. "What might that be? Pure*?*"

The boys smirked.

"… *she* is not ashamed to be seen in *her* clothes. Should he be?"

"No," They all said brusquely, one guy adding that she'd look a damn sight better without 'em. Enthused assent ensued with calls of "take 'em off baby", and "strip, strip, strip".

"But how do you like his clothes?"

Millions of big fingers shot out to feel Rodney's clothes along with other parts of him. The men agreed that this was the sweetest broad they'd ever seen.

"I am truly happy to hear you say that."

"Yeah, but what's the point?"

"Well, only that you accept HIM for doing HIS own thing."

The Gulpo Plains Construction workers stopped petting Rodney. They looked down on the ersatz girl, scowling deeply.

Echoing across Main Street, like thunder, came the sound of a multitude of lunch boxes clanging to the ground. If this wasn't nearly enough to make Rodney's head explode from fright, the sight of many hamlike fists being rubbed with palms of hands was.

"Forget about that job, sister. I don't need no limpwrists," a voice whispered in his ear.

"Yes, sir!" continued Benny Fossert. "This is ROD RODOGGIO, a male citizen, from over on Gulpolina Drive! Rod is asking for our understanding."

Nobody listened to what Benny was saying, and even Benny himself lost interest when he spotted Sheila Golasher walking across the street. He happily ran over to join her, and while Rodney was having a deep, penetrating encounter with the men from the Construction Company, Benny was escorting this real live girl to her nifty little flat over on Strumpet Lane.

TWENTY-THREE

Rodney felt it.

Not quite enough of a sensation to qualify as pain, but enough discomfort to make walking a real big nuisance. He hobbled along, splay-legged and hurriedly, down Main Street toward the Church of Our Lady of Perpetual Misery as the hooting laughs, crude comments, and catcalls from The Barrels O' Fun Bar & Grill faded into the distance. Feeling confident now that the men were finished beating the shit out of him and that he was safely away, he reached up under his torn and soiled miniskirt to extract the remnant of a big, smelly cigar from his butt. That was better. He could walk normally now.

Soon he was in front of the venerable stone church, the oldest structure in Gulpo Plains, standing at the bottom of wide concrete steps looking up at the massive black birch doors. These heavy doors were set deeply and securely in the stable stone, giving everyone an impression of enduring strength and reliability in worship.

When he was a kid, Rodney was talked into a little mischief by his then-pal Oogie Cabalette. Rodney spray-painted *Jesus Saves* on the left hand door while Oogie wrote GREEN STAMPS on the right. Unfortunately, Oogie spelled green as grene, the same way he spelled it on the Sunday School Quiz just the previous week when answering a question about church offerings. He was captured and questioned by Father Yorrick. Poor Oogie warbled like Maria Callas with her hand caught in a meat grinder, blaming Rodney for the whole sordid affair. Rodney was never quite welcome in the church again.

Up the wide concrete steps he went, down the steps he tumbled. The same damn thing that greeted him at home was now here at the church.

"Ah, Rodney Rodoggio. Come in, my son." A voice soft, compelling, comforting, invited.

Rodney instinctively checked for a collection envelope in his pockets, or rather where his pockets should be if he was wearing pants. He gingerly climbed the stone steps, entering the church with no problem. Looking first to his left then to the right, he was surprised to find the narthex empty. Who invited him in? Relieved, but cautious, he approached the double doors opening into the nave. Stepping through and closing them quietly, he scanned the room for his coffin. It was remarkably dark, lit only by the light from two thick candles placed at either end of the altar. He saw a thick congestion of elaborate floral arrangements in the chancel, surrounding what looked like a rickety wooden packing crate. That *thing* was his coffin? In spite of the casket, Rodney got a lump in his throat, touched that so many people would send him such beautiful tributes.

He passed the font and pews without even looking at them. At his coffin, he noticed that it appeared to have been put together either by someone with limited mental power, or by someone working quickly and with little care for the outcome. Or by three hundred monkeys locked in a room with hammers and a stack of wood.

Maybe it was by all the above.

Rodney could have done a better job making it himself in Mr. Kahduggle's Woodworking Shop, a class he'd failed more miserably than any other High School class because he never got the hang of following project plans. The sides of the coffin buckled out, the lid was longer than the box, and there were gaps where pieces were joined together incorrectly.

Altogether, it was a mess.

The most baffling feature was the litter on top, little round things and square pieces of cardboard. He picked some of it up.

"Bingo cards," he groaned. *They're using MY coffin as a goddam Bingo table.* He removed the cards and plastic chips with a backhand swipe, revealing a carefully executed logo plus some sloppy words branded onto the coffin's lid with what looked like the use of a child's wood-burning set.

GULPO PLAINS WOODWORKS CO.
—J. MILFUNCH, PROP.—
"Lumbering Along With Progress Since 1953"
HERE RESTS

RONALD RAGGIEO
b. 6-8-73 d. 1-12-73

Dignity in death, he thought bitterly. Someone behind him gave out the wolf-whistle. He spun around quickly.

"Hey, cutie-pie!" said the vampire, sitting in a front pew with his feet up on the armrest looking very comfortable and at home.

Rodney backed away. "*You?*" He thought vampires couldn't come into churches.

"How did you get in here?"

"Same way you did, sonny. I was invited. One of the padres asked me if I wanted to win some easy cash."

"Sooo, did you?" Rodney smirked.

"Are you *kidding?*" He got up and came over to the coffin. "I'm never that lucky. Neither are you, I see. Neat little box your loved ones got for you, eh?"

Rodney had no intention of being molested yet again tonight. He put himself on the opposite end of the crate. "They have those Bingo games rigged, you know," he said to distract the creature.

"I KNEW IT!" the vampire screamed, slapping his hand down in a fit of anger. The box creaked and threatened to collapse in on itself. "Anyway, I knew you'd be here eventually and would need an invitation to get in, so I was just killing time," he mumbled. Rodney's jaw dropped.

"Haven't you done me enough favors?" He opened the box. Wood creaked, hinges squealed. The weight of the overly large lid unbalanced the box, tipping it over. Rodney went to close it, but the heavy lid slipped out of his grip falling back. This promptly snapped the rusty metal hasp. The lid rebounded off the crate and crashed to the floor, nicely chipping an altar rail in the process.

"Shit!" Rodney hissed, more worried about having to pay for the damaged rail than about the condition of his coffin. It would be the best thing just to get his clothes and get out of the church as quickly as possible.

The dark inside the box was extremely thick and apparently all that was in there. The vampire wandered over to the altar and was playing with a candle as Rodney continued feeling around inside the box, finally asking the vampire to bring the light over so he could get a better look inside. Moving slowly toward Rodney, waggling the candle under his chin to let the flickering shadows play across his pallid face, the creature made goofy expressions with his mouth.

Rodney clucked his tongue. "Would you please stop that crap?" He snatched the candle away and dipped the flame down into the box. Moving his hand across the cheap fabric liner on the bottom and sides, he peered deeply into the corners and saw that it was as empty as he had feared. The vampire absently asked what he was looking for and Rodney told him, adding the salient line, "Do you think I dress like *this* all the time?"

"Hey! What's wrong with it? It's kind o' sexy, if you ask me."

Rodney put a little more distance between himself and the grinning ghoul.

Off in a corner, folded down into a crack between slats of wood, he found the sleeve of his suit jacket and pulled excitedly at it, but it was stuck in place. Then he spotted the nails. The Gulpo Plains Woodworks Company used his good blue suit for the coffin lining. It was nailed into the wood in about five million places.

"Hmm," the vampire said. "That is a problem." He chuckled under his breath.

Shifting the candlelight all around, Rodney found that his clothes were all here although there was no trace of shoes or socks. Shirt, pants, tie, and jacket, everything seemed to be in one piece; those lumbering scumbrain bastards didn't even take the time to cut the lining for a proper fit. Thanks be to God for American labor.

He tugged at the cloth, trying to get his suit free.

The vampire waved his arms frantically. "Wait! Stop! You'll rip it all to shit!" Bending down into the box and using his pointy teeth, the undead thing pried out the nails one by one. With each shrieking creak of each nail pulled, a chill traveled up Rodney's spine. Eventually his own pointy teeth began to ache.

Standing upright, the vampire arced his head. He began spewing out the nails into the air and watched them shower down all over the chancel. He laughed hysterically. Rodney was appalled by the vampire's disrespectful conduct in church, and ended up pulling out his suit more roughly than he should have. With little to hold the crate together now the sides collapsed inward. The coffin became a heap of unfinished rough wood, a very sorry sight indeed amongst all the pretty flowers.

The vampire shrugged. "I had good intentions, Brother."

"The road to Hell is paved with good intentions, asshole." Rodney shot back, highly irritated, kicking at the pile of junk.

The vampire bellowed a laugh, gusting out the redolence of decomposition and sour blood full into Rodney's face. Rodney clutched his nose shut with both hands. When the vampire's merriment subsided he took it upon himself to inform Rodney that come dawn he would need that coffin, so it was probably best not to scatter it to the wind. Rodney sarcastically inquired what he expected him to do about it and the vampire kindly offered to help reassemble it.

"You gather up the nails, I'll be right back."

What a pain, Rodney ruminated, trying to find all the scattered nails. He counted his miserable blessings: a crappy coffin, a suit filled with more holes than the President's alibi, no shoes or socks … and don't forget that now he was taking orders from a grim Mr. Fixit, an undead *Boss*. It was the very last thing he needed in his afterlife, a vampire up his ass in more ways than one. The creature returned with a tremendous brass cross. Rodney recognized it as being the one that was affixed to the inside wall above the nave door. The vampire carried it slung over his shoulder like a rifle. Rodney was aghast.

"What are you doing with that cross for cryin' out Christ!?"

"It's to bang nails in. What do you think they have hanging on walls in churches? Hammers?"

"Can you touch it?" The vampire looked at him funny. "The *cross*! Aren't vampires allergic to them or something?"

"Well-l-l-l, you see," he explained, knowing full well that most of it would be lost on Rodney. "It's not just crosses, son. It's all the icons humans use to worship their Gods. Crosses, Stars O' David, Cows, the whole lot. But faith is the ruling factor, otherwise these things are mere objects. Some pious asshole waving a cow in your face, now that's a problem." He waited for Rodney to ask why because he was prepared with a hilarious answer.

"Yeah, but don't crosses make your skin pucker and burn and get all gooey?"

"Forget it," the vampire said, disgusted.

They reassembled Rodney's coffin. Rodney held the slats together while the vampire pounded the long spiky nails in with the cross. The brass ornament was so big and unwieldy that accuracy was a problem; several times Rodney got whacked on the fingers. When they were done, the coffin was almost as good as new, except the sides were not quite even. They seemed to tilt inward making the opening tight, and the lid closed at a definite slant. Rodney appraised it disapprovingly, picking up his blue suit and shaking off the sawdust. Candlelight shone through his jacket and pants.

"It looks like Clyde Barrow's last suit," he complained. Wanting someplace private to change, he ducked behind the altar.

"What are you so worried about?" the vampire told him. "I'm not going to bite you." The humor struck him and he let loose another foul-winded bellow. Rodney dropped his pants and grabbed for his nose.

"Man o' live! It smells like something crawled in your mouth and died."

"See what your breath smells like after a few meals, Brother."

A few meals? "What are you talking about? A few meals?"

"You're one of us now, chumly."

Rodney looked at him questioningly.

"You're a wyampyr."

Still nothing.

"Nosferatu … Wurdalak …"

Rodney's slackjawed face contained all the comprehension of a chipmunk's who's just been read Longfellow's *The Midnight Ride of Paul Revere.*

"Vampire, ninny!"

Rodney dropped his bundle of clothes yet again. "A vampire!" he cried. "I'm a lousy, stinking, smelly, dead VAMPIRE?"

"What did you think you were? Do you think everyone who dies just gets up and walks around? Jeez! You know, it could be worse. You could be a ghost."

"At least ghosts are invisible! And they get to walk through walls and stuff!" He was very disappointed. Rodney had entertained a notion that he was a ghost, although he hadn't fully worked out the dynamics in his mind to warrant that opinion. He'd been looking forward to trips into Betty's bedroom, the girl's locker room at the High School, and, of course, the changing room at the women's clothing store Oo-La-La Lady on Main Street.

"Well, we can go through walls. Sort of. Just turn into vapor and float through cracks."

Rodney was hopeful. "Yeah? How do I do that?"

"You'll find out in your own time."

"Wow. Thanks," Rodney said bitterly, gathering up his duds and changing clothes. "You're a big bundle o' information, aren't you?"

The vampire shook his head disdainfully. Several flecks of dried blood fell off his chin. His long tongue darted out instantly and caught the flakes in midair. Sucking them back into his mouth, he smacked his lips loudly with satisfaction.

Charming, Rodney said to himself.

"You young ones. You always think you have the tiger by the tit, don't you? I stayed behind here tonight out o' the goodness o' my heart to impart some wisdom about your new existence, and this is the gratitude I get?"

Rodney scoffed. "What kind o' wisdom? Name one thing."

The vampire thought for a moment, absently licking his chin and scratching his head. "Well," he finally said. "You cannot enter a dwelling without being invited by someone from within."

"I've already heard that one. Tell me something I don't know."

"Elephants are the only mammals that can't jump." Rodney stared at him dumbly. "You wanted me to tell you something you didn't know, and I guessed you didn't know that elephants are the only mammals that can't jump," the vampire said defensively. "Well, did'ya?"

"I meant tell me something I need to know! How in the name o' God do jumping elephants help me?"

There followed a litany of things sounding vaguely familiar from movies. Crap like not being able to cross running water, not being able to cast reflections or shadows, not being able to function past sunrise when you must return to your coffin where, although your senses are fully active during the day, your body lies in the immovable state of death until nightfall.

Rodney looked for something to shove up the vampire's ass, something not as pleasant as a big smelly cigar, something more like one of those three inch diameter candlesticks, preferably one with a chubby lit candle.

"Why, what's the matter, Brother? Aren't you happy with the gift I bestowed upon you?"

"Gift?"

"The Gift o' Eternal Life! Isn't it exciting?"

"Oh, yes. It's just swell. I especially enjoy the long list o' can'ts that goes along with it."

"You can drink blood," the creature told him enthusiastically, balancing all the negatives with this one mighty positive. "'Blood is the life', and you'll find the need to feed quite enjoyable, especially since we have supernatural powers that aid us toward this end." He went on to tell Rodney that vampires are the true shape-shifters, that they can change at will from human form to beast and to bat."

"What about ... you know ... bathroom stuff? I mean, am I going to be pissing and dumping blood from now on?"

The vampire could not believe his ears. Obviously, the supernatural intelligence that was part of becoming wurdalak was lost in the vastness of Rodney's stupidity. Bathroom indeed!

"You're dead, idiot! You don't go to the bathroom anymore."

"Yeah? Well how come when you attacked me as a friggin' bat you were crapping all over the place?"

"The forms vampires take, bat or wolf for example, are corporal. And if dawn comes upon you in these forms, there you remain vulnerable until nightfall. Only in your true form—that of human—do you have supernatural powers."

"So, if I'm a wolf, say, and I lift my leg to a tree. Am I going to piss plasma?"

The vampire was losing his patience. "Look, when you are in the form of a creature you are bound by that creature's natural physical tendencies. Bats crap all the time. That's what they do! Wolves don't go around pissing …" Rodney had that droopy-mouth vacant look on his face again. The vampire sighed, defeated. "No, you will not piss blood when you're a wolf. Also, not that it's going to help *you* much, but our superior intellect gives us control over mortal minds."

"That green fog?"

The vampire sucked in breath as if rammed in the solar plexus. He exhaled, then moved very close, pushing his face directly into Rodney's, speaking sotto voce. "That power comes from the Kingdom. The green fog is a Glamour spell that can make mortals perceive what we want them to. I can make you see me as a gay caballero, for example …" he said, leading Rodney. "… or as the girl of your dreams."

There was no response.

"If I went after your sister, as I should have done, I probably wouldn't have needed to use it because of the natural attraction power we have over the opposite sex."

"If you were supposed to get *her*, how come I'm the one who's dead??"

The vampire laughed. "I couldn't resist! You were so frightened and sooo funny! My vampiric nature got the better o' me." He frowned deeply. "But I'm probably in deep-shit hot water now because I screwed the pooch."

Rodney's mind wandered as the vampire regaled him with information about the Kingdom of the Undead. Snatches of information, however, like the fact that there are these twelve foot tall, horrible, green-skinned Goblins ruling the Kingdom, eked through into his brain. The one thing impressing Rodney most was that apparently there is a *Head* Goblin, an awesome figure respected by all the Kingdom's population and not a fun guy to deal with.

"These damn greenies are everywhere," the vampire told Rodney in a very, very low voice. Rodney stared intently at him. "There's millions and millions of 'em, everyplace you look."

"Whew!" Rodney said, frowning. "Are you ever ugly."

"Too bad you can't see yourself in the mirror." The creature made a pretend scared face. "Whew!" he added mockingly.

Rodney was devastated. Outside of what he considered to be fairly good looks, he always felt he had little, if any, other redeeming qualities. Now with the pointy teeth he felt popping through his gums digging into his lips plus the tightness of recessed eyeballs and nostrils flaring like a bull's, even that was cruelly and permanently taken away from him.

"Thanks a bunch for turning me into an ugly, smelly monster," he said bitingly. "Just what I need to turn chicks on."

Sensing the kid's dejection, the vampire reached out to put a comforting arm around his shoulder. Rodney was swift enough to avoid the aggressive action. The vampire was hurt, still he offered encouragement.

"Are you kidding? Rodney, old chum, women love us. It's the scheme o' things ..." but he was cut midsentence by a voice calling to them from behind the nave doors.

TWENTY-FOUR

"What's the *problem*, Sassi?"

Novice priest Father Jerome Sassi, startled, turned on his wide heels to see Father Horatio Yorrick glaring at him. Because his ear had been pressed to the nave door, listening intently to the activity inside the church, he didn't hear the minister creep up behind him. The presence of his Superior gave Sassi a mother of a problem to deal with: should he spare Father Yorrick the horrifying truth of what he just discovered? Jerome feared the shock would be too much for the old man's tired heart, but he was so very unsure over what to do about this dismal situation. It would be a noble, heroic thing to keep the news that criminals were looting the church to himself, but an even bigger feather in his own cap to handle the problem proficiently.

"Well?" Yorrick said impatiently, grabbing a chunk of flesh on Sassi's flabby upper arm and twisting it hard. "What's wrong?"

"Uh … I heard voices in the church," the young man confessed, spilling out his guts in one long rush of excited words. "There are robbers in there cleaning us out!"

Father Yorrick's craggy face flushed, then drained of color. His lips took on a purplish hue. "O, God!" he implored, then trembled with excitement.

Nervously, Jerome asked if he should call the police. Father Yorrick's eyes revolved up into his head. He clutched his chest and fell over backwards.

"Aww! Nuts-in-spring-g-g!" the young priest twanged, stewing over the new dilemma of whether he should first call the police or an ambulance. It was a delicate balance of which emergency should be handled with the most swiftness, which contingency would hurt the church more ... a robbery or the old man's demise?

"Wait here and try to hold on, Father. I'm going to call the police."

"Come back here," Yorrick ordered with a clear wheeze in his voice. "That is not the way we deal with robbers. We're not cath'o'lics, you know. Didn't they teach you *anything* at that damn seminary?"

Jerome Sassi looked down at his big hands, thinking that Father Yorrick's mind must have snapped from lack of oxygen due to this sudden heart seizure, in which case it should be permissible to ignore him. He continued on his way to the telephone.

"Don't you dare call the police," Yorrick growled between clenched teeth. Sassi stopped dead.

The elder priest regained some strength and rose to his feet. He tottered to the nave doors and took a good deep breath, clearing the mucus out of his throat with a hacking cough and swallow, usual procedure before sermons. He called out sweetly, "Is there anyone in our Church? Feel free to stay and enjoy the company o' God!"

Inside, the vampire's attempt to comfort Rodney was aborted.

"Now you've done it, you crazy bastard," Rodney said quietly, but with heat. "Father Yorrick is out there. Any second he's going to come in with his great big collection plate, and I hope you have moolah, 'cause I sure don't!"

"No!" the vampire moaned. "I spent my last shekel on those overpriced Bingo Cards."

"Always remember, my friends," Father Yorrick's soothing voice echoed throughout the church, "that God welcomes you with open arms. He wants to share your heartache and strife. There is a *collection plate* on the *altar* for your convenience."

"Yes, Father ... Yorrick," Jerome Sassi's weak voice intoned, strained with strange pauses and hesitations, as if he were reciting back a speech by lip reading. "It is ... a wonderful ... thing to ... know that the church ... door is always ... open to God's ... children ... who can ... count on spiritual ... aid and comfort any ... time o' the day or night ..."

"I don't know about you, but I'm going to find someplace to hide."

"Why?" the vampire asked fearfully.

"Because, two priests ask for *twice* as much."

The sermonizing voice continued: "Let us pray that whoever is in our church feels the welcome warmth of God's love, and will leave a small thank'ee in the collection plate. The *collection plate* there on the *altar*. Right, Father Jerome?"

Silence.

"Right, Father Jerome?" echoed impatiently through the church followed by something that sounded like the smack of leather against a casaba melon. Then came Jerome Sassi's rushed words, "Oh, yes! Right, Father Yorrick."

Rodney lifted the lid of his lopsided coffin. Before he could enter, the vampire pushed up against him, jockeying in. They got stuck in the narrow opening, wiggling and squirming until they both tumbled into the box. The lid slammed down, leaving them pressed closely together face to face in darkness. Pinned under the weight of the vampire, all Rodney could see were glowing yellow eyes peering down on him. The creature panted heavily.

Father Yorrick creaked open the nave doors to have a looksee. There wasn't a soul in sight. *Good,* he chuckled, closing the doors again. *They're probably hiding behind the altar, shaking with fear! A job handled with superb technique and polish,* he congratulated himself. *Heh-heh-heh. It pays to be old and experienced. This will come out wonderfully, no thanks to this lummox standing here staring bug-eyed at the back o' his hands.*

"Sassi, you look like a frightened baboon with your eyes popping and that moronic tongue hanging out. You'd screw up the second coming o' Christ with your sour attitude."

"But, sir—the robbers?"

"What about 'em?" he barked. He barked so hard that it brought on a coughing fit.

"Why didn't you let me call the police?" he asked quickly, getting the whole question out as the aged priest gakked away. "You acted like you were happy they were robbing us blind."

Yorrick regarded the young man silently. *The first chance he gets he should see about replacing this nitwit with someone a little brighter, someone who didn't need to have the facts of life explained at every turn. Too bad the assbackwards church elders sitting pretty in Rome (Wisconsin) didn't approve of women ministers. He could be very comfortable with a nice young girl under him.*

"In the first place," he expelled, "we don't know that they are robbers! They could be SINNERS for all we know, which is why I took the time to remind them of their obligation to leave an offering. Secondly ... eeeakkkkk-*hooo,*" here he stopped to spit some blood onto his sleeve. "Secondly, if they were robbers we'd encourage them to think we're empty-headed pushovers."

Sassi knitted his brows and frowning deeply stuck his hands into his pockets. Father Yorrick could almost swear he had dead mice in those pockets, that he was stroking them with his big bulbous thumbs as he listened. It wouldn't be surprising to learn that Sassi had a roomful of rabbits either. Yorrick suddenly felt very weary. It's been a long, long life in God's service, getting longer still with each moment he had to spend with this refugee from pinhead island. He dragged himself over to the coin-operated confessional, where he could sit and rest on the uncomfortable wooden bench, a gift from those annoying Daughters O' Gulpo Plains ladies, and indicated for Sassi to join him. But, of course, the numskull was too dense to understand the gesture.

"Sit down over here," he yelled. The young priest quickly shimmied over, his dark robe flapping behind him, his arms banging together, looking like a trained seal coming to get a fish-treat.

"Jerry," Father Yorrick said as kindly as he could muster under the circumstances, "I was once a young, inexperienced priest …"

"Like me?" Sassi asked brightly.

"No, not like *you* at all … although I admit that I was a little foggy on some things. I served in a church in Dumfry. As you should know from seminary school, some of the nicest and richest churches in the country are in Dumfry. Billionaires live in that goddam town! I happened to belong to the richest church of them all, the Church of Count Our Blessings."

Sassi gasped in recognition at the name.

"Late one night, just before I retired for bed, I thought I heard a noise in the chapel upstairs. I was young, strong, and brash. I flew up those stairs from the sleeping quarters like a canary with a firecracker up its ass and discovered a crook at the altar. Three of his wetback buddies were trying to crowbar the marble font off the floor. Oh, we didn't call them *wetbacks* in those days," he reminisced, "probably *amigos* or *caballeros*, but whatever we called 'em, they were plenty worried o' God's retribution so it was easy to scare 'em so they left empty-handed."

"Jesus jump up and kiss me!" Sassi exclaimed, impressed. "What happened?"

"I was sent all the way to Rome. For an audience with the Big Cheese."

The novice priest whistled between his teeth. No longer did he think of his superior as a worn-out old fart, but as a figure to be respected and admired. To think, this dried out, cranky old prune actually stopped a church robbery and had audience with the worldwide leader of the Church of United Sillificationalists in Wisconsin!

"Wow! Did he thank you?"

"Thank me? He THUMPED me on the top o' my head with his knuckles! That blasted heavy ring hur-r-rts!!" Yorrick rubbed the spot, still sore after all these years. "That's when I learned the *proper* way to deal with church robbers."

Sassi's dull eyes clouded with puzzlement. The old man placed his knurled hand on the younger one's knee. "Now, listen up. The stuff we have here: the altar, the crosses, the font—what are they? Certainly not that important when you stop to think of the bigger issues. The altar is made from cheap plywood, for example. Oh, it looks real, real ritzy when you're sitting in the pews with your hands in your pockets fishing out a collection envelope, but it's only the dressing that makes it look like its worth something. And except for that big brass cross that I swiped from Count Your Blessings, all the others here are plastic. The font is cheap bathroom porcelain ...

"I could go on, but the point is, all this stuff is worthless. Dixie Paper Goblets have no street value, you know. So, some misguided soul breaks in and steals this valueless junk. What happens? We discover the theft after the fact and call the police *and* the newspapers. Because we're a church, we get special attention in the news, which makes the cops act quickly. They usually get the crook while he's trying to unload the stuff, and not making out very well I might add. Now what happens? We get all the crap back. The robber's family, naturally, is embarrassed as all hell by the newspaper and tele'o'vision coverage and feel they have to atone to God. They generally make a hefty contribution to the church, which outrages the community. To think that the family of worthless criminal scum is getting more forgiveness from God than decent folk like them! It is not to be tolerated. Heh-heh. Before you can say the Apostle's Creed, good citizens from all over are making their peace with God. The police department donates heavily, too, wanting to keep God on their image index."

A smile spread across Sassi's lumpy face.

"That's not all. The case comes to court. We can expect another healthy Soul Soother from the family and the community due to the hardnose investigative stories appearing in the press ..."

"And even the press sends donations!" Sassi joyfully announced.

"Shut up and listen!" Yorrick warned with the same menace he's used on Sunday School children for the past sixty-odd years. "We have to *give* money to the lousy extortionists at the newspapers in order to keep the boring story alive. They're the *real* crooks, if you ask me. Anyway—where was I?—oh, yes. The case comes to court. The thief is found guilty, o' course. And as we pass the plate around the jury box, we make a spiel for mercy. When they see our Godliness and charity for the deadbeat who wronged us, everyone hates the guy even more." Here Yorrick cackled a mirthfilled little laugh. "They really hate his guts! But to please us and God, the Judge gives him a light punishment. No prison time, just paying back to the church the cost of all our missing property."

"Huh? But I thought we got it all back."

"O' course we got it all back!" Father Yorrick exploded. "But the Court doesn't know that! The jerky jurors don't know that! Even the idiot robber doesn't know that! The cops and us are the only ones who do know. We won't tell, and the cops don't care what happens to the criminal."

"What if the robber tells the court he was caught with all the things still in his possession?"

"The court's going to believe a disreputable defendant? His own family doesn't believe him, and they're real sick of him to'boot. He's costing them a bundle o' BURRITOS! They'll have to mortgage property or sell their cars to keep up, and that doesn't put smiles on their philistine faces, let me tell you!"

"We itemize a list at the court's request, outlining the value of the stuff ..."

Father Jerry snickered. "Ooo! Big-g-g deal! What? Thirty-four dollars for the font, five bucks for the altar ..."

"What are you Sassi? A complete buffoon? I said we tell the court the value of the stolen items, not what we actually paid for them from GodSend Distributors mail order!"

The old holyman felt a sudden twinge. Pangs of nausea swept through his body. Breathing heavily, he panted out "You're really something, Sassi, did you know that? What the hell kind o' dummy are you? You should be reading your catechism for Kelly Christ's sake instead of making me explain it all to you! Does it say in that slim little chapbook to charge the *cost*? Nooo, it does NOT! Thirty-four hellhumpin' dollars for the font, huh? They'd laugh our asses right out of court. We'd be lucky to get thirty-four *cents*! Brilliant! For your information, DeeLuxe Marble, hand carved and designed by a bunch o' geepy spaghetti vendors over there in Italy runs about six thousand big green dollars."

"Hey! It all comes out so clean for us!" Jerome Sassi's visage took on a new, almost intelligent look.

He looked like he just read a book ...

... *and* understood it.

Yorrick smiled warmly. "And when the judge hears the total value of stolen church property, he throws the sap in jail anyway. Hee-hee! That guy's not going to be sitting easy for a while, that's for sure. So," Yorrick counted off on his wrinkly fingers, "we have our junk back, we're getting full restitution of the retail value of all new equipment, and the born-again family continues to make donations annually when feature stories with color photographs tracing the robber's embarrassing life appear in the Sunday paper supplements."

Sassi's spirit lifted to the height of Father Yorrick's. Together they basked in the glow of Eternal Truth.

"Do you really think we had robbers here?"

"I hope so, kid. Let us pray."

TWENTY-FIVE

Putrid gas filled the coffin. Even after the vampire stopped heaving out grave stench, a layer of foulness hung in the air like DDT over a cornfield. When the voices in the lobby ceased, and the vampire pushed open the lid, escaping death-breath wilted several floral arrangements nearby.

"Aw, look at my flowers," Rodney said unhappily. "They were the only decent thing about my funeral and now they're ruined."

"*Your* flowers?" the creature chided.

"O' course they're my flowers. Tributes from family and friends who'll miss me. Whose else's flowers do you think they'd be?"

"I assumed they were the bride 'n' groom's, here for the wedding."

"Wedding? What wedding?"

The vampire shrugged. "The Bingo ladies were all in a'twitter about a wedding ceremony taking place tomorrow at the same time as your funeral service. They were calling it a double header."

Rodney was aghast. "Man! Now I've heard everything. Who in HELL would have the bad taste to get married during a funeral?"

The vampire chuckled. "Nobody in *Hell*, that's for sure." When he saw that Rodney was not amused, he added testily, "Why don't you look at the cards attached to the flowers?"

At first Rodney found only pre-printed greetings with such banalities as "Good Luck" and "Happy Blessings", none had any kind of personal sentiment, but all had signatures from people Rodney knew. The Argroodie family (Mike, Paulette, Enid, and little Salusa), Henry and Doris Greel, Hank Heidihaw and his wife Bettina, the Arthur Youncellays, Steven and Nubian Vecutt, Sid Harpi and Howard Hemp-Bluntkins, and, naturally, those asskissing brown-nosers, the social climbing Mufflin family from over on Golliwogg Street.

Finally he found a card with some handwriting.

A Merry Marriage!

to:

Betty Bunz and Martin Martex

from:

Helen & Bob Seersucker

The card fluttered from his fingers. His knees gave out, sending poor Rodney to the floor snuffling dryly. Rodney's lips moved, but no sound issued forth. He pointed dumbly to the discarded card, so the vampire bent over to pick it up.

He read it aloud. Several times. Punching home different elements of the inscription with each new reading while Rodney blubbered away. After several minutes the vampire stopped performing, flicking the card from his fingers as if it were a snotball.

"So?" he asked.

"So? That's my girlfriend," Rodney choked out.

"So?"

"SO! Don't you understand? I'm an undead thing, a creature that has to have disgusting blood for food instead o' good stuff like hot dogs and Twinkies, and now I find out my girlfriend, my own true love, is going to walk down the aisle with that asshole creep Marty Martex."

"What do you mean, walk *down* the aisle? I thought it was UP the aisle to the altar." He led Rodney back, away from where they were standing, then turned him and pointed his gray finger at the chancel. It was a raised, carpeted area, very much like a low stage, which extended from wall to wall. A small wooden railing with an opening as wide as the center aisle separated it from the nave. "If you look at that part of the church, it resembles the cross beam of the crucifix. This big middle aisle is like the main beam."

"So?" Rodney said.

"So," said the vampire, "if that way is down, it would sort of indicate Christ was crucified standing on his *head*."

"But they always say walk *down* the aisle."

"Something's not right, and I'll bet if you ask a Holy Man he won't know either," the vampire sneered. "They'd give you the runaround, same as they do that goddam Cain 'n' Abel story."

"Huh?"

"Jeez! I can't believe you don't know about Cain 'n' Abel. Look, in the beginning there was only Adam and Eve, right?" Rodney nodded, and the vampire continued. "They had two sons, Cain and Abel. Cain got pissed off and slew Abel. Okay, now they're a threesome. Adam 'n' Eve 'n' Cain UNTIL Cain goes off to get married." Rodney cocked his head to the side, distracted, but pretending to be thinking.

"Well, unless someone was creating people over in another garden—who on earth could Cain marry?"

"Let him marry Marty Martex," Rodney said sourly.

"Oh, now I get it. That dish with the big woo-woos. That's the one you're hot for." He made that repulsive tch-tch sound out of the corner of his mouth, elbowing Rodney in the ribs simultaneously, the same way all males with disgusting thoughts of women do when they are packed together in places like football stadiums. "Wowzer! The size o' those things! Kowa*bunz*a!"

Rodney yowled like a wolf in pain. He ran down (or up) the aisle to the chancel. Grabbing floral arrangements and biting them in a perfect frenzy, he tore at them, mutilating the pretty decorations beyond recognition. He pricked his undead fingers on some sharp rose thorns and watched the green goop seep out of the open wounds and spread across his fingertips. He thought this discomfort was far too good not to share with the one who brought all these good things to him, his wonderful *benefactor*, so he gathered up some flower remains, ones with the thickest, thorniest branches. *That bat will be crapping roses for weeks ...*

But sorrow overcame him. He fell back against the altar, which creaked almost as badly as his coffin did. The branches fell from his hands to the chancel floor. Words tumbled out of his mouth in a rush of emotion and loss, "I never even got to hump her!"

"So?"

Rodney re-gathered his bouquet.

"If that's all that's bothering you, take heart. Chicks dig vamps in a purely sexual way. They can't get enough of us! For some damn reason, they think we're really hot stuff."

Rodney halted. "Yeah?" he asked skeptically. Maybe it's true. Girls in movies are constantly mooning over vampires, letting those thin little straps on their skimpy nighties fall off their irresistible, creamy-smooth shoulders. A bright new future dawned.

"Of course it doesn't do much good, having a *dead* pecker and all, does it?"

The Lord giveth and right away the Lord taketh it away ...

"You mean to tell me everything works except my pecker?" Rodney was practically spinning with vexation.

"Hold on, hold on … simmer down. I was just pulling your pud. Of course it works! We have full sexual powers, Mortal Privilege it's called in our existence, but we can lose it if we don't play our cards right. Just another half-assed gift from the greenies."

"Mortal Privilege?"

"Sex, m'boy! It so happens that intercourse with mortals produce issue that populates part of the Kingdom. You don't need that Betty Buzz …"

"Bunz," Rodney corrected firmly. "Betty *Bunz*."

"… there are millions of pretty female mortals that would beg to have a rollaround with you now. There might even be some here in Gulpo Plains, although I wouldn't count on it. Take my advise, get out of this hick burg and see the world."

Rodney felt sudden shame for his lousy attitude. He apologized, excusing himself by saying that suddenly becoming dead with no hope of ever getting screwed pushed him over the edge.

The vampire smiled and said with slow deliberation, "Don't worry, Brother. You'll get screwed all right."

Rodney, attempting to exercise a new-found friendliness toward the fiend, although it was difficult because he was a very annoying fellow, asked his name.

"'Call me Ishmael.'" the vampire joked.

"What kind o' jerky name is that? Foreign?"

"Actually, I don't have a name anymore. Why don't you pick one for me?"

Rodney didn't have to think very hard. The vampire reminded him of a magician he saw long ago, when he was two years old and life pre-Roweena with his parents was sweet. In Rodney's funhouse mirror of a memory, Count AlliBabbi took on the coloration of a cuddly uncle, although he's been told time and time again by his parents that the man was a fraud. "A regular charlie-chan," Ralph often bleated, meaning *charlatan*, when talking about the event. The only trick Count AlliBabbi performed that day at the Old Gulpo Civic Center Auditorium was making the entire audience vanish from their seats and reappear at the box office screaming for their 25¢ refunds.

"Count AlliBabbi," Rodney whispered wistfully.

The vampire snapped his lips, following it with a long, deep tongue cluck. "That sounds like a bathroom cleanser … just call me Master if you can't think of anything decent," he said sharply. "Better yet, call me *Maestro*." Continuing, condescendingly now, befitting his new title, the Maestro announced "and since you're my little apprentice, I shall go over the myriad details relative to your new existence."

Rodney yawned. While the Maestro rattled on with one boring dissertation after another regarding afterlife in vampirehood and in the Kingdom, Rodney conjured up thoughts of beautiful girls with skimpy nighties. Girls like Celeste Yahootie melting in his arms, swooning to his irresistible charms.

He licked his lips.

Sensing that Rodney was not paying very close attention, the vampire slapped him on the side of the head. "Are you listening?"

"O' course I am!"

"What did I just say?"

"Uh ... something about everlasting life in exchange for something?"

The Maestro repeated his last statement, this time a little more forcefully, pinning Rodney with his sallow eyes. "In exchange for everlasting life you have Kingdom duty, as voted by the lycanthropes, passed by the Goblin Committee, and approved by Head Goblin, to bring into the Kingdom one female initiate per mortal month, by feeding with transference of blood, and also at *least* one impregnation of a mortal female per mortal month, give or take six or eight months depending on werewolf census."

"Sounds like the Vampire-Of-The-Month Club," Rodney laughed. Maestro ignored him and went on (and on) to explain that all inductees brought into the Kingdom through blood transference shall be his responsibility. This somehow led to the discussion of known methods of destruction to vampires. There's the wooden stake through the heart, which Rodney knew about, followed by stuffing the vampire's mouth with garlic flower, wolfsbane, or seasalt, then chopping off the head. Rays of sunlight and the intake of Holy Water from Rome (Italy) also end eternal life. The vampire finished his speech with a flourish, spreading his arms and turning into a bat. Flying merrily around Rodney's head in circles, farting out bat shit everywhere, he made quite a mess on the already messed up chancel. Re-transforming into human shape, Maestro asked if there were any questions.

Rodney shook his head to get the droppings out of his hair, but Maestro misunderstood.

"Excellent! I will now teach you to feed."

"What's to learn? It's your basic bite 'n' suck. Like in the movies."

"Bite 'n' *Suck*! What do you think we have these sharp teeth for? Do you think they're drinking straws? Watch me." Maestro took a big chomp of air, shook his head like a terrier with a chewtoy, then opened his mouth wide, gulping.

"Got it?" he said, ready to go on to the next subject. "The only difference is blood transference. You regurgitate blood back into the throat opening, then drink down the mixed fluids. Pump some in, slurp some back. Everybody gets something out of it. You get a meal, your inductee passes over into the Kingdom, and the greenies get an initiation ritual for their jolly green joints."

Rodney looked puzzled.

"You know, you're a funny little guy, Rodney. I like you very much, but you're starting to get on my *nerves*—what is it you don't understand."

"The whole thing."

He started explaining about regurgitating blood when Rodney stopped him with, "No, I mean about feeding,"

The vampire rolled his eyes upward and shook his head disbelievingly. What little lifeless hair he had on his scaly head wagged like bulrushes in the breeze. He did the pantomime over again, this time slower, pausing at key points to highlight detail.

"I still don't get it."

The Maestro made an angry gurgle in his throat.

"You're not exactly Marcel Marceau, you know." Rodney said dryly.

"Do I have to use PROPS for your stupid benefit, like some crappy *method* actor?" The vampire angrily pushed Rodney toward the huge font. Pushing him down to sit on the edge of one of the back pews, he instructed the tenderfoot nosferatu to observe carefully as he demonstrated the art of tearing open a jugular vein and sucking out the life's blood. He leaned over the font and started tearing at the burlap covering cloth with his pointy teeth. His mouth ripped and tore at the fabric, making a frightful sound. Rodney was quite alarmed.

"Hey! I don't think you should be doing that …"

"Don't worry. It's harmless. These cheap bastards would never spring for real holy water." He continued tearing at the burlap.

"… they'll make us PAY for that, you know …"

The Maestro ignored him. "Now once you've torn out a nice big chunk o' flesh, press your mouth over the opening and suck away like this." He slurped nosily at the cloth, drawing in a great quantity. He stood up straight, wiping away a few drops of Imported Roman Holy Water from his chin. "See," he smiled. Then, almost at once he started glowing like a fluorescent bug light. Gaseous steam billowed out of his mouth, ears, nose.

The vampire let loose an unwholesome scream of unmitigated suffering. He ran turbulently down, or up, the aisle to the apse, his body dissolving around him. Maestro was flowing down onto the floor and onto the altar steps, and all around the chancel, into a gooey pus-yellow puddle mixed with bright red blood from his last meal.

That's my blood, Rodney thought, looking down at the trail of stuff, gulping hard as he followed Maestro's path. He wondered what went wrong, and somehow got the impression that whatever it was, it was supposed to teach him a lesson far greater than anything the vampire had told him.

Hearing the unearthly caterwaul, thinking some unGodly *animal* got fingers caught in the rat trap by dipping their hand into the Poor Box, Father Yorrick, backed by a frightened-looking Sassi, flung open the nave doors.

Yorrick clucked his tongue with deep, deep disgust. Rodney, at the altar, froze like a deer caught in the headlights of a pickup truck full of gun toting rednecks.

"I might've known. It's that Rodney *Rodoggio*. Adding collection plate pilfering to your list o' crimes, my boy?"

Sassi babbled an oath to God. "But, you … you're dead! We're officiating at your funeral tomorrow … ooo-ahhhhhhh-ooo," he trailed off into hysterical screams, waving his arms wildly.

"Oh, sweet Johnny Jesus!" Yorrick moaned, realizing himself just what was before him. Certainly, the Rodoggio boy was a nuisance, acting up in Sunday school and passing rude comments during service, but who would've thought he'd arise from the dead an unclean monster? The old man clutched his chest, stumbling forward, bumping into the Vend-O-Candle machine, praying. Then he saw the font's torn covering and the Holy Water sloshed out all over the floor.

"Oh, my GOD! That's REAL Holy Water! Sassi! What have you been ordering? Imported?"

He stopped shrieking long enough to shake his head fervently. "No … no … no … I've been buying domestic, 17¢ a keg … taste it, you'll see."

"I don't have to taste it! I can smell that oily perfume they lace it with! And it costs $170.00 a gallon, you nitwit! I'll take care of YOU after I deal with dead young Rodoggio here."

God-diddly-dammit! His church was a mess! What was this unholy monster doing in here? Having some kind of hellish party? Floral arrangements ripped apart and scattered everywhere, the font desecrated, the big brass cross laying sloppily across the backs of two pews … and that awful smelling puddle of gook on the floor. What was that? Yorrick lifted the heavy cross, huffing and puffing under its weight as he advanced on Rodney for an exorcism the young hoodlum will never forget.

Rodney smiled sheepishly, starting to apologize for leaving his collection envelope at home. His sharp teeth glistened. At a complete loss for words, he asked the priest if walking toward the altar was going down or up the aisle.

Yorrick stopped for a moment, considering the question. He leaned the back-breaking cross against a pew and rested his elbow on it. "Up," he said finally.

"But a bride walks *down* the aisle."

"O, THOU DEMON!" Yorrick shouted, then began squealing words in Latin, waving the cross from side to side at Rodney.

Rodney backed up against his coffin. Maybe he should have asked the Cain and Abel question instead? Holding the lid open he wiggled in, getting stuck once again in the narrow opening.

"Get thee out," Yorrick intoned, taking a giant stride toward the devil spawn, stepping into a splotch of dead vampire. He brandished the cross at his uplifted shoe, chanting things in Latin to exorcise the stuff off his foot. Failing, he ripped pages from a nearby hymnal and scrubbed.

Rodney tumbled into his coffin.

TWENTY-SIX

Father Horatio Yorrick returned the hymnal to its rack while Father Jerome Sassi began a fresh round of hysterics. Coming up swiftly on the young priest, he gave him a good sobering swack with the edge of the cross. "Cool it, Sassi," he hissed. "I'm in no mood for this crap."

Jerome fell to his knees, praising God for delivering him from this overwhelming evil through the hands of Father Yorrick. He kissed the old man's feet reverently.

"If I'd have known you were going to do that, I wouldn't have ruined a perfectly good hymnal," Yorrick snarled, then shifted to his most officious voice. He condemned the coffin and its contents as contaminated by unholiness, and ordered the thing out of his church. Striding through the nave doors to the narthex with the young doofus in tow, he then pushed open the massive wooden front door and went out onto the street.

The night was still, warm and dank, with an overhanging smell of swamp. Still, Yorrick felt chilled to the bone and turned up the collar of his clerical jacket, plunging his hands deeply into his pockets. He looked at his young apprentice standing there dumbly in front of the church steps like a cigar store Indian without the cigars or the personality.

"Haven't you forgotten something?" he asked crossly.

"Huh?" said Sassi, then exclaimed, "Oh!" and galloped back into the church, returning moments later with a fresh collection plate. It wasn't long before three off duty construction workers came by. They were headed across the street to Bitsy's Bar and stopped to exchange greetings with the ministers.

"Hulloo, Fodders," said one as they lined up and reached into their pockets for change.

"No, my sons," Yorrick said, with a welcoming smile, refusing their kind offerings and shocking everyone. "Sometimes the greatest gift to make is your time. Would you strong lads help us remove a little something from the church nave?"

The men pocketed their money with relief. To give away what little their wives allowed them would mean an early end to their night out. "We'd be dee-lighted to help you," rasped one warmly. "It's our civic duty," said another.

They filed into church behind Father Yorrick, much like they used to do when they were wee lads attending church school. Sassi attempted to step inside, too, but an angry squint and head tilt from the old man gave him the clear inclination to remain outdoors, holding the collection plate out to any barhopping passersby.

He looked down the long street, first left, then right. There didn't seem to be much action on Main Street tonight, unusual for a Friday going into Saturday morning. Usually the night was rife with the sounds of breaking chairs and clanking bottles.

But tonight it was quiet. Very quiet indeed.

Supernaturally quiet.

Sassi shivered. Seeing that Rodoggio kid had given him the heebie-jeebies. Those yellow eyes, and the picket-fence teeth …

Someone screamed.

It sounded like a little girl, high-pitched and sissified. With a hysterical giggle, Jerome realized it was himself screaming. Teeth chattering, pressing against the stone wall of the church so that nothing could sneak up behind him, he wondered if his brain was snapping. What's it like to go crazy, anyway? When you do crazy things, do you know they're crazy, or do they seem normal and rational? How could you tell if you are embarrassing yourself, if what you're doing seems normal?

Dammit all! He should have gone into law like he wanted to, instead of being pushed into the friggin' ministry by his ambitious father. Still, dad was right about the money to be made doing the Lord's work.

"Yeah, but lawyers don't have to deal with actual demons from hell."

"Who said that?" he asked nervously, gazing around. His thick upper lip starting to jitter.

"*I did,*" he answered himself. His face spread into a big, beaming smile. He started laughing in long, deep gulps. Jerome thought it would be a good idea to put the collection plate on his head like a helmet and march merrily up the street singing "Roll Along Prairie Moon". *That* would protect him from all creatures great and small ... but it would have to wait for later. Right now, he was supposed to stand outside the barn, watching to be sure no one came along while daddy was inside doing funny stuff with the cows. He wished he had remembered to bring along his sunglasses. The sun shining in his face was sooo bright, it hurt his eyes.

To Yorrick's great discomfort, the first thing the construction workers did was complain about the evil odor in the church. Maestro had become rather graveolent, and was commanding the house with his presence. When they saw the big wooden crate in front of the altar, the smallest of the three assumed it was filled with garbage, the source of the stench. It was important to get these dolts out of here *very* quickly, so quickly that they wouldn't have time to notice much of the unholy mess and ask millions of unanswerable questions, so Father Yorrick didn't bother correcting their misthinking.

"Who'd leave a box o' garbage inside a church?" one of them wanted to know as they walked through puddles toward Rodney's coffin. "What? Did garbage men come in to pray and forget to take it with 'em?" the other asked facetiously.

"That's exactly what happened, my sons." Yorrick said rashly, trying to halt this dangerous line of talk. The men exchanged skeptical glances. "When you walked to the altar just now, were you walking *up* the aisle or *down* it?" Yorrick asked quickly for distraction. The men huddled together, conferring like meatheaded football players. Yorrick tapped his foot irritably.

"Uh ... down?" one offered without the consent of the others.

"You go UP the aisle, jackass! Nobody goes *down* for communion!"

Everybody looked at the third man. "It depends," he said sagaciously. "Does the middle aisle run north and west, or south and east?"

This discussion went on for many, many nervewracking minutes, until Father Yorrick finally yelled at them to stop debating. It was a hung jury anyway.

"What *is* the right answer, Fodder?" Three sets of eyes, six raisins in three doughy buns, regarded him.

"Who cares? Stop futzin' around and pick up the box! Hurry, now! Chop-chop!"

With a burly man on either end of the crate, and the smallest one in the middle for support, they hefted the box high in the air, lifting it above their heads in a moronic show of strength. Rodney was bounced around like a doll in a washing machine.

"Don't drop it," Yorrick warned with a nasty edge in his voice. Catching himself, he chuckled theatrically. "It'll make quite a mess if you do!"

Moving forward, looking like overfed packboys in some low budget *Tarzan* movie, the last man's foot slid in a thick collection of melted Maestro. He nearly fell on his ass. The other men let out bursts of laughter. The embarrassed individual lifted his foot and saw red-yellow gunk covering his nice new loafer.

"Aw, *fuck*! Look'it my SHOE!" he rasped heatedly, trying to keep the box aloft, his balance, and his temper all at the same time. He waggled his foot vigorously, shaking stuff off onto pew seats.

"What is this anyway?" the lead man asked.

"It looks like some kind o' shit," said the gorilla in the middle.

"You're ga-ga! Shit ain't yellow and red."

"Haven't you ever seen a parrot? What color do you think their shit is? And don't call me ga-ga, unless you'd like all yer teeth knocked inta yer fat belly."

"Boys, boys!" said Yorrick. "Please!" But the workers were too caught up in their conversation to hear him. They stood there, arguing, holding the wooden box above their heads, coming out with one asinine theory after another about what could possibly be on a church floor this time of night. Finally, the middle man released his hold on the box and crouched down low to examine the pool. He took a long, hard look. "It's puke," he decided.

"Your head is filled with puke," the lead man yelled. "Who'd have the balls to throw up in church?"

"Yeah," said the last guy, really losing his temper at the stupidity he was hearing. "This is the House o' GOD! Nobody would throw up in a fuckin' CHURCH!"

Yorrick was getting nervous. He wanted that coffin and its contents out. He goosed the lead man to get him moving, but it was like goosing a refrigerator. Nothing happened. They fully ignored the elder until one of them, probably the trouble-making smallest one, got the bright idea to incorporate *him* into the What's-The-Puddle game. If he so much as hinted to these thick-headed animals that they were stepping in ect-O-plasm they'd blab it all over town. By tomorrow evening everyone in Gulpo Plains would know about it, his church would be the object of ridicule, and Yorrick would be summoned to Rome. He'd have to come before the Big Cheese to answer why he was allowing unholy demons to run amuck in his church, and then he'd have to face the sanctimonious council. Wouldn't that be ducky?

Shit.

His church would lose credibility. Those damn ambulance-chasing Lutherans would get in and sell his congregational flock a bill of goods based on the fact that they've never had to perform an exorcism in all their long history, let alone worry about hell's bells ringing in their belfries.

He had to get these monkeys off his back, so, sweating, he improvised a story about pizza pies and the Bingo Ladies. The pizzas ended up falling all over the floor in a jubilant burst of excitement when one of the regulars hit big. Yorrick bit his lip with apprehension. No one, no matter how stupid they are, would buy this. The story was just too far-fetched to be believed since everybody knows nobody wins church Bingo. He was framing another elaborate lie when ...

"Pizza sloppings!" the men shouted happily. Without pause, save to dump the wooden box, each grabbed a handful of pizza to sample.

Father Horatio Yorrick sighed in relief and thanked God for little green apples and men with little green apple*sauce* in their heads in place of brains.

"Wish I had a beer," one of them groused.

"Yeah, to get this awful taste out o' my mouth. This is the worst pizza I've ever had." He coughed up the gunk and spat the remains down onto the floor. "Goddam garbage!"

The smallest man's face had gone purple. He stopped breathing. His throat spasmed as he fell face-first into a pizza puddle. His pals picked him up and plopped him down onto a pew seat. They slapped his beefy face until he started breathing again. When he found his motor skills, he feverishly wiped his mouth with the sleeve of his Gulpo Lanes bowling jacket. He said to one and all in a loud, incensed voice that if this was pizza, he was the Virgin Mary.

All of them were anxious now to get this job done, and get over to Bitsy's Bar where they could fill their mouths with something *good*. They didn't waste any more time critiquing pizza, or asking questions, or wondering about down and up the aisle. They took their stations and hoisted the crate.

While they juggled the unwieldy box through the double nave doors, Yorrick barked directions to them so that protruding nails and big splintery chunks of wood didn't leave deep scratches in the doors' finish or in the walls. There was a close call when someone sneezed and, bending forward with the force, his butt tipped over a large candle stand which arced down scraping against the middle of one of the doors. Fortunately, there was no candle on it that would have dented the wood, and the worst thing that happened was that the cheap metal alloy stand bent upon contact and left a superficial, cosmetic, black streak on the door which Yorrick easily wiped away with his handkerchief. Getting the crate outside, they set it down almost upon Jerome Sassi's toes because he was standing right in their way. He danced back, bumping into Yorrick, who gave him a hard poke. "And take that collection plate off your head," the old man whispered sternly.

It was requested that the men move the box closer to the row of garbage cans from next door which always, somehow, ended up on church property. There, at least, the mourners will have a place to sit during the alfresco funeral service.

After they placed the coffin down to Yorrick's satisfaction, the men said good-bye and wished the priests a pleasant evening. A bunch of cold ones were awaiting them over at Bitsy's, and they dabbed their mouths with the back of their hands thinking about those big frosty mugs. Their strong legs pumping, they hastened onward, like Christian Soldiers going off to war. The old man's loud wheezing and familiar throat clearing stopped them in the middle of the street. They turned to see a grinning Sassi extending the collection plate. They came back and got on line, basking in the glow of Father Yorrick's beaming face. The first man up plunked two quarters into the plate.

Yorrick had recently removed the felt liners in every single collection plate that crossed his threshold. When those two coins hit the naked copper bottom they made such a deep resounding cacophony that Rodney, uncomfortably jammed in his box, thought one of the burly bovines had dropped his lunch bucket.

Yorrick winced at the sound, covering his ears and looking offended. "Please, my sons ... for the sake of the community ..." he hinted. "Be *quiet*," he finished boldly since construction workers do not take hints.

The second man put the silver half dollar he was holding back into his pocket. Instead, he drew out his wallet and extracted a dollar bill. Gently, he placed it in the dish. When the man stepped aside to allow the next member of the flock to approach, Yorrick jostled Sassi's hand so that the two quarters bounced off the side causing another loud disturbance. "Ohh," he wailed, "that metal money is going to wake up all of Gulpo Plains!"

The man who thoughtlessly donated the two quarters received nasty stares from everyone. He begged forgiveness and took out his own wallet. Lamentably for him, the smallest bill he had was a five, part of the money he'd been saving for a little something special Bitsy offers in the backroom; he invested in this kitty instead. Grabbing back his two quarters, his hand was slapped roundly halfway out. His mitt sprang open and the two quarters fell back from whence they came. After the clanging subsided, Father Yorrick reminded them all that greed was a passport to Hell.

"What is needed here is some *padding* to silence those coins."

The man reached into his wallet again and brought out more green money, slipping it under and around the damn coins, padding the plate so well in fact that the third man could gracefully replace his wallet and drop a dime into the plate noiselessly.

Father Yorrick had many years experience in service to Our Lord, and this was not the first time he had encountered such heathen opportunism. With a whack on the plate from underneath, all three coins were sent heavenward during which time his practiced hand deftly rearranged the paper cash. Three coins hitting the copper plate from such a height caused a triple clang that bore deeply into the soul. The third man promptly took out his wallet and made a proper offering.

"God thanks you my Sons!" Father Yorrick said exuberantly, his booming voice rattling garbage cans up and down Main Street. The three construction workers said goodbye to the priests, as well as goodbye to their night out, going off in the exact opposite direction of Bitsy's Bar, back to their homes and to their wives for a night of nagging and television.

Yorrick cackled until a violent mucousy cough overtook him. He sat down for a moment on the coffin, regrouping his energy. The exorcism, and especially dealing with the moronic construction workers, took a lot out of him. Once he started feeling better, he grabbed the full collection plate out of Sassi's pudgy paw. His old pale eyes gazing down into the pile of money took on the luster of a child seeing his first post-baby food meal. He made happy little squealing noises in his mouth, licking his slubby lips, counting and re-counting the dough. Joyfully, he tucked the bills under his clerical collar. He tossed Jerome the three silver pieces.

"What about that ... uh ... *Rodoggio*?" Sassi asked. He pronounced Rodney's name as if it were something foul in his mouth.

"What about him?" the mentor replied. "He got a free exorcism, what more can he want?"

"I mean ... will he rest now, being unholy and all? Or does the exorcism cure all that unholiness? Will he get a proper burial?"

"With the Gravedigger strike still on? O' course not! No one is getting buried unless their loved ones are digging holes ... and I doubt anyone will want to dig a hole for that hooligan." Righteous anger clouded his face. He slapped his palm down on the coffin lid next to his dangling leg. "That's the trouble with this world today," he yelled. "Here we are, sitting in the nineteen-seventies, the country is almost two hundred years old, and people are getting more and more avaricious! Strikes! Walkouts! Labor disputes! Anything and everything to inconvenience good, God fearin' folk!" The man of God was so riled that he actually bounced up and down on the crate, farting up a storm. Several bills fluttered from his collar. "If the Good Lord *intended* man to have money, He would *not* have made churches!"

Sassi bent to pick up the fallen bills from the sidewalk.

"It's our duty to protect the people of Gulpo Plains from this wickedness," Yorrick said with passion, crunching Jerome's fingers under his shoe. He bent over to retrieve the bills himself.

The priest fell to silence, contemplating. Jerome frowned, distressed and wondering why they were still outside in the dangerous night, especially with all that good stuff tucked away in the old man's collar. He rubbed his big hands over his knees, timorously waiting for Yorrick to make a move.

Father Yorrick suddenly tilted backward, falling and striking his head on a garbage can cover. It appeared as if he stopped breathing.

Frantically, Sassi searched for a pulse. Finding none, he put his fingers to the old man's jugular where he could detect a slight throb. Yorrick opened his mouth, garbled sounds eked out. Sassi leaned over to hear the dying man's words.

"Get your hands out o' my collar," Yorrick said.

TWENTY-SEVEN

It was just after the *Little Lucy* fiasco. Rodney was calling the Bunz house almost hourly, then started showing up unannounced on their doorstep. All in order to make amends for the humiliation he'd put them through. His efforts were fruitful, for he was eventually invited to the Bunz household for dinner.

Why did *this* memory have to creep into his mind now?

Rodney opened his eyes. He must have been dozing. *Do vampires sleep?* He should have asked the Maestro when he had the chance … then, like a light bulb un-dimming after an execution at the state penitentiary, he brightly remembered that during daylight hours vampires sleep the sleep of the dead. But, if he was awake now, how could it be daylight? *Perhaps it's tomorrow night already?* He clucked his tongue over this bit of stupidity; but just how long has he been cramped up in this box anyway? It must be hours since the priests went back into the church. Just how near dawn was it?

Through a split in the box lid, slightly down from his eye level, he could see that it was still plenty dark outside. He just lay there, staring out at the sky, bored out of his skull, and let his mind wander. It meandered back to the niggling memory of dinner at the Bunzes.

Knowing it was important to make a good impression, Rodney dressed as well as could be expected for someone who didn't give his clothes much consideration. For this special social gathering, punctuality was in order, which meant leaving his house extra early, assuring his arrival at Cowbell Place in a timely manner. Flowers for hunchbacked old Mrs. Bunz would be a nice, ingratiating touch, so he took a moment to trample through Mrs. Loodelay's garden. She grew hybrids, some of which actually won prizes at county floral shows, and due to this distinction she became the closest thing Gulpo Plains ever had to a celebrity. Her yard was certainly one big colorful showcase of flowers starring her prized plant, a cross between the Evening Trumpet Flower and a Pigtail, which she lovingly named after her dear mother. It was a rare and delicate bloom taking years to mature since the splicing of the two plants, like her parents, resulted largely in an incompatible marriage. Rodney's eye glommed onto it because it was pink and yellow and had big bulbs, reminding him of Betty.

It was ten minutes to five in the afternoon when Rodney arrived for his seven-thirty dinner invitation. After she expressed her consternation at his early arrival, Mrs. Bunz accepted Rodney's proffered gift hesitantly. "My goodness! These flowers look just like Lorina Loodelay's Caliantfir!" she said, then sneezed … and sneezed … and sneezed until a disgusted Mr. Bunz took the flowers away from her and threw them into the trash outside.

This memory hadn't gotten any better since last he had it. The old emotions were still too close to the surface, and still mighty raw. Soon Betty would be lost to him forever, locked in a marriage most likely arranged by Marty Martex and his psycho mother. Why couldn't they have focused on someone else, dragged another girl into their miserable trap? Roweena, for example. Why did it have to be Betty? *His* sweet Betty. The bitterness at this injustice was salt in the wound. It felt to him like someone was rubbing a cheese grater over the tender, fleshy part of his heart. *Betty-y-y-y-y*, he wailed, which was as close to crying as he could now come. *Bettttttttteeeeeeeeeeeeeeeeeeeee … hooooooooo, hoooooooooooooooooo …*

Betty was not expected home until six-thirty, Mrs. Bunz explained to Rodney. Perhaps he would like to come back later, say *closer* to seven-thirty? Rodney clucked his tongue at this ridiculous suggestion. "O' course not! I'll just sit in your living room and wait. I don't mind." Rodney bulldozed past her and went into the living room, where he plopped himself down on the sofa. And there he sat, while Mr. Bunz read his newspaper. Soon, Betty's father was grunting and making comments to himself, which Rodney chalked up to being reactions to the news he was reading. When the mumbling got very angry and very loud, Mrs. Bunz hurried all the way in from the kitchen and asked Rodney if he would care for a soda, hinting that he might enjoy drinking it in the dining room. "No, no," Rodney protested, "here is plenty good enough for me." She gave him a strong look of displeasure, squinting her wart eye, then trotted off. She returned a moment later with a large ice-filled glass of soda.

Rodney took one sip and knew it was that awful diet crap his sister drinks—*NoCal*. It tasted like cardboard soggy with seltzer, so smacking his lips to get the taste out of his mouth, he relegated the still-full glass to the coffee table. When Mrs. Bunz, who was speeding up the cooking of dinner, checked back on their guest in the living room, she was horrified to discover the glass leaving a big wet ring on the bare wood. At the moment Mrs. Bunz gasped, Rodney reached for the glass intending to take a big sip, showing how much he was enjoying the drink, and accidentally tipped it over. Ice cubes skittered across the table onto the carpeting, fizzy liquid bubbled away on the tabletop. He tried mopping it up with magazines, but the slick pages merely pushed the soda around, covering a larger area of wood and splashing against knickknacks. That got Mrs. Bunz even *more* upset, so he sat back and let her do all the cleaning.

"*Honestly* …!" she rasped over and over again with her construction worker's-wife voice, highly perturbed as the finish peeled off her coffee table from the *NoCal* chemicals eating through it like paint remover.

Rodney lifted the lid of his coffin. Looking at the night sky and all the stars, he reflected upon how everything was absolutely quiet and peaceful. He wondered about his future …

… which was exactly what Herbert Bunz was curious about. Slapping down his newspaper, too agitated to read, he asked the boy in no uncertain terms what his plans were. "We*l-l-l-l,*" Rodney said carefully, weighing each word. "First we'll have some dinner, and then I can spend some time with Betty. Alone." He smiled and winked at the girl's father.

"Your *life*plan, *ACE,*" Herbert Bunz said loudly enough for Grace to call "Yes?" from the kitchen.

Rodney told him that he thought he'd go to New York City to become a powerful businessman, live in a Penthouse Suite and drink martinis for dinner every night.

Herbert Bunz stared at him, dumbfounded.

"One thing I *don't* want," Rodney said with animation, sitting on the edge of the sofa, rubbing his hands over and through his hair like an ill-mannered orangutan. "I *don't* want to stay in Gulpo Plains and end up a *chowderheaded* construction worker!"

Mr. Bunz was not thrilled to have Rodney Rodoggio sitting in his living room, on his very own sofa, calling him a chowderhead. Thank *God* Betty couldn't stand this jerk: he would hate to have to bury a son-in-law in a concrete foundation. He wanted to smack his wife good and hard for coming up with this hair-brained scheme, her last-ditch effort to put an end to the nutty kid's obsession with their daughter.

For Grace, it was a matter of her sanity. If she looked out her picture window one more time and saw that unkempt stringbean staring at the house from behind the Agroodie's hedges, she'd go mad. Her family was less than delighted with her idea that once the boy came to dinner and got a little taste of what he thinks he wants he'd lose interest. Both Herbert and Betty were dead-set against this plan, and Grace had to threaten them with terrible retribution to get her way, yelling and screaming and stomping her tiny feet up and down like Rumpelstiltskin. Betty found the idea of Rodney in her own home so repulsive that she pouted for days, and then forgot about it. She forgot about it so completely that when she got home from a sweaty date with Hal Miggley that afternoon, as she walked through her front door to see Rodney jump up from the sofa like a Jack in the Box, the afterglow disappeared from her face and the first words tumbling out of her sweet mouth were, "Aw, *fuck*—what's HE doing here?!"

"*Betty Grable Bunz!*" Grace screamed, outraged, marching her daughter into the kitchen for a mother/daughter chat. Whatever passed between the two women did the trick, for Betty was civil to Rodney throughout the whole rest of the hideous evening. An evening that included undercooked pot roast, overcooked vegetables, and almost raw potatoes.

Too bad they don't have a dog, Rodney thought, innocently dropping bits of inedible food off his fork onto the floor and mashing it into the carpet with his shoe while pretending to chew. Except for some uncomfortable grunts and sighs, there was silence around the dining table. Apparently, the Bunz family did not engage in dinner conversations. Rodney's attempts at light banter, such as bringing to everyone's attention the fresh gravy spot on Mr. Bunz' shirt, were met with harsh glares and plenty of tongue clucks. Words like "slobbered" did not tickle the family funny bone.

Betty herself was noisily clanking her silverware against her plate in a feeding-frenzy rush for protein, smacking her lips with each bite.

When it finally came time for dessert, Rodney made what he felt was a slight *faux pas*. Grace Bunz had whipped up her special Raspberry Fool, the only item on the menu that wasn't ruined by mistiming. The texture of the stuff—Raspberry Jello whipped with milk and something gritty—did not agree with him.

The first spoonful caught in the back of his mouth refusing to go down his throat no matter how hard he swallowed. A sip of milk did little more than dribble out the corner of his mouth. En mass, suddenly, the whole mess slid down his gullet and stayed there, refusing to travel any further. Gakking on it, nearly coughing up onto the table, he started slapping the back of his neck until it slid down into his stomach. The heave from the bottom of his belly began almost instantly. Rodney felt the gelatinous stuff bubbling sourly up, up, up into his esophagus and then into his throat. The Raspberry Fool had come back! He gakked again, slapping his throat hard. Luckily, it slithered back into his stomach and stayed there this time. It would have been awful to have barfed on the pretty lace doily table cloth.

Rodney insisted on helping clear the table. He quickly made a precarious pile of dishes over everyone's objections, and as he scooped up the stack his index finger hooked into a dainty lace opening so that when he lifted the plates, he was also lifting a good amount of the table cloth with them. The mostly full gravy boat tipped over, as did a serving bowl of limp vegetables. Not paying much attention, and thinking everyone's shouts were more polite protestations, he turned from the table. Plates flew from his hands on a magic carpet ride of table cloth, falling to the floor and breaking with the pure crystalline sound of fine china.

"*GET HIM OUT O' MY HOUSE!!*" Grace Bunz shrieked harshly, sounding like one of David Seville's Chipmunks, Theodore with a sore throat.

Betty jumped up from her seat and pushed Rodney to the front door and practically tossed him out onto the porch. She sat him down on the swinging love-seat. Hovering over him, her tight fists pressed to her hips, she said, "Okay, Rinty, if I give you som'thing to get you off, will you *pul-l-leeze* stop hounding me??!"

Rodney thought she was offering an after dinner brandy and nodded his head suavely.

"Unzip 'em," she said to his great befuddlement. "Unzip your *pants*," she repeated.

Betty belched out one of her disgusted sighs. "Oh, never mind! I'll do it!" She dived into his crotch. Rodney's left eye fluttered. He stretched his legs and lifted his pelvis to give her better access. She was having trouble getting the metal tab down the track because fabric of his tucked-in shirt was caught in the zipper.

"Ooo, ooo," he said sexily. Betty appraised the pencil-like bump in his pants with distaste.

"It's *stuck*, goddamit!"

"Let me try."

Betty watched his stupid fingers fumbling around forever with that zipper. Finally, she smacked his hand away and gave the zipper a good quick zip-p-p-p, pulling the track clear of the fabric and clipping off some shirt and some foreskin.

"Eeee-oooo-YOWWWWWW!!!!!" Rodney screamed into the warm June evening. Everyone on Cowbell Place came out of their houses to see the hubbub; the light above Betty and Rodney clicked on, flooding the Bunz porch with yellow bug light. Betty hurried back inside, so neighbors, as well as Grace and Herbert Bunz, had an unobstructed view of Rodney Rodoggio's obscene dance as he hopped around clutching his injured pecker.

"I knew that boy was a pervert," Herbert Bunz said, going for his hunting rifle.

"Get out o' here," the old hunchback hissed, and this time Rodney took the hint.

It would have ended differently, Rodney cursed to himself, if it wasn't for that *crappy* shirt. He spent the next few minutes thinking up possible endings to that memory, and soon fantasy replaced the real event. His mortal privilege stirred awake. His mind fuzzed over with thoughts beyond Betty Bunz and Gulpo Plains, thoughts of glamorous New York City.

In that patch of sky within his vision were the bright lights of Broadway! And there he was at the world-famous Playboy Club, sitting at one of those little round nightclubby-type tables as Bunny Celeste came over to serve him.

"Ohh," she squealed. "*Rod*!" She made him stand up from the table so that he could embrace her. Soon her Bunny suit fell to the floor around her ankles, people at other tables ooed and ahhhed at her beauty, jealous of the lucky man for whose attention she was begging.

Rodney deftly unzipped. Mr Weasel poked out his head. Rodney's clammy, undead hand wrapped around him.

Celeste Yahootie was fondling Rod's massive tool, oooing and ahhing herself now. There was a stir in his groin. He lifted his voice in hosanna. "*Oh, yes! I'm cum …*"

But the words halted in mid-whoop, his body functions stopped.

All that had come was the dawn.

TWENTY-EIGHT

Deafening loud and frantic church bells pealed above him, heralding a new day in Gulpo Plains. All the familiar sounds of Saturday morning life followed, and Rodney counted them one by one, an effort to stave off the boredom that was driving him out of his skull. He wondered *when* he'd go into his deathsleep … his active mind, trapped inside this body filled with inertia, was producing hours of imaginary itches on his legs and arms although he could not even sense any part of his body at all. He even forgot that he was clutching his mortal privileged dong in his dead hand.

What a drag, he complained to himself, watching the little bit of sky and church cornice that was afforded him and listening to the escalating din of Main Street. He heard every little noise, but his sight was limited to what he could see through the split in the box lid directly above his face.

The six a.m. sanitation department truck, chugging its diesel engine and belching greasy black smoke, rumbled past, sloshing stagnant cleaning water over the macadam *and* over early risers out for their newspapers, who, in turn, shouted invectives back. Next came the cheery rasps of night shift construction workers mingling with the grumbles of day shifters. There were screams from the swamp … shopkeepers along Main Street rattled keys into padlocks, dropping heavy chains to the ground and unlocking several dozen doorlocks on each of their doors, underscored by the one or two burglar alarms inadvertently set off.

A doggie barked somewhere, probably that pain in the ass Cooglin dog, Stumpy. From down the street, the cacophony of trash cans being jostled and thrown against buildings was followed by the snap, crackle and crunch of mulching refuse—garbage men at work.

The truck pulled to a screeching halt in front of the church. A couple of Neanderthal garbage men jumped off it, hootin'n'hollerin' for all they were worth (which wasn't much in Gulpo Plains hierarchy). Rodney's view of the world suddenly changed. He saw the stone church wall at a nauseating angle, followed by a whip-pan view of the church door and then the back of the garbage truck, and finally the sidewalk. Then, a spin-o-rama view of Main Street and Rodney was looking up at the sky for a moment before prying eyes stared back at him.

"Hey! There's a *dead* stiff in this box!" a very surprised voice said. The box was dropped with a thud. "Don't those church guys know we don't handle this type o' trash?"

"It's because of that balls'alickin' strike over at the cem'o'tery." Another gruff voice said. "People are trying to get rid of their corpuscles …" He was cut off in mid-sentence.

"That DON'T mean *we* got to handle 'em! It would be one thing if we was getting paid to haul 'em out to the swamp or to dump 'em at a research lab. So …" *He* was cut off.

"SO, keep your whiskers on! We simply refuse the damn thing. Big Effin' Deal! It's no skin off *our* snoots."

A pre-printed Garbage Refusal Form #60118-B was nailed to the box, splintering wood, poking some sharp rusty points into the coffin above Rodney's face, and effectively narrowing his field of vision. The large, brightly colored legal notice also covered nicely the Gulpo Plains Woodworks Company logo and Rodney's epitaph. After dumping the trash cans and tossing them onto the box, where they ricocheted off into the street, the guys got back onto the truck and shouted, "Okay Buddy!" The truck rumbled off. "*And Awa-a-ayy we GO-O-O-O!*"

More people were on the street now, stopping just close enough to his coffin to be irritating with their idle chit-chat and asinine conversations, making Rodney want to leap out of his skin. In the near distance, there was the frightening tap-tap-tap-*boom* of Crazy Eddie blowing up things on his morning constitutional—not as much a concern as was the disquieting sounds of romping children coming closer. The breaking glass, guffawing over dirty jokes, and cursing galore was almost upon him.

"Hey! Look'it this!" a boy screeched, obviously right on top of the coffin. "A big wooden box!"

"So?" asked a chorus of squeaky adolescent voices.

"Sooo let's SPRAY PAINT IT!"

"*Sooo* eat my ass!" screamed an obnoxious little voice. "I'm saving my spray paint for the friggin' train. I'm not wasting it on a box that's getting ditched into the goddam garbage."

"It's not getting ditched, hooplenose! Can't you *read* ? The garbage guys refused it."

"Yeah, well the train's more *fun*."

There was heated discussion and dissension. The children broke into two camps of preference, bickering heatedly back and forth before things got really ugly.

"*I* tell you, this here box would be more rewarding to dec'o'rate."

"You don't know what you're talkin' about, assface," a little girl chimed in. "This screwy box isn't going nowhere and the fuckin' train is going everyfucking-place."

"So what the hell is good about *that*? Nobody can see the words on an idiot train when it goes zipping around at a thousand miles an hour! At least this box will be sitting here for the next twenty years—with all our stuff written on it!"

Spray painting a moving train is risky, especially for small children. One of them could easily fall onto the tracks … or they could have their fragile arms caught on the fast-moving train and ripped clean off while trying to put the cross stroke on the *f* in *fuck you*—precisely why Rodney wished fervently for the train vote to win. Let the little bastards have to go to *Chicago* to get their body parts back. That ought to teach them a *good* lesson for entertaining thoughts of desecrating someone's coffin.

"… I say we do the train …"

"The box …"

"Train …"

"Box, scumnuts."

"Train, *turdlicker*."

Rodney heard the hiss of an aerosol can.

"*Oooe-eee-OOUCCH! My eyes! … My eyes …!*"

Laughter abounded.

"We're spraying this BOX, Mr. Blue Paint Face, and *don't* call me a tur-dlicker!"

After twenty minutes of steady work, Rodney W. Rodoggio's coffin became a Technicolor conglomeration of the unfettered expressions and thoughts of Plain-sian youth.

TWENTY-NINE

Members of the Wedding Party and guests began arriving at one o'clock in the afternoon. They boorishly congregated around the front of the church at the crate laughing and chatting away, having a high old time. Often one of the cosmetically enhanced, overly dressed neighborhood women came into Rodney's limited view. Jesus! They were *hideous*. He wished he could shut his eyes against them. They made vampires look like movie stars.

Except for Mrs. Martex, who planted herself in the exact spot to give Rodney optimum exposure to her face and hair-do, she did indeed look like a movie star.

Gabby Hays.

When she laughed—which was often given this momentously happy occasion—her high-pitched, ear-smarting, whinnywheeze cachinnate made her little pug nose crinkle up, flaring her nostrils wide enough for Rodney to be able to count each of her extra-long nose hairs, which, amazingly, were the same peroxide color as the tufts of hair on her cheeks and chin. For today's joyful occasion she wore a dark purple minidress a size or two smaller than her waist demanded, plus festive green vinyl boots upon which she creatively affixed some artificial daisies. To complete her ensemble, she had on one of those Mary Quant white plastic caps with a groovy matching belt.

Marty's mother made it her business to grab the ear of anyone unlucky enough to stray near her, regaling them with story after boring story of Marty's geeky childhood and all the cute little things he did. She mercifully drifted out of view frequently, dashing after some poor slob or another, but always returned, making her virtually the only person Rodney got to see since her arrival.

"What a bee-*yooo*-tiful day!" a woman, whose voice Rodney recognized as Sylvia Ennui, said gaily. "Thank the Good Lord it isn't raining."

"Knock wood," joked some asshole, probably Hank Hedihaw, pounding down his knuckles on Rodney's coffin. There was a round of hearty laughter. Suddenly, Mrs. Martex's face zoomed down, filling Rodney's entire sight. She apparently was reading the crude slogans spray painted on the box, and finding them quite distasteful she frowned deeply, her thick red lips curling downward like an unhappy clown's mouth. Sighing a sigh of disgust mixed with a slurry attempt at a tongue cluck, she provided Rodney with the aroma of mouthwash-covered booze. Along with a dose of face powder, a furry kind of sweat and some very sweet perfume, Mrs. Martex had the effluvium of a billy goat that has rummaged through a perfume shop after having a few beers.

"Ooo," she squealed suddenly, like the teenage girl she thought she was. "Here come the *Bunzes*!"

Everyone complimented Betty's dress. Rodney mentally urged her into his line of sight. He could only imagine, judging by all the rants and raves, how truly gorgeous she looked. He wanted to see her desperately.

"Oh, Betty, dear," sighed some old lady. "You do make a lovely bride. And that color is so becoming on you ... but, dear," she whispered dramatically, "isn't it a *tad* low cut?"

"No," Betty said sweetly. "And besides, Marty picked it out."

"That's *nice*," the old woman said tartly. "But who IS Marty?"

"Why, Auntie *Roo*—he's the man I'm getting married *to*!" After a moment Betty giggled. Somewhere a lightbulb clicked on as she realized that her syntax fell together in a lyrical fashion. "That RHYMES! I'm a PO*ET* and nobody knows *et*!"

"Just the same, honey, you don't want your *bozoom* seen too soon by your *groom*!" Auntie Roo said sourly. "You know what it says in the sampler on my living room wall: '*Why marry the cow when you can get all the milk you need at the supermarket?*' Let me help you pull it up a bit."

Betty's protests were drowned out completely by the sound of cheap crêpe de chine ripping. Women let out started little gasps, Betty screamed, somebody (probably Hank Hedihaw) whistled and exclaimed, "Holy Mother o' God! Look at those *GAZZOOBAS*!"

All Rodney got to see was the dopey look of horror on the face of Mrs. Martex. He noticed something round and fuzzy adhered to the corner of her mouth, stuck in a thick glob of lipstick. It was so repulsive that he felt like gagging. *O, please move ... let Betty shift into that position ... please God ... pul-l-eee-zzze ...*

"LOOK WHAT YOU DID TO MY WEDDING DRESS!" Betty sobbed. "IT'S *RUINED!!*"

"Don't cry, sweetheart," Herbert Bunz rasped. "Daddy'll take care o' it!" Rodney heard more fabric tear, more shrieks, more sobs and many, many more whistles. Nearly everyone was surprised to find that Betty Bunz wore no underwear—at all.

"OH DADDY! YOU RIPPED IT ALMOST OFF! AND HERE COMES MARTY!"

"That lucky sonuvabitch *bastard*," a man said.

"Would I like to be in his friggin' shoes," said another.

"Forget the shoes …," said a third.

"Oh, boy!" Marty Martex said. You could hear his mouth water.

"Please don't look at me, Marty!"

"Why not, baby?" He said with lust in his voice. "I'm your *hubby*, after all, aren't I?"

"Be-ee-ecause," she whined, "Look'it my *dress* … I'm a *mess* … Hey! I *am* a poet! How'd'ja like that couplet?"

"I like 'em real fine, baby." There were some wet, slurpy kissing sounds.

"Not now," Betty pleaded. "PULEEZE MARTY! *Not* in front of our guests!"

"Then come into the church …" Martex grunted. Over this dialog was a strange sound. A click-clacking on the sidewalk approaching quickly from a small distance away. Rodney thought at first that it was Crazy Eddie's blind cane tap-tap-tapping along, but without the small accompanying blasts it was difficult to tell. Then, too, the sound was not really like the tapping of a cane, but more like the annoying sound of a dance-school recital.

"Oh, look," Mrs. Martex grumbled dismally. "Here come the Rodoggios."

"The *Rodoggios?*" Grace Bunz asked with a nasty intonation in her voice. "*Who* invited *them?* Did *you*, Hillary?"

Hillary Martex shook her head violently.

"The Rodoggios? Sounds like a team of acrobatic dancers," said Lennie Subbule, someone's cousin from out of town.

Ralph Rodoggio click-clacked up to a group of people, a group which included both Mr. and Mrs. Bunz and Hillary Martex. He performed a little tap-whirl, spinning completely around on his heel, coming to rest facing them with his arm extended. "How d'ya like my new Gene Kelly Tap Shoes? Just got'em yesterday at *Houf & Mawth's Shoes 'N' Snacks!*" He lifted his foot to show off the highly polished black shoe. He tapped away from the ladies to huddle with the other males.

Rhonda and Roweena said their hulloos, air-kissing cheeks, basking in the collective glow of respectability. Congratulating Mrs. Bunz and Mrs. Martex, Rhonda said, "You must be very proud."

"Oh, yes!" Grace told her exuberantly, with a big smile. "Betty is a *very* lucky girl. It is so comforting for a mother to know that her daughter has found someone to take care of her."

"Oh, yes," Helen Seersucker added, "Getting married is such a magical thing. All girls should take that little stroll up the aisle ..."

"You mean *down* the aisle," Grace Bunz corrected.

"*No*, I do *not* ... wait ... is it down or up the aisle?"

"I am quite certain that it's *down* ... as long as the altar is on the left, otherwise its UP ... or is it the other way around?"

"It would make sense if—"

This conversation went on, naturally, for quite a few rounds, involving quite a few people, until, miraculously, Helen Seersucker brought it back to where she had left off, at this most important point:

"... well, which*ever* way they walk, every girl should get married whether they like it or not, unless, o'course they are a totally unacceptable pariah of society."

Pitying eyes drifted to Roweena.

"Well, my goodness! Roweena, dear!" Malta Youncellay warbled. She lifted a gloved hand to her sunken cheek demurely. "I didn't see you there! How *lovely* you look."

Ralph, overhearing, called over. "Thanks! That's a *new* dress I bought just for today's special ossification. One hundred and fifty smackeroos."

"You know, Roweena," Nancy Schlonggker added. "I saw a dress just like that on *The Mary Tyler Moore Show*. I hadn't noticed until this very moment how much you look like Mary Tyler Moore. My, my, *my*! How our little kiddies grow up! Roweena, do you remember my son Stephen?"

The image of Stephen Schlonggker passed through Roweena's head: a big, thick bulletheaded boy. She shivered.

"He's got a *fabulous* job on the construction crew night shift and will *certainly* become FOREMAN before long. I'm sure he'd enjoy hearing from you. Perhaps he *might* even consider taking you out on a date. Ooo, you'd *like* THAT, eh? Let me give you his phone number so you can call him up." Eagerly scribbling out Stephen's phone number on a slip of paper, she sighed wistfully, "All our kiddies have grown *so* much."

"It was only yesterday my Martin was starting school," Hillary Martex said, upstaging Nancy Schlonggker. She wiped a crocodile tear away, smudging amber eyeshadow and glitter over her cheek. "I'd dress him up in his little sailor suit with his cute cap and short li'l pants, and how we'd run off to the school house together! I'd sit with him throughout the ENTIRE school day, holding his little hand, helping him understand his lessons! Now ... he's getting *married*!" Seeing that some attention was still upon Roweena, she added loudly enough for heads to turn in her direction, "And here is little Roweena Rodoggio dressing up like Mary Tyler Moore, and looking oh-so-adult ... yes, indeed, our kiddies have grown up—and have turned out so wonderfully well."

"All but *one*," Ralph said bitterly.

"Whoever do you mean?" Doctor Monklee's wife Fellâre said, shocked. "Not little Benny Fossert? Georgie Kilnorris? Edward Scrotagg? Patrick Flipkin? Bobby Frogner? Leonardo Lummy? You *can't* mean Andrew Bobachhian?"

"No," Ralph said. "I meant *Rodney*."

"Rodney? Rodney who?" asked Hillary Martex.

"Uh ..." said Ralph.

Fellâre clucked her tongue. "Oh, you remember! That disgusting boy who tried to violate Betty during the school play."

"Oh. *Him*. Is he out of prison now?"

"He wasn't sent to prison," Rhonda said, attempting to put up a united front for her family honor.

"Good God!" Hillary Martex screeched, blinking her eyes with enough force to loosen her artificial lashes. "NO? Where is he then? Running around violating innocent girls I imagine!" She crossed her arms over her chest protectively.

"Naw," Herbert Bunz put in, lightly and jovially. "He's *dead*. Drug overdose, right Ralphie?" Ralph nodded enthusiastically.

"Oo, *good*," Hillary Martex sighed with relief. "You know how these s-e-x maniacs are! They can't *control* themselves! None of us girls are safe with such a *person* roaming the countryside! Consider yourself *lucky* he didn't attack Rhoda or little Mary here ..."

"Roweena," Roweena said.

"And that's *Rhonda*," Rhonda added.

Mrs. Martex raised her eyebrows, disapproving of the correction. "Of course," she said coldly. "Yes. Well, anyway, more to the point ... what are you people doing *here* at my son's nuptials? It seems nobody invited you."

Rhonda blushed deep scarlet. She wished Main Street would open up and swallow her whole, or, if that was too much to ask, that a full bottle of Old Hen's Foot would drop out of heaven into her hands. Now, because of *Rodney*, everyone in Gulpo Plains is going to think that she, of all people, would show up some place where she hadn't been invited.

"We're *here* for my brother's funeral service," Roweena countered, equally cold.

Grace Bunz saw the storm clouds brewing and intervened. "Oh, well in that case," she said cheerfully, "have a nice little service. Perhaps you'll still be here after the wedding to see the newlyweds off? Did you bring some rice?"

"Say!" Herbert Bunz exclaimed, clapping his hefty hands together. "We're having the Wedding Reception outdoors over at the Gulpo Park Picnic Center—why don't you folks come along?"

Ralph beamed with excitement. His feet clickity-clicked merrily around until he remembered. He smacked his hand with his fist. "Aww, nuts! I *can't*. Those LOUSY gravedevils are on strike, and my wife wants me to dig a hole to bury the boy."

"Well, bring him along. You can bury him in the Picnic Center, they got plenty o' dirt there."

"Ahhh, it'll take too long," Ralph sulked. "I'll *miss* everything."

"Not with HERBIE BUNZ helpin'! Me and some o' the boys will give you a hand. We'll have it done in no time flat! It'll be a BLAST!"

Ralph brightened. Rhonda poked him in the ribs and whispered, "I can't go to the reception dressed like *this*! I'll have to go home and change out o' these slacks."

Gluupick, the junk miser, arrived with his family for the wedding. "Hey! What's in this box?" he asked Grace Bunz, running his graspy little hands over the lid and down it's sides, feeling the contours and enjoying its colorful appearance. He was obviously very interested. "Is it a wedding present?"

"Noooo," Grace said, sustaining the ooo sound smoothly. "I don't think so. Let me look." With Gluupick peeking over her shoulder, she opened the lid. "Isn't he supposed to holding flowers instead of *that*?"

The junk miser shrugged his shoulders. "Who knows? At any rate, this is nothing I want." Grace Bunz let the lid crash back down.

"Ah! Kitties!" cried Ralph, seeing Betty and Marty coming down the church steps. Betty wore her dress backwards, which covered her front but was so droopy in the back that the seat of her personality was clearly on display. Marty's fly was undone, his shirttail sticking out over the rented tux pants. He was flushed and panting.

"Congratulations!" Rhonda offered to Betty. "Marty is a fine, fine boy."

"Thank youuuu," Betty gushed. "I wish *every* girl can be as fortunate as me! I'm soooo happy and so is my *pappy!*"

Everyone looked at her with puzzlement.

"It's a *rhyme* you dodos. *Jeez!*"

"There IS someone *almost* as lucky," Ralph announced, his voice a symphony of pride. Rhonda tried to hush him. "My ROWEENA!"

Hillary Martex sneered. "Why her? Is she getting her own TV show?"

"RO'S GONNA HAVE A *BABY!*" he chuckled with delight. A gossipy buzz broke out over the congregated merrymakers. "MARTY'S BABY!!"

All chatter stopped. The only sound audible was a long, hard gulp from Marty Martex's throat.

"Really?" Grace Bunz asked with disbelief.

"You're SO lucky!" screamed Auntie Roo.

"I'll say," Hillary Martex said, warming up to Roweena and the Rodoggios. "Just imagine! The Rodoggios will finally have someone in their family worth something."

The excitement continued until it was time for everyone, except Ralph, Rhonda, and Roweena, to go into the church for the wedding ceremony. To Rodney, the celebrants entering the church sounded like a herd of buffalo going up those steps, everyone fighting to be first in for best seating. Soon came the sounds of garbage cans pulling up to his crate and his family sitting down upon them. It was many moments before anyone spoke, and when someone finally did it was his mother.

"This is the happiest day of my life. At long last we'll have our rightful place in Gulpo Plains Society."

"It's just too bad that the Mayor couldn't be here to witless our upheaval."

"What?" Rhonda asked.

"I said, it's too *bad* the *Mayor* wasn't *here* to sodomize our joy."

"Oh, I don't know WHAT you're talking about!"

"I'm saying what I mean," Ralph said irritably. "It's too bad the MAYOR could NOT be here to see our upsweep ... what could be plainer than that?"

Witless, Rodney repeated to himself, reducing the words to a formula he'd worked out long ago, *plus sodomize divided by joy plus upheaval equals upsweep: Too bad the mayor wasn't here to witness our upraise into society and solemnize our joy.* The instinct to say aloud the correction was in place, but the muscles moved not.

Ralph was too happy to care what he was saying anyway. He was pleased that God chose to reward them in this manner, that they would have a grandchild that will bring them to the forefront of society and the respect of all Gulpo Plains. "Life is bland!" he cried, hugging his family tightly together. Rhonda, on the outside, nearly toppled off her garbage can and Ralph pulled her in. The family laughed together, cried over their marvelous good fortune, and Rhonda wept openly into Ralph's armpit. Roweena had to shelter her new dress from the slobbering tears of her mother's eyes. Ralph broke away in a giant burst of gaiety. He climbed atop the rickety wooden box, balancing precariously. "LOOK AT ME," he screamed at the top of his lungs. "LOOK AT ME GULPO PLAINS! I AM RALPH RODOGGIO!" He tapped his toes on the coffin lid and soon began dancing.

"Ralph!" Rhonda scolded with amusement. "Don't make a spectacle of yourself!"

He jumped from the box, spun on his heels, ending by facing his family, right knee bent, left hand extended. There was some playful applause behind him.

Father Jerome Sassi, with his prayer book tucked under his arm and the collection plate tucked between his knees said, "Well done! You should have been in show business."

"And a hap-hap-happy day to you, Father!"

Sassi handed Ralph the collection plate. "Shall we begin?"

The service was short. Ten words or less expressing sorrow for Rodney's dismal life, and regret over the fact that since he was now a demon from hell cannot reside in the Lord's arms.

"He had an unproductive life; now he's an unclean demon."

"Amen," said one and all.

Later on, as Father Yorrick tallied the takings of the day, he found Stephen Schlonggker's phone number on a bit of paper masquerading as a cash offering. Although Stephen hadn't been invited to the wedding and did not come to the funeral and, in fact, consistently avoids walking anywhere *near* the church day or night so as not to part with any of his hard-earned money, the Long Arm of the Lord had tapped him smartly on the shoulder, which he discovered Monday morning when, with very high expectations placed into his bullet head by his doting mother, he answered the telephone.

THIRTY

Aside from the abundance of annoying flying insects, the Gulpo Park Picnic Center was an ideal place for an outdoor wedding reception, although if Grace Bunz had more time for planning, that is to say if Marty's lunatic mother hadn't been so gungho for a *speedy* wedding, Grace would have preferred a Lake Loon Country Club reception instead; a wedding always seemed classier when someone else did the cooking.

"I didn't buy hamburger buns," she said. It was the fourteenth time she put those exact words together to make that communication. Fourteen times in the space of less than half an hour.

Rodney started counting after the first half-dozen times he heard her say it. What else could he do to keep from going insane? They were using his box as a condiment bar, and Mrs. Bunz and Mrs. Martex acted as serving hostesses while, several feet away, Herbert manned the barbecue grill. Rodney suffered through one batty conversation after another, but this one, about hamburger buns, was the worst yet. He wanted to scream.

People waited for the newlyweds to appear, engaging in small talk and utter banalities. Impatient Herbert Bunz started grilling, so some folks stood around with hamburgers and hot dogs in their hands, letting them get colder and colder, not knowing what was the proper protocol, while others gobbled them down and came back for seconds. Many used their food to swat away insects flying too close to their faces.

"I didn't buy hamburger buns," Grace said yet again, in case Hillary missed it all the other times. "I figure why bother when there are plenty o' hot dog rolls.

It's the same dough they use after all. It *tastes* the same. So, you cut the hamburger up and put it on a hot dog roll. What's the big deal?"

"It makes a *tasty* sam'wich." Mrs Martex concurred. "Who needs to have hamburger buns?"

"I *didn't* buy *any* hamburger buns. You can eat a hamburger on a hot dog roll."

"I can't stand people who are sooo fussy! Hot dog rolls are good enough. Why would anyone want a hamburger bun unless they were *real* fussy. They shouldn't be here if they want hamburger buns. Let them go to some swanky restaurant and get their hamburgers on hamburger buns. Hot dog rolls are good enough."

"That's *exactly* the thing. They use the same dough to make hot dog rolls as they do to make hamburger buns. It makes a tasty sam'wich. You cut up the hamburger. What's the big deal? It's the same flour, the same ovens. Hot dog rolls taste just like hamburger buns. Only someone very, very fussy would have to eat a hamburger on a hamburger BUN. That's the way they give 'em to you at that awful Manny's Jewyburger place. Hamburgers on *Hamburger* buns!"

"Disgraceful!" Hillary Martex clucked her tongue in disgust at the idea.

Yes sir, who needs hamburger buns if you're serving hamburgers? Half-Assed is First Class.

Adele Anasambole in her pretty pink dress approached the condiment bar with a mushed-up hamburger on a hot dog roll. Mrs. Bunz conversationally told her that she did not buy any hamburger buns, that hot dog rolls are made from the same dough and are cooked in the same ovens and taste the same. Adele replied that they should have made sloppy joes then instead of hamburgers.

"You can put sloppy joes on any type o' bread in the world. But the thing about a hamburger is having it all together in a patty on a *bun*." She took a bite of her mushed up hamburger on a hot dog roll dripping with mayonnaise and ketchup. The hot dog roll, softer than a hamburger bun, broke apart all over her dress.

"This is SO typical of the thinking in this goddam town!" she screamed. "First you have to burn your hands all up breaking the *fucking* right-off-the-grill hamburger apart, then you have to make it *all* fit on a stupid hot dog roll, and if THAT'S not enough—you got to try to get the ketchup 'n' may'o'nnaise on it without slopping it all over the place!" Adele stormed off, ranting and raving all the way out of the Gulpo Park Picnic Center, telling the trees, the squirrels, the fucking grass all about it.

"She's sooo fussy," Hillary Martex said. "It's no wonder she's not married."

"What's the BIG-*G-G-G* deal, anyway? Hamburger buns are made from the same dough as hot dog rolls. It *tastes* the same, right? What's the big deal?"

When Herbert Bunz and the other merrymaking men pushed the box into the hole they dug, it in flipped over dumping Rodney belly-first down the long drop. The crate hit bottom with a hard thud, jiggling his dead flesh, wobbling it around like spilled jelly. His body was pressed flat to the coffin lid, while above him came the rapid fire thud-thud-thud of shovelfuls of dirt, each one shaking the box and cutting off more and more light until there was nothing but confining darkness around him, a tight, black void. He figured he was down about twelve feet, under tons of dirt. But, the most horrible thing of all was that he could still hear the dreadful accordion music and rejoicing jackaloons at the party.

The festivities continued through dusk. When at last the party began winding down, about eight o'clock, Rodney's muscles had tightened, pulling together with imbued animation. Gaining control, flexing his legs and arms and stretching his neck, he wondered how he'd get out of his box, let alone this godforsaken hole. He tried to turn over on his back, but there was not room enough to maneuver. Fretting over this new and dismal predicament, wishing with all his heart that he was up top *on* land instead of *in* it, he felt a cooling sensation tingling over his body. It was sort of like being covered head-to-toe with Vick's Vapo Rub; it stung after a bit, getting stronger by the moment. When it was totally unbearable Rodney was engulfed in that luminescent green fog Maestro had brought with him. It cleared, sucking back *into* Rodney and he was amazed to find himself standing in the park looking down on a fresh mound of dirt littered by the remains of partially eaten soggy hamburgers on hot dog rolls. Someone had fashioned a makeshift cross from Popsicle sticks and stuck it into the head of the mound. There was a crossword inscription on it, too:

R
o
R o d n e y
o
g
g
i
o

He recognized Roweena's handwriting. He swallowed dryly, thinking fondly of his sister and her nice gesture. He went to touch the cross, and it seared his hand with an angry sizzle. Black smoke curled up from his fingertips.

Son of a BITCH! Rodney fanned his hand in the air until the hurt subsided.

The park was quiet, save for one or two party stragglers in the distance, drunk and arguing over the up/down issue. Rodney didn't quite know where he wanted his resting place to be, but he sure as hell knew he didn't want it here at the scene of Betty's wedding reception. He then made his first decision as an independent creature of the night—to unearth his box. Working quickly and tirelessly for forty-five minutes, digging with his bare hands, he located the crate and brought it out. Not bad considering Herbert Bunz and four of his construction worker pals took well over an hour to dig the original hole using the shovels Ralph brought. But they were having fun doing it, fooling around, throwing dirt at one another, so Rodney did not take it as an accurate measure of mortals against the undead. He put the coffin under a big oak tree where it would be safe for a while.

Now he was free to enjoy the evening.

THIRTY-ONE

Forty some miles north of Gulpo Plains is Siftracht City, the statewide shopping mecca and melting pot. The main thoroughfare here was called Memorial Boulevard for the many area sons who served our country valiantly in all the Great Wars; locally, however, it was known as Mammarial Boulevard for all the topless joints that serve into the wee hours of the morning. Unlike other main streets, including Main Street in Gulpo Plains, Memorial Boulevard is vibrant, alive with lights and color, teeming with commerce, goodwill, and (very much like all the others) crime. There was a constant people flow on the street ... shops, eateries and amusement areas never closed their doors ... there were no blue laws.

Rodney, gray with gravedirt and smelling of death, merged into the throng unnoticed and practically invisible. It was nearly ten o'clock. He traveled swiftly from Gulpo Plains, walking as only the dead can with feet not touching the ground, legs hardly pumping, but covering a large distance in surprisingly little time. When he came upon Memorial Boulevard, gawking at it like a rubbernecked tourist, he could not get enough of the exotic sights and sounds and smells of the myriad of people. The sidewalk itself was almost as congested as the street, with bumper-to-bumper traffic slowly creeping inch by inch. Cripples, panhandlers, and immigrants passed him in an endless parade; there were young couples on dates, teenagers, a lot of military personnel ... and even some small children wandering alone and unattended. It was a smorgasbord of humanity.

The exotic and upscale shops held little fascination for him, but the sharp city girls, braless, *liberated*, girls, their nipples poking through the material of their blouses, going in and coming out of those shops caught his attention all right.

Watching a long-legged redhead bounce freely past he collided into a newsstand, one of those kiosks like he saw in dozens of movies and television shows. Magazines hanging from the uptilted roof swayed back and forth from the impact. He was amazed at the quantity of papers stacked in front of the booth, each pile held down from errant breeze by a heavy lead disk. Stopping to admire this bit of Americana, taking in the tang of newsprint mixed with the horrid pungency of unwrapped cigars in a wooden box (*Dom de la Caballa 2fer 2bits*), Rodney's eye caught a small column headline on the Siftracht Sun:

DISGUSTING MESS FOUND
ON CHURCH FLOOR

He snatched up a copy of the paper and read:

> GLPO PLNS. According to the Lutheran cousin of a Gulpo Plains construction worker, a mass of unidentified slime was found on the floor of a church here late last night. The cousin, a Loodyville Fire Marshall, alerted media, who checked out the story based on his recognizance and fine morals
>
> Father Horatio Yorrick, chief priest of the Sillificationalist Church of Our Lady of Perpetual Misery, showed great excitement over the slime's appearance and told reporters that he intends to apply for its status as a Miracle from the Almighty.
>
> If the Leader of the Church of United Sillification, which is housed in Wisconsin, declares it a miracle, Gulpo Plains will achieve parity with the Tarsville Church of Saints Alive who discovered the famous crying portrait of Kathryn Khulman in their chancel several years ago.
>
> Father Yorrick further stated that souvenier vials of Miracle Slime are available. A two ounce bottle is free for a donation of 75¢, a $3.00 tribute will get you a six ounce bottle, and thank-

ing the benefactor of the Miracle to the tune of
$20.00 or more nets you the jumbo ten ounce size.

"Hey! Punk!" someone harshly addressed him, a voice so gravelly and deep
with menace that Rodney instantly looked up from the paper thinking that it was
his Aunt Malaysia. He was relieved to see that it was only a skinny little old man
dressed in tatters behind a stack of piled newspapers inside the newsstand.

Having the boy's attention, the man waved his wrinkled fist as a preview of
the pummeling in store for you if you didn't watch out. "You want dat nudes-
pap'pa? Fork over some MOOLAH. This ain't no liberry where ya get to read for
free."

Rodney ignored the newsdealer and turned to the obituary page.

"I sez put dat dere *mutha*eatin' pap'pa *down*, cheap creep! Some folks gotta
earn a *livin'*, ya know." He threw one of the lead paperweights at Rodney's head.
Batting it away with the back of his hand, Rodney continued looking for his
name in the paper. The deadly frisbee zoomed back at the newsdealer.

"*HELP—HELP—HELP! COPS ... POLICE ... I'M BEIN' ROBBED!*"

"Aw, keep your skin on," Rodney hissed. "I'm through with the goddam
thing." Leaving it open to the Rodney-less obits page, he creased the paper in half
and tossed it back on the pile as he fled the scene of the crime.

"*VANDAL ... VANDAL ... VANDAL ...*" the old man screamed after him.

He drifted over to an alley between two storefronts and stood deep in the
shadows watching the populace, feeling very sorry for himself. All of the people
alive and so very lucky—especially the guy waiting at the curb to cross the street,
who was approached by a beautiful blonde girl wearing a very short skirt and high
leather boots. She seemed very affectionate, and something about her struck Rodney as vaguely familiar.

A toss of her long straight-hair snapped it into focus. *Nancy Sinatra!*

He couldn't believe that he was seeing a real celebrity, and wished he could get
a better look at her. She turned toward him, staring in his direction for a
moment. Rodney noticed that in person she didn't look as good as she did on
television in those dreadful shows he was forced to endure. For one thing, she was
wearing an awful lot of face make-up: shiny red lipstick, blue eyeshadow, round
pink rouge cheeks ... why would Nancy Sinatra go out of her way to look like
Clarabell the Clown? And what in the name o' hell did she see in this guy? He
looked like a doofus, a version of one of Benny Fossert's dippy friends. Vernon
Fosleaf twenty years from now. Old Vern was crossing the street now, arm in arm
with Nancy Sinatra. They were headed toward a seedy looking place called *The*

Club Yummy. Rodney's supreme powers of observational reasoning quickly kicked in and he surmised that the internationally famous entertainer was traveling through Siftracht City incognito. The Vernon Fosleafy-doofus must be her agent, who was meeting her for a little business drinkie at *The Club Yummy*. Perhaps she even had a contract to perform there.

He thought it would be nifty to get her autograph, so crossing the street at an angle, weaving around cars and cabs, he stepped up onto the curb in front of the club and was both surprised and *dee*lighted to see a small placard in the draped-off window reading <u>Totally Topless Dancers!</u> *Maybe Nancy Sinatra is in there right now, topless dancing with her agent!!* He pictured a swanky night club dance floor with couples dancing cheek to cheek and all the women with their shirts off. His tongue flicked out and darted hungrily over his lips. He tried to get a look inside when the door opened to eject a happy looking army sergeant, but the muscle-bound bouncer fixed Rodney with a no-nonsense stare. He told Rodney to scram or pay the $5.50 cover charge to come in. "We got a *four* drink minimum, bub," he said bluntly. Rodney, unconcerned, still tried to peek inside, but it was impossible since a wall was blocking his view. The wall held out his hand for the cover charge, and Rodney moved off down the street autographless.

He eventually came to a place called the *Lady Luck Restaurant*. Gazing through the large plate glass window he decided that it was more like a glorified coffee shop than a restaurant, but supposed that Lady Luck *Coffee Shop* didn't have the same ring of joie de vivre as Lady Luck *Restaurant* did. Either way, the place was devoid of customers. At one of the back tables a middle-aged waitress with bright red hair sat counting through a small pile of coins laid out before her. She scowled frequently, re-counting the change, sliding the coins around on the table with her finger. At the other end of the *Lady Luck* was the cash register stand, and behind it, sitting on a high stool, was an attractive girl engrossed in a paperback mystery by Dorkis Wallingford. Rodney stood, transfixed, looking through the window at her. He felt his eyes glow hotly, willing her to look up from her book and see him.

Her head tilted up smoothly, looking at him through the window, her face a mask of pure animal want. Rodney gulped hard, his eyes stopped burning and he looked down uncomfortably. She returned her attention to her book, seeming somewhat confused by the interruption, but the novel bored her now. Glancing around, as if seeing Rodney for the first time, she smiled warmly at him and gestured that he should come in. Naturally, the Invisible Vampire Shield was working. The cashier looked amused, then furtively checked to see if the waitress was watching, and when she was sure it was safe said in a loud whisper, "Come on in," flexing her index finger rapidly.

Rodney, the teenage vampire, stepped through the door quickly before something rotten could happen to screw it up for him. Once inside, he smiled broadly, then remembered his awful, predatory teeth and closed his lips tightly. The girl's eyes were up and down him, as if he were something delicious she'd been waiting for. He went up to the cashier, searching his brain hard for an opening line.

"Slow tonight?" is what he came up with.

"You could say that," she said.

"Table for one, sonny?" the waitress called from the rear.

Rodney reiterated his opening line, then blathered about the weather and the people he saw out in the street. He was just telling her about Nancy Sinatra at *The Club Yummy* when he felt a bony finger poke into his back.

"Table for ONE, *sir?*"

The girl shifted her eyes, indicating to Rodney that he should take the table. The waitress led him to the middle of the restaurant, even though the place was a ghost town, and seated him at a postage-stamp-sized table that was rich in decor. All the other tables were relatively clean, but not this one. It had the customary grease and tar-like stains marring the light colored faux-marble tabletop just like the others, but it also boasted the added attraction of many foodcrusted plates. The yellowing remains of some gooky sauce ran over the edge of one of the plates, forming a little muck lagoon that Rodney did not want to look at. The sugar dispenser, a thick cut-glass canister with a silver top, was badly splattered from past banquets, as were the matching salt and pepper shakers. Cigarette butts floating in cups of unfinished coffee laced with curdled cream and crumpled, mouth-wiped napkins finished the appetizing appearance of the table. Altogether it was repulsive, even for an undead creature no longer interested in mortal sustenance. The waitress thrust a sticky menu into his hands then picked up all the plates at once, dumping some of the leftovers onto the table. She didn't bother cleaning any of it up before going off on her merry way. He opened the menu, which made a prolonged teeth-grating *t-t-t-ccch-h-h-h-t* sound, like tacky tape peeling off leather. The laminated pages were dull and the words printed on the paper almost indecipherable, so he pretended to read while peering over the top at the cashier, who was similarly looking at him over the top of her book. She scrunched her nose cutely. Rodney flirted back, mouthing silently the question, *What time do you get off work?* She shrugged her shoulders, puzzled. He tapped the back of his left wrist with his right index finger, pantomiming his question, then tried to indicate to her that he'd like to see her after work. She was beginning to understand the first part when he felt another sharp poke, this time on his shoulder blade.

"I don't have time to play charades. Just *tell* me what you want to order."

Rodney studied the menu.

"Wel-*l-ll*-l?" the waitress asked with strained patience. "Think I have *nothing* else to do but stand here? I've got work to finish."

Rodney wanted nothing. He looked at the girl, and she encouraged him to order something by pretending to eat, and then pointing at the cash register. She had to do this over and over until Rodney got the hint. The waitress, meanwhile, was tunelessly humming, making it louder and faster with each note, displaying her growing annoyance.

"I'll have a peanut butter'n'jelly sandwich," he told her finally.

"Oh," the waitress said sarcastically. "A real gourmando. I hope you *tip* better than you eat." She yanked the menu out of his hands; if he was human, he'd have some nice friction burns now.

"There oughta be a *law* about letting teenage hoodlums into decent places," she mumbled going off to the kitchen.

The girl behind the cash register had placed her book down flat on the counter, now totally uninterested in it. Her soft brown eyes were glued on Rodney. For many moments they watched each other, Rodney with his mouth open and tongue just about lolling out of his head. She played with a strand of her dark hair, running the tip over her full lips, touching it to her tongue, and finally drawing it in and sucking on it.

She was unbearably sexy, so compelling to look at that he didn't notice the waitress return with his order. She stood there holding a chipped and scuffed dinner plate, her coin dirty thumb rested against the crust of the sandwich. She waited for Rodney to move his elbows so that she could put the meal down in front of him, but he was not getting the hint. The unappealing sandwich, thrown together undoubtedly by a chef who'd rather be hanging from a tree than working the night shift in this dump, was hardly centered on the plate. A gaily colored toothpick with yellow cellophane decorating the visible end was driven squarely into the heart of the uncut sandwich.

"Do you want this or don't you?" the waitress inquired nastily. Since there wasn't enough room for his elbows plus the plate, she flipped the sandwich off onto the slimy table. Rodney's food landed in the lagoon of slop. "You'd better be planning on leaving a BIG tip, honey." She ripped a check off her pad and placed it down on the only clean spot on the table. "All that work for a crummy sandwich."

She huffed through her skinny nose when Rodney didn't enthusiastically dive into the meal. "Well? Aren't you going to *eat* it?"

He looked down at it. A mass of purple, brown and yellow gunk. Picking it up by the corners, the soggy bread fell apart.

The waitress clucked her tongue. "Don't expect me to get you another one! I don't get paid enough to walk my tootsies off for people like *you*!"

Rodney stood up from the table, staring her down. She frowned deeply back, then tapped the check with her finger. At the cash register, making a big pretense of trying to pay, the girl told him that she was taking care of it. She scribbled something on the check and gave it back to him, asking if he had a nice dinner. Grinning, digging his pointy teeth into his lower lip, he nodded and felt like he blushed.

"How 'bout some dessert?" she murmured, ringing up his check dishonestly as a No Sale. "... I'll be home at midnight ..."

"That bum owes us $6.75, including my 25% tip!" the waitress yelled from her table at the back. "Don't let him B.S. you about any returned food!"

"You better go. I'll see you later."

Outside the *Lady Luck Restaurant* Rodney was about to release the check onto the ground, but something caught his eye: the girl had written her name, *Joanni Ygorski*, and her address, *The Mohambi Arms #3G*, on the check, making each "o" a tiny little heart.

It was no fun killing time walking up and down dirty city streets, being bumped into by low-life foreigners and drug addicts. He had an hour and a half to kill, and as excited as his libido was over the prospect of Joanni, his body didn't stir in the same old way. He wondered if, in a fit of humping passion, he might do something terrible—like bite open her throat and drink her blood. That would certainly put a nice little crimp into her pleasure.

Feeling very low, not sure if his fears were legitimate, he tried to bolster his morale by convincing himself that being a blood-drinking obscenity in the eyes of God didn't mean he couldn't control a murderous feeding frenzy if it came on him. Rodney didn't really feel inspired to suck up somebody's blood anyway, so he relaxed a little. If he didn't think like a vampire, he wouldn't *act* like one. Right? He nearly convinced himself, but it didn't help his esteem much when he stopped in front of the sales window of the *Really Big Shoe Shop*, looked in the relective glass and saw only really big shoes. Cursing loudly to himself, like many another citizen on the street, he walked on, passing the *Explo Mod Shoppe* next door and then the *Do Me Hard Massage Parlor*. At the end of this row of buildings was a long, dark alley. Accustomed to see even in the lack of light, he discerned the supine shape of a bulky mortal at the far end. Alive, he sensed—but barely. A flabby arm extended upward, waving a bottle-sized brown paper sack. Rodney nervously checked to see if anyone was watching him from the street, then tip-toed into the darkness of the alley. Coming up on the figure, he saw that it was an old, bloated woman. Dry and broken strands of matted gray hair stood straight up from her grimy head. Her face was soiled with dried vomit and snot, and when she smiled at Rodney, she jiggled a loose front tooth with her tongue.

"Gotta drink on ya, sweetie? I'll make it worth yer while." She hoisted her raggy skirt temptingly. Rodney got down on his hands and knees and crawled toward her. She fell into some kind of stupor, starting to sing *Be My Little Baby Bumble Bee* in an off-key and grating voice. Thoughts of Joanni left his mind as soon as he got his hands around the woman's head. He turned her jugular toward him, appraising the flesh for a place to bite through her blubbery jowls.

Finding the spot, he sunk his teeth through crusty skin into mushy-soft flesh. It was like biting into a stale and sour jelly doughnut. A gush of sickenly sweet warm liquid laced with a hint of gin entered his mouth.

"Oh, HONEY!" the oldie cried out with lust. She wrapped her arms around his torso, dragging him over atop her, then gyrated her hips against him, dry humping like mad.

At the end, right before she died, the woman thrust her hips one last time, surprising Rodney. He involuntarily released some of what was in his mouth and slurped it back. He stood up, satisfied, and wiped his mouth as he looked down at the corpse on the ground. He wondered why Maestro made such a big fuss about feeding, because this was easy. Nothing to write home about. A piece o' cake, really. A walk in the park.

New vitality coursed through him. He felt supremely confident, virile—

—and also a little tipsy.

THIRTY-TWO

Rodney counted twenty-six stories. He whistled in awe, never dreaming that a building as grand as the Mohambi Arms could be located this close to Gulpo Plains. He glided up the curving walkway, passing the neatly trimmed hedges and plantings, each step he took illuminated by round light cast onto the concrete just where his feet fell by hidden walkway lights.

Entry into the Mohambi Arms was through a huge plate glass door. Rodney pressed his nose to it, peering in. The posh foyer was even more impressive than his first view of the building itself had been. Everything inside was done in earth tones, to give a woodsy, nature-like ambiance. There were seven brown velvet settees, flanked by large terra-cotta sofas, a few fluffy pastel yellow easy chairs (tastefully arranged around a cherry coffee table), and all of it on a floor covered in rich wall to wall sand-colored carpet. Oval shaped lavender ashtrays, probably bone china, dangled from the ceiling over the furniture on silver tasseled chords at convenient levels for ash receiving, and some large potted palms along with rubber tree plants were spread throughout. One whole wall was devoted to a mural of lines crisscrossing one another forming squares and triangles of pink mixed with orange stripes and red cubes. The painting was hideous, and Rodney looked to see if the artist had balls enough to sign his work. He searched, and what he saw that looked like a signature on the bottom right was obscured by a pile of dirty clothes and rubbish on the floor. A very peculiar place for laundry to be left, he thought, but who can argue the ways of the rich? A gigantic crystal chandelier illuminated the room with soft, clear light, emulating bright sunshine.

He wondered how a young girl like Joanni, a cashier in a dumpy coffee shop, could afford to live in such a fabulous place.

There was no one inside who could furnish him with the necessary invitation. It was nearing midnight, and it didn't seem likely that any residents were going to come downstairs to pick up their mail or sit in the chairs smoking cigarettes. Rodney paced with anticipation outside the door. It occurred to him that he'd better have handy some sort of ploy to get inside should someone come along. Moments worth of hard thinking, of stopping to stare inside at the pristine furnishings and empty foyer brought him no closer to a solution, until he realized that perhaps he was looking at his answer. A sly smile crossed his lips. The carpet was the key: if Rodney told whoever approached the door that his shoes were a little dirty, did they think it would be okay for him to walk on that nice carpet, the only response to his polite consideration would be *"O' course! Come on in!"*

In Rodney's estimation, it was practically foolproof.

Fifteen minutes later, Rodney saw a skinny little child coming up the long cement walk toward the entrance. Rodney soon realized that it wasn't a child after all, but a very small man. A very small man who fixed Rodney with a nasty stare. He extracted a key from his tattered pocket, a key attached to a very long watch chain wrapped several times around his waist. He put the key into the lock, his beady eyes on the miscreant outside the door.

"Uh, excuse me, sir, but my shoes …"

"Too cheap to buy a stinkin' pap'pa, but mighty *free* to beg favors, eh?" the little old newsdealer said. "Lousy delinquent."

The man pulled open the door and was half through it when Rodney squealed out quickly, "… can I walk on that carpet with dirty shoes?"

"What are you? A *pig*? Were you brought up in'a BARN? Walk on dat carpet with dirty damn *shoes*!" He pushed in and slammed the door in Rodney's face, making extra sure it was locked. Rodney watched him go to the elevator and press the up button; as the old man was stuffing his door key back into his pocket, a wad of his cash tumbled out onto the thick carpet. The elevator doors slid open and the man stepped inside, when he turned to face forward, just as the doors closed shut, he had the perfect view of that grinning, moronic teenager outside shooting him the bird.

Rodney cussed, voicing the wish that someone, some*thing*, would be inside to help. Just then, as if Rodney's supernatural powers were calling forth a being made from inanimate objects, the pile of old clothes and rubbish stirred. At first it moved stiffly, forming itself from the materials at hand, Rodney thought. It shifted, stretched and moved, taking a definite human shape.

It was scary to see this, and now that it was standing in front of the mural, yawning, looking through the glass door at him with blank eyes, Rodney wished he could take back his wish.

"Hey, man," it said. "Is this '*Nam*?"

Rodney shook his head in answer. Now he saw that it was only a derelict, a male human and not some nightmare creature of his making.

The guy looked around, puzzled, scratching his long scraggly beard. He had a moth-eaten woolen cap on his head, pulled down over long hair. Tufts of that greasy hair sprouted out of the moth holes like crab grass on a pitcher's mound. His dark trench coat reached all the way down to the tops of his combat boots and looked like it's seen more action than MacArthur. Rodney found those glassy and vacant eyes disconcerting, and wondered if he had damaged the guy with a vampire spell.

"Jeez, looks *just* like 'Nam." He pulled his beard thoughtfully, studying the mural. "Especially this sunset ... whoa! I didn't know it was so late in the day! He turned and saw the sitting area, then seemed to grasp the idea of where he was. "Wait a second ... are you inside? Or am I outside?"

Thinking swiftly, Rodney called through the thick glass.

"What?" the guy said, cupping his ear.

"You're outside."

"No good! No good, man!" he moaned. "There's snipers out here!"

"Want to come in?" Rodney asked.

The concept was as foreign to him as soap and water. "Come *in*?" he asked.

"Don't mind if I do," Rodney said, delighted, accepting the invitation. He pulled at the door but it would not budge. Inside, the hophead was pulling at the handle likewise.

"Let me in, man! LET ME IN!" He stopped, snapped his fingers and said brightly, "Wait, you gotta open it from the *inside* for me. I don't got no *key*."

"Just turn that handle, shithead," Rodney barked.

"What?"

"Pull!"

"Pill? Naw, man, I got *grassss*. Ooo, baby, go*ooo*od stuffarooni."

Rodney clucked his tongue. "Just PULL the door, jerk off!!"

"Pull my dong and jackoff? Man! How's *that* gonna get me inside?" He shrugged, reached into his disgusting clothes and pulled out his dong.

"No, NO, pull the DOOR open, asshole!"

The guy stared at Rodney. "Put my *dong* up my *asshole*? Jesus *Post-Toasties* Christ! I don't think it'll reach." he began tugging and twisting his organ, trying to pull it around behind him.

"The DOOR," Rodney shouted. "Open the DOOR!"

Now he pushed his pecker against the keyhole, dry humping the door. The communication problem, Rodney believed, wasn't due entirely to the muffling effect of yelling through thick glass: this guy was a real, dyed-in-the-wool, jackass.

He tried one last time. Motioning with a turn of his wrist, he said loudly with strained patience, "Twist-the-door-handle." Rodney was gratified to see that the pile o' rags did exactly that. "Now, *pull* !" The door breezed open releasing Freon-scented air conditioning. Rodney rushed into it.

"Weee-ooo!" The guy grabbed his nose with both hands. "You smell like the killing fields!"

"Great, just great," Rodney hissed. "What the fuck am I going to do *now*?"

"Fuck you now? I don't think so, man! *She-e-it*! You need a wash-up first, baby! Come back to my 'partment and you can use my bathroom."

Rodney was amazed. "You *live* here? How the hell can *you* afford to live here? What's the rent? Twenty-five bucks a month?"

"Twenty-five my hairy beansack! Try *eight* twenty-five a month. Government foots most of it, and I supplement with my sales managerial position."

"You were in Viet Nam?." Rodney asked sympathetically.

"Fuck NO! I was in *Canada*! I wasn't going to no 'Nam, no siree! Wanna buy some grass? Goood stuffarooni!"

Rodney wanted to ask him why the Government was footing the bill if he was a goddamn deserter, but any answer he got along those lines would bound to lead him into a deeper quagmire than he was already in, so he decided to forget it. He let his host guide him down the long hallway to a public washroom. "Here we are. Make yourself at home."

"*This* is your apartment?" Rodney asked.

"Hell, no! Mine's upstairs, but I didn't want you smelling it up with your slaughterhouse odor, so I brought you here instead." Rodney gave him a dirty look and went right for the sink where he filled a basin with water from the tap. Dipping his face into the water, glugging around, he was surprised to find that his face felt very, very warm, on fire almost. His eyes stung as if they were flushed with Listerine. Quickly coming up from the sink, eyes smarting, he walked blindly around, groping for a towel. He rammed into a toilet stall door. Changing direction, he brusquely asked for a little guidance. The jerk sounded like he was answering him from a billion miles away. Rodney wasn't aware that a cloud of rancid green mist was engulfing him.

THIRTY-THREE

Rodney found the towel. Blowing his nose into it first, then wiping his eyes with the rough fabric, he thought: *What lousy towels for such a ritzy place.* They smelled terrible, too. Vile, stale, like they haven't been washed since before Lucille Ball's been on television. His eyes hurt less. He tentatively squinted open one eye and saw that the towel was a cheap red burlap, soiled with gummy streaks. He tugged it, hoping that the towel dispenser had a clean spot further up the roll, but there was no metallic grinding of gears, no draw of cloth into the machine's take-up. He opened his eyes wide, and tugged harder. A monstrous green face zoomed down at him, red eyeballs blazing, pointed devil-ears waggling. There were a couple of sharp-tipped, lethal-looking, horns on top of it's lime-textured bald dome. The thing smiled. Long ivory tusks jutted out over a sagging, juicy, bottom lip.

"Yikes!"

"Ah! Brother Vampire" the thing said, puffing a blast of noxious gas out of it's mouth right into Rodney's face. "Welcome to The Kingdom!" Rodney pressed his nose flat with the palm of his hand, averting his face. Insulted, the goblin stood upright to his full twelve foot stature. "I am Goblin Emergent. Head Goblin is awaiting audience with you." Rodney noted with disgust that the stains on the thing's red burlap robe fell right in line where underneath would be its big green pickle.

His new surroundings were equally dismal: a misshapen stone room, like a cavern in a cave lit by flickering verdant light from some unknown source. The air was heavy and wet—and a trifle *too* warm. Rodney could only guess where they rented this space, and it turned out for one of the few times in his life and afterlife that he was correct. This was an antechamber in Hell, where you'd wait to take up any official Kingdom business. Goblin Emergent said that it would not be unusual to be cooling your heels waiting here for decades since Head Goblin is *very* busy. The place was filled with castoffs from the real world, old and discarded furniture that had been replaced on earth due to wear or by something more modern. The care with which things were arranged gave Rodney the impression that either these creatures were attempting to make a comfortable environment for the newly dead, or that the designer had tremendously bad taste. The idea of thrift never entered his head.

"Uh, do you think I can come back some other time," Rodney said meekly. "I've got an appointment ..."

He was ignored. The goblin lifted his hands and although he had no thumbs, snapped his fingers. An opening appeared in the wall beside the ornate, but warped, Louis XIV reception table upon which sat a tarnished Proctor Silex coffee pot and some saucer-less Melamine cups plus an open jar of Creamora. He was led—literally—*down* a passageway, going deeper and deeper underground at a severe angle, to an area at one end of a long platform situated in a tremendous cave. This platform divided the cave into two distinct portions, the larger to his right. He felt like he was waiting in the wings to go on stage.

"Looks like Radio City Music Hall," the goblin said proudly.

Except for the bumpy and sharp-angled boulders instead of those soft velveteen padded seats, Rodney thought gloomily.

The platform, a tremendous dais, where the stage would be, was lit by an amber baby-spot focused dramatically down on it.

Spectators were arriving. The auditorium filled with the sounds of chatter and of disagreements as everyone looked for comfortable boulders. Soon, the house lights dimmed and blacked-out completely, then bright light filled the dais area and sitting now up there was a huge throne, and sitting on the throne, attended by ten carbon-copy creatures all dressed in the same cheap red burlap, was Head Goblin. His cheap burlap robe was decorated with what looked like cheap gold Christmas Tree tinsel on its shoulders, like epaulets. Miscellaneous creatures entered from the opposite side, emissaries from various demonic groups. They knelt in front of the throne and offered human sacrifices and other goodies to Head Goblin.

It seemed as if this groveling went on forever, but finally the creatures were done and took seats in the audience. Goblin Emergent then shoved Rodney out into the light, following closely behind. It was a packed house; you could hear the scrapings of feet-against-stone, grunts of effort, as the audience tried to stay put in their seats and not slip off them. There was a smattering of applause when Goblin Emergent appeared, and he acknowledged this with a polite nod, then turned to the throne. Bowing deeply—so deeply, in fact, that his beeky nose nearly touched the floor—he said, "Sire, this is Brother Vampire Robrooneo."

"Rodney Rodoggio," Rodney said.

"*Silence*, underling," the Head Goblin commanded quietly, but with great authority. "I am Head Goblin, Supreme Ruler of Time, Space, Destiny and *YOU*. These are your kith and kin," he lifted his mighty arm, stretching his powerful green hand out over his Kingdom. Under his arm was a dark sweat stain. Wet'n'Fresh, went through Rodney's mind. Several kith (or were they kin?) up front shrank back on their rock seats, fanning their noses secretly.

"Meet now *THE GOBLIN COMMITTEE*." The large green goblins at the dais lifted their pompous chins to him. "Most of the Goblin Committee is out in the field," Head Goblin stated, trying to make it sound like a valid excuse for their small goblin population

Rodney heard some sniggering. Goblin Emergent stepped closer to the front row and it ceased.

"—but I'm happy to report that we have *full* attendance otherwise. So, without further adieu, here are your brothers, *THE VAMPIRE LEGION*." Hundreds of maestros stood up in the audience. They began hooting, hollering and shape-shifting, much like democrats at a caucus, changing forms from wolf to bat and then back to the familiar human. Several vampires honored the newcomer by staying bats and flying into Rodney's face, squeaking and farting up his nose. Some other ones, not to be upstaged, turned wolfen, wagging tails happily. Rodney's attention was caught by several human-form vampires sitting apart from the rest. They winked at him, blowing baby kisses in the air.

Head Goblin saw them too, and he clucked his tongue. "Fruit Loops," he said, and not so softly either. "*Vamp*ires ..." He didn't bother waiting for them to stop showing off before presenting the next group.

"*THE FRATERNITY OF GHOULS.*"

All the vampires sat down now and behaved themselves; in their place, extraordinarily thin creatures of almost equal number limply arose from the audience. The ghouls had sickly yellow skin hanging loosely over their skeletons, they looked like dribbling melted candles. With bulging eyes and thick saliva running down their lips and chins, and showing all the stamina of wax beans boiled several hours, they didn't do much in the way of welcome except stand there looking awful. And *hungry*.

"*THE WARLOCK SECTOR.*"

There were less warlocks than there were vampires and ghouls. When they were called, they levitated up from their seats in a showy fashion. Apparently, warlocks thought of themselves as wizards, for each one of these ersatz Merlins wore flowing navy blue silk robes emblazoned with yellow stars and moons and traditional matching conical hats. The shamans all sported flowing white mustaches, too. They got to be very annoying with their magic wands, which they pointed and waved continuously, tapping each other with them, and poking the heads of those unlucky enough to be sitting in front of them. When they turned their attention to Rodney, he felt like the first string under a Boston Pops of Arthur Fiedlers.

"Last and very least," Head Goblin said with absolutely no interest, "the Lycanthrope Litter," A handful of scruffy werewolves at the back of the house stood up, scowling. Anyone could see that they were a pack of malcontents.

"There are others," Head Goblin sneered. "The *distaff* side. The Sisterhood of Witches and some female vampires, but they're barred from our business meetings since we are a fraternal group," he shot a look over to the Fruit Loops, "more or *less.*"

Rodney wondered when they were going to get to the point of all this; it seemed like hours since he was whisked out of the Mohambi Arms bathroom.

There was some commotion as three late coming goblins pushed through the crowd from the back, displacing a few werewolves who slipped off their seats and landed their hairy keesters painfully on the floor. They pushed and shoved and bullied their way through the assembly to the dais, joining their brethren by the throne. A hush fell over the house.

"Quorum!" someone said mockingly. Many incensed goblin eyes searched the audience but everyone was sitting stock still, hands (or paws) crossed in their laps so the wag got off scot-free.

The three new greenies gave Rodney the once over, rolling their red eyes and faintly clucking their tongues. Rodney self-consciously brushed at his blue suit and felt very much out of place. Two of them made a big show of standing century while the third conferred with the Chief. A smile crept across Head Goblin's evil face. He looked down at Rodney, who by now was shuffling his feet nervously.

"I am informed that you have brought us an initiate! I dearly hope you do better in that department than your late lamented predecessor." Goblins chuckled.

"By the way, I heard he had a little *accident* with holy water." There were outright laughs from the Goblins. Head Goblin was on a tear. The next one should bring the house down.

"That's what happens, I guess, when you aspire to be a *Pizza* party." It fizzled and died to some forced coughs and throat clearings. Head Goblin's mood turned a little sour. "Be that as it may, you will find that we are very forgiving and can be quite helpful to you. Helping you out of your coffin was just a sample of our generosity."

Rodney's jaw dropped open. "That was *you*? I thought it was *my* power! You mean to tell me that you were *watching* me?"

"Did you know I control the elements? Did your recruiter tell you that?" The werewolves mumbled and groaned, mouthing along silently the often heard and tiresome litany: "I control time and space, the earth, the stars, the moon."

Goblin Emergent cleared his throat. He was recognized. "Of course we were watching. We are aware of everything. Want to see something funny?" Rodney was not so sure that he did, and when he didn't leap at the opportunity, the goblin bulldozed ahead anyway. With a flick of his wrist, he motioned one of the goblin lackeys over. This seven foot tall green creature with red eyes and badly stained red burlap robe, folded his arms into his chest, then holding his left elbow in his right hand, his chin in his left, looking for all the world like Will Jordan about to launch into his Ed Sullivan impersonation, he turned his back on Rodney. When he turned back again, he was—

Mr. Pursnikky, the merry mailman!

"How'dee'doodle'do, Master Rodoggio?" Rodney was flabbergasted. This was Mr. Pursnikky in the flesh, not some pale impression. The goblin had actually shrunk himself down, changed clothes, and was smelling whole lots cleaner.

"Sire, shall we proceed with the Rite of Initiation?" asked the mailman.

"In a moment … I'm enjoying this!" The green bastard fairly glowed, his good spirits restored.

"Wha-a-at?" Rodney stammered when he was able to speak. "You goblins impersonate people to spy on us?"

"No-o-o-o, not exactly. Some people you know as people are really GOB-LINS."

How do you know who are people and who are goblins? Rodney was seriously creeped out by this new knowledge. *God! What next?*

"Oh, you can tell." Head Goblin answered, reading his mind. "Unless, of course, you're *very* stupid." He relished the look on Rodney's face. Priceless!

The goblins were getting antsy to see the delicious treat awaiting initiation, and under their duress Head Goblin ordered the Initiation Altar to be brought forth. He snapped his four-fingered hand. Rodney, asleep as usual, missed it: he wanted to see *how* goblins were able to snap with no thumbs. He was trying it himself, keeping amused during the boring parts of the meeting, and the best he was able to do was make a sick little *th-h-wwwkk* noise with his index nail off the bottom of his middle finger.

Off in the wings came a sound like squeaky casters. The throng at the throne parted and two disgruntled werewolves huffed and puffed, pushing what looked like an old industrial hotel bed from the 1930s, brass grill headboard and all. It was covered by a bedspread of red burlap.

"NOW ...," Head Goblin said as every one of the goblins rubbed their hands together. Their collective leathery skin made a sandpapery din echoing throughout the arena, setting many a preternatural tooth on edge.

"... BRING ON THE DELECTABLE INDUCTEE!!"

"Here come the *Rockettes*," a ghoul in the front row grumbled.

A great puff of green smog appeared in the midst of the dais. Lute music started playing; it must be piped in from a purloined Muzak machine, because there wasn't anyone in sight playing an instrument—at least one that makes music. The smog dissipated, slowly lifting and spreading away to reveal a gaggle of haggy witches in ring formation, their backs to the audience. Because they wore ritual transparent gowns, their puckery posteriors were in full display. They held this ringed position for several beats of lute music, then started to sway their hips very slowly. Subtle lighting changes, from full bright to a muted fuchsia, mercifully dulled detail. Rodney stole a glance over at the goblins, and in the spillover light saw that they were actually drooling with anticipation. The ugly witches were reconforming into a line, treating the audience with a frontal view, performing a geriatric version of a south sea island passion dance. Slowly, the line parted. Lights went dim. A bright spot appeared, but someone missed a cue because it revealed nothing. Two witches frantically maneuvered the inductee into the light then stepped back quickly into the darkness.

Hands immediately stopped rubbing. If anyone had the guts, they would have shouted to bring back the witches because as bad as they were to look at, what was now in their place was much, much worse. It was, of course, the same woman Rodney supped upon in the ally. She'd been cleaned up, her hair was combed, and she now had the customary mouthful of pointy teeth. Outside of this, death hadn't done much for her. Her initiation robe, a gossamer baby-doll nightie, highlighted her body to a frightening degree. In the bright light, and being so close to the dais, Rodney noticed the hasty alteration to the gown: apparently, it had been originally made with a much smaller figure in mind and had to be enlarged to suit the need.

"*This* is what you bring us?" Head Goblin complained. "Since you brought her, you initiate her." He raised his arms and green fog encompassed Rodney. "And be *quick* about it!" Coughing from the fumes, eyes stinging, he was transported to the time and space he'd occupied before being brought to the Kingdom. Roughly. It was now thirty minutes later than when he left. And he did not return alone.

"Are you going to initiate me now?"

"Uh ..."

"Call me Norma, my *maestro.*"

The stall door swung open, Harry Hophead was sitting on the toilet taking a dump even though he'd forgotten to pull down his pants. "*Norman*! Man! Is that *you*? I thought they got'cha last month, threw your ass right over to 'Nam!"

It's too bad, Rodney thought, that he couldn't arrange to use the one hump to hump the other hump and get both humps off his back. "Hey, man," Rodney said, affecting the parlance of the disenfranchised and sounding hip. "Wanna meet a *real* groovy chick and get laid?"

Harry jumped up from the toilet, rubbing his crotch lustily. "Yeah! Bring it on! ... and get a girl for my buddy, Norman, huh ... oh, and one for the guy with the teeth, he's waiting inside ..."

Rodney pushed the female vampire into the stall. "Meet Norma!" He tried to close the door, confining them together, but Norma's undead ass got in the way and the door wouldn't close.

"Hot diggity damn, Norman! What the *fuck* did those 'cong do to you? You look like shit!"

Rodney pushed at Norma, all his supernatural strength was needed to cram her into the tiny stall. "Have a good time you two!"

"Where's my peckerpleaser?" he moaned, trying to see past Norma.

"Here," Norma said, itching for initiation.

"What? NORMAN? You're a *fairy*?" He sounded edgy, shielding his crotch against invasion. "Hey, like, I don't wanna get *involved*. Know what I mean? I'm not into long term relationships ..."

Norma backed off, highly insulted. "Watch it, sweetie-pie," she hissed. "Or I'll have the maestro bite the blood right out o' you. You have no right interfering with my initiation!"

"Initiation? What's this? The Elk's Club? Am I an *Elk*, man?"

"No," Norma stated, raising her voice, "you're a wigged out asshole".

Rodney left the bathroom, happy to know that the two of them hit it off better than he expected. He went back to the foyer, heading for the elevator. What was her apartment number? He reached into his pocket for the slip of paper and it was gone. But how? He thought he was being toyed with, a definite possibility after seeing those goddamn goblins at work. Concentrating, he conjured the image of Joanni's handwriting, picturing the sexy little hearts in place of *o*'s. It came to him: 3G. *Yup!* He smiled, then gulped.

What if Joanni's a goblin?

Get it out o' your mind, out o' your mind ... forget it ... forget it ... get it out ... asswiping ... dirtlicking ... sonofabitch ... jesushumping ... GOBLINS ...

At the elevator, he pushed the Up button and waited. And waited. Nothing happened. He pushed it again. Still nothing, not even the rattle of the car moving from some other floor. He pushed the button yet again, harder this time. The indicator above the door was stock-still. He pushed the button again and again in rapid succession until he pushed so hard the button jammed. Still the elevator did not come.

Screw THIS!

There had to be a service stair entrance somewhere, so Rodney started looking until he found it. This took quite a while, and his search led him back to the bathroom door where, thankfully, all was quiet inside. The service stairs were, ironically, next to the elevator, the one door he assumed was locked. Rodney raced up the gray cement flight of stairs until he found the third floor. Pushing open the heavy door, a low, droning noise greeted him. *Whoosh*-clunk-*whoosh*. *Whoosh*-clunk-*whoosh*. *Whoosh*-clunk-*whoosh*.

The second thing Rodney noticed was that this floor was dark and dreary as compared to the brightly-lit and well-kept foyer. Ten-watt bulbs in fixtures set in the ceiling fifteen feet above shed economic light down on a carpet that was old, badly worn and stained. It might have been a golden color when it was first installed, but now it had the hue of rotten egg yolk. The walls were a nasty stucco, painted orange, apartment doors a lawn green.

The *first* thing he noticed, of course, was the dead body laying across the elevator threshold, blocking the door from closing completely. As it begins to close, the sliding door smacks into the body with a disturbing contact sound the Three Stooges would relish, the body jiggles, the door zips back. *Whoosh*-clunk-*whoosh*. Over and over again.

He might've guessed *exactly* who it was who would drop dead coming off the elevator, causing him so much grief. Who else but that pain-in-the-ass newspaper dealer, Mr. Moolah with his tattered clothes and wads of cash. Rodney wondered bitterly if *his* name would make it to the obituary page in the next issue of the Siftracht Sun.

Joanni's apartment was past the elevator, the second door on the left side. *Hello Lover* was written on a note taped to the door, a tiny hearts in place of the *o*s. He suddenly felt tense. Although it was not possible, his hands felt clammy. Did he need an invitation? Reason said to stop being ridiculous: he's in the building by invitation, and that was that. He grabbed the brass door knob. An electric shock, like a spiteful joy buzzer, ran through his hand and up his arm.

GodDAMMITshitshitshitFUCK ... *GodDAMMITshitshitshitFUCK* ... *GodDAMMITshitshitshitFUCK* ... *GodDAMMITshitshitshitFUCK* ...

He shut up after several moments, when he realized that he was cursing to the rhythm of the elevator. Those green bastards had a hand in this. He knew it. He could see Head Goblin grinning, flashing his big yellow tusks. Rodney shook his fist at the ceiling, first to show God his displeasure for allowing goblins, vampires and the whole damn Kingdom for existing, then took out his anger at the floor to cover *them* as well. He kicked with frustration at Joanni's door and the barrier sent him spinning across the hall, knocking into the door of apartment 31. The naked man who opened the door did not look at all happy to see Rodney sprawled out in front of him on the floor.

"What do *you* want?"

"Me?" Rodney asked, innocently.

"Listen, creepo, I ain't gonna play no games with you. *Either* you tell me why you're bothering me this time o'night, or I punch your face down yer THROAT."

"Who IS it, Alvin?" an annoyed woman called out from inside the apartment.

"Some punky kid playing games with the door!"

"The NERVE!" she bleated. "Call the police. Imagine! Playing games with peoples' doors!"

Alvin yelled back, "I don't need to call the cops! I can take care of this cocklicker by myself!"

"Don't be foolish! He might have a *knife*. Throw a shoe at him."

"Throw a *shoe*, Selma? Give him something he can pawn? That's what he WANTS, you know, to rip people off. Why else would he be prowling around at one damn thirty in the morning? He's looking for things to steal ... to pay for his SEX and DRUGS. That's ALL these young bastards can think about." He poked Rodney with his foot. "Isn't that right, young punk? You ain't nothin' but a PIG."

"Alvin! Come back to BED for Christ'sakes. You'll catch your death o' cold out there in the hallway."

The man wrinkled his brow angrily and his hairpiece rippled up, sliding down over the back of his head. He licked his dry lips, flexing his muscles. "Now, punko pig, I'm gonna fix your ASS."

The service stair door opened. A shrewlike woman, grunting and groaning while hefting a large suitcase, came into the hallway. She looked with disgust at the elevator, then she spotted Alvin. Dropping her bag to the floor, she said: "John! What are you doing out in this hallway with absolutely no clothes on? What's that *silly* hairy thing on your head? Who is that *boy*??"

"Why—hulloo, hon," he said, grinning nervously. "I thought you'd be at your mother's a few more days …"

"Who's out there NOW, Alvin?" came a playful voice from the apartment. "Ooooo! I hear *another* woman!"

"Uh … uh …" Alvin called back.

"And *who* is that in my house?" the woman with the suitcase asked.

"Uh … uh …"

She lifted the suitcase, gave him one doozie of a smack with it, and pushing him inside slammed the door behind them. Rodney heard a lot of yelling. Objects, some very weighty judging by the sound of them, hit the door. There was breaking china, and loud "uh, uhs" of protest. During this, yet another woman came from the service stairs, looked in disgust at the blocked elevator, then hearing the din from the apartment and seeing Rodney, hightailed it back down the service stairs.

"Don't worry, Mister," he said loud enough to be heard through the door and above the racket. "I'll fix my own ass now. Thanks for the offer anyway." Then he added mischievously "Oh, and there's *another* lady out here looking for you." He waited a moment, heard the waning bombardment begin anew and felt satisfaction.

Back at Joanni's door, he contemplated knocking but ruled that out as being very uncool. He wondered if there was a fire escape he could climb up. He could knock on her window, and she'd think he was being daring, adventurous and romantic.

Flitting down the steps, two at a time, he got to the foyer very quickly. The resident druggie and Norma were sitting on the floor in front of the glass door, smoking and leaving ash all over the carpet.

"Maestro!" Norma shrieked with unearthly joy.

"Christ aw'mighty, Norman! You should be eating *Airwick*! Your mouth smells like a friggin' ginmill!"

"Get out of my *way*," Rodney hissed, unsuccessfully trying to push past them. Norma grabbed hold of one of his legs.

"I think we're outside now, so if you're goin' outside you're goin' the wrong way."

"I'm trying to get up to 3G, freako …" Rodney stopped talking. He bit his tongue as hard as he could.

"Is that *inside* …?"

Rodney broke Norma's hold and rammed open the door. He went left first, keeping in mind the elevator's position inside the building, and Joanni's apartment in relationship to it. The rusty metal fire escape was relatively easy to find; it took Rodney only about half an hour to do it. Climbing up, he lost count of the floors and ended up way above where he needed to be. Working his way back down, gazing into bedroom windows looking for Joanni, he considered himself lucky that almost everyone was asleep. He kept better count and this time had no doubt he found the right apartment.

Inside the dark room a lone figure stirred on a bed. Rodney tapped the glass window. The table lamp flicked on. A fierce-looking, bald-headed man angrily scoured the room with his eyes until his steely gaze fell on Rodney. Rodney was busy reconstructing his movements in his head, wondering how he went wrong, as the man got out of bed and came toward the window. Rodney hastily climbed up another flight, but the guy was quick. The window flung open, a meaty hand reached out, Rodney's foot was grabbed, and then Rodney was tugged off the fire escape, falling four stories to the ground below.

This time, he counted *carefully*. Now on three, looking in the window, he could plainly see Joanni laying naked on her bed, a silk sheet hardly covering her. Her bedroom had been romantically lit by candlelight, although now the dozens of candles were mere stubs. As he lifted his finger to tap, her door opened and Rodney heard a disgustingly familiar voice.

"Hey, maestro, man, are you in here or out there?" Rodney noticed that Harry Hophead held in his hand the restaurant check with Joanni's address.

Joanni sat up. "Why, hulloo," she said. The sheet slid away from her body.

"Wowie! Hulloo girlie-girl, man! Am I inside or outside?"

"Outside, *now*," she patted the place on the bed beside her. "Just put a little donation on my dresser." He tossed onto the dresser the wad of cash he picked up from the carpet in front of the elevator. Soon nobody had any doubt, not Rodney nor Joanni,—and not even Harry himself—that he was inside.

THIRTY-FOUR

"Go back to your alley, for cryin' out creepers," begged Rodney of Norma as she followed close at his heels, leaving the Mohambi Arms far behind them. Norma dropped back several paces. They walked along the Great Alouba Parkway, leaving Siftracht City and heading toward Loodyville on the way back to Gulpo Plains. Norma kept yoo-hooing to Rodney and offering reminders galore of Head Goblin's edict, all of which Rodney ignored until it got on his nerves so badly that he finally snapped. He stopped dead, turned on his heels and yelled in her face.

"Listen, I'm not doing *every*thing those goblins say. What do you think I am? A *werewolf*? Something to jump through hoops for their warped fun? I'm a *vampire*. I've got a mind o' my own! Get it?"

"But Head Goblin said …" she chidingly cautioned, wagging her thick forefinger at his face.

"Sca-a-*roo* Head Goblin and all those little green goblinettes too—!"

Before he could finish this sentiment, Rodney was spirited away in an angry green cloud. When it cleared, he was laying at the oversize, smelly feet of Head Goblin himself.

"You were saying, Brother Vampire?"

"Wel-l-l-l.…"

"We do not tolerate insolence and insubordination. There are *severe* penalties for those that do." Thick black smoke came out of his tusky mouth, his nose and his ears. He twirled his head thrice. A bell clanged. Rodney felt something vanish, pull away completely from his body, removed as if it never was there.

"Whoa-a-a," he screeched, three octaves higher than his usual squeaky falsetto. He had the sudden urge to blow air kisses at the hairy werewolf just coming up to the throne.

"O, Noble Sire, King of the Kingdom, Ruler of Undead, Master of the Unknown. Have a heart, O Wise One." He had a southern accent, a definite laconic drawl just like Huckleberry Hound. Bowing and bending, making a real brown-nose spectacle of himself to the Head Goblin, the werewolf continued, "Removing Brother Vampire's Mortal Privilege will cause terrible ramifications to the werewolf population. Please remember, Sire, we are an endangered species."

"Down, boy!" Head Goblin chortled. He didn't stop at the verbal put-down either. He reached out his grandiose hand and scratched the lycanthrope behind his shaggy ear. The werewolf pretended to pump his leg. Head Goblin bellowed laughter, then patted him on the head between both ears. The werewolf bit his tongue and stood there obediently until it was over.

Turning his attention back to Rodney, the Supreme Ruler of the Kingdom of Undead said, "Too bad I don't have a pair of slippers he can fetch." Then he sighed. A big, drawn-out huffy sigh from the bottom of his goblin guts, smelling of brimstone, ether, and something familiar that made Rodney think of Kix cereal. "I'll be lenient with you this time."

The bell in Rodney's head clanged twice. Head Goblin sucked that black greasy smoke, now pulled from the matrix, back into his being through every hole in his head. Twirling his head counterclockwise thrice, the spell was undone and Rodney's Mortal Privilege returned. Green fog swirled at his feet.

"Uh, your Highness, a moment with Brother Vampire, please?" the fog stopped. Head Goblin smiled at the werewolf. "Why, certainly! I hope you can impart the *wisdom* of following my orders to our young friend." To Rodney he said with a theatrical whisper behind his hand, "You should thank Brother Werewolf for the return of your Mortal Privilege. Have you got any Milk Bones?"

Several of Head Goblin's consorts laughed heartily. Rodney followed the hairy creature into the privacy of the deserted auditorium, where he sat down on one of the more trustworthy looking boulders. It was so slick with unworldly gunk that he nearly slid to the floor, so he tried one not so shiny. This had rocky jags that dug into his crotch, but to show dignity he made a pretense at looking comfortable. "Thanks, Brother Werewolf," he said sincerely.

"Listen, selfish shithead," the creature growled. "My race is steadily diminishing. There's suddenly an awful lot of Lone Rangers out there and *we need new werewolves.*"

"Don't you *bite* people to make werewolves? 'Even a Man who's Pure in Heart …'"

The werewolf clucked his tongue. "Freakin' movies! What a *jackass*! Because so many of you vamps are *queer*, and those that aren't are selfish louts who think more of *feeding* than *fucking*, my race has become low-man on this damn totem pole." Seeing the blank look on the idiot's face, a look that indicated Rodney needed some new lightbulbs in his three-ways, the werewolf asked exactly *what* was told him about Kingdom responsibilities.

Rodney shrugged. The werewolf rolled his eyes upwards. "Boy, you're a *gem*, aren't you? Weren't you told that vampires create new werewolves by having union with mortal females?"

Rodney was horrified. "You mean, every time I … you know, a *werewolf* comes out?" The creature nodded.

"And the host mortal dies, don't forget that little tid-bit."

"Jeez! Isn't there any other way werewolves are made? Like, what happens when *you* do it with mortal girls?"

The werewolf snarled in disgust. "Where the hell do you think those green goofballs come from?"

"Well … what happens when mortals do it with vampire women?"

"They get the *clap*! What d'ya think happens, dumbo? Nothing happens! Sheesh!" He was rolling his eyes and about to cluck his tongue when the familiar fog started to form around Rodney.

"Do your duty," the werewolf was saying as Rodney was carried off, floating suspended in air. "Get laid, get laid …"

The fog did not gently drift away this time. It just utterly vanished, leaving Rodney high in the air above the Gulpoville Little League Field, which was out in the middle of nowhere, caught between Loodyville and Gulpo Plains. The Little League field was one of the more popular spots for the dog populations, as well as being a constant source of friction between the towns, each claiming it as their own. It was an ideal dumping ground: even strays two towns over found their way here to use the facilities; the overly large pitcher's mound (from where right-handed Tommy Gurgin pitched the famous knuckleball that beaned Solly Solé—who was sitting in the bleachers along the third base) was actually the living testament of this canine fascination.

Norma was sitting roughly where Solly Solé had been. As if watching a descending pop fly, she traced Rodney's path with her eyes, jumping up as he splat-landed squarely onto the pitcher's mound.

"Is it time for my initiation?"

He ignored her and just walked, brushing and flicking at his clothes as he went along. Norma followed doggedly. Going from one Loodyville street to the next, Rodney tried to lose her with his vampiric speed and find his direction home. He crossed railroad tracks just as a graffiti embellished train whizzed by. When he looked back, certain that she was on her way to Cleveland now, he was dismayed to see her floating in the air high above where the train had been. She landed softly behind him.

"Whew," she said. "I didn't know I could do *that!*"

It wasn't long before they came to the intersection of Abelard Avenue and Heloise Drive, right at the junction where Loodyville became Gulpo Plains. Gas stations did business on three of the four corners, but the fourth corner belonged to a greasy looking bullet-shaped silver railway car diner. Saucer lights lit the front of the building, spilling reflective light out onto the tarmac making the street look oil-slick. Blood red neon above a small door spelled out:

Corky's
OPEN 24 HOURS EAT ALL NITE

Rodney knew of this place. It had the reputation of being a hangout for lonely old men, insomniacs, and winos. During Manny's closed hours, truck drivers and other roughnecks also frequented the place. Fights started here quicker than you could order a cup of coffee, and death was often the blue plate special. Or so Rodney believed.

Just the right place to find Norma a boy friend.

He installed her in a dark recess of the building's shadow by a street mailbox, and told her to stay put, then went back to the door, waiting for someone to come out. Soon, a glazed-eyed old man with ketchup smeared over his mouth and the remains of his meal on his shirt hobbled through the door.

Rodney asked, "Is it busy in there?"

"Naw! Plenty o' room! C'mon in!" the customer replied. He noticed Norma, creeping out of the shadows, licking her lips. "Bring yer wife, too. She looks *hungry.*"

Rodney flicked his hand at her then dashed up the small stone steps to the door, crossed over the threshold squeezing past the old man. The place was packed almost to capacity. Harsh fluorescent lighting playing off grimy chrome and Formica gave the place an almost metallic sepia look, like a memory of the nineteen fifties. Silverware rattled against dishes, raucous conversations and juke-box music filled the smoky air. A stocky man with thick jet-black dyed hair came out from behind the cash register. He was wearing a dark green apron embroidered with "Corky's" in yellow stitches over a greasy white tee-shirt and dark work pants. He wiped his hands constantly on those pants and on his shirt but not once on the apron, which was spotless. He had the largest hooked nose Rodney ever saw.

"Welcome to *Corky's*!" he shouted over Dusty Springfield. "I am *Corky*! Corky Corkanapolis! My friends call me CORKY! This is *my* eatery. Let me find you a table so you can eat in comfort my friend!" He stood up on tip-toes and gazed over the narrow diner. Aside from a long counter with shorter ends on either side, customers were at the booths lining the walls plus at a couple of the freestanding tables crammed into the corner by the entrance to the bathrooms. "Ah, yes!" Corky said, pointing to one of those loose tables. "That one is free!" Corky gave him a playful shove in the right direction, and Rodney wormed his way through the crowd. From his jammed-in position, Rodney scanned the place for a likely candidate, which he found right under his nose seated at the counter's short end beside his tight table. Half-blind and smelling of Old Hen's Foot, the geezer didn't respond to repeated p-s-sts or pokes. Rodney stood up, intending to lean over and yell in the senile old bastard's ear when Norma squeezed in and sat herself down on a recently vacated counter stool all the way in front.

She stared across, diagonally, at Rodney, and Rodney gave her an angry farewell wave that caught the attention of the serving girl behind the counter. "Just a *moment*," the girl said wearily, returning to her business at hand. She was a thin little thing with short mousy brown hair and big round glasses. She raced back and forth serving orders and placing new ones with the short-order cook.

Norma looked over to see what Rodney was looking at, scowled at the girl, showing her predatory teeth. This was seen by a rail yard worker, seated in one of two stools at that short end of the counter. He executed the perfect spit-take with his coffee. Danny Thomas would have been envious. Corky noticed and came over to see what was wrong. "That *woman*," the customer said, positively shaking. Corky thought he was referring to something that the counter girl did, and in front of the entire place fired her on the spot.

"Let nobody say that *Corky* does not treat his customers right!"

The girl, meanwhile, standing perplexed with an order of eggs in one hand, a greasy black-grilled hamburger platter in the other and grasping new order slips between her teeth saw Norma's evil grin of satisfaction directed at her. Startled, she dropped the plates.

"Kat!" Corky screamed, making her name sound like a Greek cuss word. "That comes out of your paycheck … your *last* paycheck!" He began apologizing to his house full of friends, most of whom could not give a rat's ass about what was happening around them, let alone about the screwups of an insignificant young woman.

Now the first customer was chanting, *evil, evil, evil* over and over again, his eyes fixed in horror on Norma.

"Don't you worry, Corky will get you a *fresh* cup o' coffee." As he took the coffee away, the customer gurgled, "*Lamia* ..."

"No, not *that* cheap stuff! It's Chock Full O' Nuts, the *Heavenly* coffee. Better coffee a millionaire's money can't buy, my friend!"

Another customer overheard and looked up from his food. "Lamia? Where?"

Several others said, "Where, what?"

Someone else ordered a steak.

"Yes! A hardwood stake!" said the knowledgeable one.

"Hey!" Corky said indignantly, "Corky's food is *good* food ... you can eat it all night ... Beef that'll melt in your mouth, it's so tender!"

"For God's sake, get me a *stake*," the man hissed, looking frantically around for a cross.

"Me too," said a truck driver who was finishing his order of eggs, bacon, sausage and pancakes. "Make it *rare!*" Pretty soon everyone in the place was asking for steaks, and Corky was doubly-dee-lighted since his new distributor, Bastardos, had overstocked him on expensive cuts of meat. He was looking to un-fire the girl now, since he was going to need a lot of help getting these steak orders out, but she was nowhere to be seen. Corky moved to get behind the counter just as the railway man, using a makeshift cross of two dirty knives, leaned over and pressed it against Norma's cheek, which sizzled in a more healthy manner than anything Corky's ever grilled. Norma screamed, her undead flesh bubbled and turned to goo under the cross and she wrenched the man's arm out of its socket, slinging it clear across the room where it landed on a booth table.

"Hey," growled that patron, "I ordered a friggin' *steak!*"

Men grabbed Norma, attempting to confine her but her strength was too much for them. More customers got into the act, more customers got hurt. Norma snarled and growled frightfully.

As bedlam ensued around him, Rodney said to himself that this particular adventure was going to end very badly. His best bet, as always, was to try to look as inconspicuous as possible and keep his nose clean. The drunk, half-blind, deaf old man turned on his stool seat and looked at Rodney. Then clucked his tongue.

Blood was pouring out onto the counter from so many different directions that. Corky, wiping frenetically with a dishrag, implored everyone to calm down. The one-armed customer weakly gasped that they needed to drive a *wooden* stake through the creature's heart in order to vanquish it. "Oh, THAT kind o' stake," Corky said. He rummaged under the counter and came up with a rolling pin. "Will this do?"

As the lynch mob held Norma down onto the blood-drenched counter, Rodney saw his chance to slip away unnoticed. The last words he heard before the diner door closed behind him were: "You're driving that rolling pin into my *hand*, shithead!" and within seconds the shrill, unearthly screech of pain.

The men stood up from their task, surveying their handiwork. Norma, her mouth agape, hair ajangle, had the rolling pin driven neatly into her stomach.

"Oops," someone said before she was up and on them in a new wave of bloodshed.

When it was finally done, and Norma's body was riddled with countless tries and one successful staking, Corky wiped his brow. "Who do we call to get rid of this ..." he started to ask, but was told that the procedure was not yet finished.

"No!?" he asked incredulously.

"You must remove her head and fill her mouth with garlic."

Corky, beet red, sweating profusely, winded, huffing and puffing, managed to get out a real big tongue cluck. "What the hell you think this is? An Eye-talian restaurant? I ain't got no *garlic*!"

"Wolfsbane, then."

"Nope, none o' that either."

"Sea Salt?"

"How about Saltines?"

The expert nodded. Corky went into the kitchen to get a meat cleaver and a box of Saltines. He told the short order cook to put on some fresh coffee. "We got a *lot* of complaints about that last pot."

THIRTY-FIVE

Rodney smelled something, something calming and very pleasant at first, but was becoming quite heady. It was driving him crazy with distraction. He looped back to walk the same ground he already covered, seeking its source. Whatever it was, he wanted it. Moving with his zephyr-like deathspeed, he passed unseen and unheard the counter girl from the diner, who was walking herself with mortal swiftness.

It was her—that wild scent was emanating from *her*. It was the smell of fear, and he liked it.

He slowed almost to a stop, appearing before her like magic.

"Where did *you* come from?" she asked nervously, shoving her hand deep inside her strapped pocketbook. Rodney couldn't think of an answer. "Don't give me any grief, I'm in no mood." She looked directly at Rodney, "I remember you … the impatient guy in the corner."

She stepped up her pace, looking from left to right, watchful. She kept her hand inside the pocketbook now, and hurried along looking like someone who expected to be mugged. He kept his gait slow to match hers, drinking in the essence.

"I don't know what your game is, but I'm getting out of the night into my home as quickly as possible, and you'd be smart to do the same. I'm *not* looking to be picked up, you know."

"No … no … yes … I know … I wasn't trying to," he stammered, apologetically. Her redolence was much too attractive to leave behind. It flowed in waves, delicate tendrils of appealing aroma, with a complex subtlety and an underlying musky tang. The intensity was all around his face and head; Rodney drew it in to himself, amazed that she continued producing more and more of it with each second that passed. He didn't stop looking at her, watching.

"Do you have any idea what was back there at the diner?"

"Uh ... no."

"Vampires." she whispered hoarsely. "Real *vampires.*"

Rodney, intoxicated and delirious, grinned.

"What? Don't believe me? I ought to know. My parents are vampire hunters." The more she talked, the more excited she became, the more prominent was her manner of speech. She talked like Hayley Mills. "If you're smart, you'll come home with me and wait to leave until dawn."

There were several reasons why the girl's offer was not a wise one to consider, not the least of them being that Rodney might find garlic in the mouth of his severed head before morning, but his need to sop up this effluvium was overwhelming. "Okay!" he said without hesitation, sidling up to her. She became calmer.

"What's that smell?" she asked, suddenly stopping in her tracks, distracted.

Rodney shook his head, puzzled: could she sense it now? For him it was growing dim, a tenuous memory.

"It's like a *kennel.*" She sniffed the air. "Wait. It's you, your *clothes.* Even if you don't believe there are vampires, you have to believe that you need a real thorough clean up. You'll be safe *and* clean by dawn." She smiled. Being this close to her home, bemused by the silly looking boy, and just the fact of *human* companionship, lulled her fear to a controllable level; to Rodney, her fear had completely gone south.

"Your parents?" he asked cautiously.

"Away. On business. Newport in Rhode Island. I think some of the old ones woke up or something. They'll be gone for weeks." Then she added, sternly, "But this is not an invitation for funny stuff, get it?"

He breathed a sigh of relief.

Pointing to a modest little cottage she said, "My house is right over there." They were on Clabbough Road in Loodyville, close to Netherland Avenue in Gulpo Plains. Rodney used to make supermarket deliveries here, and he wondered why he'd never seen this girl before tonight. He asked if they grocery shopped at the EverRipe Supermarket.

"Oh, *that* place," she said angrily. "Dad and Mum went there after we first got settled and some *rude* stock boy insulted them." She fished out her house key.

Rodney remembered something that happened months ago involving canned vegetables and a fat English woman. It was a blistering hot day and he'd been bringing produce in from the landing dock out back. They had been sitting there most of the morning while Rodney goofed off, and just as he finally got around to taking care of it, the asshole store manager, Tony Chuckhuck, told him to re-price all the cans of vegetables and fruits some*one* mispriced. While Rodney was kneeling on the floor to get at the cans on the bottom shelf, his legs were run over with a full shopping cart. He dropped the can he'd been working on, as well as the price stamper and magic marker, yelping in pain. He rubbed his injured legs frantically while the woman, an ugly white-haired old bag, snuffled out an insincere apology, talking, it seemed, through her nasal passages. Then she absent-mindedly backed the cart over his legs again, clucking her tongue with disgust.

"Where *are* the canned asparagus?" she demanded to know, drawing out the word *canned* so it sounded like it was being spoken through a Gatling gun. Can-n-n-n-n-ed.

"Next to you," he moaned. "On the *shelf*."

By this time her husband, a thin little man with a derby hat and big walrus mustache, joined her. "Why, the idea," she said to him. "This young man told me to look for the can-n-n-n-ed asparagus *myself*!"

"He *did*, did he? Well, we'll soon see about that!"

It wasn't long before Tony Chuckhuck was brought onto the scene, giving Rodney a long public lecture on customer service, and kowtowing to the offended couple, offering fistfuls of double-value coupons to ease their indignation. But the damage was done. They left the store in a huff, deserting their full shopping cart with at least three hundred pounds of merchandise in it, most of it refrigerates. To top it off, crows got into the rotting produce sitting outside in the noonday sun and made a terrible mess he was forced to clean up *after* he put the groceries from the abandoned cart back on the shelves, which he did *after* re-pricing all the cans.

Those bastards couldn't be her parents.

Could they?

"I suppose you have a lot of crosses and garlic hanging all over the place inside," Rodney said, thinking of the cheerful decor vampire hunters would have.

"Don't be *stupid* ! They don't bring their work home, and, besides, vampires must be invited, so as long as you don't *ask* one into your house you're quite safe." She opened the door. "Won't you come in?"

He stepped into the house with her. Over a hunt table in the entranceway there was a small round mirror, which Rodney did not want to look at so he gazed down at the table and saw that it was emblazoned with a gaudy crest and the letters *V D*.

Vampire Destroyers?

When she closed the front door against the night she said, "I suppose we should introduce ourselves. I'm Katrina Von Droggler." She waited for him to respond, but Rodney was looking around, slackjawed, trying to think what else V D could stand for. "Well?" she said sharply.

"Oh, I'm Rodney. Rodney Rodoggio."

"What an *awful* name!" she laughed.

Inside, the house was as tidy as the outside. The living room was snug and cozy, with very big, overstuffed easy chairs in front of a fireplace. Bookshelves were everywhere, and these shelves were lined with books. Hundreds of them.

"You can call me *Rod*, or by my middle name, Winthrop." he offered.

"Winthrop! I have an Auntie named Winthrop! Dear old Auntie Wint. No, I don't think I'd like to call you by a woman's name, Rodney. And 'Rod' sounds too *whippish* for my taste." She was not as homely as Rodney first perceived. In fact, there was a definite style to her that was becoming more and more winsome. The short hair, so dull a brown in the garish lights of Corky's, looked somewhat more vibrant here, and her eyes, an unremarkable sort of bluish-green color behind those big round black-rimmed glasses, were less pale now.

"Huh?" he said.

"Make a fire ..." she repeated. "I'm going to change, and I think you should get those dirty clothes off. I'll bring you one of my father's robes. In the meantime, make that fire."

After she left, Rodney stared dumbly at the fireplace. There was a scuttle of wood next to it, so he put several logs on the grate. He found some long wooden kitchen matches on the mantle, struck one and poked it under a log waiting for it to start burning. Nothing happened.

Katrina came back with a man's dressing gown. A yellow silk one, with black trim collar and cuffs and blue fleur-de-lis pattern. The thing would look almost feminine to Rodney if he hadn't seen Basil Rathbone wear something similar in one of those Sherlock Holmes movies they run late at night on television.

"You *might* want to use some kindling ... now, get out of those clothes and call me when you're ready."

Rodney removed his miserable funeral ensemble and slipped the robe on over his naked vampire body, then called to Katrina to say that he was ready. She collected his clothes, and holding them away from her, left to wash them in the machine in the basement.

There were no newspapers or magazines laying around that he could see, so he took down a book from one of the shelves and ripped several pages out. They should go up in flames real good, because they were very, very dry. He looked at the book. Some boring piece of crap by Charles Dickens. The book looked about a hundred years old, and was probably available in paperback anyway. Nobody would miss a few pages in one book, not with all these books around. To be sure he had enough kindle, he tore out several more pages from several other books.

Soon the living room was ablaze with the cheery orange light of a fire. Katrina re-appeared wearing a ratty old bathrobe and big fuzzy slippers. She sat down on the carpet before the hearth. She gazed out the big picture window.

"Look how pretty," she said, indicating. Rodney looked. There, on the horizon behind Loodyville houses and trees, was the rosy pink glow of encroaching dawn.

"Holy SHIT! Where's the basement??"

"Through the kitchen ... why?"

He was up in a flash, running, looking for the goddamn kitchen door, then down the stairs into the basement. He tripped over a Punch doll, and kicked it angrily out of the way. He flung open the front loading washing machine door. Soapsudsy water sloshed out onto the floor and kept coming as the basket churned away. He reached in to pull out his clothes, then struggled to get into the sopping wet things. He galloped up the stairs, trailing water behind, sprinted into the living room, waved goodbye to Katrina, and was out the door.

Rodney's step in the predawn light was a sluggish one. Although his top speed was that of a very fast mortal it was a tremendous effort for him to move. The ease of flight he was accustomed to made his running feel like crawling and his vitality was draining through him quickly. A veritable conveyor belt of vim and vigor, from his being's center down through his legs to his feet and into the earth with each step he took, as if the earth itself was grabbing the lifeforce from him.

Struggling through the park, looking for the oak tree under which he left his coffin, his shuffling feet attracted bunches of nocturnal woodland creatures out and about in search of food. Field mice, raccoons, squirrels, skunks, and a whole flock of pain-in-the-ass chipmunks danced around him, snapping and gnawing as he became more animated dead meat and less ethereal. For such little things, they sure were mighty big ballbusters, especially those persistent chipmunks, who refused to be kicked out of the way and doggedly attached themselves to his heels until he stepped on them.

His tree was up ahead, which was good because dawn was just moments from breaking. He could see the rough yellow wooden box, the one with graffiti spray paint slogans on it, the one with cracked sides, the one with the open lid, although he didn't remember leaving the lid open.

Coming up on it with every bit of mobility he could muster, he saw that inside a family of chipmunks had made a new home for themselves. Two of the ratty bastards were cavorting around among the leaves and twigs and dirt and grass they used to make their disgusting nest. There must have been a house-warming party, too, because chipmunk shit was everywhere. More chipmunk shit than it would be reasonable to expect from just these two leftovers. It was all over the inside of his crate, smeared on the sides, little turds stepped upon with tiny chipmunk feet. God! What *pigs*! Rodney was too weak to spill the buggers out, or even to stomp the living bejesus out of them; all he could do was manage a weak sort of shooing motion with the back of his hand and lay down, closing himself in with them. They were not happy campers, those chipmunks. They cooed and cried and made little *gnack-gnack* noises by his ears the whole day, objecting to his presence in their domain and to the wet detergenty odor they were forced to endure. They did, however, enjoy nibbling on Rodney's face.

THIRTY-SIX

Rodney dozed and dreamed of werewolves. Big, hairy, mean-spirited, snarly faced werewolves. These werewolves yanked and pulled at Rodney's pecker, wrenching it off him to push into Katrina. Rodney became a Fruit Loop vampire for eternity, sitting apart from the normal vampires and blowing air kisses at all the new Brother Vampires welcomed into the Kingdom. Katrina gave birth to a werewolf baby named Huckleberry, an ugly little thing with big floppy ears and a long brown snout. Katrina waved goo'bye to the world and was dead and gone, while Huckleberry went to live with Katrina's parents. Rodney saw them going on jaunts to supermarkets and running over stock boy's legs while looking for the canned asparagus. That oh so merry, chuckleberry, Huckleberry Hellhound was laughing so hard the pointy ears on top of his head waggled and spittle flew out of his snout in all directions. At home, the lad excelled in staking and head-chopping lessons. Head Goblin's annoyed face, his thick tongue clucking with disgust over Rodney's werewolf offspring, appeared superimposed over the whole thing, like a scene in one of those lousy ABC Movie-Of-The-Week TV movies.

Then he was waking up, slowly coming back into the world, not really remembering the dream, but having questions that he wanted answers for, and thinking about the unfair dictates that the Kingdom has imposed on him and, to a lesser degree, on the human race.

If he humps a girl, she dies and the Kingdom gets a werewolf. He could hear his Uncle Barb saying, "*So? Ya humps the gal and she croaks? Big DEAL! You gets some jollies, they gets a wolfie, and everybody is hap-hap-happy! Right?*"

But if he feeds from her, she can become a stupid vampire PLUS a goblin lovedoll. "*So? Ya eat something and it croaks? Big DEAL! You get yer food, they gets their wicks dipped, and everybody is hap-hap-happy! Right?*"

Rodney guessed so, wondering what difference it made in the long run, except that one way the werewolves are hap-hap-happy and the other way the goblins are. Talk about being caught between the devil and the deep blue sea.

Sunset.

Rodney's first order of business was the removal of his grave to a more comfortable location. He'd given it some thought during the day and now, as healing green slime covered his chipmunk ravaged face, he picked up his casket and carried it to its new home: behind the screen at the Gulpo Plains All-Weather Drive-In Movie Theater. Instead of digging a hole, Rodney pushed his box under the bottom lip of the screen's back, making sure the lid was firmly *down*.

Rodney chose this area, actually a four foot wide by one hundred and fifty foot long strip of land bordered on one side by what looked like a twelve-foot high dam made by amateur beavers and on the other by the Pisa-like movie screen, because this land was the driest in town. Years ago some of the Samuel A. Gulpo Memorial Swamp leeched into the ground behind the drive-in, settling behind the big screen and causing it to tilt backwards. Had the Gulpo Plains Construction Company not stepped in, that screen would have toppled over completely. They created a method of diverting the swamp overflow toward the Main Street businesses and residential homes so that the drive-in movie theater would be safeguarded from further swamp attacks. Nobody, however, thought to fix the severely angled screen, so movies from that day forward had a funny, distorted look and Gulpo Plains was treated to a constantly *abnormal* view of the world. For many a Plainsian it was quite a shock to see James Stewart on television lean and lanky, when their view of him had always been that of a barrel chested pinhead.

When Rodney was satisfied that all was secure, he left the drive-in to go to Loodyville, to the Von Droggler house.

"Who *is* it?" came her firm response from inside.

"It's *Rodney*."

"Go away! Aside from vampires, you are positively the last thing I'd let in here. I'm still cleaning the mess you made."

"I can explain. Please let me in," he said calmly.

The door flung open. Katrina's angry face pressed against the storm door's screen. "How? How can you explain?"

His eyes glowed warmly and she softened immediately, as he suspected she would. "I'm a vampire," he told her, testing the waters. "I had to leave by dawn to get back to my coffin."

She laughed. Then she opened the door to him. "Okay, now you know," she said. "I'm a pushover. But *you're* still a blighter. I spent the whole day cleaning up the mess you left me with, plus hating you for what you did." Standing in the entranceway, he saw that everything inside the house was covered with a fine layer of soot which Katrina was obviously trying to clean. There was probably something wrong with the fireplace. The carpet looked ruined from soot and water.

She saw him looking at the mess and said: "The damper," fixing him with a look.

Rodney stared back, then got the message. He felt his sleeves and pants. "No, they seem dry enough now."

"The *fireplace* damper! It wasn't open, and there was a big puffback."

"Oh," he said and deliberately placed himself before the circular mirror. In the silver glass he could see the front door directly behind him as well as part of the wall and the elephant-foot umbrella stand next to the door. He put his arm around Katrina's shoulder and pulled her cheek to cheek to look into the mirror. What Rodney saw now was Katrina, leaning against invisible air, playfully struggling to be set free.

"What do you see?" Rodney asked.

"I see me, of course," she said.

"And?" he asked, already guessing the answer.

"Well, you—you big fool! What *else* am I supposed to see?"

"What am I doing?" He quickly opened his mouth very wide and rolled out his tongue over his bottom lip, like a hanged man.

"Smiling like a fool," she laughed.

He turned her to face him, grimaced so his pointy-toothed mouth could not be overlooked, and still there was no response. She could not see the truth. *This* was the vampire power, as it occurred to him today. That the predominantly evil nature of the undead was hidden by an illusion of life mortals are too willing to accept. Their superficial natures made them unaware of the danger. Silly sitting ducks, ripe for plucking. Rodney thought that if he could feel emotion in human terms, he would probably feel very sad about this.

"You're just too cute to be mad at for very long," she grumbled, then hugged him, pulling Rodney's head to her shoulder so that his mouth happened to be at her neck. He pressed his lips against her firm, delicate throat. "Oh," she said. He nibbled, tasting the salty, scent-laced flesh.

"Harder," Katrina urged.

Rodney chomped, and the next thing he knew, blood was flowing into his mouth and down his throat. He gagged, surprised by what he was doing, spitting up some of her blood, but the momentary lapse didn't last very long; soon, Katrina Von Droggler left his thoughts, and eventually this life.

THIRTY-SEVEN

"Well, well!" said Goblin Emergent. "Another tête-à-tête with HG? My, aren't we the lucky one?"

The sarcastic goblin led Rodney from the antechamber down a path that brought them to Head Goblin's private sanctum, a facsimile of a lofty personage's office from the 1930s. The rock walls were painted a sort of robin's egg blue, the ceiling an off white color. A big desk, all marred and scratched, with a mismatched chair sat in the center of the room. There was a ratty white sofa and some folding chairs. The most remarkable feature was a carpet, once snowy white now a grayish matted mess, that ill fitted the rocky floor. It was bunched up in some places, in others the bare stone was exposed, but all over the lumps and bumps on the cave floor underneath rippled the carpet like the back of the Loch Ness monster. Representatives from all the councils were in attendance, lounging on chairs, relaxing on the what they thought was a luxurious sofa, and generally feeling pretty spiffy to be in this exalted place.

"I understand you've brought us another initiate," Head Goblin said unenthusiastically. "Your first has been inducted, has she not?"

"Uh ... there was a slight problem," Rodney said.

"Problem? What kind of *problem?*" Head Goblin sounded peeved. "We cannot tuck her away into the Sisterhood until she's been initiated."

"She's been destroyed by mortals," Rodney stated as a matter of fact. This sort of stuff should happen all the time, and since no one cared much about Norma to begin with he didn't think it'd be a big deal.

"*DESTROYED!!*" Head Goblin screamed. "*WHY WAS I NOT INFORMED?*" The Supreme Ruler of the Kingdom of the Undead was so angry, his eyes glowed a hellish red and licks of flame issued from both tips of his tusks and the horns on top of his head tooted as steam escaped through them. Goblin Emergent came forward.

"Oh, worthy Sire! It must be a terrible oversight. Goblin Sources *must* indeed have reported the incident to the Census Committee, and I'm sure *they* have a reasonable explanation as to why the information has not been passed on to you."

A werewolf approached boldly. "Actually, your highness, the report we received from a field *Goblin* was sketchy to say the least. Apparently, Brother Vampire here," he hooked a clawed thumb in Rodney's direction, "failed to follow your instruction of induction and instead brought the Sister into an establishment filled with violent mortals. Then he proceeded to incite them into destroying the poor neophyte."

There were startled gasps and some nervous titters. Goblin Emergent said, "This is most serious. To betray one's own kindred shall not be condoned. There will have to be severe punishment."

A ghoul approached and whispered something into the werewolf's ear. The lycanthrope sucked in his breath, then turned to speak to the Head Goblin, who was now deep in concentration.

"Your Majesty," the werewolf said. "King of all Afflicted Dead, Leader of all that is supernaturally inflicted …"

Head Goblin did not respond; the glow in his eyes was gone, in its place were dark coals, blank and unrecognizing. The werewolf continued, speaking very softly, out of earshot of all, although Rodney was close enough to overhear. "… shitiest of the shits, Assholiest of the Universe, Greenest of the Greens, Sucker of Big Fat Hairy Devil Cocks, Eater of Turds …"

"What!?" Head Goblin asked, coming forth again from the deep recesses of his trance. "… Lover of Evil, Mightier than Might, Captive of Souls …"

Head Goblin clucked his tongue. "Get on *with it!*"

"It has just come to my attention that there was a witness to the Sister's unfortunate demise. It is none other than the new initiate Brother Vampire has brought into our fold. According to a communiqué just received from the Inner Chamber of Witches to the Census Council, of which I am Chairwolf, Brother Vampire had no hand in the tragedy."

"Yes, yes. I removed myself to the time of the incident and saw what befell the vampire woman for myself. I must say, Rubeego, you looked mighty stupid sitting there at that table with your mouth hanging open as your neophyte was being slaughtered."

After the last Sister Rodney brought into the Kingdom, the unfortunate Norma, nobody was much interested in this new one; the open gathering consisted of just the bare minimum required from each faction, and there were grumbles aplenty when Head Goblin called forth the inductee. When the witch dance was over, and the circle parted to reveal Katrina, Rodney, along with the entire assemblage, were stunned. In her induction gown, her skin a luminescent white with ruby red, full lips, she was quite a sight. There were wolf-whistles, enchanted sighs, and many a mouth watered over her. Head Goblin's burlap robe tented forward, he licked his forked tongue over his tusks and lips.

"Brother Vampire," he said in awe. "This is superb! I'm granting you Special Ceremonial Place of Honor."

"First?" Rodney asked eagerly.

"Noooo *last!*" Head Goblin chuckled. He whipped off his stained and damp robe and tossed it into the air, galloping to the initiation altar at high speed. The robe floated down over Rodney's head and covered him completely. While struggling to get out from under it, he heard a loud cry of *Yahoooooooooo*, followed by the sound of creaking springs. When he finally untangled himself, he was dismayed to see that the ranks had swelled considerably; every member of the Kingdom must have been alerted, for they all seemed to be here now, hundreds of thousands creatures waiting their turn.

Even the witches were lined up.

THIRTY-EIGHT

"Ahhhhhh," said Head Goblin, leaning back on his throne enjoying a smoke. Fluffy tendrils of white smoke puffed out through his nose, which he sucked into his mouth, inhaled, then exhaled back out through his ears.

"When will I get my turn?" Rodney asked. So much time seemed to have passed already, and there were still thousands of Goblins left, not to mention the rest of the Kingdom.

"Due to our number, Brother, Goblins take a lot of time, but we're fairly swift. Straight initiation, you know, no funny stuff like those damn warlocks." He bent toward Rodney and spoke confidentially. "They're into that kinky stuff with their pointy hats and wands. *That* takes a long time. Then of course the ghouls are big on oral initiation ..." Head Goblin trailed off. There was a pause.

"And the werewolves?" Rodney asked anxiously, falling into the dunderheaded trap.

"*DOGGIE STYLE!*" he shouted with glee. After several minutes his laughter subsided. "It's going to be a while. In the meantime, go practice shapeshifting or something. We'll call when we're ready for you." He snapped his thumbless hand and—*woomph*—Rodney was behind the screen at the Gulpo Plains All-Weather Drive-In Movie Theater, standing around in the darkness by his coffin. He sat down on the rough crate and waited.

It wasn't long before he became bored. Shapeshifting started looking like something fun to do, and turning into vapor seemed the most interesting of all the forms he could think of. He set his mind on becoming gaseous, closing his eyes and trying to imagine himself drifting upward, weightless and spreading. It was very relaxing. He found that he was seeing in many directions at one time: looking out over the top of the dam toward the swamp while seeing the back of the screen plus over its top at the cars parked down below. He was directing his swirling mist up, trailing wisps from where he stood before, reaching for the sky.

Car horns blared, headlights blinked. Someone screamed *Fire* and Rodney saw a host of citizens rush toward the screen and then run around behind it. He shifted, dipped and eddied, watching dismally the scene below at his coffin. The mob was stomping the weedy dirt with their feet, pouring sodas everywhere and finally one of them said, *Good work! Fire's out!* and they scampered away leaving their empty cups behind.

With the rabble gone, he reassembled to human. It was a tricky procedure because he found that he needed to force the insubstantial vapor to conform to his contour in the reverse order of the way he disassembled. Mastering that, he took form slowly, coming into himself naked with tendrils of vapor clinging to his being instead of clothes. He focused on the texture as well as the form of the clothes and they took shape around him, as they had been before his transformation, except that now his goddamn shirt was on backwards. He corrected the situation in the time-honored human way: by cursing and taking off the jacket and shirt and then re-dressing.

He surveyed the do-gooders' damages. His coffin was soaked with sticky wet soda. Big dribbles of the fizzy crap were dripping down from the ledge above directly onto it with an annoying splish-spl-a-a-attttt-*splush*. Rodney used his foot to push the box away, thinking that wolf form might have been a better shape-shifting choice. An animal would be innocuous, not so *smoky*. There shouldn't be a problem with that shape, as long as he kept himself in the darkness by his coffin. There was plenty of room to run around without being seen.

Feeling his body contort, expanding in directions he didn't think possible while contracting in others, he was brought swiftly to his knees. Tufts of coarse hair popped out of him in all directions, but most of his fur came from his clothes. Soon he was sauntering around on four paws. Unlike werewolves who walk on two legs, Rodney was a full-fledged animal, not a man/wolf combo. And he *felt* animalistic, with the pull of an animal's instinct. Little of Rodney survived in this form. His dopey personality integrated into the wolf, and that was about all. Almost immediately he lost touch with the human portion of his mind and he loped down the strip of land behind the screen, coming openly around to the parking area, curious about everything he saw.

The wolf meandered his way through rows of cars, smelling tires and eating dirty drive-in snacks that had been tossed out car windows onto the ground. This was stuff a mortal wolf wouldn't bother to *lick* let alone ingest, but Rodney gob-bled it down eagerly. Liking the smell of one car's front wheel, he lifted his leg to it and let loose a mighty stream. He turned to look at it steaming in the cool night air and then pushed his nose right into the puddle. As he was sniffing up his scent, the car door opened and the owner yelled at him to scram. Rodney stood there staring at the man until a Shrimply-Delicious EggRoll, hard as a wood peg, was thrown at his head and then he sprinted off.

In front of the refreshment building were several picnic-style tables, arranged so patrons could sit on balmy nights and enjoy their snacks while watching the movie. There used to be an outdoor speaker which spewed out echoing sound, but it hasn't worked since 1965 when Crazy Eddie tossed a cherry bomb into it. Subsequently, the tables went largely unused, except as a tryst locale. The wolf sniffed under these tables, enjoying the various odors of food and human secre-tions while three high school girls plopped themselves down for a chat. They were dreamily discussing someone named Roland Grigglic and his tongue, when the girl wearing pink hot pants felt Rodney's cold nose push against her bare leg.

"Ooo, what a cute doggie," she squealed. "C'mon here, doggie." She snapped her fingers for his attention, tapped her bare belly, and generally acted retarded until he came over and looked up at her delicious throat. She wrapped her arms around his head and pressed his snout into her young chest. Rodney felt her hard little nub of a nipple right through the sheer fabric of her cutoff shirt, and mov-ing his nose slightly a button opened. He flicked out his tongue and wormed it inside, feeling the warm, smooth flesh of the underside of her breast. If any thoughts of procreation danced in his head, they were canine, not human; it was only the salty flavor of her skin that was enticing.

"What IS that dog doing, Cynthia?" one of her friends asked.

"Looks like he's trying to bite off her tits," said the other.

"Naughty doggie!" Cynthia said, slapping his nose.

The two friends flagged down a drive-in security officer passing on his scooter and told him what was going on. The wolf stood there dumbly, wagging its tail and contemplating the urge to stick its nose in the officer's crotch. Onlookers started to gather.

The officer radioed to the security office. "Got a mad dog here," he said into his two-way, speaking loudly and enunciating slowly. The onlookers heard buzzes, pops and beeps coming from the scooter's radio. It sounded like: *What d'ya want us to do about it?*

"… well, send a dog *catcher*, I guess."

bzzzzzbeeeeeeBOOOP*Find out what the dog's doing.*

"Yeah … uh-huh … wait." He turned to the girl. "What did you say the dog was doing?"

"It tried to bite her tits *off*!" said one of the friends. The crowd was getting larger by the moment.

He clicked down the button of his radio. "The dog was trying to bite her, uh, *bazooms* off."

beeeeeeeeeeeeBOOOOOOOOObeeeeeeezzzzzz*Are you NUTS?? Bazooms? Ask if she's sure about that.*

"Okay … I'll ask … Miss? Are you sure it was your uh … uh …, you know— those," he pointed gingerly, "that the dog tried to bite off?"

"Of course I'm sure. Do you think I don't know what my *tits* are? I'm in the fuckin' tenth grade, you know!"

"She's sure," the security officer reported.

booooooop-ooooooeeeeeeeeeee*I'll call the shelter, so long as she's sure that there was an attack, but it's your ass on the line, Security Officer Nuksford. Find a way to restrain the dog so it can't do any more damage … Over* screeeeeeeee-bleeeeeeeooooopp.

"Over and out." Officer Nuksford said to dead air. He slid off his pants' belt, and looped it around the wolf's neck. He tied the excess leather lead to one of the table braces. "The Gulpo Plains Dog 'N' Cat Shelter will be coming," he announced.

"Is *that* all?" someone in the crowd asked derisively. "*You're* not going to do something else?"

"Yeah, aren't you going to shoot the beast?"

"Forget about that. What about the *girl*."

"What—shoot the GIRL?" a wisenheimer said.

Amidst the laughter there was a clucking tongue. "*No*, dummkopf, the girl is injured."

"I better have a look at the injury." Nuksford said authoritatively.

"Take your shirt off," the girl's friends suggested. "Let him see."

Cynthia took off her shirt, and since she was a modern, liberated woman, wasn't wearing a bra underneath. She stood there highly visible in the garish light spilling from the refreshment building, bare chested in the night air in front of just about every single patron and worker at the Gulpo Plains All-Weather Drive-In. The security officer took out his flashlight and shined it's beam on her chest. "Hmmm," he said, licking his nervous lips. "I do see bites, but they look more human than animal."

"That's not MY problem," Cynthia screamed. "Any MORON can see how vicious that doggie is! Look at it!" The officer pushed his face closer to her chest, basking in the soft warmth.

"I mean the DOGGIE!" she insisted.

Everyone looked at the wolf, who was sitting there dumbly with his mouth open and his tongue lolling out of his head.

"It's probably rapid," an observer yelled.

"You mean rabbit, don't you? That dog is definitely *rabbit*," said another party.

"Aw, you're both wrong. The disease is rabies."

"I don't think that dog is going to have *babies*, it doesn't look prega-nant."

"Kick it and see if it growls," a helpful person suggested. "That's how you can tell if its a mad dog."

"You mean a *rabid* dog? That can be a problem if the girl was bitten. She can get rabies, too."

"Yes," agreed Nuksford. "I'm gonna have to give you some first aid, miss, suck the rabbit venom out of that wound before it travels to your brain."

The girl was receiving plenty of first aid when Cal Abattoir arrived from the Shelter. He was a thin little guy in his forties, with big feet and hands and an Ichabod Crane nose. The left corner of his mouth twitched constantly.

"Whew! This is *bad*," he said, looking down at Rodney who was wagging his tail and playfully chewing on the belt leash. "I'm gonna have to take him in and gas'em for being a public menace." He led the wolf away, pulling the belt strap even though Rodney happily pranced along with him. Cal worked his way through the crowd, many of who reached out to pat Rodney's furry head.

"Watch it, folks!" the shelter man warned. "Mad dog comin' through! Mad dog walking … ma-*a*-ad dog-g-g-g a'walkin!"

At his vehicle, a pick-up truck owned by the town's public works department, he tried to lift Rodney up into the wire cage in the flatbed, but Rodney was too playful to oblige, so Cal threw some dog treats onto the floor of it and Rodney jumped in after them. He slammed the cage door shut, locking it with a big padlock. The wolf looked up, puzzled, then went to eat one of the treats and Cal Abattoir zapped him good on the snout with an electric prod he called *The Whacker*. All of Rodney's head fur stood up on end and there was a buzzing sensation he didn't like in his nose and jaw.

With sirens blaring, the truck zoomed through the streets of Gulpo Plains to get to the Gulpo Plains Cat 'N' Dog Shelter before nine o'clock, when Cal's shift ended, otherwise someone else would get to gas the mutt. Arriving at the squat shelter building, he screeched around back to the receiving entrance and parked at a sloppy angle then jumped out of the cab, leaving the wolf in its cage. He hurried to enter the stray in the register, filing the necessary report that would justify the animal's immediate destruction. Returning to the truck, he opened the cage door.

"Here, boy," he coaxed, blowing some air kisses, but the animal did not want to leave. Dog treats did not work the second time around, so, clucking his tongue with impatience, Cal charged up *The Whacker*. Seeing the joy stick coming at him, Rodney jumped out of the cage and ran toward what looked like the only way out—the receiving door leading into the shelter. Cal Abattoir was hot on his heels, but as the wolf entered the area of threshold, it flipped over backwards, propelled by an unseen force. Rodney tumbled into Cal, and Cal tumbled backwards onto the ground.

Rodney stood there, dazed, some of the wolfiness leaving his brain. He pushed Cal's hand with his front paw so the tip of the prod rested under Cal's chin, and Cal was treated to a good jolt. With very little effort, Rodney was shifting into a bat. As he flapped away, leaving the belt leash on the ground below, he dumped a stream of liquid guano onto the woozy Cal Abattoir.

Flying high above Gulpo Plains, seeing all the familiar landmarks below, he soon was soaring over Tarsville Heights, a town away. Bat speed was very fast, and Rodney now knew why bat was the preferred vampire choice of shapes because he retained much of his intellect in this form. Over Demimonde Street, familiar from the many news reports on television about escalating crime there, he swooped down low enough to see a woman standing in front of Goocannko's Pizzeria. She was dressed in a micro-miniskirt and a pink transparent blouse. She leaned against the building smoking a cigarette, which she held between her thumb and index finger. She looked like the perfect mama for a werewolf, someone just right for a hump'n'dump, or, as it occurred to him now, a lie'n'die. He found a dark place to reform to human, then walked right up to her.

"Well, hullo beeg boy," she said in a strange accent, a cross between Charo and King Farouk. "Interes-teed in havink a goot times with Margarita Belledejour?"

"Goot times?" asked Rodney.

She clucked her tongue and rolled her eyes. "Yah, a *goot* times! A very GOOT times?" When she saw that he still didn't understand her, she said with a twinge of nasty sarcasm: "Don't you vont to FOOK me?"

"You bet!"

"Twenty-five green American doolars, then" she said, holding out her hand. "Hoory up, soony boy" she said angrily. "I hoven't gots all good-dom night!" Rodney glowed his eyes, attacking her with supernatural power to eradicate resistance to him.

"And doon't give me any of that *vompeere* crep, either," she hissed. "Twenty-five green American *doolars*."

Seemed like a fair deal, but where was he going to get twenty-five bucks?

THIRTY-NINE

It was the Annual Night O' Repenting Your Sins Service at the Church of Our Lady of Perpetual Misery. Everyone who is anyone in Gulpo Plains was there, and Father Yorrick was in rare form; he had the bull by the nuts and was squeezing hard.

"… and God does surely love us. On that you can *rely*," he orated. Even after three solid hours of preaching, his voice did not waver or warble. Young Sassi's arm, on the other hand, extending the collection plate time after time, was throbbing and sore.

Yorrick leaned forward on the pulpit, his craggy face beatifically lit by the HolyGlo pulpit light. He extended his right hand out to his flock.

"That *wonderful* God in Heaven loves us to TEARS …" he paused for emphasis.

Sassi sighed and rubbed his sore arm: his next cue would be coming up in a moment.

"Yes! To TEARS! He loves us to *tears*, as He loves the lambs in the fields, the birds in the skies! He loves the trees, the flowers, the waters. He loves them *all* … but He loves US best of all! Yes indeedy-do! *Best* of all! We are His own dear little kiddies, and He wants what is best for us, for our *souls*.

"But are we worthy of such love? Have we earned it? Can we *accept* such a love as the Lord God offers? Can we??

"*NO!*" Yorrick screamed, pounding the pulpit with his gnarly old fist. "*NO!*" he repeated, pounding once again. "*NO!*" a third time, and this time a fissure erupted in the plywood. He paused now, took a sip from the glass of gin nearby, smacked his lips, then said in a calm, controlled voice: "And do you know why we cannot accept the love o' God into our lives? Because you worthless hunks of animal flesh, you rotten excuses for the sanctity of life, you *have not* made the sacrifice God demands of us all."

Quiet sobbing could be heard throughout the church as unrepented sinners realized with horror that their paths were leading them straight into a Hell greater than Gulpo Plains.

"You must dig deeply into your selfish selves and give unto God that which you love more than God ... and what is that? What is that *thing* which you love more than God? Ask yourselves: *What do I love more than God?*"

"I love *Lucy*," a voice chirped, followed by some sniggering. Yorrick's old eyes searched the place for the infidel, and spotted that grubby little bastard Joseph Woogle with a shiteating grin on his face.

"Open your bibles to *Ecdysiastics* 18:24," Yorrick improvised to Sassi's chagrin. He rustled open the pages of his bible, although no one else did, which was not unusual since no one ever bothered bringing their bible to church and there were none left out in the pew-back hymnal racks for their perusal. "Ah! What does it say? Let us read:

> '... and, lo!, God came out of heaven
> and dashed upon the earth, asking one
> and all if they loved God; and one-eth by
> one they said unto the Lord God that that
> which is in their pockets they loved more;
> but one citizen came forward, emptied his
> pockets to God and said, "Aw, mighty *God*
> I love you more than these green slips o'
> paper!" And God said, "This is good," and
> cast all the rest of them directly into Hell,
> declaring for all time that a Woogle shall lead
> the way.'

He snapped the book shut. "A Woogle shall lead the way. Whatever does that mean? A *Woogle* shall lead—but, wait! We have a Woogle here, do we not?" All eyes shifted to Joseph Woogle, squirming in his pew. "Well, Mr. Woogle ... lead the way! Empty your pockets for God, unless, of course, you love *Lucy* more than God."

"Come on, get on with it!" Sassi hissed, his arm very tired stretching across three people to get to Woogle. When the man didn't do anything, Sassi shouted with annoyance, "Forget it father! Just have God cast all these sinners down into Hell!"

Six burly construction workers jumped on Woogle, beating him silly, renting his clothes and tossing the contents of his pockets out toward the young priest. In the collection plate was a plastic Hopalong Cassidy penknife, a terribly damp and soiled snotrag, a keycase, some coins, and, the jackpot, a wallet containing pictures of Howdy Doody, Flub-A-Dub, Dilly-Dally and eighty-five dollars in cash.

"A Woogle shall lead the way! Who among you does not want to go to hell and roast for eternity? The contents of your pockets are your only salvation, your ticket to the Kingdom o' God Aw Mighty! Remember: *He Who Loves Money Cannot Love God.*"

Sassi was besieged with repentees dumping all the crap out of their pockets into the collection plates; elderly Mrs Cossblah delicately placed into the kitty a quarter. "I'm sorry, Father. This is all I have."

"Where's your *checkbook*?" he said with disgust. "Make it out to 'Father H. Yorrick', and don't get funny replacing the *r* with a *u* and adding a *p* this time."

Father Yorrick gazed out over his congregation; it looked like a prison riot, the sure sign of a successful evening. "The choir," he announced, "under the direction of Mrs. Lenora Snucklebrass, will now perform an original hymn composition entitled *Devil Don't Roast Me* by Harvey Snucklebrass."

During the hymn Sassi brought the collection plates to Yorrick, who separated the wheat from the chaff. This round of soulsaving netted about seven hundred dollars, which he folded and tucked into his collar for safekeeping. There probably weren't any more holdouts this night, so he figured he might as well wrap it up with his big finale. As the last discordant notes of the hymn ended, as everyone sat transfixed in their seats by the awfulness of lyric and voice, Father Yorrick climbed up behind the pulpit and held aloft what looked like a twenty dollar bill for all to see.

"God hates this evil paper because it takes *your* love away from Him, so tonight we will burn this evilness to cinders in HELLFIRE!" Taking out a Bic disposable lighter, he flicked up a big flame. Stage money from the Hat O' Rabbits Magic Shop has a certain *je ne sais quoi* to it, and as soon as flame touched the flash paper it whooshed up in a big noisy poof of technicolor smoke, and out of that smoke a bat circled downward, whisking past the old father's shooing hand, and plucking out the wad of cash from his collar. Father Yorrick was so astonished that he forgot to release the smoldering ember of flashpaper stage money and burnt his fingers.

"*Goddamit to hell'n'back again!*" he sang out loud and clear.

Sassi and the entire flock watched the bat circle high above their heads, spraying little drops of liquid batshit onto their heads like manna from heaven.

"Get that bird," screamed Yorrick. "A *free* vial of miracle slime for whoever catches it!"

From the commotion in front of Goocannko's Pizzeria it was evident that something evil had happened there. Walking toward it, seeing the flashing lights in front of the place, Rodney hurriedly counted out twenty-five of the bucks and tossed the bulk of the wad down an alley. A large Police van was pulled up to the curb and three Tarsville city cops with rifles and handguns were pushing Margarita Belledejour into it. She was handcuffed and shouting something in a foreign language which nobody understood. "*Óµjjcha poplÅ eecheÇh Îöïæñþ!*" she said.

"Wait!" Rodney screamed, holding out his handful of cash and running toward them as at that same instant he was summoned to the Kingdom. He ran right into the squishy, jellied body of Head Goblin.

"Ah!" Head Goblin said, "A gift? For *moi?*" He snatched the money out of Rodney's hand and tucked it inside his robe. "Brother Vampire, we are so pleased and delighted with your inductee that I decided to call you here to offer you something *very* special."

Rodney looked at the long line of creatures waiting to induct Katrina. "You're going to let me go next?" he said.

"Noooo. We're delegating you Chairman of the Membership Committee! Isn't that nice?"

"When do I get to initiate my inductee?"

Head Goblin shrugged his shoulders. "She's very popular, she even makes the ghouls smile … "

He was interrupted by a werewolf who toadied up, salaaming as if he was in the presence of Mahatma Ghandi, flicking out its big purple tongue to lick the floor at the Ruler's feet.

"O, worthy sire! We lowly werewolves would deem it a GREAT honor if you took one of our turns."

"Splendid!" He trilled, trotting off and leaving Rodney alone with the lycanthrope.

The werewolf arose to his feet, brushing brimstone ash off its fur and spitting the wicked taste out of its mouth. "Even though you are a tremendous fuckup …" he started to say.

"Me??" Rodney asked, looking around.

"Do I see any *new* werewolves here? Nope, so I guess I AM talking to a tremendous fuckup. Even still, we wanted to thank you for that inductee. Mmm-mmm! Is she ever a sweetie-pie! We damn near sharpened a stake in your honor, but having this Sister join our Kingdom made us reconsider our overwhelming dislike of you. We're willing to let bygones be bygones—so long as you keep bringing 'em in." He held out his huge, horrendous, lethal-clawed paw for Rodney to shake.

"Go hang a full moon," Rodney snarled. He pushed away from the stunned werewolf and weedled his way through the mass, attempting to get to the front. A sudden vice-like grip engulfed his skull and he was lifted off his feet and spun to face an unhappy looking goblin.

"Do you not know that HG is performing the solemn and sacred rite of induction?"

"Ooooooo, baaayyyy-beeeeee," Head Goblin chanted somewhere close.

The goblin pinched Rodney's head hard. "So, what is the meaning of this intrusion?"

"I wanted to ask Head Goblin to send me back ..."

"Is *that* all?" He dropped Rodney, lifted his arms and green mist flooded all over the place. When it lifted, Rodney found himself on a sidewalk somewhere familiar, but no place he knew. Neon was everywhere, making it bright with gaudy colors. Automobiles were zipping and weaving around garbage cans left in the middle of the street, knocking down pedestrians *before* honking their horns, and driving over traffic islands and sidewalks to hasten their journey. Seedy looking characters lurked in doorways. Steam swirled up from manhole covers, just like in the movies. At the corner he looked at a street sign.

E 59th

and wondered just where the heck he was. He passed a very familiar building, and it took moments to register, but it eventually did reach his dead brain that he was standing in front of the actual Playboy Club.

"Holy Hell!" He yelped. "I'm in New York *City*!!"

The neon Bunny Head seemed to wink at him. Inside was the one and only *Celeste Yahootie*, wiggling around in her little Bunny outfit, dipping and smiling at everyone. God!—he just *had* to get an invitation to get in there to see her. Pressing his face to the etched glass, straining to see through the blur that the stupid textured glass made, he could barely discern a dark blob coming toward the door. It must be a Keyholder ready to leave the club, and Rodney rubbed his hands together anxiously. Not only would he force an invitation out of the mortal, but he'd also use his vampire powers to make the man hand over his Playboy Club *Key*. The figure stopped just short of the door and was joined by another blob, this one lithe and slim and pink with long ears ... a real-live Playboy Bunny!

The Bunny chatted with the guy. It looked like she was trying to sell him one of those famous Playboy drink mugs, because she kept waving something that looked black and onerous at him. Several times Rodney thought that the customer was breaking away from her, but she managed to pull him back into conversation. Finally, the Bunny put her hand out to open the door for the Keyholder and things got even more blurry, drenched in green light. When the door at last opened, the tempting Bunny in the doorway was Head Goblin.

"So sorry, Brother. That was an apprentice goblin and he sent you to the wrong place. Lucky I detected the error, eh? We must make allowances for the inexperienced, although *mine* is the only absolute power." He snapped his fingers and Rodney found himself at the Mohambi Arms, in its bathroom. *Absolute power, my ass.*

He walked all the way back to Gulpo Plains and his coffin at the drive-in, cursing God, the Kingdom, every goblin, ghoul, werewolf and vampire that ever was. His mood became even darker when he approached his coffin and saw that the lid was open and inside four goddamn field mice were mating, crapping, and generally having a high ol' time. Rodney tilted the box over, scattered the rodents and tried stomping their furry little asses, but they were too quick. He got in, slammed the lid shut and waited for dawn.

FORTY

Rodney's return to mobility on this, the fourth night of his afterlife, was accompanied by the sound of impatient tapping on the box's lid. He opened the lid expecting to see a woodpecker, or a squirrel cracking its nuts, but was greeted by ugly Goblin Emergent, whose big feet were planted in the soft dirt, and who was forced to crouch in order to fit underneath the lip of the movie screen's base. He wore the Royal Ceremonial Garments of an Official Kingdom Messenger: red burlap robe decorated with silver and gold abstract lines crisscrossing higgledy-piggledy, wide brocade lapels and matching hem, plus a large Santa Claus-like belt of shiny black plastic. A chef's hat, redressed to look like a serious headpiece, sat upon his head.

"Hear Ye, Hear Ye!" He knocked on Rodney's box yet again with a scepter that looked like it just was purchased at a Pennsylvania Flea Market. "Greetings, Brother! I bring thee glad tidings! Time is at hand for ye to participate in the Sacred Ritual of Induction." He raised his hand and pointed out his middle finger. A stream of green ectoplasm snaked out from the blunt fingertip, and by careful manipulation he drew a childlike sketch of stairs in thin air. With a wave of his scepter the sketch became solid, growing upwards step by step to make a gigantic stairway leading higher than the eye could see, going all the way up toward heaven. With pompous ceremony, the goblin led Rodney slowly up these steps, invoking some power or another with each step. Hours and hours later they were at the top and Rodney was greeted with delegates from all the leagues, factions and clans. They applauded him and joined, hooting and hollering and applauding, in a march forward led by Goblin Emergent, who handled his staff like a drum major. Light emanated from the green smoggy stuff that hung in the air like car exhaust all around them, and there was nothing solid to walk on, nothing Rodney could see above or below or around but dark air. He bounced along, hardly moving his feet, being carried forward by some force. They marched along in this manner for quite a while, until the goblin stepped aside to let Rodney proceed all by himself. All the other marchers halted. Rodney was carried on the automatic walkway alone, leaving the others further and further behind.

This is IT, he thought, finding himself with a myriad of excited emotions. He rushed forward, impatient of the force propelling him, peeling off his clothes as he went, dropping them haphazardly into the void. Now taking giant steps, Rodney stepped into a gap in the green and was sliding on his ass down a long twisting slide. Down he went, picking up speed at an alarming rate, traveling for moments that turned into minutes that became hours, twisting and turning with nothing to hold on to or to slow his descent. Eventually, he was deposited nude on the craggy floor in front of the throne of Head Goblin. Several unearthly voices chuckled.

"Well, Brother—I see *you're* ready."

"Where is she?"

"Not *here*, that's for sure. You will find Sister Vampire at the place where you brought her into the afterlife."

"You mean to tell me that you put me through all this CRAP for nothing? Why couldn't that asshole Goblin Emergent just *tell* me where she was instead of making me go up three thousand steps, and then march in that stupid parade, and THEN slide down that goddamn thing??" Rodney was very excited and angry, much to the delight of the onlookers, until he went too far and referred to Head Goblin as *Shit*head Goblin.

Head Goblin immediately summoned a lackey werewolf, who came forward with Rodney's clothes and threw them at the ingrate. When Rodney was dressed, the Supreme Ruler snapped his fingers, and—*voilà!*—Rodney was back on earth, in Gulpo Plains, sinking rapidly in the Samuel A. Gulpo Memorial Swamp miles and miles from the Von Droggler house.

Katrina awaited his arrival. She lounged in her bedroom, dressed in a fresh initiation gown, laying atop her bed seductively. Rodney was startled by the many changes in her physical appearance. Her hair was no longer that limp, mousy brown. It was full, rich and very complimentary to her face which now, without glasses, was a terrifically eye-catching one. She blazed with unearthly vitality and wanton hunger. Her red lips parted, her tongue snaked from between them and caressed the outer contours with long, sensual strokes.

"You will be the last," she said, her voice, low and deep. "My link to the mortal world will sever and I will never have the pleasures of the flesh again. Make it a *good* one." She patted the bed with her hand, and Rodney sat down on it next to her. He kissed her lush mouth clumsily, groping her undead form with his undead hands. His libido took a giant step forward.

"I thought about *you* with every ghoul, every goblin, every werewolf," she murmured in response.

"And the Warlocks too?" he eagerly asked.

"Actually no ... the Warlocks were too *good* to remind me of you." She gave him a toothsome grin, then she sighed disgusting death breath into his hair. "Now ... please ... hurry ... take me ..."

Rodney was working hard to rid himself of the swamp-crusted blue suit, taking forever and a day because everything adhered to him like glue. His shirt and jacket seemed to have merged together. She clucked her tongue.

"Hurry," she urged, hissing fiercely. "There isn't much time."

Giving up on the conventional method of undressing, he started pulling the shirt and jacket over his head. It was half on and half off him, stuck in a position where his arms winged up and his head was buried when he felt helping hands reach out to aid him. "It's about *time* ..." he said, but couldn't finish because instead of pulling the clothes off, *he* was yanked back and pushed away, spinning uncontrollably until he fell onto the floor.

"Get away quickly, m'boy." Rodney heard someone say. "You don't know what you've stumbled into here."

It was a man's voice, theatrically modulated with a thick English accent. It sounded like one of those boring actors in those ultra-boring Educational Television dramas. Through a hole in his shirtfront he could see an old woman with a shock of white hair and flabby jowls. She looked like Alfred Hitchcock in drag, but sounded like Margaret Rutherford. "Yes," she said agreeably. "Listen to my husband. This creature is no longer our daughter Katrina, but an undead fiend, a danger to all mankind."

Rodney struggled to get to his feet. "Hold him, papa! He is deep under the spell of the *wurdalak*."

Mr. Von Droggler held Rodney down, not a difficult thing to do since the missus was mumbling some transfixing words in Latin which rendered both him and the vampire girl motionless with terror. Katrina's mum removed from her canvas shopping bag a long wooden stake honed from briarroot plus a well-used croquet mallet. Except for the hand-sharpened tip, the twisted stake was just as it was when cut from the tree: moss, bark and all.

"Don't do that!" Rodney screamed, hoping that would be enough to stop them.

It wasn't.

The woman used good, swift blows to pound the stake through the center of Katrina's chest, right between her delectable breasts. She shrieked, of course, blood shot out of her chest in a gory geyser, nearly reaching as high as the ceiling.

"Sorry, Sonny Jim," the man said briskly. "Had to be done. We arrived home earlier this evening and found our daughter in this state, sleeping and satiated from a foul meal no doubt. We would have been back *sooner,* but *we* have to go all the way into the *city* to the grocer's since the local market is run by ruffians. We were completely out of wolfsbane, you see. Thank the Dear Lord we got back in time. Undoubtedly, you were to be her next poor victim."

Rodney sat stunned, his jacket and shirt bunched up around his head, his eye peering through the shirt-tear at Katrina pinned to the bed with that hideous branch coming out of her. He noticed a small, green twig attached to the end of the stake. A little leaf which will never flourish twitched in the air current of the two oldies as they moved smartly, setting up for the next step in making their daughter ready for proper burial.

"She's at peace, papa."

"Put her glasses on her, please. Ooo, she looks so lovely, like Pamela Franklin in *The Prime of Miss Jean Brodie.*" He started humming that annoying Rod McKuen song.

"We just have to nip off her noggin and stuff her mouth with wolfsbane, and that will be that."

Those were chilling words to Rodney, especially the way the woman prolonged her *n* sounds. So horrifyingly familiar. *N-n-nip ... n-n-n-ogin-n-n ... wolfsban-n-n-e.*

"Thirty cents a stalk," she grumbled, breaking apart the flower from the stem. "Absolutely criminal!"

"Yessss, m'dear. It *was* cheaper at the other store ..."

"Twenty-three cents a stalk," Rodney said under his breath.

"... twenty-three cents a stalk, as I remember."

"Yes, and ten shillings sixpence of *rudeness.*"

Rodney couldn't stay there a moment longer; he became vaporous and seeped out of the house.

The drive-in was hopping.

Apparently, a new Christopher Lee Dracula film had opened tonight; the screen vampire was about to suck the blood out of a fantastic looking chick in a low cut gown. As Rodney watched the scene unfold, memories of his own miserable existence flashed before his eyes.

Lucky Katrina, he thought. How nice it would be to be dead. Really dead. And buried, although *that* might be asking for too much around here. Dead, at least, with the bliss of eternal sleep. Thoughts of self-destruction leaped into his head: pounding a stake into the ground and falling upon it. If he didn't miss his heart, it would work. All he'd have to do is figure out a way to chop his head off and stuff his mouth with garlic or wolfsbane.

The movie was too unrealistic and depressing for him to want to stay and watch, so went around behind the screen to his coffin and once again found the lid open.

"God-d-*dammmmmm* these ANIMALS!" he shrieked. He found a big, heavy rock to pummel their brains out, and creeping up on his coffin discovered that it was occupied by a mortal couple copulating.

"Get the FUCK out o' there," Rodney said rudely. The guy on top looked over his shoulder. It was not a very happy expression on the face attached to that crew-cut bullet head.

"Keep yer skin on, mack. Unless you want my fist on your nose."

Rodney recognized him. Harold Sazmanion, the star fullback of the Loodyville Louts, the High School football team. His picture was always in the sports section of the newspaper.

"What's the matter, Harold?" asked a frightened voice under him.

"It's nothin', honey. Relax."

"Is it the *police*? What will my parents say? This is terrible! I *knew* I shouldn't have let you talk me into coming here."

"Aw, cool it! It's just some crumb-bum out to get his jollies spying on people. I'll take care o' him, don't you worry." He got up to get out of the coffin.

Rodney backed up instinctively, then held his ground. "Listen, pal ... if you don't get your goddam ass out o' there, I'm gonna call someone *worse* than the police. I got friends in high places."

"Close your eyes, baby, this isn't gonna be pleasant." Harold instructed his date.

"The Gulpo Plains Construction Crew are *very* good friends o' mine ..."

Harold's big fist dropped to his side. He went pale. "Okay, Okay, man, we're going. Better get out of there baby ... we're gonna have to leave, just as the gentleman wants."

Walter Androdginy, the quarterback for the Gulpo Plains Gauchos, got out of the crate and hunkered down behind Harold for protection.

"And don't come back here again!" Rodney threatened. "I'm gonna have my buddies keeping watch, so BEAT IT!"

The lovebirds slinked away.

FORTY-ONE

Inundated with self-pity, and finding little comfort within the confines of his coffin, he got up to take a late night walk around the quiet streets of Gulpo Plains. It was even more depressing seeing the familiar areas of his mortal life than it had been tossing and turning in the animal littered, human stained, bug infested crate, but Rodney's ennui reached its apex on Main Street, directly in front of the Church of Our Lady of Perpetual Misery. Moving stoopshouldered, dragging his feet past the wide concrete church steps, a familiar voice called out a cheery greeting.

"Hulloo to you, Ronnie!"

He looked up. Even the sight of Betty Martex, née Bunz, could not brighten his spirits. "It's been a long time, Betty," he said with mysterious tragedy.

"Yes, it has …" She stopped mid-sentence, refusing an ending that rhymed. Ever since her wedding day, Betty has rhymed her speech, much to her groom's displeasure. Sitting alone and unhappy on the cold steps, she was too teary-eye to versify.

"Whatever happened to *us?*" she sighed. "We grew up together, went through school together, and then drifted far apart. We lost *touch* of the things that meant so *much*. WAIT. Scratch that. MOST. The things that meant so *most*. Here I am, a married woman, and you have some kind o' life of your own."

He laughed bitterly.

"I'm … I'm … so unhappy, Ronnie."

Rodney watched a fat tear form at the corner of her right eye, hanging there like Harold Lloyd on a clock.

"I shouldn't tell you this, but … but … I can't stand being married to Marty. I'm leaving him, running away from home. All he thinks about is—" she looked around to make certain no one was eavesdropping, then spelled it. "S-e-x. And what's more, he's been cheating on me with another woman. My very own Auntie *Roo!*"

Rodney watched the tear. It wavered, threatened to spill down, but clung there for dear life. Another glob of moisture formed and pushed past the clinging orb, trickling down her quivering cheek and into her mouth.

"Poor, poor Betty," he said. "Things are never what we think they should be, are they?"

She sobbed and whimpered and told Rodney that in her whole life there had only been one boy who ever loved her unconditionally. Now it was too late, her golden chance at happiness has slipped through her fingers forever.

"He was sooo sweet. Gentle and understanding. I don't think you'd know him though because he was much too fine a person to hang around with scummy guys. His sister and I have become very good friends. She's going to have a baby, my stepchild-in-law, or something."

"Not Roweena Rodoggio?"

"Why, yes! *How* did you know?"

"And this guy you're talking about? Her brother?"

"Why, yes," she said quietly. "Rodney. Rodney Rodoggio …" She sobbed. "I'd do anything, if only … only …"

Rodney knew then and there conclusively that Betty was a whack-o. A real nutburger. He pictured her features on a little boy, only with the addition of a long furry snout and big pointed ears and hair all over.

"Betty … it's me. Rodney."

She clucked her tongue. "Rodney? Rodney *who?*"

"Rodney …"

He didn't get to finish. "Oh, *that* Rodney," she said irritably. "Rodney Rulalenska. Puke up on any school bus trips lately?"

Rodney patiently explained to her that he was *not* Rodney Rulalenska, a repulsive kid who brought tuna fish and prune sandwiches to school with him every day, and then made up an elaborate story about being returned to the land o' life on God's command because mankind needed him. He laid it on thick about Joanni, and especially about Katrina, who loved him to death with a love that surpassed even that of Sonny & Cher. Norma became a sultry cocktail waitress who couldn't keep her hands off him.

"… but it's you I've always wanted, Betty. Just you."

"Oh, Rodney! You've made me so happy! I thought I lost you forever and ever." She laid back on the cement steps and beckoned him with batting eyes. "Let's show Mister Marty Martex a thing or two," she said.

Something echoed in his head, something that sounded like a steam calliope playing horror movie music. Was something going on he should know about? He asked nervously, "Did you hear that?"

She blew little air kisses to him.

Now came the dreaded voice of Head Goblin, overlaid with the fright night music: *The charge is the willful destruction of a Sister Vampire. The Powerful and Supreme Head Goblin, Ruler of the Kingdom of the Undead, decrees that Brother Vampire Ragland Rolloputti shall hereafter suffer the extreme punishment of the permanent loss of Mortal Privilege.*

The bell sounded, just as Betty reached out to touch him. "What happened to your whatchamacallit? I can't find it!"

He sensed the Kingdom tug. "Stay here, Betty," he squeaked quickly with his eunuch falsetto voice. "Don't move ..." He was sucked away in green fog.

Goblin Emergent looked down at Rodney with disgust. "There's no way you can talk your way out of this one. We all saw you cowering underneath your clothes while those monsters destroyed our poor Sister Vampire. You ought to be ashamed of yourself. Head Goblin is so angry, he won't even see you."

"Nice going, lunkhead," growled a werewolf, the only other creature with them in the antechamber.

"I was about to get *Betty Bunz*," Rodney wailed.

The werewolf and goblin exchanged a conspiratorial glance. "What Mr. Big doesn't know won't hurt him," cajoled the werewolf. "Go for it."

"Very risky," returned the goblin.

"Not to *you*. Since you've been next in the accession line, GE, we've come to expect you to bring good things to afterlife. Start now. Give the geek back his things. Let him go hump the girl ... it'll put you in good stead with the werewolves—and with all the werewolf sympathizers. Need I remind you there is a revolution going on?"

"But what if it goes south?"

"Nobody'll care much, just the Big Cheese and his core group of toadies. Then we'll storm the Kingdom for a takeover, put you right up there on the Throne. Now admit it: you'd *like* that, wouldn't you?"

Rodney was appalled at how really slimy werewolves were. He tried to follow the thread of their conversation, but discovered that not only was he missing the base knowledge to understand such devious politics, but he also didn't give a rat's ass about any of it. He stood there, listening, rocking on his heels, humming show tunes until finally Goblin Emergent addressed him, asking that if his mortal privilege was returned could he manage to bring in, before dawn, *both* a baby werewolf plus a new Sister—and one even more spectacular than the last.

Rodney gulped. That was quite an order. But, hey, he could worry about that *later*. "Sure! No problem."

"And one other thing. Bring us some *Cremona*."

"Cremona?" Rodney asked. "What's *that*?" He was thinking that it was some rare spice or herb. Or a potion made from yak teeth that could only be found in the goddamn Himalayas during the Jumpin' Juniper Celebration, or something else equally exotic.

Goblin Emergent clucked. "*CreMOna*, idiot!"

"He means Cremora," the werewolf said disgustedly. "You know, that powdery shit you use in your coffee when you're too *cheap* to buy milk. For *some* reason we're just about out of it."

"It's you *werewolves*! You drink coffee like there's NO tomorrow, and GOD FORBID you drink it BLACK!"

A disgruntled hairy face turned to Rodney. "I've seen them, those GOBLINS, taking spoonfuls of Cremora right into their ugly yaws, sucking on the dry powder like it was Lik M Aid, for Christsake! Ree-pulsive, to say the least!"

"Eeee-yuuck," said Rodney, remembering the time at home when they ran out of milk and his mother mixed some of that Cremora crap with water for him to use on his breakfast cereal.

"How can you eat that stuff *dry*?" He asked Goblin Emergent.

"Have you tried it?" He snurffed back, huffing. "You really ought to, it's very good. *Better* than Lick A Maid."

Lik M Aid *was* disgusting, and memories of *that* shit plus the thought of Cremora was making blood a very attractive commodity. Lik M Aid was a fruit flavored gritty powder that came in little 25¢ packets. You were supposed to mix it in a glass of water to make a tasty drink, but instead of mixing, the stuff floated on top of the water like fish food. What most kids did was eat it out of the packet one way or another: tilting the whole thing against their mouth, or licking a finger and dipping it into the packet so the crap would stick to it then sucking their fingers like lollipops. When they were children, Benny Fossert always had a Lik M Aid mustache and his fingers were stained and sticky. In those days, Benny found great joy in putting those tacky digits all over Rodney, who hated sticky with a severe passion.

"I guess I would rather have a spoonful of Cremora than Lik M Aid," Rodney conceded.

The werewolf shuddered. "One time I ripped into a kid's neck who had just finished a whole package of *lime* Lik M Aid, and it was all gooped-up in his throat. It got into my mouth big league." He flexed his jaw, smacking his lips in unpleasant memory. "I had that pasty grit stuck between my teeth for days and days."

"That's the thing with Cremona," Goblin Emergent said. "It's smo-o-o-th and dissolves sooo easily. My-*tee* fine!"

"But, it tastes like *chalk*," Rodney said.

"Well," Goblin Emergent said nastily, "*you* don't have to like it, you just *have* to bring it. And remember, before dawn: a baby werewolf and a new inductee, otherwise we're all *screwed*." He performed the Returning Spell.

"Thanks," Rodney said sarcastically with his normally high, non-eunuch falsetto, voice, happy that the score of *My Fair Lady* finally left his brain. He asked to be sent back and realized a beat too late that he inverted his words. Instead of saying, "Now, get me the hell back," he actually said, "Now, get me back to *hell* ..." and the crackling of flames drowned out his words. A plump red demon poked a blazing hot trident into his ass. "Very FUNNY!" he screamed.

"Careful what you ask for," Goblin Emergent said as Rodney was returned to the Kingdom, on his way back to Betty.

Main Street was quiet. There was no sign of her anywhere, and it was obvious that she was gone and not coming back. She did leave smudges of HotPink Day-glo lipstick on the sidewalk, a note:

> Rodnee,
> Marty found me here,
>   (the dere)
> And home is where he's taking me
>   exzactly where I ought to be.
> Acting stoopid and like a child
>   would drive any loving hubby wild.
> I reely trooly love him so!
>   Oh, and please say hullo to Ro.
>   Godby and Good Bless,
>   Betty B. Martex

So went his werewolf connection.

It was close to one a.m., and besides being pressured, frustrated, emasculated, vampirized, abused, sick, and unhappy, Rodney was also getting hungry. With the little activity on Main Street prospects here did not seem bright. The bars were closed. Street stragglers were at a premium. He cruised Main Street from one end to the other not seeing a soul and he was about ready to check out Siftracht City when the sound of high heel shoes clacking on the sidewalk hit the air. He was near Fernillda's Cards & Gifts Shoppe, the doorway of which was deeply recessed between two show windows filled with displays of junky Gulpo Plains souvenirs. Hopefully he would be camouflaged as his intended paramour approached. He spied her through a gap in a pyramid of plastic coffee mugs as she drew near the opening: none too shapely, rather thick-in-the-waist, with a skin-tight skirt that did not flatter her figure. She also wore a large plumed hat and a boa wrap, something like what old ladies from last century used to wear.

He frowned. What a letdown this was going to be for him. His first time at bat was going to be with someone who looked like, but was probably much older than, one of his ancient aunts. Aw, so what? The idea was to get a werewolf made, not to have jollies. He bit the bullet.

Rodney leapt out onto the woman, knocking off her hat, offering random kisses while trying to undo clothing.

"What-t-t-t?" The victim exclaimed nervously, glancing around to make sure there were no other people involved in this onslaught. The voice was very masculine and very familiar, a voice that Rodney was used to hearing orate.

"Uh ... Mayor Pindoughie ... I was .. uh .. expecting someone else ..."

The Mayor of Gulpo Plains smoothed down his strained leather skirt and fluffed out his bright red wig, then bent over to pick up his hat.

"What makes you think that *I* am Mayor Pindoughie, my fine young man?" he asked in a shocked soprano. "I am but a sweet young Plainsian maiden out for an evening stroll. Our beloved Mayor—the People's Choice—Gulpo Plains's favorite son—would *hardly* dress like a woman and walk the deserted streets of his town at night! I am *appalled* that you would even think such a thing! Do you not remember that it was Mayor Pindoughie who saved the swamp when the state wanted to drain it ... and who passed the Civil Rights laws that gave our Gulpo Plains Negroes equal rights?"

"There are no Negroes in Gulpo Plains, the town council voted against letting them live here," Rodney reminded him.

"That is BESIDE the point! If they *were* allowed to live here, they'd have equal rights with the rest of us! And what about the school? And the taxes? And everything else that wonderful man has done for us? A vote for Pindoughie is a vote for you, my friend!" He reached into his purse and pulled out a *Pindoughie For President* button, which he pinned on Rodney's raggy lapel.

Over the mayor's shoulder, he saw the figure of a girl heading toward them. There was no mistake about it this time. "Here comes my date," Rodney fudged.

"In that case, I shall be moving along. See you at the polls! Toodle-dee-doo!"

The Mayor's high heels clicked away very quickly. Rodney took his post in the doorway.

FORTY-TWO

Rodney nervously cooled his heels in the antechamber, wondering what he can say to justify the fact that dawn had come and half his assignment was left uncompleted. It didn't help, sitting there nervously on a sofa of faded and stained silk, jitterly dancing his feet around and clutching his hands, to see various Kingdom creatures pop in to have a look at him and then vanish without saying a word.

After a bunch of giggling witches tried to unobtrusively peek in, a warlock appeared in a great puff of choking smoke.

"Hot *damn!*" he said, looking Rodney up and down. "Hot *diggity* damn! You sure know how to pick inductees, boy!" He poofed out, leaving Rodney alone again with his worries until sometime later a slavering ghoul appeared.

"Ho-l-l-l-l-y *sh-e-e-e-e-e-it!* This one's even better than the last," he whispered. "How do you do it?"

"Did the initiation start?"

"Not *yet*," the ghoul tried to cluck his tongue, but his mouth was too filled with saliva. He wiped dribble from his horrid lips. "The witches are so thrilled they can't keep their yaps shut. They're letting everyone in for a sneak peek." He started drooling anew. "Wowwie-wow-wow-WOW!"

"What are YOU doing here?" Goblin Emergent's angry voice sounded behind them. "You know it's forbidden to consult with waitees."

"O, your Grace," slurped the ghoul. "So sorry, so sorry. I stopped in for a cup o' coffee, that's all. I'm leaving now, very quickly." The ghoul bowed as he moved backward, his outstretched hands slapping the floor humbly with each new step away. When he was gone, Rodney was alone with the goblin.

"I didn't do it," Rodney said in a rush. "I mean, I did half of it, or probably three quarters of it."

The goblin clucked his tongue. "What *are* you yammering about?"

"Well, I had sex with a girl. At least I think I did. It happened so quickly, and I had my eyes closed. I wanted to make a werewolf, but then I *bit* her and ... well, you know, the rest is the rest."

"Okay, so you canoodled a mortal and then fed off her. The werewolf gets canceled out, no big deal. They're a little twisted, but they'll get over it, especially since this new Sister is phenomenal. Head Goblin is delighted," he puffed himself up.

"He's given me a raise for *my* foresight in reinstating your mortal privilege. Everything works out for the best." Putting his massive green arms around Rodney and drawing him close to his face, he giggled Cremora scented goblin breath up Rodney's nose.

"I used my new clout to bend the rules and have a little peeky-boo at the Sister. Mmmmmm-mmmmmmmm! She's *scrumptious!* Don't be surprised if you become Vampire Emergent as a result of your effort ... you *know* what that means, don't you?" He gave Rodney the goblin equivalent of a wink, rolling his fat eyeball up and back since goblins don't have eyelids. "If the current Head Vampire cannot perform his duties for one reason or another, you step into his shoes. Quite an honor, I should say!"

Rodney asked, just to be sure he was out of the woods, "So, nothing bad happens when you hump a mortal girl, and then feed off her? Even if you bring them into the Kingdom?"

"Well the werewolves get rankled, but that's about it. Unless, of course, the mortal female is with mortal child. *That* can be a sticky mess because what is produced from the corruption of parasite mortal life with an undead host is a creature none of us can deal with. It's hard politics, but, basically, we have to eat crow and strike a deal with Satan to take the brat off our hands. Naturally he wants the Sister too, and it's a hard barter for us to keep *her.* It's workable. Just very, very tricky. Fortunately, that sort of thing rarely happens."

He stood up straight, hugging Rodney tightly and smiling broadly. "Soooo, Brother Vampire ... soon-to-be Vampire Emergent ... future HEAD Vampire— did you bring the Cremona?"

"Uh ..."

The goblin dropped him like a ton of hot crosses.

"The stores were closed," Rodney jabbered. "They're all closed at night."

"Oh, all *right*," Goblin Emergent said unpleasantly. "I'll send a werewolf out for it. At least *they* can move around during the day." He started walking away, snapping his fingers for Rodney to follow.

When they got to the meeting place, Rodney could tell that this was a very special occasion. Colored bunting hung over the dais: for the goblins, a bright pea green one, the exact same color as their skin, trimmed in gold; black with yellow trim for ghouls—the yellow matched their jaundice complexion; black with little drops of blood red for the Vampires; and for the Warlocks, black with smoke-white curls. The werewolves' bunting was black, too, but with a tasteless silver bullet trim.

Head Goblin was already seated on his throne. He gestured to Rodney. "I want you to sit up here with me, Brother!" He tapped his knee. Rodney climbed up and Head Goblin grabbed the back of his neck then started twisting Rodney's head. "Hey, everybody!" Head Goblin said with a Mickey Mouse voice and not moving his lips, "I'm Rudy the Vampire, hee-hee-hee!"

Some of the fraternal order gathered in front of him, laughing.

"Oh, pul-l-l-eeze don't take away my Mortal Privilege! hee-hee, hee-hee." He was disappointed that not more of the audience was coming over to enjoy his impromptu show, so he got bored and stopped playing. In a moment, he got downright nasty when he saw that there still were a great many stragglers.

"C'mon," he shouted, "let's get this thing rolling."

There was rushing now to fill seats and to bring the festivities to a start. Head Goblin began rubbing his hands together, and soon the whole place sounded like a cricket convention.

Music was heard, but not the same lute music as before, something more contemporary. Familiar music that Rodney could not place at first, but when it came to him he felt sick to his stomach. It was the self-same Muzak tape that EverRipe has used for the past ten years, containing sloggy instrumental versions of songs that Petula Clark made famous, along with a sprinkling of fifties Oldies-But-Goodies hits. Someone did a hatchet editing job on several of the numbers to create a half-assed medley the witches were attempting to dance to, but it was so jumpy and nonsensical that not only couldn't they keep up with it, they kept bumping into one another trying. It was during the crescendo to *Downtown* that the witches parted to reveal the new vampire sister. A reverent hush fell over the house, for she was absolutely radiant, glowing with unearthly sexuality.

"Oh, SHIT!" Rodney screamed.

"What?" Head Goblin asked, with just the right amount of intolerance.

"That's my *sister!*"

"She's everyone's Sister, jackass."

"No, no ... you don't understand. She's *Roweena*, my mortal sister."

Head Goblin gulped. "Well," he said weakly. "At least you didn't try to make a werewolf with her."

"As a matter of fact, Sire," Goblin Emergent said nervously. "He did, but he fed upon her, so that should be all right. Right?"

"And she's pregnant by Marty Martex," Rodney said miserably.

"What the hell is a martymartex?" Head Goblin asked, shaking and visibly pale. "Not a mortal?"

Rodney nodded. Head Goblin jumped to his feet, throwing Rodney off him. Spinning crazily, hooting with horror and yelping with fear, he started a chain reaction that had everyone screeching like a banshee during prohibition. That's the last Rodney remembered because he felt sleepy. Suddenly very, very sleepy. He could hardly keep his eyes open and he drifted into blissful oblivion.

FORTY-THREE

Rodney awoke suspended in green, icky slime. It bubbled and churned around him, carrying him along a current of movement in a direction he couldn't even guess at. Bobbing along, floating uncomfortably, he started to feel physical pain more intense than he remembered when he was alive. His body stretched and ached; he felt older somehow, more used. The slime was evaporating into dense green fog, swirling and twirling him in a whirlpool of motion, taking him on an elevator ride down, down, down further still. Dizzy, immersed in a green cloud, he stopped somewhere hard and felt cold air hit him. When the fog cleared, he found himself standing almost naked in very familiar surroundings. He was by a window. It was night. He looked out, and two stories below saw a broken alarm clock on the ground. It came back to him in waves, the familiarity and the knowledge merged, dawning on him that he was in Roweena's bedroom. He didn't like the looks of this.

"Uh-oh," he sighed.

There was a chuckle behind him. A very familiar, very theatrically evil chuckle. He spun around.

"You!" Rodney said, amazed.

"Shhhh," Maestro said. "Don't wake up your parents." He was lounging on the bed, his opera cape wrapped around him like a cocoon, his silk top hat resting on his chest. He looked dead and rightfully so.

"I thought you were gone for good."

"I was, but thanks to you I'm *ba-c-c-ck*! Man, you *really* screwed the pooch. You had those greenies scrambling like ants on a hotplate." He tried to get up from Roweena's deathtrap bed but was having trouble. He flailed his arms about, looking for balance, while trying to push up. In a final gesture of frustration, he turned into a bat, flew over to the window and reappeared as the Maestro.

"We haven't got much time before dawn, and I've got a lot to tell you, so listen up."

"Meet me at my coffin tomorrow night," Rodney yawned. "I've had *enough* for tonight."

"Your coffin won't be there tomorrow. It's not even there now. Hell, technically *you* won't be here tomorrow."

"What?" Rodney broke out in a cold sweat. "What are they going to do to me?"

"It's done already, pal. Nothing can change it, but I wanted you to know what's going on ... just a little *thankee* for bringing me back from the Really Dead." He shuddered. "Do NOT drink Holy Water, it is lousy for the system."

"So, what did they do? Get to the point! *Jeez!* Talk about suspense ..."

"Wel-l-l-l," he prevaricated, trying to find the words. "You are a mortal again for one thing ... those Kingdom Kreeps monkeyassed around with time and have brought you in time to the exact instant you met me. I'm NOT supposed to be here, but what-the-hay, huh? At dawn you're slated to forget all about me and vampires and the Kingdom. You'll forget about everything that happened during your afterlife. Wel-l-l-l, almost everything ... you're going to know that goblins take human form and walk the earth." He gave Rodney an uncomfortable, embarrassed smile. "They left that in your already screwy brain so you'll have some nice neurosis and paranoia and be suspicious of mailmen for the rest of your mortal life. Goddam Green bastards!"

"I'm not going to forget seeing Nancy Sinatra, am I," Rodney wailed, remembering the one and only celebrity he's likely ever to see.

"That wasn't Nancy Sinatra, *jerk* ... that was some skanky ho, a real Springerette, and YES you're going to forget her. Hey! Nancy Sinatra herself was in *Playboy* magazine back in the '90s ... va-va-va-*voom*. Too bad you missed it. I'd loan you my copy, but I unloaded it on eBay for a few bucks."

Rodney thought about what a lucky bastard E. Bay was, then it hit him. "The *90's??*"

"See, they had to find a way of undoing the complete mess you made." He giggled, not an attractive sight on a vampire. "Feeding from your mortal sister, even bringing her into the Kingdom, was not a bad thing ... in fact, considering the source material, it was a very *good* thing. It was the werewolf factor that threw the fly into the ointment. The product of that particular combo: vampire plus mortal of the same bloodline divided by werewolf product containing goblin heritage plus mortal fetus equals something that scares the *crap* out of goblins. Christ-on-a-Cruise! You managed to break every taboo in existence plus create some new ones! I wish I could have seen 'em trying to figure out what to do. They must've looked like a bunch o' monkeys trying to hump a football!

"They needed to get rid of you with a passion. QUITE a little problem, that one. Sending you to hell was totally out of the question because Satan is no dope: even *he* passed on taking you. The Executive Committee of Goblins were sooo desperate that they even applied to the Almighty, but His entrance fee was too stiff to cough up. Lucky for you, Rosemary's Baby-times-six hundred sixty-six-billion was the problem de jour, otherwise you'd be in some sort of limbo right now, floating in green ooze forever and ever. One of the warlocks came up with the bright idea of time shifting, placing Roweena back in time before you tampered with her. Ha! It wasn't long before they saw that they could kill two birds with one stone, and, hey! ... it worked for me too, although they think they got me to believe that they brought me back out of the goodness of their hearts.

"So, Rodney, I've been waiting for you to show up for over thirty-five years! By the way, welcome to the millennium, the *new* dark ages."

"What?! They kept me in suspended animation for thirty-five years? Jeez, that would make it 19 ... uh ... 93? Wait ..." he was counting with his fingers from 1973. "1996."

"You weren't suspended in time! HEL-L-O-O, Calvin Klein!—welcome *back* to the future. You've been *returned* to the moment right before you died, only chronologically, its years later."

"Huh?"

"To be succinct, you were *dumb* before, but now you're positively moronic, thanks to those green goons. Oh, and you aren't nineteen years old anymore. You're in your twenties." He scratched his chin. "Let's see, you died at nineteen years of age in 1973, but was born in 1979 ... how's that for culture shock?"

"I died before I was born, and now I'm an older mortal in the future with no memory of anything except what was in my life before I was-uh-born??"

"Yup. That's about the size of it."

Rodney kept repeating the formula, changing and altering it with each recital until it became a jumbled mess of thinking. His eyes practically rolled up into his head, his lips quivered.

The Maestro explained it all, from beginning to end, ignoring all the blank stares, all the stupid open-mouth vacuity, and even the disgusted tongue cluckings he was getting in exchange. After many attempts, he decided to boil it down in the most simplistic terms imaginable.

"Look, while they were trying to figure out how to correct the mess you made, they plucked you OUT of time ... think of time as a continuously running stream. You're a rock. They lift you out of the stream, leaving a gap where you've been. Got that?"

Rodney nodded.

"All well and good, except that the stream moves onward carrying twigs and crap along with it that quickly fills in your space. So, *another* place has to be found to put you down. It could be up the stream or down the stream, but a place where the rock will nestle just right without causing the stream to divert. Unfortunately, it also means that everything attached to you in your life has to come along for the ride, but if you think of all the people you ever knew, and all the places familiar to you, as weeds wrapped around your rock, trailing off it as it were, then you have a picture of what I'm talking about. Okay, now think of all that trailing debris still in the water as it flows, progressing and changing with nature, while *you*, completely out of the stream, are not altered or affected at all. Naturally, this sort of stitch in time can only work if collective memory of the *other* time in which they existed is eradicated and the new timeline replaced, which it does automatically *in the current*, but, unfortunately, you were not in that current, so all your life experiences will stay exactly as they were prior to your removal. Wonderful and amazing, isn't it?—although its not a flawless thing. There's been an awful lot of déjà vu all over Gulpo Plains for years, driving lots of people loony. Lymon Fossert is nuttier than ever because of it."

Rodney struggled hard to understand. "Everybody and everything is the way it's always been before, just in a different time now?"

"Wel-l-l-l, not *exactly*. There have been some subtle changes due to the stitch, little odds and ends of rough places that had to be smoothed to fit. Let's see. Hmmm. Roweena isn't knocked up, and never has been ... your girl friend Betty Boobs didn't get married ... in fact, Marty Martex ended up marrying someone else, a rich bitch from Loodyville, that snotty little socialite Sherri Netherland, whose father owns most of Gulpo Plains. In this new life, Daddy's installed his brilliant son-in-law as the manager of the EverRipe, so Marty Martex is your boss now, bunky. How's that for a hoot? You're still a shitass stockboy there, by the way, and the store is called The Netherland-EverRipe. Ready for some good news, though? Minimum wage has gone wa-a-y up! That's right—you don't earn that crappy $1.60 an hour! Now you get something like a cool five, or six bucks and change, I forget which, but that's *great*, huh?" His jollyass smile turned to a frown very quickly. "Oh, but prices on everything are much, much higher than what you're used to."

"God O'mighty! How am I ever gonna keep up with all this? Is everything automated now? Do they have cars that fly? Is television 3-D?"

"Wel-l-l-l, no, but you don't have to lick postage stamps anymore. They've made the little buggers peel'n'stick."

"That *is* good ... stamps always had a bitter taste."

"Yeah," the vampire said dismally. "But they're closing in on 50¢ a pop. How's that for leaving a bad taste in your mouth?"

"Jesus KAAAY-rist! FIFTY CENTS!! It was EIGHT FRIGGIN' CENTS A STAMP!! Did the church take over the FRIGGIN' Post Office? That's highway robbery! Fifty cents to send a *letter*! How the HELL did it get soooo HIGH? What the hell does a *record* cost now? Seven*teen* dollars??"

"Uh, they don't make records anymore. They've been replaced by CDs, little shiny silver things, round and flat like a 45rpm, smaller though ... bigger than a drink coaster ... ummm, smaller too than a saucer. Anyway, they cost ... well, yeah, about seventeen bucks. They *sound* good, though. Eee-*gad*; what do you think of when I say 'CD'?"

"Civil Defense," Rodney said plainly. "Do NOT tell me its wrong, because its one of the few answers I got *right* on my High School finals."

He saw the look on Rodney's face and thought it best to change the subject.

"Gene Kelly. The only taps relating to him now are ones played on a bugle. Elvis may or may not be dead as of 1977. And Lucy won't be making any new shows, although they're talking about computer generating her into new projects so we're probably not off the hook yet. And Lennon was shot and killed."

"I knew *that*. That's OLD history ..."

"You knew about John Lennon, the BEATLE?"

"Ohhhh, I thought it was Lenin, the Soviet leader. Hoo boy, this is depressing."

Maestro clucked his tongue. "Nobody gets out of this world alive—you know that. Instead of the Fab Four they're now down to the Teriff Two. Want to hear about a bunch of new consumer products?"

"Not really."

"There are things you'd never dream existed! Home Video? How 'bout that? Everybody's got DVD now ..."

"A NEW venereal disease ..."

"Actually, AIDS is the only game in town is these days."

"What? That awful diet candy that tastes like rubber?"

"No! ... a disease without cure. Its a mutated strain of the rabies, and came out of the area in Africa called Zaire—you'd know it better as the Congo. There's a more potent version of AIDS called Ebola that people catch from fruit bats. Ebola blood has a sweet flavor, so some of the vampire wags are calling it Kool Aids."

Rodney was confused. "*Kawabonga*! My head is spinning."

The Maestro grimaced. "Oooo, careful! You've got to be politically correct about just about everything these days. It's women's lib to the nth degree in every conceivable direction, and Indians hopped on *that* wagon, one of the few they'll ever be on, that's for sure. 'Kawabonga' is a discriminatory term now, demeans the *Native Americans*, which is what you have to call them unless you want to be scalped, although we're all getting scalped at their damn casinos. See if you can guess what they call Negroes in Gulpo Plains today."

"Hmmm. They used to be called *colored*, then it was *Negro* and *black* ... what else could it be? Not—"

"Definitely NOT."

"Okay. I give up. What *are* Negroes called in Gulpo Plains today?"

"*New Yorkers*! It's one of the few things that hasn't changed here. Not one of them that is sane would want to live in Gulpo Plains anyway, so screw 'em. The term is African-American, by the way. Keep in mind that women today are called *Distaff-Americans*, children are *Li'l-Americans* ..."

"Aw, man! What are just plain Americans called?"

"Latino."

"I don't think I'm going to like this very much."

"It'll take a while, but you'll get used to all the things that have come into being since 1973. There's attention deficit hyperactivity disorder, for example. NEW math, too! It's much easier than old math except once you know old math you can never do new math ... ATMs. Everybody has a personal computer and is linked to the world wide web on the internet. We all travel on the Informational Super Highway nowadays. Those goblins just *love* chat rooms, so DON'T talk to anyone who uses GreenGob as a handle. There's nouveau cuisine: white pizza for starters. California has got us all Pucked up. The Four Food Groups have been stacked into a food pyramid, not that anybody cares since they still sell Twinkies. Try a deep-fried Twinkie sometime. Yummy." His expression soured. "The words *Nouveau cuisine* reminds me of the name Keanau Reeves, who isn't some Los Angeles noodle dish but an actor. See *The Matrix* sometime, but skip that faggy version of *Dracula*."

Rodney was looking for pen and paper so he could write some of this down. "Is Christopher Lee still making *Dracula* movies?"

"God, no! Those are as old as the hills! We're into new age vampires, slick do-gooder heroes with great fashion sense. Angel o' the morning types who gotta be in by dawn. Whiny, wimpy things they are too, but they throw in some token badguy vampires. You can always tell *them* because they don't dress as hip and have lousy hair styles and even worse makeup. They get their asses kicked real good by a teenage girl named Buffy in *Buffy the Vampire Slayer*. First that was a movie, and then a TV series ..."

"You mean like what they did with *Bob & Carol & Ted & Alice?*"

"Ah, yeah. Sure. Anyway, one or both of those Buffys can slay me *any*time! The movie *Buffy* is some deadly friend let me tell you, but the TV one has got *cruel* intentions!

"But I digress; there's also personal alarms, car alarms, ebonics, ergonomics, *Jaws*, Karaoke, theme restaurants. Event movies, flight simulators, Velcro, and shrink-wrap in today's world. Cable-TV took off real big. HBO is a powerhouse. You can shop at home on cable with QVC—that is if you can stand watching those sweetsy, cutesy-wootsy show hosts long enough to see something to buy."

"What happened to Katrina," Rodney asked suddenly. "She wasn't destroyed, was she? I mean, now that things have *changed.*"

"Of course not. She was never a vampire because she never met you. She lives over there in Loodyville with her daffy parents, works in a library though, not at Corky's Eat All Night Hellhole."

"Maybe I should see if I can try to meet her," Rodney said eagerly.

Maestro shook his head. "Don't bother. The only reason she gave you a nod in the first place was because of the spellcasting we vampires can do on mortals. Hey! You'll be interested to know that your pal from the Mohambi Arms is now a rich advertising exec on Madison Avenue in New York City. All he did was ask one stupid question, and his career took off." Here the vampire affected the guise of the stoned-out jerk. "'*Hey, man, that Intel thing, is it inside or outside?*'" Maestro laughed, his big, ugly, horrible vampire face twisting up in mirth.

"Charming," Rodney said with disgust, looking at how hideous Maestro is.

"Yeah, well Stephen King didn't invent us, you know. His vampires may have manners, but this is real life."

"Steven who?"

"Author o' books, my boy, a modern Mark Twain. Oh, and for a huge laugh, try to catch a rerun of *Charmed* on TV. It's a show about these three cute witches. I'd go to those stupid initiations more often if *those* witches were dancing instead of the ones *we* have to look at. And, I don't know how on earth they did it on such a small budget, but they REALLY captured the Blair witch's sense of humor in a movie!"

The only Blair witch Rodney could think of was Janet Blair in a cheesey black and white English movie called *Burn, Witch, Burn.*

"No, no," the vampire said. "*THE* Blair witch … you know, that lard-ass heavystepper in the initiation dances?"

"Oh!" Rodney said, remembering a particularly goofy-looking witch who was always chuckling to herself as if something struck her as very funny all the time. "Her?? They made a movie about *her?*"

"Wel-l-l, everyone thinks it was a made-up movie that was just pretending to be real in order to fool people into thinking it was real, but the joke's on everyone because as it turns out, the movie *was* real. One of the producers is a goblin with a grudge. He stepped on a pile of those rocks she leaves all over the place, stumbled and nearly dropped his image of self-importance right in front of the whole damn Kingdom, so he tried a *60 Minutes*-like exposé on her to get even. His sour grapes became *wine*, though, because the movie made a lot o' moolah and shook up things in Hollywood. *Variety* sez they're bringing ol' Blairie back for some more sequels, and guess what? She wants to play HERSELF! She thinks she's Al Jolson. That reminds me!" He grabbed Rodney firmly by the back of the head and drew him closer. Rodney, thinking he was going to be bitten again, struggled as the vampire dug his long nosferatu thumbnail into his forehead and etched a jagged opening.

"What are you doing?" Rodney hissed. "That HURTS!"

"Don't be such a sissypants! I'm making a lightening bolt scar on your head, and we've got to get you a pair of those big round glasses. Think you can speak with an English accent?"

"I don't know," he spit out, rubbing his sore forehead. "Why?"

"If we can turn you into Harry Potter, we can make a TON o' money."

"Jeez! What does that old guy on *M.A.S.H.* have to do with anything, that Colonel Potter guy?"

"Colonel Potter … *Oh*, now I see! *Harry* Morgan played Colonel *Potter* … Rod, old boy, I think I'm finally getting an idea how your mind works. Say something in an English accent."

"'ello, gov'nor."

"Crap! Forget it. It would be easier to turn a penguin into James Bond." Getting over his disappointment relatively fast, the vampire went off on one boring, complicated jag after another, describing all the joys of this brave new world. He virtually lost himself in talk, blabbering about such things as microwave ovens, video games, airbags, boom boxes, crack, Snapple, and Swatches. The maestro mentioned a show called *Lord O' The Dance*, which Rodney assumed was a ballet version of *Jesus Christ Superstar*. He explained the la Macerena, Yugos and Valley Girls, and as he was tearing off on mosh pits, timeshares, pet rocks and cabbage patch dolls, Rodney saw through the window the rosy glow of approaching dawn. His mind started to get hazy, and with it came brilliant insight. He finally understood exactly what has happened to him, and what it was going to mean to try to get along in the world after he loses his memory of being a vampire. The undead fool pontificating in front of him was responsible for all the misery to come, that's for sure. Rodney stood there in his last moments of knowing about the terrible injustice being forced on him, about having to remember life in America during the merry 1960s and 1970s as he grew up while trying to fit into an incomprehensible and scary future. He contemplated warning the Maestro of the encroaching sunrise, or letting him yak away and then having to get plenty of towels to mop up what will be a mysterious mess.

THE END

978-0-595-41420-8
0-595-41420-6

Printed in the United States
90997LV00003B/81/A